"Utterly fascinating and meticulously researched, *The Woman with Two Shadows* is a riveting tale about a town and its people that officially never existed and the secrecy behind one of the Manhattan Project's top-secret cities responsible for creating the atom bomb used on Hiroshima and Nagasaki. James's debut is beautifully written and captivating!"

—Kim Michele Richardson, *New York Times* bestselling author of *The Book Woman of Troublesome Creek* and *The Book Woman's Daughter*

"*The Woman with Two Shadows* is a twisting, atmospheric page-turner. Sarah James's debut, which is set against a part of America's World War II history long shrouded in secret, feels fresh and new, filled with complex characters and plenty of intrigue. You won't be able to put this one down!"

—Julia Kelly, international bestselling author of *The Last Dance of the Debutante*

THE WOMAN WITH TWO SHADOWS

• A NOVEL OF WWII •

Sarah James

Copyright © 2022 by Sarah James
Cover and internal design © 2022 by Sourcebooks
Cover design by Sandra Chiu
Cover images © Joanna Czogala/Arcangel, Anatartan/Getty Images
Internal design by Danielle McNaughton/Sourcebooks

Sourcebooks and the colophon are registered trademarks of Sourcebooks.

Published by Sourcebooks Landmark, an imprint of Sourcebooks
P.O. Box 4410, Naperville, Illinois 60567-4410
(630) 961-3900
sourcebooks.com

Library of Congress Cataloging-in-Publication Data

Names: James, Sarah, author.
Title: The woman with two shadows : a novel of WWII / Sarah James.
Description: Naperville, Illinois : Sourcebooks Landmark, [2022]
Identifiers: LCCN 2021042271 (print) | LCCN 2021042272 (ebook) |
(trade paperback) | (epub)
Subjects: LCSH: World War, 1939–1945—Tennessee—Oak Ridge—Fiction. |
Manhattan Project (U.S.)—Fiction. | LCGFT: Historical fiction. |
Novels.
Classification: LCC PS3610.A4539 W66 2022 (print) | LCC PS3610.A4539
(ebook) | DDC 813/.6—dc23
LC record available at https://lccn.loc.gov/2021042271
LC ebook record available at https://lccn.loc.gov/2021042272

Printed and bound in the United States of America.
VP 10 9 8 7 6 5 4 3

Lillian was seven minutes older. Small in the span of a lifetime, but large in that those seven minutes set the Kaufman line of succession as Father, Mother, Lillian, Eleanor. One, two, three, four—a perfect order of operations.

The chain of command only lasted six years, until 1930, when the twins rounded the corner of East 86th Street to find that the shell of their world had collapsed on itself in an instant. Father had left behind Mother, Lillian, Eleanor. One, two, three. And when Mother left, too, in her own way (Lillian could still remember the threads of shirtsleeves, floating down around her like snow as Mother sat in the closet holding silver scissors, weeping), Lillian was at the top, the one to take care of all the others.

It wasn't good or bad or wrong or right; it was just the truth. It was just the way things were.

ONE

Once again, Lillian found herself annoyed at the inexplicable behavior of another person.

It wasn't her classmate Irene's presence she found irritating, not exactly. It was that Irene had chosen—for utterly unfathomable reasons—to do her homework at the desk directly next to the one Lillian had selected for herself when she arrived that morning. The mass departure of the boys of the department left the entire spacious laboratory with any of thirty-plus workstations available, and yet every time they found themselves in the lab together, Irene hovered mere feet from Lillian, sighing and coughing and—worst of all—attempting conversation. Irene seemed to believe that because they were the only two women in the physics department, Class of 1946, they had much in common and should be friends. Lillian knew that Irene was married and had children and lived not in Manhattan but in New Jersey, and therefore their lives couldn't be more different, regardless of their chosen field of study and the coincidence of their gender.

Lillian could have moved to another desk herself, but she'd arrived early and specifically chosen her favorite spot by the window, and after all—it was the principle of the thing. Any reasonable person should know to leave a small zone of privacy when the space permitted it. It was the same concept as not sitting next to someone on the train when an open bench was just a few feet away.

As Irene sighed her irritating sigh, Lillian flipped to her next worksheet and wondered if she was the only person left on earth with any common sense.

If a body weighing w lb. falls in a medium offering resistance proportional to the square of the velocity (ft./sec.), then the differential equation of the motion is $\frac{w}{g}\frac{d^2y}{dt^2} = w - k\left(\frac{dy}{dt}\right)^2$ where the positive direction of the y-axis is downward and g is the acceleration due to gravity (ft./sec.²). Find y as a function of t if (a) $\frac{dy}{dt} = V$ when $\frac{d^2y}{dt^2} = 0$; (b) $\frac{dy}{dt} = 0$ when t=0; (c) y=0 when t=0.

She glanced at the clock, making note of the time. Ten problems in six hours left thirty-six minutes per problem, which shouldn't have been an issue for this particular one. It seemed to be a rather simple differential equation. Of course, it was the problem's apparent simplicity that was giving Lillian pause. It surely couldn't be that easy, could it? Again, she looked to the clock, although the second hand had barely moved five notches. She raised her pencil to begin scratching out the solution, but hesitated. Should she read through the problem again, more carefully this time, to make sure she'd gotten it all? Did she have the time to do that? Did she have the time *not* to?

Thunk.

The sudden noise wasn't particularly loud, but it echoed throughout the empty laboratory. Lillian jumped in her seat, the pencil in her hand scratching a deep lead mark off the paper and onto the black stone tabletop. "What was that?" she heard herself ask, purely reflexively—she'd never purposefully give Irene an opening for conversation.

"There's a leak," said Irene.

As if to underscore her point, another drop echoed: *Thunk.*

"A leak of what?"

"Water."

Lillian had to tap her tongue to the roof of her mouth to keep her patience. "Obviously. But where is it coming from?" The building was getting old, with radiators that made horrible sounds and sinks that sputtered out brown water, and a leak wouldn't have been surprising on a rainy day. But it wasn't raining; in fact quite the opposite: the sun radiated on the courtyard outside, oblivious that the strife of a world at war would make gray clouds and dense fog far more appropriate.

Irene shrugged. "Must be coming from upstairs."

Another brilliant response. "Should we do something about it?" asked Lillian.

Thunk.

"I did do something about it," countered Irene. "I put out a bucket."

Lillian craned her neck to see the bucket, a heavy metal thing that was only amplifying the sound to the level of a hammer on steel. She sighed and looked back at the clock—a precious minute gone to this insipid conversation. She could afford no more. Besides, it didn't matter to her if the ceiling caved in. Only one more year and she'd bid farewell to Columbia University forever, off to the much greener pastures of Harvard, of graduate school. A real doctoral program with real research involved. After that, a hole in the ground could open and swallow 116th Street entirely, for all she cared.

The fragile carbon paper torn by the careless slip of her pencil, Lillian moved to the chalkboard at the front of the room with a frustrated sigh. She had barely begun integrating when she hesitated, returning to her desk to read the problem again.

If a body weighing w lb. falls in a medium offering resistance proportional to the square of the velocity...

The word *body* was hitting her in a strange, uncomfortable way. The phrasing was completely irrelevant to the problem—*body* could mean any object, really—and yet she found it impossible to shake away the vision of a corpse falling through water. She read through the problem again and found that absolutely none of it stayed in her brain besides that grotesque image. She read it again, and then one more time—

"Are you practicing for the Allerton Prize?" asked Irene, quite suddenly.

Lillian looked up. "Yes," she answered, resisting the urge to add *obviously*. The question had interrupted the spiral of her thoughts, which was both an annoyance and a relief.

"Is that one of the old problems? How did you get a copy?"

Thunk.

Lillian gave a half-hearted shrug. "Just found it somewhere."

Irene chuckled. "I don't know anyone who wants to win as badly as you do."

Lillian's hand gripped the chalk tighter as she returned to the chalkboard and continued the integration, not at all confident she was reading the problem correctly but determined to press on nonetheless. Last year she had *wanted* to win the Allerton Prize. This year she *had* to. But the distinction was far more than she wanted to get into with Irene.

Thunk.

Each drop in the steel bucket seemed to hit right in Lillian's temple and radiate out, as if someone were driving a nail directly above her right eye. She rubbed the throbbing spot and stared at the half-finished integration. It seemed shaky, the numbers lacking her signature crisp confidence. She fought the ridiculous impulse to erase the whole thing and try again, to write until the solution appeared as crisp and collected as she wanted her mind to be.

Harvard, Lillian, she told herself. *If you win the prize, you get to go to Harvard.* That mattered more than the neatness of her handwriting, and yet it looked so *wrong,* somehow—

Thunk.

The chalk slipped from Lillian's hand, fell to the floor, shattered. She stared down at the broken pieces and realized her heart was racing.

"Goodness, what was that?" asked Irene. When Lillian didn't respond, she went on: "Are you all right?"

Lillian nodded, her eyes glued to the bits of chalk on the floor, to the center point of impact with shards and dust radiating outward in a tiny circle of destruction. She reached up to rub the string of pearls that always hung around her neck, comforting, constant—until she was reminded of the identical one hanging around the neck of—

Thunk.

"Well, no use in doing this anymore," she announced. "Four entire minutes wasted on the easiest problem in the bunch. I might as well go home."

Irene tilted her head in self-congratulatory sympathy. "You

should go home. You look exhausted, poor thing. It'll be easier when your sister gets back. That should be any day now, right? Now that we've shown Germany what we're made of."

Lillian did not answer this. She found details of war victories neither interesting nor cause for celebration. The end of a war did not send back the same men it took away.

"I'll see you tomorrow, Irene," was all she said.

The sun and fresh air provided a bit of relief to the throbbing in her forehead. The campus was actually quite beautiful in its way, even though it was crammed among the crowded city blocks like a blade of grass stubbornly growing through a crack in a sidewalk. Harvard, although she'd never seen it, would certainly be different: acre after acre of sprawling green lawns, ancient brick buildings, all with plenty of nothingness in between, like an atom made of mostly empty space. At Columbia, there simply wasn't enough room for one to garner the reputation of an eccentric genius, but at Harvard, she could stroll the grounds when she was stuck on a problem, stretch her legs and mutter to herself. She could already imagine the undergraduates whispering: "There goes Dr. Kaufman again. I wonder what brilliant thing she's working on."

Maybe this strange feeling means a letter has come today.

The thought appeared in her mind fully formed, as if plucked from elsewhere and deposited in her brain. Perhaps it had. Quantum physics had already shown that the world behaved in ways that could hardly be comprehended by humans. Entangled particles could affect one another simultaneously from across the planet, as if there were no arrow of time pointing relentlessly in one forward direction, as if time itself were meaningless. Why shouldn't she sense the arrival of a letter before it had arrived, sense the presence of the person who shared her very chromosomes?

Her hope was proven false one short taxi ride later, when Lillian flipped open the black metal lid of the box that hung outside the Kaufman family town house.

It was empty. She let the lid clang shut, then closed her eyes.

She would hear from Eleanor soon, she reassured herself. Given all that had been in the news of late—the end of the Battle of Berlin, the death of Hitler—celebrations in the streets of Europe had lined the *New York Times* for a week and a half. What use could the army still have for Eleanor?

Yes, Lillian was certain of the fact. A letter would arrive soon.

Mother shouted from upstairs as soon as she heard the door open: "Lillian?"

Lillian despised the way she said it like a question these days. It was always Lillian. Despite Mother's hopes, it would never be anyone else for the foreseeable future. "Yes, it's me."

"Was there a letter today?"

Lillian wanted to tell the truth, wanted to let her mother deal with something unpleasant for once. But she couldn't. She was aware every day of the line of succession in the Kaufman household. She, the highest up, had to do the protecting, frustrating though it might be.

"Yes, there's a letter," Lillian called up the stairs. "I'll come up and read it to you."

Like she did every day, Lillian stopped at her desk first to grab an old piece of paper to bring to Mother's room and read by her bedside. After all this time, she was getting good at making up its contents on the fly.

Eleanor had never written. Although Lillian had spent countless hours crafting letters to her sister—tireless accounts of her and Mother's day-to-day life—they remained unread, stacked in a desk drawer that was becoming difficult to close, waiting for the arrival of an address to which they could be sent. Lillian had not heard from her sister since they stood on the curb of East 86th Street together, watching a cab driver load her maroon suitcases into the trunk of his car.

That was March 30. Two months ago.

───────

Even before March 30, it had been several weeks since the twins had even had a meaningful conversation. A small, perfectly understandable mistake on Lillian's part had been exploded wildly out of proportion by her twin sister, and by the time Eleanor received her train ticket to Tennessee, they were barely even speaking. The days that passed during their silent feud went by both achingly slow and far too fast: slow because their time together was agony, fast because Lillian knew they did not have much of that time left. Each day, Lillian would turn her key in the front door and expect to see Eleanor waiting in the front room, a sad, apologetic look in her eye. *I've been a fool,* she'd say. *Can you possibly forgive me?*

Yet each day Eleanor would only sigh deeply at her twin sister's arrival. Growing up, they'd spent every second together, sleeping every night in the same bedroom in identical brass beds, and now the days leading up to their separation were merely a chore for Eleanor to wait out. Eleanor had even taken to sleeping downstairs on the couch some nights, as if to say her fury was so deep, she didn't even want to be unconscious in the same room as Lillian.

It was tragic. It was also annoying. There were things that needed to be discussed before Eleanor departed, logistics—and the silent treatment wasn't going to accomplish anything.

On March 29, with their time almost entirely slipped away, Lillian attempted one last stab at a reconciliation. She considered outright apologizing, but decided against it since she had nothing to apologize for. All Lillian had done was *participate* in a mistake, the details of which hardly mattered. So instead of an apology, she went with an overture. An invitation for the two sisters to pick up where they had left off, a remark that seemed innocent on its surface but which served as an olive branch, simply offered, easily accepted:

"Do you know what the weather is like down there?"

Weather. The stalwart of conversation topics between two people who wanted to let each other know they didn't despise one another.

Lillian posed the question as Eleanor went through their shared closet, attempting to pack. In happier times, Lillian would have teased her sister for leaving such an important task to the last minute, but unkindness of any sort was far too risky to do now.

Eleanor did not take the question as the friendly overture Lillian intended it to be. "It's weather," she replied sourly. "Sometimes it's warm, sometimes it's cold."

"I'm sure that will be one of the enjoyable things to figure out."

"I'm sure it will be. Weather is always *so* fascinating."

Lillian sighed. She had anticipated having to be the more mature twin—she normally was—but she didn't *want* to be. It was so tempting to leave it there, go back to her book, ignore her sister's childish mood. But time in the nonquantum universe only moved forward, only moved toward their separation. "We still need to talk about your plan."

"My plan is to go to Tennessee and work for the army."

Goodness, was she obstinate. "About Mother. You are aware that nothing has changed. I'm leaving for Harvard in the new year. You'll need to come home by December."

"I'm aware," said Eleanor, with an affected air of the casual.

"I can't help but note that's not a promise to do so," said Lillian.

Eleanor shrugged as she continued flipping through the dresses in the closet. Then her fingers stopped, lingered.

The green silk dress was a prized possession. New silk was a rarity these days, but Eleanor had acquired this dress secondhand and hemmed it from full length to the shorter cut that was popular now. The skirt was fuller than the fabric-rationing dresses of the last few years and seemed to swing around even as it hung still on the hanger. A row of tiny buttons stretched all the way down its back—another extravagant detail lost to war. Everything about the dress spoke of an elegance no longer possible, or at least no longer fashionable to display.

"They'll spit at you on the street for wearing something so opulent," Lillian had said when Eleanor first showed off her handiwork. Eleanor had replied simply, "Not when they see how good I look in it."

The dress did look good. Irresistible.

Eleanor's hand clasped the hanger and pulled the dress from the closet.

Lillian inhaled sharply. "Oh, I don't think you'll need that," she said, as casually as she could muster.

"How do you know?" said Eleanor.

"That's a dress for New York City," said Lillian. "It should stay in New York City."

"But it's not like *you're* going to wear it." Eleanor had always offered her side of the closet to Lillian freely, but the two had such separate tastes it was mostly a gesture. "Have you worn it before?"

I have, and it looks better on me. Lillian managed to hold her tongue and ignore the question. "You won't need it in Tennessee. You're going there to work."

"I'll be taking it anyway. If you want something, you should take it. That's what you believe, right?"

Lillian rolled her eyes. "Stop being dramatic."

"Oh, am I being dramatic? Dreadfully sorry. You'll have to excuse that I have emotions."

"You're letting your emotions drive the facts, which are: this is a dress to wear out in Manhattan. To stuff it in a suitcase and take it to Tennessee is unconscionable."

"That's right. It's a dress to wear *out.* Out to dates, out to parties. You don't go out to dates or parties. So I will be taking the dress."

It was a cheap shot, and Lillian couldn't help but respond with something equally low. "At least I'm doing something important in my life, when I go to school," she snapped. She immediately regretted saying it—not because it wasn't true, but because she knew it would upset Eleanor, and they still had not reconciled enough to discuss anything important.

But instead of being upset, Eleanor laughed.

Eleanor *laughed!*

"All the important things I've tried to do in my life, you've ruined!" she cried, arms flailing about. "You don't want me to do important things. You want to be the only one doing important things."

Lillian scoffed. "You think dating Max Medelson is important?"

"Do not say his name!" All of a sudden, Eleanor wasn't laughing. Her face was white with anger as she brandished the green silk dress like a weapon, clenched fist shaking. Lillian marveled that pure rage could be unsheathed so quickly, quite out of nowhere. The range of human emotion was truly fascinating, from a scientific perspective.

Lillian wanted to assure Eleanor that she had no intention of saying Max Medelson's name on a long-term basis, and if Eleanor knew what was good for her, she wouldn't either. Instead, she waited for Eleanor's breathing to even out. She waited for her to stuff the green dress in her suitcase, unfolded. She didn't mention the nasty wrinkles that would follow.

"We need to talk about your plans," said Lillian again, after Eleanor had turned back to the closet. "We need to talk about Mother."

"What about her?" came the muttered response.

"What if the war's still going on when I graduate from Columbia? What if you're still in Tennessee when I need to leave for Harvard?"

"You haven't gotten into Harvard."

"I will."

"Well then." Eleanor tossed a handful of undergarments into the suitcase and slammed it shut. She flicked the clasps closed. "You'll have to figure something out. Shouldn't be too difficult. You are very, very smart."

———

Still in her clothes, Lillian lay in bed, staring at the ceiling. She shouldn't have left campus so early, she thought. There was nothing to do except stare, stare and run scenarios through her mind like equations. Problems as complex as the ones that would appear on the Allerton test, but that stood no chance of being solved in a mere six hours.

What if the army base in Tennessee is so secret Eleanor is not allowed to write? What if she's forgiven me and she wants to send a letter, but she can't?

Plausible.

The location was so secretive that Eleanor had not even been given an address, just a train ticket to Knoxville and the promise that someone would meet her at the station. Yet even soldiers stationed in Germany and Japan and France could send letters home, however infrequent and vague.

Plausible turned to implausible.

What if she never had plans to go to Tennessee? What if she and Max have run away together and she had no intention of telling me at all?

Also plausible, and unfortunately, Lillian's evidence for this unpleasant scenario held up. Before this Tennessee nonsense, Eleanor had no interest in joining the war effort. She'd barely blinked at a newspaper. More importantly, Mother needed care. The only way to avoid that responsibility, to leave it squarely in the lap of Lillian, would be to disappear entirely, start over somewhere unknown. And Max Medelson was enough of a lapdog that he would certainly do whatever Eleanor asked.

The only evidence in the contrary was the pearl necklace. Eleanor and Lillian had been gifted their identical pearl necklaces, with matching diamond-adorned fishhook clasps, when they were children. Lillian couldn't remember a day when the necklaces hadn't been draped around their necks. In happier times, the delicate strands had been an unspoken symbol of their connection. Lillian would reach up and touch hers for strength, when she needed the courage of her sister. After their fight, Lillian fully expected Eleanor to take hers off, leave it pooled up on the top of her nightstand, another way for Lillian to be punished.

And yet, Eleanor had left the necklace on. It gleamed in the low morning sun on the day she hailed the cab to whisk her to Penn Station. It was insubstantial evidence, of course, but there was a chance Eleanor didn't want their bond permanently broken. There was a chance that one day, things would go back to the way they were.

Or perhaps she took the necklace to sell it. There was also a chance of that.

Then Lillian ran through the explanation of why Eleanor hadn't written that scared her the most, even though she prided herself on her rationality and independence and hated to admit she was frightened of anything at all.

What if something has happened to Eleanor?

The Kaufman family didn't have the best history when it came to service with the army. Lillian would always remember the way Father's eyes would linger at the fire in the hearth for far too long, seeing things that weren't there, things that could send him flying into a terror in only a heartbeat. And she would always remember the way she hadn't been surprised at all, walking home from school and rounding the corner onto East 86th, to find the police and the doctors and the world around them changed forever. It felt to her, even at age six, inevitable.

Plausible. It was certainly plausible.

Lillian returned to the lab the next day determined to solve the integration problem in under half an hour. To win the Allerton Prize, she would have six hours to solve ten problems and secure her future. Without the scholarship, Mother could refuse to pay for Lillian's education, use it as ransom to hold her hostage in New York City. But nothing and no one could keep her away if she won a full scholarship to Harvard.

She had only just begun working when she heard a woman's voice call her name from the doorway. Lillian looked up to see the red-haired, freckled secretary from the department office looking at Irene. "Lillian Kaufman?"

Irene blinked, then pointed at Lillian. The red-haired woman's gaze shifted over. "That's me," said Lillian.

"There's a telephone call for you in the office."

Eleanor. Lillian's heart leapt even as her brain assured her this hope was foolish. Eleanor may have memorized the telephone number for the physics department office (as well as any telephone number she came across—really, her sister was far too obsessed with the silly telephone), but she'd made it quite clear before her departure there'd be no way she could call from Tennessee. Unless—Lillian's mind raced—there'd be some kind of emergency, some kind of... She couldn't imagine what. The red-haired woman's heels clacked as she led Lillian slowly down the hall, making offhanded comments about the chill in the air, blissfully unaware of the somersaults turning in Lillian's mind. Sometimes Lillian wondered if she was the only person on the planet to move with some sense of *urgency*.

In the office, Lillian was handed the receiver to a phone placed on the very low desk of the secretary. The cord strained at its coils as it stretched to her ear. "Hello?"

"Lillian?"

It was a man's voice. That was a surprise. Of all the possibilities, Lillian hadn't considered it would be a man's voice on the line. "Who's this?" she asked.

"It's Max? Max Medelson? Look, I don't have long—"

"Max Medelson?" Lillian had the urge to slam the phone

back on its receiver. Max Medelson had to be last person in the world Lillian wanted to speak to, now that Hitler was dead, at least.

"Don't hang up," he said quickly, as if reading her mind. "It's important. Have you heard from your sister?"

She did not want him to have the satisfaction of knowing that he was in more regular contact with Eleanor than she was. And yet, there was something about his voice, some hitch of desperation, that made Lillian fear honesty was required. "No."

"She's missing. Eleanor's missing."

The rest of the office faded away. Lillian clutched the phone tighter. "What do you mean?"

"She disappeared from the facility. Almost two weeks ago. No one's heard from her since then. Did she tell you where she might have gone?"

Lillian had been shaking her head for a few seconds before remembering the medium of the telephone required a verbal response. "No," she said, although the problem could be solved quickly enough. Two weeks was long enough that if Eleanor intended to come home, she'd have been here by now. *My god, she really did it. She really left for Chicago. She really is taking Harvard from me.*

"Max, I have to go," she said. "If you give me your telephone number, I'll ring you if I do hear from her."

"Wait," he said. Now it was more than a hitch, now his voice was sick with panic. The sound made Lillian swallow, made something tug at her lungs. "I think you need to come to Tennessee."

TWO

SEPTEMBER 1944

As soon as Lillian saw Max with Eleanor, she knew.

It was the beginning of Lillian's third year at Columbia University—an important milestone. Finally, she was free from the school's insipid requirement to study composition, literature, philosophy. Not that she had a problem with composition, literature, or philosophy, but they were a distraction from what she was there to do. Why couldn't the university trust that she could read some poetry and think about it on her own time? Physics was marching on, with new theories and insights into the quantum universe being published at breathtaking speed. They'd recently discovered that the atom behaved in ways that could not be described by any of the rules that had been in place for *centuries*. This was the most exciting time to be working in science since the days of Isaac Newton, when the laws of gravity and motion were first being worked out. And while *other* scientists edged closer and closer to the grand truths of the universe, Lillian was stuck in literature class analyzing the poetry of John Donne. But no more.

Lillian was so eager to dive into some actual research that she often lost track of time in the laboratory, and that day was no exception. It was half past one when she realized she was supposed to meet her sister for lunch half an hour earlier.

She did not expect to see Eleanor and Max sitting together on a bench across the quad when she pushed open the science building's heavy wooden door. Why would she? Two completely separate parts of her world, colliding in that way—how could she have expected such a thing? Even so, as soon as she did see, she knew. She *knew*.

Her first, uncontrollable reaction was a leaden *thunk* in her chest. Her second was anger at this uncontrollable leaden *thunk*. Just a few moments ago, she had been a promising physics undergraduate at an eminent university excited about her research. And *Max Medelson* was the one to ruin that good mood? Absurd. Lillian didn't care one bit about Max Medelson, who was half the physicist she was anyway. (Still, she did brush off some of the chalk dust from her gray skirt before heading over to the two. What good was not caring about someone if you weren't superior to them in every way?)

Making her way across the grassy courtyard, she carefully eyed her sister, who was examining with a smile an unfinished wood carving. The dopey look on Max's face made Lillian's anger melt to sympathy. It wasn't Max's fault that he was so boring. (Only a very boring person would find chipping away at a block of wood until it somewhat resembled an animal a worthwhile hobby.) At least he was pleasant, kind. And (by standards of beauty relevant to their current culture) not unattractive, although he didn't have much control over that either. Still. He was so far out of his element talking to charming, witty, talented Eleanor Kaufman.

Eleanor was midsentence when Lillian arrived at the bench and cleared her throat, startling both of them. Lillian rolled her eyes. It was one thing for Eleanor to jump at a sudden appearance, but Max was supposed to be a trained observer of the world around him.

"Lillian!" squealed Eleanor. "I was beginning to worry I'd never see you again."

"I lost track of time," explained Lillian. "I see you've met Max."

Eleanor turned back to Max imploringly. "Do you see it now? Now that we're here at the same time?"

Max made a little show of looking from Lillian to Eleanor, back to Lillian, back to Eleanor. It was a performance the twins witnessed nearly every day of their lives. Eleanor always found the confusion amusing, but Lillian did not—probably because it usually ended with her being told that the only difference between the two of them was the width of Lillian's hips. "No, I still don't see it," Max said finally. "You don't look a bit like twins to me."

"Unbelievable!" cried Eleanor. "You're a liar. No one else can tell us apart."

"I mean I see it, obviously," Max clarified. "You look similar. But not identical. I can definitely tell the difference."

Eleanor turned to Lillian to explain. "Max saw me sitting out here and knew right away that I was your twin. Didn't think for one second I was you."

Lillian pretended to gasp, turning to Max with awe. "Wow, Max! How remarkable of you to remember that you'd seen me one minute before, in the laboratory, wearing a different outfit."

"No, I didn't," said Max quickly, glancing to Eleanor to make sure she believed him. "I wasn't in the lab. I was in a meeting with Dr. Peters."

"When I saw him coming over here, I was worried I'd have to apologize for not being Lillian," gushed Eleanor. "But he said he already knew!"

"Wait a moment. So you're not kidding? There's people not able to tell you two apart?" asked Max, with a painfully obvious attempt at feigned confusion.

"Even our own mother has trouble with it sometimes!" exclaimed Eleanor.

"Really? Because I could tell, just, right away."

Lillian had to stop herself from rolling her eyes again. She didn't know what was worse: Max's terrible attempt at flirtation or that Eleanor seemed to be falling for it. "My nonidentical sister and I were just about to go for lunch, so we'll see you later, Max," she said.

"Max, you should join us," said Eleanor. The precise five words Lillian did not want to hear. "You can tell us all about your wood carving. Oh! Show Lillian what you're working on."

Max held up for Lillian's examination what appeared to be mostly a block of wood. "It's going to be a cat," he said.

Eleanor seemed to sense that Lillian was about to respond with sarcasm and jumped in. "It's very sweet. I love cats. Max, are you free for lunch?"

Max nodded, nearly dropping the pathetic cat as he leapt to his feet.

Lillian clenched her jaw. "Let's get this over with, shall we?"

———

"Is she seeing anyone? Your sister?"

Max barely waited until the doors of the science building shut behind them to ask the question that had clearly been on his mind for all of the dreadfully uncomfortable lunch.

"I haven't the slightest idea," Lillian replied coyly. "Why do you ask?"

"Why do you think I'm asking?" snapped Max. Lillian sighed. It was useless, trying to quip with Max Medelson. He finally caught up a few moments later. "You're infuriating. Is she or not?"

"She's not. Your lucky day."

They entered the laboratory. Lillian thought that would be

the end of the conversation, but Max followed her to her desk.

"She doesn't have someone overseas?"

"I said she wasn't seeing anyone."

"Yeah, but what if there's someone who's not exactly a boyfriend, but they were flirting before he shipped out?"

Lillian sank into her chair, staring up at Max. "Are you even listening to yourself? Why would that matter?"

Max chewed on his lip. "I just... If the only thing keeping one of our boys alive is the thought of Eleanor waiting for him at home, I don't want to take that away."

"For god's sake, Max, you haven't even asked her out yet."

"I know," he said, glancing toward the window as if he might catch a glimpse of Eleanor outside—foolish, since she'd gotten in a cab home. "But I think she's the one. So I want to do this right."

"If there is some poor soldier who returns for Eleanor and finds her taken, he can always marry me instead," joked Lillian.

Max didn't even crack a smile. "You know, to me, the two of you don't look anything alike."

———

Although she thought him unworthy of a relationship with the Kaufman family mailbox, Max's courtship of Eleanor didn't bother Lillian too much. Eleanor would come to her senses eventually, drop this whole Max business, and get to work on falling in love with somebody *practical*.

It *did* bother Lillian that Eleanor now spent the majority

of her evenings away from the house. It was a particular sort of sting to know that she was seeing her beloved sister far less only so Eleanor could waste her time. It would be quite different, of course, if Eleanor disappeared for a serious romantic prospect. And, yes, it bothered Lillian when Eleanor brought home that stupid cat carving and placed it proudly on the bookshelf in their bedroom—but only because the dreadful thing resembled a cat about as much as Winston Churchill did. It had looked better as a block of wood. At least a block of wood wouldn't stare at her with lifeless eyes while she undressed.

But these were minor annoyances, comparatively speaking. Minor annoyances that Lillian was happy to put up with, knowing that the relationship would only last a week or so.

And when a week or so turned into a month or so, well, that wasn't so much worse.

But when a month or so turned to two months or so…

When fall began to drag on and on…

When the air got chillier and when mornings began with a thin layer of frost on the ground and when students began making holiday plans…and Eleanor *still* hadn't moved on…

Lillian wouldn't say she was "worried," exactly. She was still certain that Eleanor would come to her senses. But she did begin to wonder if there was something she could do that would hasten that decision.

One December night, Lillian lay in bed awake, having spent yet another evening utterly alone. She didn't like being alone, but tolerated it because she knew she would have to get used to it. A woman dedicated to her career was destined for spinsterhood, especially a woman who happened to have a prettier, more feminine carbon copy. Who would settle for Lillian when Eleanor was nearby, such a perfect model of what Lillian could be if she only bothered to try?

It was long past midnight when Eleanor finally returned. Lillian was still wide awake, her mind capable of doing nothing but ruminate on where Eleanor had been and what, exactly, Eleanor had been doing. "Welcome home," she said as the door creaked open.

Eleanor jumped a little. "I thought you'd be asleep."

"I should be. It's so late."

She heard Eleanor unzip her dress, pull it over her head, and drop it on the floor. "We lost track of time," Eleanor said.

"Who's 'we'?" teased Lillian, although she knew the answer. She could practically see her sister blush even in the pitch-dark room.

"Me and Max," answered Eleanor, just as playfully. She pulled the sheets down on her bed and crawled in.

"You must really like him," said Lillian cautiously, a toe in the water of her intentions.

Eleanor sighed, like she'd certainly seen the romantic heroine of a movie do many times before. "I do. He makes me feel so special, like I'm the most fascinating person in the world."

Lillian knew she only had a few words to convince Eleanor

that she could do far better, only a few words before genuine concern for Eleanor's well-being began to look like petty jealousy. So Lillian uttered the one sentence that would definitively cause herself to lose interest in any romantic prospect, should it be told to her:

"He's not a very good physicist, you know."

Eleanor went quiet, and Lillian worried for a moment that she might have drifted off. But finally her sister responded, "Is that something I should be concerned about?"

"All I mean is he's far from the best in my class."

"I'm not hiring him for a job."

"I know," said Lillian. "I just always imagined you with a man who excels at his chosen profession."

Again, Eleanor was quiet. Lillian could hear her twisting her hair around her fingers in the dark, pondering. She decided it was safe to go on. "You know, either the very *best* physicist or the very *best* violinist or very best...what have you. You are," she added for charming comedic relief, "my baby sister, after all."

Eleanor laughed. But Lillian's words didn't sink in. "I'm sure when you get to know him, you'll come around," Eleanor said. "He's quite sweet."

Lillian did not agree with either of these sentences. A few days ago in the laboratory, knowing that Max had taken Eleanor to a play the previous evening, Lillian had politely asked him if he enjoyed the performance. "It was *Julius Caesar*," he replied darkly. "No one enjoyed the performance." Lillian did not appreciate either his depressing opinion on the state of the American theater-going public or the bitter tone of voice with which he asserted said opinion. The more chances she gave Max Medelson, the more she disliked him.

But there was nothing more she could say to Eleanor tonight. She could only hope that she had planted in Eleanor's brain an inkling that she deserved better. As a scientist, Lillian knew that if one were expecting a particular outcome, she would see evidence in support of her hypothesis even where no evidence existed. It was a fate to be avoided inside the laboratory, but for the sake of the greater good when it came to Eleanor's personal life, it could be allowed. If Eleanor expected to see the faults in Max, she would start to see them. Lillian had to trust the process to work.

For a few more weeks, anyway. If nothing changed by the new year, she would reassess. She had to take care of Eleanor, after all. The order of succession said so.

MAY 1945

According to Max, the train to Knoxville would take a little over a day. Lillian could depart Penn Station first thing Saturday morning and arrive in Tennessee (after what she was sure would be the worst night's sleep she'd ever had) Sunday afternoon. This worked out well for Max, who said that Sunday was one of the only days he could "usually" get away from work. It seemed obvious to Lillian that he was exaggerating, and in a way she found the boasting comforting. If Max was still worried about impressing her, perhaps Eleanor's situation was less dire than he'd made it sound. Either way, she knew that no project of any importance would require the around-the-clock use of Max Medelson.

Apparently, others Max had spoken to believed Eleanor was unhappy in her new job and had simply left for greener pastures. Max did not. "She wouldn't just run away," he insisted. "Something's happened."

"Have you called the police?" Lillian asked. The word *police* made the redheaded secretary's eyebrows creep toward the top of her head, although to her credit, she immediately put on quite a good show of being intensely interested in a nearby stack of envelopes.

The line crackled as Max insisted, "It's not that simple. We're in no-man's-land out here. Local police don't even know the plant exists. And the security they've got here…" His voice trailed off, but Lillian understood. The army's security was there to protect the army, not the workers who did their bidding.

Lillian massaged her right temple, which hadn't yet begun to throb, but it was only a matter of time. "I come to Tennessee, and then what? If she's not there, she's not there. And if it's something more serious than that—"

"I know what happened," said Max. "But I can't tell you on

the phone. I have no idea who might be listening." There he was, trying to talk himself up again, as if anyone in the world were interested in his telephone conversations. Were it not for the gravity of the subject matter, Lillian would have enjoyed quite an eye roll at his expense. "You need to get down here so we can talk freely. If you leave on the next train out of New York, you can be in Knoxville on Sunday. I'll meet you at the station. We can go to a hotel. Please, Lillian."

There were muffled voices in the background, and Max reassured someone with an "okay, okay" before turning his attention back to Lillian. "I've got to go," he said. "You'll come? You are coming?"

Lillian stared down at the redheaded secretary whose phone line she was tying up. The woman smiled up at her as she licked an envelope. It was so strange, how they were mere inches apart, yet this woman had no idea of the consequences of the phone call happening above her. "Yes, I'll be there," said Lillian.

"Sunday, at the train."

The line went dead. Slowly, she lowered the phone from her ear. Slowly, she handed it back to the redheaded woman, who was still smiling.

"All done?" she said brightly.

"I'm going to Tennessee," Lillian replied.

"That sounds fun!" chirped the woman. "Family down there?"

"My sister," said Lillian. "I have to go get my sister."

Normally, Lillian would never make small talk with a secretary. But she felt as if she had to practice saying the words out loud.

What on earth was she going to tell Mother?

———————

"A trip to Knoxville? Whatever for?" Mother had lowered the book she was reading onto her lap. Its pages curled upward and threatened to fold over, burying her place.

"For our birthday next week," Lillian replied evenly. She'd considering using a more upbeat tone, but it sounded false passing through her lips. She couldn't take the risk that Mother would grow suspicious. *'How odd, Lillian. You've never much cared about your birthday before…'* "I'll leave Saturday, and I'll be back in a week. I've already paid Dot Greeley next door to look in on you."

"I don't need Dot Greeley's help," snapped Mother. Both were aware that this was painfully untrue, but to argue would have been pointless, so Lillian remained quiet as Mother chewed on her lip. "You should have told me sooner."

"I know," said Lillian. "I'm sorry for that."

Mother harrumphed in a way that indicated she either did not believe Lillian was sorry or did not care, but said nothing. Anxious to leave before she changed her mind, Lillian backed toward the door as Mother resumed her reading. If she noticed at all that the threatening pages had at last slipped over, that at least fifty of them had cascaded to the incorrect side and launched her narrative forward in time, she didn't seem to mind.

———

On Saturday morning, Lillian rose early and pressed one week's worth of white button-up blouses and gray wool skirts into the mustard suitcase with the torn lining and the squeaky clasp. (Eleanor, of course, had taken all the good suitcases.) It took her only five minutes to pack, after which she stood by the open suitcase and stared at the two neat stacks of gray and white. It had taken Eleanor hours to round up her makeup, her hairbrushes and curlers and pins, her earrings and berets and snoods. She'd laid dress after dress on the bed to analyze: This one or that one? She'd muttered to herself for hours. *These shoes go better with the yellow dress, but these shoes will go with the yellow dress and the blue polka-dot dress, so even though they don't go as well with the yellow dress, perhaps they'd be a better use of space...*

Lillian shut her case. The street outside was silent, most of its usual inhabitants taking the weekend to sleep in a bit. The sound of the squeaky latch echoed throughout the empty room.

To Lillian's surprise, when she went into the kitchen for a piece of toast before departing, she found Mother at the table, sighing and wringing her hands. Mother rarely managed to get herself out of bed, let alone all the way downstairs to the kitchen. Lillian cursed her decision not to have skipped breakfast and headed directly for the train. She should have known any minute she spent in this house was a minute Mother could distract or delay her.

"Good morning," said Lillian, heading directly for the bread box, afraid to even look her mother in the eye.

"I'm not a fool," said Mother.

Lillian tried not to register a reaction as she lifted the tin lid. "Oh? And who said you were?"

"I thought about it. I'm still capable of doing that, you know. Thinking. You announce two days before you are to leave that you'll be going away? That's not like you. You decided at age five where you would go to school, at age ten that you would never marry, at age fifteen the exact outfit you would wear every day for the rest of your life. She's in trouble. Isn't she?"

Lillian kept her back turned as she weighed her responses. Perhaps Mother deserved finally to know the truth. That's what one of those philosophers (for the life of her, she couldn't remember which one) from that ridiculous humanities course had argued: people deserve the truth because they are human. Lillian had been denying Mother's very humanity by pretending that Eleanor had written, by reading fake letters out loud, by writing down Mother's dictation on notes that would only see the inside of a wastebasket, by pretending now that Eleanor was safe in Tennessee and not a thing was wrong in the world.

But does a person still deserve the truth if it's become clear they can't handle it, if it would be better off for them not to know?

"It's possible that she's in trouble," said Lillian, slowly, choosing her words ever so carefully: the truth, but not enough to cause either upset or undue hope. "I'm going to find out." She turned around and watched her words hit Mother, watched them travel through her like a wave. Mother reached up to grab at her heart as if she could slow down its beating. She stood slowly, shakily, crossing the distance between the table and the countertop until she stood right in front of Lillian and placed a hand on her shoulder. The weight of it was strange at first, but after a moment Lillian was surprised to find it comforting.

Lillian's heart swelled with pity. For almost a year after his death, Mother had refused to box up or get rid of any of Father's clothes, as if he were away on business and would be back in the morning. One day the facade became too much. Mother found a giant pair of glinting silver scissors, sat in the master bedroom closet, and wailed. Lillian had found her clutching a piece of destroyed white cotton, kneeling in a mess of fabric scraps a foot deep, loose threads floating down around her like snowflakes. To live through two wars, to watch the army take away everyone she loved, one by one... Surely this was not the life she'd wanted for herself.

Lillian reached up to take Mother's hand in her own.

But Mother snatched her hand away.

"It should have been you," she said.

And just in case the gravity and the cruelty of the words hadn't pierced the armor around Lillian's heart, she repeated

THREE

JUNE 1945

Lillian watched the trees of some unknown state blur into one another as the train rushed through the darkening dusk sky. Behind her, a child complained to his mother how he couldn't wait to be home; in front of her a pair of businessmen in crisp blue suits smoked and flipped through newspapers. It occurred to Lillian that she might be the only person on the train who hadn't the slightest idea what would be in store for her when she stepped off. Was Max right that Eleanor was in trouble? What on earth could he possibly have to say that couldn't be discussed over the telephone? Lillian, usually so good at developing hypotheses, was at a loss.

To distract herself, she thought of the theory of relativity: how a train's passengers can't feel themselves moving forward because they are stationary relative to the train's motion.

A passenger who didn't know better might believe he was on a perfectly still train, that it was the trees outside that flew by at fifty miles an hour.

She wondered if she could trick her body into believing the same thing. Willing her eyes to soften and then come back into focus, she concentrated on telling her brain that what she knew to be true wasn't. She was surprised to note that after a moment it required almost no concentration at all. Even Lillian—educated, intelligent Lillian—really believed (for a heartbeat, at least) that she wasn't moving an inch. It had been easy. Shockingly little effort was required to believe something just because she decided to try believing it. Utterly fascinating.

Fascinating, but with horrible ramifications for science, of course. Lillian considered herself fortunate to be one of the ones who could be aware of the self-deception as it was happening. She had the rare power to stop it in its tracks. In this instance, it was quite simple to reorient herself to the truth. All she had to do was pay attention to the sound of the wheels.

OCTOBER 1944

Lillian arrived on campus early, hoping to take advantage of the quiet laboratory before her noisy male classmates arrived. Silence was a necessity today. Today, she held in her hand a copy of five problems from last year's Allerton Prize.

Five problems was an enormous get—unheard of, really.

Although the sponsors of the prize provided a general sense of the areas of mathematics that would be tested, actual problems from previous years were kept under lock and key. Test takers entered the room empty-handed and left it empty-handed—not even scratch paper was permitted outside.

That didn't stop a few enterprising individuals from attempting to memorize the problems, hoping to sell their efforts to next year's students who looked to get a leg up. Lillian, of course, would *never* pay for problems half-heartedly scribbled in the margins of a newspaper. That would be cheating. Furthermore, she didn't trust any of her classmates' memories enough to hand over her money. But when a rumor went around that a senior from the mathematics department who had assisted in administering the test had surreptitiously made a copy of its second half... Well, if Lillian suddenly decided that she was interested in going on a date with the fellow, and then another date, and then another date, and then for heaven's sake, a fourth date, that wasn't cheating at all. It was certainly a worthwhile trade, even though it still wasn't until she took him behind the science building and let him touch under her skirt that he finally turned over the folded, yellowing piece of paper. Five real Allerton questions, in her hand. She hadn't even minded being touched by him, although she had wished he took better care of his fingernails.

Unfortunately, the laboratory that morning was not quiet at all, but filled with every last one of her loud and rambunctious male classmates. Only Irene seemed to be uninterested in participating in whatever tomfoolery was going on. (It looked to be a game of tag that involved leaping across desks and slapping each other's behinds. Boys were ridiculous.)

"What's going on? Why is everyone here so early?" Lillian asked Irene.

Irene rubbed her temples. "We have that meeting."

"Another one?" Lillian rolled her eyes. Academia was proving to be a rich and interesting world but for the onslaught of time-wasting meetings. (Although, as much as Lillian hated meetings, she loved being the sort of person who hated meetings.) "I'm not staying for that," she declared. "I'll be in the library."

"You have to stay," said Irene. "It's mandatory."

Lillian had always been one to learn and follow the rules, except in the all-too-frequent instance when the people writing the rules had no idea what they were doing. She was perfectly capable of deciding whether or not her presence was required at a meeting. Ignoring Irene, she headed for the door.

"They're going to take attendance," Irene called to her back.

Lillian dodged a classmate lunging over a desk to make it to the exit, where she immediately ran into a tall, imposing figure entering the room.

"For god's sake, can you idiots at least slow down when you're going through a door?" she snapped, just as the room behind her went deathly quiet.

It was then that Lillian noticed the tall, imposing figure was a man in an army uniform.

"Are you an undergraduate student studying physics at Columbia University?" he asked her.

"I am," she replied, doing her best to sound nonchalant.

"Then have a seat."

Lillian squared her jaw, feeling the eyes of every classmate on her. "I can't attend this meeting. I have a prior engagement."

"She has to go shave her mustache," one of her hilarious classmates fake-whispered. A few giggles and snickers erupted through the room. Lillian's cheeks burned. She tried to will away her embarrassment—why should some idiot who didn't have the guts to speak at a full volume bother her?—but she felt her shoulders sink anyway.

"Have a seat, miss," said the soldier. Lillian slunk back to her desk as he strode to the center of the room.

"Are we being drafted right now?" someone murmured behind Lillian.

"No. That's not how the draft works, dummy," came another whispered response. Lillian noted the lack of confidence in this voice, and it made her feel a little better. She may have had a trace of hair on her upper lip, but unlike anyone else with the same condition, she wouldn't be sent away on a hopeless mission to take over islands off the coast of Japan.

"Good morning, students," began the soldier. "I'm Lieutenant General Jones. I'm here to tell you about an army project that requires the immediate assistance of the brightest young minds in physics."

Lillian looked around at her classmates: Gabe Meadows, who was picking a bit of lint from his ear. Will Bannerman, who was on the verge of falling asleep. Max Medelson, who was deeply engrossed in the process of making a block of wood look more like a cat. If the lieutenant general wanted bright young minds, he wasn't going to find many here.

"At first, this opportunity was only available to students at a graduate level," the lieutenant general continued, eyeing them all with a steely glare. "But with the war effort expanding every day, our need has grown. We're looking to recruit interested students with physics and mathematics experience to relocate to an army engineer works in eastern Tennessee."

At the word *Tennessee,* many of the born-and-raised Manhattanites scoffed, including Lillian. No one just *left* the island, especially for a nothing place like Tennessee. Lillian couldn't quite think of what was even in Tennessee. Surely there were cities, but she had no idea what they were called. Was that one of the states with prairies, or one of the ones with mountains? She had never bothered to learn such detail.

Jones heard the scoffing and raised a hand, silencing the room. "You might want to hear me out before you react like that. These positions are paid, and you'll be working with some of the world's preeminent physicists."

"Like who?" asked Gabe Meadows.

"I can't tell you," said Jones. "Military secrecy."

Lillian knew that phrase surely translated to "no one good."

Jones went on. "I *can* tell you that there's housing available, for singles and families. And we have plenty of unskilled work if your wives want to relocate with you."

"Or husbands," added Lillian. She glanced at Irene for support, but Irene kept her head down, steadfastly avoiding Lillian's gaze.

Lieutenant General Jones was not in the mood. "Are you married?" he snapped, staring daggers right at the fuzz on her upper lip.

"Of course she's not. Let's move on," groaned Max Medelson from the other side of the room.

"Whether or not I'm married isn't the point—" Lillian began.

"I'll say," interrupted Jones. "Regardless. Because of military secrecy, I can't give you any information on the work you'll be doing." This didn't faze most of the room. It was the army; there were a limited scope of possibilities. Airplanes that flew faster, ships that sank slower. Stronger bullets, and stronger metals to shield against the stronger bullets the other side was building in their own top-secret army engineering works. That bit was boring; Jones's next sentence was not. "I can also tell you that should you choose to relocate, you'll be deferred other service."

A whisper went through the boys in the room. Now they were listening. One freckled student, his voice lilting with hope, spoke up. "What about our education deferments? We've already been given education deferments."

"As the war goes forward, the army can't guarantee the availability of education deferments," said Jones, as calmly as if he were a waiter informing a table the kitchen had run out of halibut for the day.

The whispers in the room turned to outright conversations. Everyone had heard rumors of this sort every now and then, but here was direct confirmation. Lillian could comprehend their anger, but not their surprise. As if the army would let an untapped pool of healthy bodies sit untouched for long. They certainly didn't care about the minds contained within the bodies they sent off to die.

"When?" shouted another student. "How long before education deferments go away?"

Jones coughed a bit. "I don't have any more information," was all he offered before passing around a stack of applications for what Lillian noted was the almost hilariously generic-named Clinton Engineer Works.

Lillian stared at her blank application. She had no intention of filling it out, of course. Unlike the men in the room, she had no service in need of deferment, and she would not be swayed by the promise to work with "preeminent" physicists. She would meet many preeminent physicists after she became one. She couldn't let anything distract from that goal, from the Allerton Prize, from Harvard, from her future.

As she balled the application up and tossed it in the trash, she caught sight of Max still studying his intently. Eventually he reached in his desk and produced a manila folder, into which he carefully placed his application before locking it in his drawer.

It was awful that a war was happening, that the course of quantum physics was being put on hold so that young men could calculate the maximum velocity of a fighter plane. And yet...if it took Max away from Eleanor... Well, was it so wrong for Lillian to appreciate a silver lining?

JUNE 1945

Lillian had never slept on a train before. None of her journeys had been long enough to warrant it. Her dreams jumped wildly from location to location. More than once she would dream about being on a train, only to have the realization that she was *actually* on a train jolt her awake, leaving her rubbing her eyes and staring at the bunk above her. It was a few feet away but still close enough to feel, combined with the curtain pulled tight at her side, like she was lying in her own coffin. She tried to comfort herself with the thought that if she were in a coffin, she would be dead and not conscious of it, but this line of reasoning—although logically sound—did not much help.

When she drifted off again, she was in a field. Or perhaps not a field (she couldn't see very far in the distance) but definitely somewhere with grass underneath her palms, poking up through her fingers. *The grass is underneath my hands,* she thought, *so I must be on the ground.* It did not occur to her dream self that she should try to get up.

There was a noise in the background, a thick static that she couldn't make out or place. She strained her ears, listening. Was it a river? Perhaps she was lying in the grass by a river.

The noise became louder, and Lillian realized with a start that it was both a river *and* Tchaikovsky's Symphony No. 4. This combination made perfect sense and she felt quite the fool for not recognizing it sooner. Tchaikovsky was one of her favorite composers. She never missed a performance of any of his pieces at the New York Philharmonic. How could she not have recognized it immediately?

For a moment, Lillian wondered if she oughtn't try to *see* this majestic, Tchaikovsky-playing body of water. She went so far as to try moving her hand, but it wouldn't budge. The more she tried to move it, the more it resisted her, clinging tighter and tighter to the grass.

Just as the piccolo was about to come in (her favorite part), Lillian realized that it wasn't Tchaikovsky's Fourth at all but rather the sound of a train. Was she on a train? She *was* on a train—

Lillian jolted awake, rubbed her eyes, and stared at the darkness in front of her.

<hr />

The first thing that Lillian noted about Knoxville, Tennessee, was that apparently its citizens were obsessed with pastels.

As her black-and-white heels clicked along the red brick of L&N Station, she realized she might have made a grave miscalculation in her wardrobe. She had worn her dressiest shoes and an exquisite black suit specifically because most passengers traveling out of Penn Station dressed in their best, and she didn't want to be out of place in her everyday attire. Indeed, most of the men and women who had boarded the train with her were impeccably put together. But apparently those stylish customers had disembarked in Pennsylvania and been replaced by women who wore only candy-colored shades of pink and yellow.

Lillian tried to keep her composure, knowing she wouldn't have to be exposed like a sore thumb for very long. Max had warned her that he wouldn't be able to get a car exactly on time to meet the train, but he hoped she wouldn't have to wait more than twenty minutes. The plan also had the advantage of giving the other passengers time to disperse, decreasing the likelihood they'd be spotted together. Lillian found a bench to wait on at the front of the station and immediately realized why no one in this town wore black. The fabric took in all the sun's heat and radiated it directly onto the skin. She started sweating immediately, the kind of sweat where every single pore seems to open its floodgates.

Waiting in the direct sun simply would not do. Fortunately, she spotted a bus shelter directly across the street. She managed to dodge the traffic (one car) to reach the shade. But unlike New York, where the shady side and the sunny side of the street might as well be in different hemispheres, the heat in Tennessee seemed to permeate the air. It was as if the warmth wasn't coming from the sun at all, but rather rising from the earth, like they were all in a frying pan simmering over the fires of hell.

A drop of sweat rolled off Lillian's forehead and into her eye. She refused to wipe it, absolutely detesting the idea a stranger walking past might think she was crying.

Fifteen minutes went by. Then twenty. Then an hour. With each passing minute, Lillian felt more and more like a fool. Her mind spiraled off into wild scenarios that she knew were not true but couldn't help but fixate on nonetheless: Had this all been a joke? Were Max and Eleanor somewhere nearby, hidden, watching her sweat while they laughed and laughed? Had Max simply forgotten about her? Did he wake up this morning with that nagging feeling of something he was supposed to do today, but couldn't for the life of him remember what it was, before shrugging and heading for breakfast?

One hour and fifteen minutes had passed. The fact that she had trusted Max Medelson at any stage of this was ludicrous. The fact that he had convinced her—frightened her, really— into traveling down here was absurd. Eleanor was fine and in Chicago and wanted absolutely nothing to do with either Max or Lillian, which for one of them at least was a perfectly reasonable—

"Eleanor!"

The voice had been shouting at her for a while before Lillian thought to look up. Standing over her were three women, each dressed, unsurprisingly, in pastels, each wearing absolutely dreadful brown leather boots caked nearly to the top with reddish-brown mud. The one shouting Eleanor's name was a pretty blond with an angelic face who looked at Lillian quizzically with soft blue eyes. "What are you doing here? Where have you been?" she asked eagerly.

She thinks I'm Eleanor, realized Lillian. She knew she should correct the woman, but maybe she could be useful first. "Where did you think I was?" she asked, forcing a smile.

"I hadn't the slightest idea. We've been worried sick," the woman replied unhelpfully. The women flanking her nodded their agreement. The blond sat down on the bench to peer at Lillian strangely, and for a moment Lillian was certain she wouldn't have to admit she wasn't Eleanor because this blond was about to realize it on her own. But all she said was a concerned, "You look tired."

In a way, she was spot-on. Lillian was Eleanor, but tired.

"Actually, I must confess…" Lillian did fully intend to tell the women that she wasn't their acquaintance, and yet she let her sentence trail off. What were the words she was looking for, again?

One of the other women, a curly-haired brunette with the most heavily drawn-on eyebrows Lillian had ever seen, took Lillian's silence as her chance to jump in. "You were with that man, weren't you."

Lillian's spine straightened. Did they mean Max? They couldn't possibly mean Max. Surely they would have noticed that Max was still around when Eleanor was gone (she had no idea how many people worked at this place, but it couldn't have been that many), and anyone describing Max Medelson would most likely choose the descriptor of *boy* rather than *man*. Had Eleanor run off not to Chicago, but with a new suitor? Lillian cleared her throat. Perhaps it was acceptable to continue the lie a moment or two longer, for information gathering only. "Which man?"

The women giggled, and the blond playfully reached up to hit her friend on the shoulder and scold her. "We're not supposed to talk about him."

Something about their laughter hit Lillian in the gut. It was the laughter of a secret joke, gossip shared between friends, *"Don't tell anyone, but I met this man."* It was the kind of laughter that Eleanor used to share only with Lillian, and now she'd gone and shared it with these strangers in frills and pastels and absolutely terrible shoes. The thought made Lillian stew in rage. *Fine*, she thought. *If Eleanor wanted to run off with a man she knew for two months and share her secrets only with this pack of idiots, let her.* Lillian stood and grabbed her suitcase. She no longer even wanted Max Medelson's no-doubt-ridiculous take on the situation. She wanted to be back in New York, as quickly as possible. She regretted not following through on her impulse to hang up when she'd heard Max's voice on the phone.

"Where are you going?" asked the blond woman. In her

rage, Lillian had somehow completely missed the arrival of a large tan bus bearing a sign in its front window reading "Clinton Engineer Works: Townsite." Lillian recognized the bland name from the application she'd binned a few months ago. This was the bus to where Eleanor lived, where Eleanor worked, and now three of Eleanor's friends were wondering why she wasn't joining them in the queue to board.

Lillian couldn't even be bothered to come up with a good excuse. "I forgot something," she said blandly. "I'll catch up with you later."

The blond woman peered at her in that strange way again, and Lillian noted an edge to a jawline that moments ago had appeared nothing but cherubic. "Are you sure?"

Lillian's initial jolt of anger had lessened a bit, allowing her to hear the question and consider it. She was a woman—a smart woman, sure—but still a woman, alone, with not much money, in a strange city. She had a ticket back to New York in her bag for a train that didn't leave for another week. She could sit on this bench forever and wait for Max to find her, she could waste a week in a cheap hotel room bored to tears in Knoxville, or she could figure out where Eleanor had gone off to from the inside.

For a moment, Lillian entertained the thought of solving the riddle and showing up at her sister's secret stoop in Chicago or Pittsburgh or Boston. She imagined the look on Eleanor's face when she realized she'd been found, that Eleanor may have thought she was smart but that Lillian would always be smarter, that Eleanor could run but Lillian would run farther, and she would be going to Harvard.

"Never mind," she said to the blond woman, joining her in the queue. "I'll come with you."

The blond smiled, rummaging through her handbag as she stepped on the bus. Lillian followed.

"ID?"

The bus driver wore an entirely khaki uniform that looked like it had been rejected by the army for being too dull. Once Lillian realized his question was directed at her, she almost laughed. She had hoped her plan would last a little bit longer than fifteen seconds.

"I take it you don't mean my driver's license," she said. She didn't have one of those, either, but that wasn't the point.

The bus driver was unamused. "Your CEW ID."

It was no doubt an army rule, and therefore worthless to try to mount a logical defense against. Lillian would have shrugged, turned around, and returned to her bench. But something deep inside her insisted that she wasn't Lillian. *You're Eleanor,* the voice hissed. *What would Eleanor do?*

It had always been easy for Lillian to imitate her sister. She'd done it a little bit when flirting with Alexander, the mathematics student who had given her the Allerton questions. Not the part where she'd let him touch her behind the science building, of course. Eleanor would have been horrified by that. But when she'd batted her eyelashes and touched his arm and acted like everything he said was *fascinating* to even get the date in the first place—that, she had learned from her sister.

She looked for the driver's name tag. "Come on, Mark, it's me," she said with a smile that felt strange on her face. Her cheeks seemed to be working overtime to sustain it; they were out of practice. "You've seen me on this bus all the time."

"Rules are rules, miss," said Mark.

"Yes, but presumably the rules are there for a reason. To stop strangers from getting on the bus. A smart man like you must know that." She fluttered her lashes up and down. "And I'm not a stranger, am I?"

He sighed. "This never happened," he said, waving her through.

Lillian made her way to the back of the bus, turning her suitcase sideways so she could squeeze through the aisle. She noted that everyone was displaying incredibly poor footwear choices: all some variety of heavy boot, more than one caked in red mud. She was now relieved she selected the black and white heels. Someone in this town had to demonstrate good taste.

She'd barely reached the last open seat when the bus lurched into motion. Eleanor's friends were safely a few rows behind her, and Lillian could drop the smile that was now starting to hurt her face. Rubbing her cheeks, she stared out the window and wondered if she hadn't made a huge miscalculation by boarding this bus.

Find Max, she thought. *There's nothing you can do until the bus stops, but as soon as it does, you can get off and find Max.*

FOUR

JUNE 1945

The bus journey lasted longer than Lillian expected, even though she couldn't quite articulate what she *had* been expecting. Downtown Knoxville had fallen away quickly, leaving behind a scenery of endless tall grass and mountains and the occasional farmhouse for nearly an hour. Just as Lillian was wondering if they'd ever arrive, the bus slowed down. She peered out the window, eager for her first glimpse of the mysterious place where Eleanor had spent the last two months.

But all she saw was a fence.

The sight took her aback. Was a fence really necessary? They were in the middle of nowhere in Tennessee. How many walk-up visitors did the army need to ensure were kept out? She blinked to clear her eyes in case she was seeing things, but it remained a fence, and a tall one at that. Twelve feet, at least, and topped with strips of ominous barbed wire. It could have been plucked straight from a prison yard, and the notion made Lillian suddenly quite uncomfortable. Perhaps the fence wasn't there to prevent people from coming in, but to make sure no one got out.

A uniformed soldier pushed a gate open and waved the bus through. Lillian was certain they would arrive within seconds to their destination, which she reasoned would be perhaps four buildings—one for the men to live in, one for the women, and perhaps one or two for whatever it was they were doing there.

What she saw instead shocked her.

To her left, there wasn't much of note, but to her right a few round hills crested above the tree line that appeared to be dotted with cement-colored houses, poking out every few feet from among the pines. It was nowhere near as dense as Manhattan, sure, but it could be Long Island, or Queens. Whatever it was, it certainly wasn't four buildings. They passed a school, and just as Lillian was wondering in amazement what kind of engineering works could possibly require a school, they passed a small white *church*. The farther in from the fence they went, the more people began to appear. Soon there were dozens of men, women, even children, walking along the road, utterly undeterred by the lack of pavement or a sidewalk. They were quietly strolling alone, or laughing in groups, or carrying shopping bags, just like they would be in Manhattan.

It was a city, thought Lillian, her stomach dropping and

her hands suddenly as fidgety as if she'd drunk an entire pot of coffee. It was a whole city, built behind a fence. She fussed with her necklace nervously, feeling the graininess of the pearls on her fingertips. How would she ever find Max here? How would she find *anything*—Eleanor's room? Eleanor's things?

The bus rolled to its first stop, an intersection at a road that led uphill to what appeared to be *another* school. The door hissed open. Lillian jumped to her feet, not even bothering to take the time to smooth her skirt. She had already grabbed her suitcase and made her way into the aisle when she was stopped by a hand on the hemline of her black suit.

The blond woman was holding her back. "Where are you going?"

"I need to get off," said Lillian. The bus suddenly felt extremely claustrophobic, a cage she needed to escape. "I'm meeting someone."

"You're not going back to our room first?"

So the blond woman and Eleanor were roommates. That was a useful piece of information—but for later. "It's quite urgent," insisted Lillian.

"But your bag," said one of the brunettes, sharing a seat with the blond. "Won't it look suspicious to be walking around town with a suitcase?"

"Suspicious?" Lillian couldn't fathom why anyone would care what a stranger thought of their possession of luggage.

"Someone might think you're smuggling out secrets," said

the brunette dramatically, raising one of her heavily painted brows. "It's out of the ordinary."

This was so impossibly ludicrous Lillian couldn't help but chuckle. "Out of the ordinary...!" Her laugh faded when she saw that neither of the women had even cracked a smile.

"Come back to the room," said the blond woman. "Whoever you're meeting will understand you needed to drop off your things."

Lillian felt trapped into forcing a smile and sinking back into her seat. She stared out the window desperately, searching the face of every pedestrian that passed, trying to will Max's familiar jaw and wavy brown hair to appear. The quantum world could be affected by the mere presence of an observer, so perhaps if the world knew she was watching, she'd recognize the face of one of these strangers—

But once again, the quantum world refused to affect her real one, and the bus moved on.

DECEMBER 1944

Lillian glanced at her watch. It was ten minutes past one. Out of the corner of her eye, she saw the waitress approach her yet again, this time under the pretense of refilling her water glass.

"You can't hold this table forever," said the waitress as ice clanged out of the pitcher. She was an older woman whose graying locks were pulled back into a woven snood—a red one, as if to match her disapproval.

"Trust me, I'm not holding it for my own amusement," muttered Lillian.

The waitress gave her a bit of a glare, but relented. "Five more minutes," she said.

The glare would prove unnecessary. It was only two minutes before Eleanor arrived at the table, cheeks flushed from the cold. She grinned and offered what was not an apology but instead a loud exclamation: "Rodgers and Hammerstein are writing a new musical!"

Lillian wanted to match her excitement, but it was difficult when she didn't know what on earth her sister was talking about. "Are those friends of yours?"

Eleanor laughed as she unbuttoned her camel polo coat, draping it over the back of the dark oak chair. The coat was from last winter, Lillian recalled. Once upon a time, Eleanor had purchased a new coat every winter, but with the same neutral wartime utility clothes replacing what used to be called "fashion," there was hardly a point. "They aren't friends of mine," she said, settling in at the table and helping herself to a drink from Lillian's water glass. "They write musical comedies. Rodgers writes the music, and Hammerstein the lyrics. Or maybe it's the other way around. I can't believe you haven't heard of them, Lil. You're so deeply uncultured."

"I think not knowing musical comedy writers actually makes me *more* cultured," said Lillian.

"Of course you would think that," laughed Eleanor. "They're really quite good. They wrote *Oklahoma!*"

Lillian happened to be taking a sip from the water glass that was rightfully hers as Eleanor said this, and the resulting snort threatened to spray water all over the table. "They wrote *Oklahoma!* Well, why didn't you say so! How could they be anything but respected practitioners of the arts with a title like *Oklahoma!* Why, it rivals Tchaikovsky's *1812 Overture!*"

Eleanor waved this off. "You didn't even see it. It was good! But *Oklahoma!* is yesterday's news. They're writing a new show, and they're already casting the workshop."

She said this last bit with a wiggling of her eyebrows that implied Lillian should be picking up on something quite obvious. This was a game at which Lillian was terrible and did not care for. "What? Don't wiggle your eyebrows at me. Just say what you mean to be saying, please."

Before Eleanor could respond, the impatient waitress arrived at their side. "Ready to order?" she asked.

"Oh goodness, I haven't even looked at the menu yet!" responded Eleanor. "I hope you'll forgive me; I'm a bit flustered! I've received some wonderful news. But I'll look right now, I promise. Oh, what a lovely snood!"

"Thank you," said the waitress, reaching back to touch it gently. "Take your time with the menu. I'll be back."

And that's how it was, how it always was. The same people who scolded Lillian were utterly charmed by her identical sister.

Lillian didn't resent Eleanor for this, but she did wish her sister knew it wasn't as easy for the rest of the world to be so beloved.

"Anyway, as I was saying," Eleanor continued, "I have an audition." She shimmied her shoulders a little and sat up quite proudly.

Lillian gasped. "How exciting! When?"

"In a week," said Eleanor. She reached into her large, black patent clutch—another generic item from several years ago, not worth replacing—and pulled out a folded sheet of paper. She smoothed it out on the table for Lillian to see. "Look at the length of the monologue I have to memorize."

"My word." There were barely any margins on the paper, it was so covered in dense prose. "Is this necessary?" asked Lillian.

"Must be," replied Eleanor with a shrug.

"Does every chorus girl have to do this?"

"Oh no," said Eleanor with a slight smile. "I'm not audition-ing for the chorus."

"You're not?" After an entire childhood of private singing lessons, Eleanor's vocal instructor had recommended her to a few producers, resulting in Eleanor booking a small chorus role in a Broadway show when she was only seventeen. The show was terrible—it closed in under a week—but she'd managed to use the experience to land two more chorus jobs over the next three years. But these had always been chorus roles: light, easy work that required little dancing and certainly no acting.

Eleanor again reached for Lillian's water as she shook her head. "No. It's a lead."

Obviously, Lillian knew that her first reaction (a perfectly reasonable question about Eleanor's ability to pull such a thing off) was inappropriate, and she had to push through to the genuine excitement. Which was there—really, truly. It was just that Lillian's logical side often overcame her emotional one. "Oh, really! Well, that's fantastic!"

Eleanor smiled again. "They liked my look, according to my agent."

"I'll take that as a compliment, too," said Lillian.

Eleanor finally opened her menu, and only had to glance at it for approximately thirty seconds before signaling for the waitress. She ordered the Niçoise salad dressed in vinaigrette, which is what Lillian had planned on ordering until she suddenly felt self-conscious about ordering an identical meal to her identical twin. Instead, Lillian opted for the Caesar salad, which she found boring as a meal—but she was too flustered to spend much time selecting something else.

"What's the part you're auditioning for?" Lillian asked her sister. "What's the story?"

"I don't know," said Eleanor. "They're keeping the whole thing under wraps. It's not even done yet. Isn't that exciting?"

"They're casting for a show that's not even done yet?" mused Lillian. "How interesting." It perpetually baffled her how people in the arts seemed to refuse to do anything in logical order.

"It's a workshop," explained Eleanor. "They cast people so they can hear it out loud while they're writing it."

"Why do they need to do that?"

"So they can see if what they're writing is good or not."

"They're professional writers. Can't they tell?"

"Well, sometimes writers aren't sure."

This sounded like utter nonsense to Lillian. "If they're unsure, I would think that means it's bad."

Eleanor laughed. "It's very common, Lil."

"If you say so. How long does a 'workshop' last?"

"Eight weeks."

Lillian's eyes widened. "That long? My goodness."

"And I haven't even mentioned the best part yet."

The best part would have to wait a little longer. The waitress returned to drop off Eleanor's salad, just as a woman in a white chef's coat appeared at their table. "Caesar salad?"

Lillian lifted her hand slightly.

The woman nodded and vanished, reappearing moments later with a tray of ingredients and giant metal bowl. Lillian tried to conceal her groan. "I forgot it's prepared tableside," she whispered to Eleanor.

The chef obviously overheard. "To prove our dressing is as fresh as possible, miss."

Lillian forced a smile. She knew *why* it was prepared tableside; that wasn't the point. She'd much rather taken their word for it and not have a stranger breathing down their necks for three minutes. She shifted uncomfortably. "What's the best part?" she asked Eleanor.

"Right," said Eleanor. "If it goes well, they might cast me in the out-of-town tryouts in Chicago."

Lillian furrowed her brow. "Chicago?"

"I know, isn't that exciting?"

"And how long would that last?"

Eleanor shrugged.

"But you'd be back before I leave, right?"

"Leave for what?"

"Harvard, obviously."

Eleanor stared at her, incredulous. "Are you kidding me, Lillian?"

The chef cracked an egg into the bowl and began to whisk. Lillian lowered her tone. "I most certainly am not."

"That's over a year away."

"No, it's one year exactly. I'm graduating early, remember? If you go to Chicago, will you be back in a year? Because someone has to take care of Mother."

"I can't believe this," fumed Eleanor. "I don't even have the part yet, and you're already making me feel bad about it."

The chef dumped a handful of romaine into the bowl and tried to act like she wasn't eavesdropping. "I'm not trying to make you feel bad," hissed Lillian. "My goodness. I'm simply asking a question about logistics."

The completed Caesar salad was unceremoniously dumped

on Lillian's plate, and the chef scurried away as fast as respect-
ably possible. Lillian stabbed a bit of romaine with her fork.
"Next time you're going to make a scene, could you pick a
time when there isn't a stranger standing over our table?" she
muttered.

In spite of herself, Eleanor snorted a laugh. The undigni-
fied sound made Lillian giggle, too.

"I really was just asking a question," said Lillian. "I do still
want you to get the part, as long as it's a good part, of course. Is
it a good part?"

Eleanor chewed her tuna thoughtfully. "I mean, it is the
lead."

JUNE 1945

Lillian's left foot hovered over the final step. Not ten minutes ago,
she'd been desperate to disembark, so eager to hunt for Max.
Now she couldn't bring herself to put her foot on the ground.

It turned out there was a reason beyond poor fashion that
the women of Tennessee wore old boots caked in mud. This
town was so new that apparently they hadn't gotten around to
building sidewalks yet, or pavement of any kind, it seemed. The
roads were mud, the walkways mud, even the patches of grass
had been trampled so sparse they were mostly mud.

"What's going on up there?" someone shouted from behind
Lillian. It occurred to her that she was holding up the queue,

but she couldn't be bothered to care. Her black and white pump was a foot away from a patch of particularly wet mud. She needed time to mourn the loss properly. They weren't her favorite shoes, it was true; she hardly ever wore them, as they were much too fancy for school. Still, they had always been in her closet, at the ready. It had been comforting to know that *should* she want to do something more exciting than go to school, she'd have the shoes to do it in.

My god, grow up, Lillian. They're just shoes.

She took a deep breath, closed her eyes. She had no choice. All this time she spent fussing over a little bit (all right, quite a lot) of mud, could have been spent looking for Max. And yet—

You don't have an option. It's not like you can take them off.

She wasn't even wearing stockings. She still owned stockings, of course, but people tended to shoot dirty looks at women wearing stockings, as if they should immediately mail their used hosiery off to Uncle Sam. Rationing nylon didn't mean the government wanted everyone to turn in their used undergarments, but Lillian found it easier to go bare-legged than to argue about anything perceived as unpatriotic. It was her naked toes stuffed into those heels, and she very well couldn't step barefoot into slimy mud.

Or could she?

"Come on!" shouted someone behind her, and in a flash, Lillian slipped off both her shoes, tucked them under her arm, and stepped off the bus.

Wet mud squicked up through her toes. The sensation was nauseating, and the sound of the mud slapping against her feet was worse. The handful of women who had gotten off before her barely tried to hide their disgust or their giggles.

The blond woman, to Lillian's relief, had a bit of sympathy for her. She took Lillian by the arm, helping her through the worst of the muddy patch. Lillian noted that it was not without a smirk, but she appreciated the gesture nonetheless.

"Forgot your boots, huh?" she said. "It's happened to all of us."

"No, it hasn't," laughed a nearby woman.

The bus had deposited them about fifty feet away from a long, narrow, two-story building, the same cement-white color as the houses she'd seen from the bus window. Two wings stretched out from a center entrance, and though Lillian had never seen it before, there was no mistaking this building for anything but the dormitory. To her surprise, however, the blond did not head for the dormitory's entrance but around the back of the building. Lillian realized there was another dormitory behind the first one, and a third dormitory off to her right, and then—goodness—was that two, three, four more off in the distance ahead?

The blond woman gabbed on about one thing or another. Fortunately, her conversation didn't seem to require much of a response from Lillian. Bare feet still sliding on mud, arms heavy from suitcases, her brain feeling like it had been put in a jar and shaken up from the sheer overwhelming size of this place,

Lillian didn't feel much like speaking. She tried to focus on her plan, on the small steps she could take next. After making it to whichever one of these drab buildings was hers, she would put down her luggage and find a way to wash her feet. *Where will you put down your luggage? Where will you find a bathroom?* Problems rose to the surface far more quickly than any ideas. Lillian, usually a realist, now clung to optimism like it was a life raft and she adrift at sea. *You can abandon your suitcase! That will be fine! It doesn't matter, in the long run. You can find Max with dirty feet! All that matters is that you find him.*

Fortunately, the building right behind the first dormitory proved to be their destination. From the size of the building, Lillian would guess it contained maybe forty rooms or so, but the noise and activity inside seemed more appropriate for hundreds, not dozens, of women. Right off the front entranceway was a laundry room, where women shouted and giggled over a radio playing far too loudly. Two long hallways stretched to either side, flung-open doors revealing girls sitting on their beds, girls talking and laughing, girls painting their nails. The blond stopped in front of the fifth or sixth door on the left, dropping Lillian's hand to dig through the small tan handbag she carried for her key.

The door swung open, and the air that hid behind it hit Lillian in the gut.

It was Eleanor. The air smelled—Lillian would have never recognized it before, but it was undeniable—like Eleanor. Her perfume, the one Lillian had always teased her for spritzing on her wrists: *Surely men know you don't really smell like lavender!* It was her hair spray, the brand she never left the house without a copious amount sprayed on. It was her, complete, indescribable, a memory Lillian hadn't realized she'd forgotten.

But Eleanor was not there. There wasn't even a dent in the pillow, an impression in the bedspread.

After sitting Lillian down on the bed, the blond woman gave a "wait here" before disappearing down the hall. Lillian took advantage of her absence to take in the room. It was tiny, far more appropriate for one person than two. The bulk of the space was taken up by the two beds, each pressed up as close as possible to opposite walls and yet still only a few feet apart. The rest of the furniture—two nightstands, two dressers, all the same bland and industrial tan—were shoved in awkwardly, clearly deposited where they would fit and not arranged with any eye for decoration.

The closet was of decent size, at least, running the length of most of the wall opposite the beds, but it had no door. Without any other storage, it had been shoved to the brim with clothes, shoes, books, cases, handbags, making the whole room appear messy and disorganized even though none of it spilled out into the room itself. The simple light fixture dangling from the center of the claustrophobically low ceiling was off, so the only light in the room came from the narrow single-pane window that seemed punched out like an afterthought above her roommate's bed. There was no desk, no armchair, no carpeting, nothing that would make this place feel anything like home.

Eleanor's roommate returned only a few moments later with a bucket and a towel. Lillian submerged her feet in the clear, lukewarm water. Swirls of mud dirtied its surface.

"Better?" asked the woman.

"Much," admitted Lillian.

Her roommate flopped down on her own twin bed and kicked off her boots. "So," she said in her same cheerful tone of voice, "why don't you actually tell me where you've been, instead of cleverly blowing off the question?"

It was so innocently spoken that it took a moment for the words to hit Lillian. She blinked a few times, aware of her spine stiffening—a guilty sign if there ever was one. Her best chance at not being caught in a lie, she reasoned, was to tell as much of the truth as possible. "I was in New York," she answered.

The blond woman smiled, and suddenly the expression was haunting rather than friendly. "Come on, El, it's just the two of us now," she goaded. "You can tell *me*."

This last syllable was drawn out in that playful way Lillian had observed women used when chatting with girlfriends, but there was nothing friend-like about the way this woman's eyes were piercing her. Lillian swallowed. "That's the truth," she said. She swallowed again. Her throat was suddenly so dry. "I went home to New York to see my mother and sister."

"Oh, please," said the woman. "You know I don't buy that

for a second! You disappeared without a warning. They'd never let someone leave out of nowhere like that."

Lillian remembered the fence, the barbed wire, the eerie sensation she was walking herself into a prison. She shrugged, and tried her best to look bored. "I don't know what to say. They let me. Anyway..." Lillian searched for something to change the subject to, but found herself quickly at a loss.

"All right, keep your secrets," said the woman. "You know what's interesting?"

"What is?" asked Lillian.

"I didn't even know you had a sister," she said with a yawn. "Anyway, Sadie and I are going to see a movie. Want to come?"

After adequately managing to hide her shock that this place had a *movie theater* and insisting that the blond woman should go on without her, Lillian finally had the room to herself. She was starting to get hungry, but there wasn't any time to waste. The answer to where Eleanor had gone had to be in this room somewhere.

As soon as the door had shut behind the blond, Lillian went for Eleanor's nightstand, pulling open the slim top drawer. The motion jerked a curious small cardboard tube, which rolled to the front. It took Lillian a moment to recognize it was the inside of a lipstick. Then a flash of memory: Eleanor would remove the tube from the applicator so she could scrape the very last dregs of the shade out with her fingernail. *Just throw it out,* Lillian would scold her. *The time you spend rooting around in there isn't worth the cost of a new lipstick.*

She'd nearly forgotten Eleanor had done this. How much had she forgotten about Eleanor? How much had Eleanor forgotten about her?

The next thing she spotted in the drawer was a picture ID badge that listed Eleanor as a "Townsite resident" and gave her "clearance level 5" for "Building Y-12." Lillian quickly pocketed it despite the meaninglessness of all these phrases. Wherever Eleanor had gone, she had decided not to take her ID with her. From Lillian's experience boarding the bus, that could only mean that if Eleanor had left the facility, she had no intention of returning.

Or she'd forgotten it. With absentminded Eleanor, that was a distinct possibility. Lillian took the ID out of her pocket and stared again at her sister's smiling face. Did the presence of this silly little card mean something, or not?

She didn't have time for the random chances of the universe, she decided. Eleanor must have purposefully left it behind.

Underneath the ID was a thin book with the phrase "Resident's Handbook" printed on its card-stock cover. Lillian could have fainted with relief. Finally, she thought, some explanation of where she was, what on earth Eleanor was expected to do here—but the handbook contained no such thing. The front page consisted of the usual "Do whatever the army tells you, or it's your fault if we lose this war" propaganda, and it was mostly downhill from there. Lillian's hopes of finding a map that might help her find Max, or even a hint or two at the purpose of this seemingly full-size city, were quickly dashed. She did, however, learn that gambling, drinking, or other "violations of the moral code" could result in losing one's housing. *How important,* she thought bitterly.

The rest of the drawers were largely empty. A few pens, a half-smoked pack of cigarettes, some clip-on earrings, more makeup, a few hairpins. She moved on to the closet. The good maroon suitcases were still there, and a good deal of Eleanor's clothes, although it was impossible for Lillian to say if any were missing without knowing exactly what Eleanor had brought with her in the first place. Regardless, she had not packed her bags, meaning she might have left in a hurry, or perhaps it really was suspicious to be carrying luggage around here. Or maybe she wanted some time to get ahead before anyone realized she was gone. Or maybe she didn't care if she left anything behind, because she was running off with a wealthy—

Lillian realized she could speculate on the meaning of the suitcases for hours. She had to leave it for now and move on. A few pieces of cheap silver jewelry were already gathering a thin layer of dust on top of the bureau, but the string of pearls, Lillian noted, was nowhere to be found. That at least eliminated the possibility that Eleanor had been snatched in the middle of the night. She glanced in the bureau drawers but found nothing except stacks of more clothes. A few things, however, were conspicuously absent, like Eleanor's black patent clutch, as well as any money.

Lillian returned to the closet, digging a little deeper this time for anything she might have missed. There was, in the back of the closet, a dress that appeared to have fallen off its hanger and landed behind the rack of shoes. Lillian kneeled and reached her hand back to pull it out to the light—

It was the green silk dress. Lillian didn't simply drop it—her hand recoiled from it, the way it would after touching an unexpectedly hot stove. She was surprised to note her own heart was racing as if she'd suffered a great fright. Ridiculous! It was only a dress.

And yet she found that looking at the horrible wrinkles in the silk, thinking about that long row of delicate buttons, made her stomach churn. Unavoidable, horrible memories danced through her head:

Eleanor's audition—

Janet Mayberry—

She was being ridiculous. It was a dress, nothing more. Lillian rose from the floor, found an empty hanger in the closet, and hung it with the rest of Eleanor's things.

She returned to her search only to realize it was over. There were no more drawers to open, no more stones to overturn. The room was so small that her entire investigation couldn't have taken more than fifteen minutes, but she was suddenly exhausted by the effort. Perhaps a quick rest before she set off to find Max would be a good idea.

But as she crawled into Eleanor's bed and pulled the sheet up to her neck, the dress seemed to haunt her—stare at her, almost, even as she shut her eyes and tried to banish thoughts of it from her mind. How ridiculous she was being, giving a few scraps of fabric so much power over her. Why should a dress bring up bad memories for her? She had done nothing wrong.

As if to prove the statement to herself, she went back to the closet and yanked the dress off its hanger, shoving it once more behind the shoe rack where it fell. It could rot there. What did she care?

It was a shock when Eleanor's roommate shook her awake. Lillian hadn't actually believed she would fall so deeply asleep. There was far too much on her mind, not to mention the stifling humidity. For a few disorienting moments, Lillian thought she might have slept all the way until the next morning, but this dissipated when she realized the blond was babbling on about going to dinner. At the word, Lillian's stomach growled. She hadn't had a bite to eat since breakfast on the train, which was hours ago.

She sat up blearily and attempted to blink the sleep away from her eyes. She needed a change of clothes, that was certain. The nap had wrinkled her skirt, and sweat had drenched her blouse. Stumbling toward Eleanor's closet, she stared for the second time that afternoon at the handful of outfits that hung there. The idea of wearing Eleanor's clothes, even clothes she had abandoned, felt wrong. This was no longer the closet they had shared in New York, with a divide in the middle that was merely symbolic. This was Eleanor's closet, shared with someone entirely new. This closet had nothing to do with Lillian.

She pulled her mustard-yellow suitcase from where she had stashed it under the bed. Its hinges cried as she propped it open, reaching for her standard starched white button-up blouse and her charcoal skirt. It was nice, too, to have on clean, familiar clothes in such a strange place. She noticed her roommate watching her with curiosity as she dressed, but paid her no mind. Sometimes people got new clothes, didn't they? One's tastes could change, could they not?

The only item of clothing she did borrow from Eleanor's closet was a pair of muddy black leather boots. As she laced them up, she could feel the imprints where Eleanor's toes had begun to wear in the soles. So close to where her own toes landed, but off just enough to feel strange.

"Are you ready to go?" Lillian asked her roommate as she ran a few fingers through her rapidly frizzing hair to fight the tangles.

"Is that what you're wearing?" asked the roommate, and Lillian fought the urge to roll her eyes. Once a person saw a woman dressed up, they believed they were entitled to view that woman only dressed up every day going forward. People could be so silly about appearances.

"I brought some new clothes from home," answered Lillian. Thankfully, that seemed to be the end of the conversation, at least for now.

The cafeteria was only a short walk from the dormitory, past three more identical cement dorms and across the street to what seemed to be a full-scale shopping plaza. A security guard on a horse, of all things, was set up near the entrance, which would have surprised Lillian if she hadn't been too busy marveling at a sign in the distance that advertised an ice-skating rink. Fortunately, she had remember to put Eleanor's ID inside her clutch and passed by both man and horse without incident.

The place was packed when they went inside, but Lillian was grateful for the chatter of people, as it masked somewhat the fact that she didn't have much to say to the blond roommate whose name she still didn't know. As she took a tray from the stack— the plastic still hot from the quick sanitization it had received— she noted that most of the people in line ahead of her were women. Of course this sight wasn't surprising back home, in the halls of Columbia or the theaters in Times Square, but she had thought that an army engineer works would look more like the army. She was so taken by the abundance of dresses and pin curls that for a moment she forgot her original purpose. Then she saw a familiar flick of a wrist out of the corner of her eye, a shaving of wood float to the floor.

Max.

FIVE

JUNE 1945

Mumbling some excuse to her blond companion, Lillian took her tray and headed for that unmistakable mop of floppy dirt-brown hair. Max sat at the only table of men in the room, although a little way apart from the group, engrossed in yet another wood carving as his colleagues threw bread and laughed and shouted at one another with mouths full of shiny scrambled eggs. Max had never quite fit in with the boys at Columbia, which Lillian always suspected was because he believed himself to be better than them. It seemed the dynamic had repeated itself anew. Incredible, thought Lillian, that not even active participation in the war effort could turn a boy into a man.

Max happened to look up when she was only twenty or so feet away, and at the sight of her dropped the wood carving in his hand, the poor creature's tail snapping clean off.

Lillian stopped in her tracks. She could hear the boys at Max's side stop their ribbing to turn their attention to him. "What happened, butterfingers?" one of them laughed.

Max said nothing. In one swift move, he scooped the pieces of the broken carving from the linoleum and headed toward the door without so much as a glance at Lillian.

Despite her hunger, she abandoned her spaghetti, side salad, and canned peaches on the nearest table and followed him.

"Are you insane?" were the first words out of his mouth when she found him outside, around the corner of the building, hidden from the main road.

"I waited for you. For over an hour," she countered indignantly. She'd been so focused on finding Max that she'd nearly forgotten how much she disliked him. It was quickly coming back to her. "Eleanor's roommate saw me at the bus stop and thought I was her. I saw an opportunity, and I took it."

"I got stuck at work," said Max. "It happens on a project as important as this one. I show up only a couple hours late to find you not there. I thought you hadn't showed." He rubbed his temple, annoyance crossing his brow. "Okay, okay. You can do your best to lay low until tomorrow morning, and then you can take the bus back to Knoxville with the night commuters at shift change. Think you can manage that?"

"Why would I go back to Knoxville?" asked Lillian, a tad annoyed Max was refusing to give her even a little bit of credit.

How many others could claim they flirted their way onto a secret army facility?

"You can't very well stay here," he snapped.

Lillian folded her arms. "Why not? Eleanor's roommate thinks she ran off with some man, and I've searched her room, which seems to bear that out. She took her money and her purse but not her ID. My train home isn't for another week. If I can figure out who that man is before then, I can figure out where she went."

"She didn't run off with some man," said Max.

"How do you know?"

"Because the man she was seeing is still here."

Lillian pursed her lips. That was an unforeseen wrinkle, certainly. But before she could address that, she raised her voice innocently. "I thought she was seeing you."

She'd hoped to get a rise out of him, and she had. "We broke up," Max said, accidentally raising the volume of his voice a bit and staring at the ground in disgust.

Lillian couldn't help but feel a rush of relief at the confirmation, which she tried to mask with a surprised expression and an arched eyebrow. "Oh? When?"

"She didn't tell you?"

Of course. Max had no idea how bad the falling-out between Lillian and Eleanor had been. "Eleanor and I have better things to talk about than men," she lied.

"Well, about a week after she arrived, someone stole her away from me," Max said.

"You can't steal a whole person," replied Lillian.

Max blustered on as if she had said nothing at all. "My boss. You'll recognize the name: Dr. Andrew Ennis."

Lillian did recognize the name. "From Caltech? The man who yelled at Niels Bohr?"

Max nodded. "The very same."

"Huh," muttered Lillian. The incident had occurred before she'd even started school, but it was so legendary it was still gossiped about in physics labs, even ones all the way across the country. Bohr, the world-famous physicist, had graciously agreed to give a lecture to Caltech's undergrads, only to be berated by a student over one of the theories he was presenting. The actual theory, and the student's issue with it, varied wildly from story to story. In Lillian's mind, this was a key part of the plot: *What if Bohr had been wrong and the undergrad right?* Her colleagues tended to find this less relevant than she did.

"He's as much of a piece of work as you'd think," said Max. "Temper. Flies off the handle at anyone, anytime. Yells at us constantly, over the most minor mistakes. I know he could have done something violent."

"Violent?" It dawned on her why Max had been so insistent she come. He didn't merely think Eleanor was missing. "You think she's dead."

"Christ." Max winced at the word, seeming surprised at Lillian's candor. If she were to be honest, Lillian was a bit surprised at it herself. Perhaps it didn't affect her because it didn't seem true. Wouldn't she know if the person who shared her DNA had died? Wouldn't she feel it in her cells? Eleanor couldn't be dead.

"She was going to leave him," Max continued. "I don't know what happened, but she told me he wasn't a good person and she wanted to end it. That was the last I saw of her."

Lillian nodded, her mind spinning through scenarios. "Maybe she decided not to go through with it? Run away, rather than risk his temper."

Max shook his head. "She wouldn't have left without me."

Lillian wasn't sure if she heard him correctly. "Pardon?"

"She was going to leave him for me," said Max.

"And she...told you this? She told you she was leaving him for you?"

"Not in so many words," admitted Max. "But I know it. She never stopped loving me. He swept her off her feet for a time, but she never stopped loving me." Lillian could hardly believe what she was hearing, and yet it all made perfect sense. She had come all this way—slept overnight on a train, lost hours of Allerton practice—on the delusional hunches of a jealous ex-lover. She pressed her eyelids closed. Max Medelson had nothing. Her sister could be anywhere and Max Medelson had *nothing*.

Max realized she was barely listening. She watched the truth as it dawned on him: "You don't believe me," he said.

"Max," she began as gently as possible, "this is an army base with thousands of people around. One of Eleanor's silly friends told me it would be suspicious to carry a suitcase. I had to show ID to have the privilege of purchasing spaghetti tonight. How would a murder happen without anyone noticing?"

"There's places where security doesn't go. There's woods," said Max, but she could hear the waver in his voice. She could practically see him calculating behind his eyes. *Was* there anywhere behind this fence where no one would hear a scream? Where no one would come across a body for weeks on end?

"What if she *let* you think she was leaving him for you? What if she was giving you a kindness before she ran off somewhere on her own?"

"That's not the case," said Max in an uneven tone that indicated he suddenly wasn't sure, not at all. "You never liked me," he lashed out suddenly. "Admit it."

He was grasping at straws, and Lillian knew it. "I don't like you," she confirmed. "But that's irrelevant here."

"It's extremely relevant," he countered, moistening his lips with a swipe of his tongue. "You don't believe Eleanor's in trouble because you can't admit she would want to be with me."

"No, Max," she said as patiently as she could muster. "I don't believe Eleanor's in trouble because I have more information than you do."

"Which is?"

"The war is ending." This was true. Germany had fallen; there was victory in Europe. The enemy in Japan paled in comparison. There was little doubt in anyone's mind that the war would be over at least by the end of the year.

"I know that," said Max stubbornly.

"So you know that when the war ends, your job here will end, too. So will Eleanor's job. And Eleanor will have no choice but to go home. She'll go back to her life before, of not getting acting parts and taking care of our insufferable mother. And when I leave for Harvard in a year, she'll be trapped in that life forever. Unless—"

"Unless she runs away," said Max.

Lillian was surprised Max finished the sentence, and looked at him, confused. He cleared his throat and clarified. "Well, I must admit... I asked Dr. Ennis if he knew what happened to her. And that is what he claims Eleanor said." Max quickly waved his hand in the air, like a magician trying to distract an audience. "You know, what you said about...your mother...and all that. He said, you know, she didn't want to go back to New York... He even said she left him an address where he could find her." He shook his head at his own words. "But he was lying. She was furious with him the last time I saw her. There was no way she would have told him where to find her. And besides. She wouldn't leave me. She loved me. I know she loved me."

He'd gotten himself so worked up that a little dribble of spit had escaped his mouth and was working its way down his chin. The Tennessee heat had caused a few of his dull brown curls to flatten with sweat and plaster themselves against his forehead. A flap of dry skin had separated itself from the rest of his lip and was dangling precariously from a thin millimeter of dying cells. Lillian could simply not comprehend how this man—this child—could think himself irresistible to Eleanor, to her Eleanor, who scraped the bottom of the lipstick tube for her perfect shade, applying it delicately with a tiny, special brush, and never left the house with a hair out of place.

There was no use in arguing this to Max, of course, so Lillian simply said: "Now you know how it feels when Eleanor decides you're no longer worth her time."

"But she...but she..." He'd run himself out of steam. His shoulders slumped. "I'll show you where to board the bus back to Knoxville tomorrow morning," he mumbled. "Do you need money for a hotel when you get there? I can give you some money."

Lillian shook her head. "I'm not going back to Knoxville. I'm staying here until my train home."

Max closed his eyes, as if the Lord were trying him. Lillian huffed. If either was tried by this conversation, it was her, certainly. "You can't do that," Max said.

"Eleanor's somewhere, isn't she? Who would have a better idea of where that would be than the people she saw constantly before she left?"

"You don't understand," said Max, shaking his bony arms at her for emphasis. "To pull that off for more than a couple hours, you'd have to be a flawless Eleanor. A perfect replica. If anyone finds out you're not her, you'd be done for. Arrested. Brought up on treason charges, most likely."

"I can do that," said Lillian. "It's only for a week."

Max's eyes bulged incredulously. "Are you joking? You're not even wearing her clothes!"

As they so often did in Max's presence, Lillian's eyes went rolling. "No one will even notice." Of course, as soon as the words left her mouth, she recalled the offhand remark her roommate had made. *Is that what you're wearing?* "I'll wear something different tomorrow," she conceded.

"No, you can't be here tomorrow. If you're here tomorrow, you'll have to go to work."

"That's perfect," said Lillian. "Maybe Eleanor has friends at work who know something. I can talk to them."

"Oh, good plan," said Max sarcastically. "Do you know where she works? Because I don't. We're forbidden from discussing that."

"She works in Y-12," said Lillian. "It's on her ID."

Max was quiet, clearly weighing his annoyance with her with the one shred of him that perhaps still did not want to see her arrested. "All right, so that means she's a calutron girl," he said, his voice dropping somehow even lower. "You might—perhaps—be able to do that. It's mostly sitting on a stool and turning a few dials. But you—I don't think you're understanding. You would have to *be* her, even when you're alone. It can't be a show; it can't be a costume."

Lillian was hardly listening to him anymore. "What are they building here, anyway?"

"You can't ask that!"

"So you don't know, then."

"I know *unofficially*," Max clarified with the customary puffing up of his chest required of men who were trying to appear impressive. "But I've never been told on the record."

"Then tell me unofficially. Please, Max. This place is so much bigger than I imagined. I need to know what I'm walking into."

He stared at her, mouth agape, for a few moments. "Unbelievable," he said finally. "You wrote this place off months ago, and now that you see it, you think that might have been a mistake. You're thinking about your career. You don't care about her at all."

The words hit Lillian like a bullet to the right temple, and she felt sudden white-hot rage fill her body. Max didn't know her, didn't know anything about the love Lillian had for her sister, the lengths to which she would go to make sure Eleanor had the best of all possible lives. He didn't know it was Eleanor who didn't care, Eleanor who ran away, Eleanor who had resisted Lillian's every attempt to do what was right for her—to take care of her, the way she was supposed to—

Before she could process what she was doing, she felt her hand raise, felt her palm closing in on Max Medelson's stupid cheekbone. What gave him the right to say such a thing to her, anyway? Because he'd dated her sister for less than a calendar year, he could say what was good for Eleanor, say who loved her the most?

The imprints of Lillian's fingers left a red-hot impression on Max's cheek, which faded back to sallow chalkiness all too fast. Instinctively he raised his hand to the mark and rubbed it as if he didn't understand. He looked at Lillian with some mix of anger and disgust. "You're on your own, Lillian," he sneered. "Good luck pretending to be your angelic sister. I swear to god, I don't know how the two of you are related."

He stalked off back inside the cafeteria, probably thinking to himself what a clever last line he'd landed. Lillian watched him go, finding herself feeling sorry for him—but just a bit.

DECEMBER 1944

Eleanor managed to memorize the preposterously dense monologue, and performed it in the front room for Lillian a few days before her audition. The writing itself (a young woman reminiscing about her deceased husband) was precisely the sort of eye-rolling schlock Lillian would have expected from a duo who saw fit to spend an entire three hours on the state of Oklahoma. Eleanor's performance of the monologue, on the other hand... Lillian could hardly find the words. Before, Lillian always assumed that acting must be quite a tedious affair: thinking about what emotion one *should* be feeling, then reminding oneself what facial expression accompanied that emotion, then contorting one's face into that expression. It was the same sort of thing she refused to do in everyday life, when a colleague told her he had gotten engaged or someone asked if she'd had a nice weekend, only big enough for everyone in a theater to see it. Positively dreadful.

But Eleanor seemed able to *feel* the emotion, not just analyze and convey it but experience it and inhabit it, as if it were really, truly happening. The effect stunned Lillian into silence.

"Oh no, was I that bad?" asked Eleanor when Lillian's only response was a few blinks and a vacant stare.

"No," Lillian replied. "I'm just trying to process it all."

"In a good way, or in a bad way?"

"A good way."

"You're lying. Thank goodness I still have two more days to prepare. Do you think I should cry more at the end?"

Her sister's incessant questions and nervous lip-biting were ruining the magical effect. "May I give you some advice?" asked Lillian.

"When you audition, do it just like that."

Eleanor beamed. "Really?"

"Yes, really. How on earth do you do that? You make it seem so real. Honestly, it doesn't look like acting at all."

"Well at a certain point, it isn't," said Eleanor. "If you pretend to feel the emotions long enough, you just feel them. It's not pretend anymore. Does that make sense?"

"Absolutely not," said Lillian. "But it's working. You're going to get the part."

At that, Eleanor shrieked with joy and threw her arms around Lillian, who patted her on the back. Her own words echoed in her head. *You're going to get the part.*

It wasn't that Eleanor's success meant Lillian's failure. But if Eleanor succeeded in Chicago, it made Lillian's success all the more difficult. That was simply the unfortunate truth. Their plan had always been that Eleanor would remain in New York while Lillian attended Harvard. This plan was solid, logical. Eleanor wasn't the sort of woman who wanted a career forever. She wanted to marry, have children. It made sense for her to stay in the city, take care of Mother, and watch over the house on East 86th Street.

Lillian tried not to get ahead of herself. After all, Eleanor didn't have the job yet. She was very talented, but inexperienced. Surely she would be up against girls who had half a dozen leading parts under their belts, or more. Even if she were cast, there was a chance the Chicago stay would not overlap with Lillian's plans to go to Harvard at all. And besides, while Eleanor might balk at coming home just for Lillian to attend school in a normal situation, if Lillian won the Allerton Prize, surely Eleanor would realize that asking her sister to turn down a full scholarship would be quite unreasonable.

All of these hypotheticals were comforting but not enough to keep Lillian from ruminating on the situation in the lonely, anxious hours between going to bed and falling asleep. She wished for a way to control the situation, to solve it to her satisfaction the way she would a problem in the laboratory. Too much in the current scenario was left to chance, was out of her hands.

She did her best to plaster an expression of joy on her face, hoping what Eleanor had said about eventually feeling it would come true.

JUNE 1945

As soon as Lillian's eyes opened the next morning, she was out of bed. There was not a moment to be wasted on tossing and turning and trying to grab a few more moments of sleep. It was still dark out, and she'd have to tiptoe to avoid waking the roommate whose name she still didn't know, but she had an important mission. Her feet hit the floor, and Lillian went straight to the mirror. It was time to take out her hair rollers.

Last night, she'd found Eleanor's set of twenty-six foam hair curlers tucked in the top drawer of the bureau. She'd squirreled them away to the bathroom down the hall, afraid Emmy would see her put them in and realize right away she hadn't the slightest clue what she was doing. Eleanor could roll her head completely in fifteen minutes flat; Lillian spent almost an hour leaning over a porcelain sink and frowning as she tried to remember how many sections Eleanor had separated her hair into. Did she position her rollers in steps across the top of her head, or a ladder around the frame of her face?

It took all of Lillian's skill at deep concentration to conjure the image: the rollers on the right, perpendicular; the ones on the left, a forty-five degree angle. *This is as complicated as an Allerton problem,* she'd almost thought to herself, and had to quite literally shake the thought from her mind. This was *simple* compared to all that, which is why she would succeed at it. She would. She reached what appeared to be a more than satisfactory placement of curlers, tied a scarf around her head, and went triumphantly to bed.

In the morning, however, she was much more hesitant. The curlers had produced a bouncy head of tight coils. But what on earth was the next step? Brush them out, or not? She held the brush an inch from her head, paranoid. She could remember Eleanor brushing out her curls in the morning, as vividly as if she were standing in front of her, and yet—what if her mind was playing a trick on her again, like she'd been able to do on the train?

Your mind doesn't play tricks, Lillian, she reminded herself. *If you saw her brush out her curls, you saw her brush out her curls. You know exactly everything that you know.*

Hesitating not a moment longer, she pulled the brush through the ringlets, twisting her hair around her thumb by pure instinct, as if Eleanor had inhabited her. The result was perfect. Soft waves across her right cheek, elongating her face, emphasizing her cheekbones, bringing out her eyes. She twisted her head from side to side to see every angle—flawless. It occurred to her that she might do more than simply pull this off. She might be a better Eleanor than Eleanor had been.

───────────

After dressing in the plainest outfit she could find in Eleanor's half of the closet, she headed out, retracing her steps through the mud to where she'd stepped off the bus the previous day and praising the innate sense of direction life as a New Yorker had given her when she found it with relative ease. A bunch of women were already queued up, standing in packs on the nonexistent sidewalk, a few talking animatedly but most yawning and tired. It was just a normal Monday morning for them, Lillian realized, just like the commuters in Manhattan waited for buses and elevateds to take them downtown. Not even working on a secret army complex in the middle of nowhere in a city behind a fence could take the dreariness out of commuting.

As she approached, Lillian scanned the faces of the women in line, looking for the other two women who seemed to be Eleanor's friends, or anyone else who might be eyeing her expectantly, as if waiting for her to join them. She didn't see any, but still figured the best course of action was to play as sleepy as possible, so if someone asked, "Eleanor! Why aren't you standing with us?" she could quickly reply, "I didn't even see you there!" All this subterfuge was certainly annoying in theory, but Lillian had to admit she found it somewhat thrilling to know that no one around her had any idea she wasn't who she claimed she was. Being Eleanor in this strange place involved layer upon layer of calculation, done at a speed nearly impossible for the average human brain. The stakes, of course, were very high—but for one week, what was the harm in allowing herself to enjoy it?

She wondered how she would spot the correct bus when it arrived, but this query was quickly answered when one pulled up bearing a placard reading "Y-12 ALL GATES." How perfectly easy! It would have been insulting to think that Max believed she couldn't pull this off, except she would never stoop to be insulted by anything that came out of Max's mouth.

This ride was much shorter than on the last bus Lillian had boarded, heading south this time instead of east toward the gate she'd come in from. Just a few minutes later, they'd arrived at the top of a long, sloping hill, at the bottom of which was a large white warehouse surrounded by power generators. It was the first building Lillian had spotted at the Clinton Engineer Works that actually looked like an engineer works. For a moment, she felt a wave of relief. This was a building from the world of science and math. This was a building that could be understood quite easily, that didn't need to be navigated and picked over like the fraught, unfamiliar worlds of a women's dormitory or a dining hall.

It wasn't until she stepped off the bus that she was able to take in the enormity of this place.

Women, none much older than she, streamed off not just her bus but at least a dozen others, if not more. Hundreds of women, all chatter and linked arms, flooding toward the large white building—and just as many coming out. There were *shifts*. Whatever was humming away at the bottom of that hill required not just the presence of an entire city, but twenty-four-hour maintenance.

Lillian wanted to know where Eleanor had gone. But now she also very much wanted to know what was happening inside this building.

She clutched Eleanor's ID badge in her suddenly sweaty palm as the flow of women carried her through the main gate. She didn't have any difficulty getting inside, but she suspected it would be harder to blend in once the work started. Instead of frightening her, the thought made her heart race with anticipation.

Lillian followed the herd into a locker room off to the right, where arm after arm reached out to grab from the top of a pile of folded khaki pants and tops. Women headed to their lockers, each emblazoned with a cheap stamped label announcing the name of its owner. As curious as she was about what Eleanor might be keeping in there, Lillian had no time to search for "E. Kaufman." She changed in the restroom and stashed her things under a bench. The women, indistinguishable in their uniforms, paraded back out of the locker room and through a set of double doors. Lillian followed.

The noise of the place hit her first. The stomp of boots on cement and steel, the clanging of metal, the static of electrical equipment all echoed around her, to the point where she half expected to see an active steel mill ahead. When she did adjust to the sound well enough to take in her surroundings, she thought that a steel mill might have made more sense. The long, narrow room beyond the doors was filled not with construction equipment or a manufacturing line but panel after panel of gauges, levers, and dials, tall enough to almost reach the soaringly high ceiling and seeming to stretch back until infinity. Approximately every four feet sat a stool, and on every stool sat a girl, monitoring the movement of a gauge's needle, scribbling a number into a notebook, flipping a switch, cranking a lever.

Lillian made her way to an empty stool, running her fingertips lightly over the equipment. The laboratory at Columbia didn't even have a leak-proof ceiling, but everything here was brand new. It would have to be. She watched one of the needles jump to the right, then collapse again to the left, an elegant ballet made more intoxicating by its mystery. There were at least forty women in this hall, and who knew how many rooms identical to this existed in the massive building? Beyond that, how many of these *buildings* existed in this giant, secret town? Five? Ten? One hundred?

A shiver went up Lillian's spine. She had always wanted to be at the forefront of physics. It was why Harvard was so important, why the Allerton Prize was essential. But suddenly it seemed like the forefront of physics wasn't in some old university building with crummy pipes and bad insulation. The forefront of physics, Lillian realized, might be happening right at her feet.

She snuck a glance at the woman next to her, a round-faced brunette who couldn't have been older than nineteen. She also wore a strand of pearls around her neck, but unlike Lillian's, they were clearly fake. The brunette absentmindedly bit her lip as she stared at the machine in front of her. She adjusted a dial labeled "J" slightly, so Lillian did the same. A few moments later, she adjusted it back, so Lillian did as well.

This proved to be a mistake. The machine in front of Lillian made a horrible cracking sound, followed by a series of large pops. Lillian jumped in fright and nearly fell off her stool, but no one around her seemed all that alarmed. From the end of the room, a slightly older woman who seemed to be a supervisor of some sort meandered over. Lillian expected to get yelled at for breaking the whole operation, but the woman merely twisted a few dials and then sauntered off.

"You're still not used to it when it does that?" asked the brunette next to her in a strong southern accent. As she swiveled toward her, Lillian could see the name on her ID badge read Patricia.

"Apparently not," said Lillian. The words came out of her

mouth a little too sour for Eleanor, so she added an awkward giggle at the end.

"What's funny?" asked Patricia, blinking slowly.

"Nothing," said Lillian quickly.

"Well, you'll get used to it." Patricia turned back to her own machine. "Try not to fall off your stool again in the meantime. Took me a whole year."

It made sense, with everything she'd seen, but Lillian couldn't help but be struck by the thought. A whole *year*, probably more, of twenty-four hour shifts of girls fiddling with dials!

But that wasn't the mystery she was here to solve. And just when she was pondering the least suspicious way to ask this new potential source for information— *"Have you ever met me before, and did I mention running off somewhere?"*—Patricia spoke again.

"Are you feeling better?" she asked.

Had Eleanor been ill? Her friends hadn't mentioned it. Had it been a ruse to get out of work, maybe? Perhaps on the day she ran?

"Much, thank you," said Lillian. Hoping to get a few details out about what exactly had happened, she cautiously went on. "Have you ever had anything like that happen to you?"

Patricia shook her head so violently, her fake pearls bounced along with her. "Oh, Lord, no," she said. "I bet your boyfriend took good care of you, though."

She hadn't qualified it, hadn't added the singsongy little "We're not supposed to talk about him!" that Eleanor's friends had. This was almost a threat, an "I know something about you that you don't want me to." That, Lillian realized with a small jolt of energy, she could work with.

"How does everyone know about that?" she exclaimed in her best impression of Eleanor: upset that people were talking about her, but also quite pleased that people were talking about her.

"You haven't exactly been discreet," said Patricia. "I think the whole town knows."

"This town is full of gossips. I bet half of what they're saying isn't even true," Lillian said with a small huff. Then, as if it were an afterthought, she added, "What have you heard?"

Patricia went quiet, studiously focusing on her dials. For a moment, Lillian wondered if she had gone too far, asked something she wasn't supposed to. She turned back to her own cubicle and stared at the needles. Then she heard a whisper barely audible above the cacophony of machinery:

"Maybe you could tell me something first."

Lillian had no idea how to respond to this. It sounded suspicious, like something she should avoid, but she only had a week left in this strange place. She couldn't afford to keep it safe. "Such as?"

"Something about this place. You must know *something* about what we're doing here."

For a moment, Lillian considered coming up with some kind of lie. She could have produced something half-plausible, based on simple deduction. It was a weapon, surely; a new weapon, one could be reasonably sure, because of all the secrecy; a highly effective weapon, most likely, based on the size of the operation, and "highly effective" to the army meant deadly. Some lie was on the tip of the tongue, some fancy about a dangerous new gas, when it occurred to her that this might be a trap.

"Oh, I have no idea about any of that," she said.

"Come on," Patricia whispered. "I'm sure he's told you."

"He hasn't," Lillian insisted. "And besides. We broke up." She still wasn't sure if this was the truth, or just something Eleanor had told Max, but perhaps it could be helpful in getting Patricia off her case.

Unfortunately, it was a bit too helpful. Patricia didn't say another word for the rest of the shift. The handful of times Lillian did glance her way, she kept her eyes fixed on her own machine as if Eleanor no longer existed.

SIX

The next day at work, Lillian looked around for Patricia, planning to sit next to her again despite the frosty end to their conversation the day before. Clearly Patricia knew some gossip about Eleanor's personal life, and maybe a couple more hours by her side would warm her up again.

Patricia, however, was nowhere to be seen, and the woman who occupied her stool today (Ruth, according to her ID badge) seemed completely incapable of holding a conversation that wasn't about how uncomfortable she thought the stools were.

Lillian debated asking Ruth about Patricia for at least an hour, going back and forth on whether or not the answer could be something like "Patricia's never here on Tuesdays, where have you been?" that would reveal her as an outsider. Eventually she decided she had no choice but to follow up, for the sake of Eleanor.

"Where's Patricia gone?" she asked Ruth, as casually as she could muster.

The look on Ruth's face—one of paralyzed neutrality, the fear of displaying any reaction whatsoever—was enough. Lillian had been worried about the answer revealing her as an outsider when she should have been concerned that the *question* would.

"Never mind," she added quickly. "We shouldn't be discussing such things."

***

Her hopes at gleaning any information from Eleanor's colleagues dashed, Lillian reverted her attention back to the giggling idiots who claimed to be Eleanor's friends. That night, at dinner, she was a flawless Eleanor, even managing to pick out (quite cleverly, she believed) the women's names (Emmy, her blond roommate; Lorene, the heavy-browed brunette; and Sadie, the mousy one whose hair was more of a reddish-brown). She could even see Max glowering at her success from across the cafeteria out of the corner of her eye, which of course only made blending in feel that much sweeter.

Not that blending in with this lot was all that difficult. The conversation was embarrassingly simple, once Lillian cracked the code on it. Each woman had her own *thing* that she wanted to discuss, and any sound made by the others was narcissistically filtered back around to her own pet topic. It wasn't so much a conversation as three record players each playing a different song simultaneously. "My hair is so frizzy today," one would say. "Maybe Roger isn't speaking to me because he doesn't like my hair," another would respond. "I tried to spray it down but nothing was working," said the first. As long as Lillian strung a few words together half-coherently now and then, she more than kept up.

Only one moment made Lillian stumble a bit, and it was the realization, quite out of nowhere, that these were Eleanor's friends. These self-absorbed, dull, dim-witted women had been the ones Eleanor had chosen to be with instead of her. She pushed the notion aside. Eleanor always saw the best in people; that was her way. She had only been here a few months. It was quite possible she simply hadn't realized yet how terrible these people were.

Unfortunately, the same trick that made conversing with Eleanor's friends so easy also made mining them for information quite difficult. "Once the war's over I'm going to travel," Lillian announced. "Weren't we talking about this recently? What cities did I mention?"

"I'm never traveling to anywhere with humidity ever again," declared Lorene, still desperately trying to pat down her locks.

"Do you think Roger likes to travel?" asked Sadie.

Lillian's best guess about Eleanor's destination was still Chicago, still *Carousel*, so she tried some more pointed questions when alone with Emmy in their room that evening. "I can't remember, Emmy darling—was it you I was telling about going to visit my theater friends, or someone else?"

"Theater friends?" said Emmy, seeming a bit surprised. For a moment, Lillian's heart leapt. If Emmy hadn't known Eleanor was an actress, she really hadn't known a thing about her. It meant they weren't close at all, that these people were nothing to Eleanor.

"Oh, did you not know—" Lillian began.

"Just call them Bev and Carol and Adrian. I've heard enough stories about them to know their names," continued Emmy. "Christ, I feel like they're my friends, too."

Who the hell were Bev and Carol and Adrian? Lillian had never heard these names in her life; she would have sworn it. Eleanor had friends, but they were more like chums, people she grabbed a lunch with every now and then and greeted warmly when she happened to bump into them on the train. Eleanor didn't have a *Carol* and an *Adrian* and certainly not a *Bev.*

The response threw Lillian so off guard that she completely forgot to ask any follow-up questions about visiting these people in Chicago, instead lying awake and racking her brain for any mention of the best friend, *Bev.*

The twins' twenty-first birthday was two days later, fortunately without any recognition from Emmy, Sadie, and Lorene. The special attention of a birthday celebration would have put a lot of eyes on her, eyes that might then realize "Hmm, something looks a little different about the placement of Eleanor's freckles." Remaining out-of-thought allowed her to slip away from her station in Building Y-12, dip back into the locker room, and finally track down the locker labeled "E. Kaufman." The flaw in this plan, of course, was that it was locked.

After a futile few moments banging at the thing with the heel of her boot, Lillian began to worry she was causing a commotion and abandoned the idea. They'd spent so many birthdays doing the same thing that she wondered briefly if Eleanor had also spent the day hitting something with a shoe, before remembering that Eleanor was probably eating chocolate cake, her favorite, somewhere without her. Maybe with Carol and Adrian and Bev.

By Friday night, Lillian had given up. Even though it was only seven thirty, and they'd only just returned from dinner, Lillian changed into her pajamas and crawled into bed. She'd have to be up quite early, she reasoned to herself, to be dressed and packed and on her way to the train before Emmy even noticed she was gone. Really, she just wanted to be asleep. She had failed, and Lillian was not accustomed to failing. She had stayed an entire week to learn information and had learned absolutely nothing, except that if you rolled your hair curlers too tight and close to your head, you'd awaken with a nasty kink that was impossible to brush out. She did not like the feeling of defeat, the powerlessness of it. At least asleep, she would not have to dwell on the reminder that there were some things she could not accomplish.

The door to the bedroom creaked open, and Emmy appeared, a towel wrapped around her body and wet hair clinging to her shoulders. She stared at Lillian, frowning. "Why are you in bed?"

Eleanor's friends had been planning an outing to a dance that evening. That morning, as Eleanor, Lillian had enthusiastically agreed to attend. Eleanor would never miss a party. Tonight, she didn't see the point. In twelve hours, she'd be on her way to the train station. It no longer mattered if her roommate thought she was behaving oddly. "I don't feel well," she said, although it came out sharp and twinged with sarcasm.

Emmy raised her eyebrows. "Oh dear," she murmured, and in a flash she was at Lillian's bedside, pressing her hand against Lillian's forehead. "You don't feel warm," she said, which shocked Lillian, as the Tennessee summer heat had left her feeling like she was in an oven all week. "When did this come about? What are your symptoms?"

"I'm fine, I'm fine," said Lillian, pushing the intruding arms and elbows out of the way so she could sit up. "Just tired, is all. I'd like to rest."

"And miss out on all the fun?" asked Emmy. "That doesn't seem like you."

"No," sighed Lillian, accepting the inevitable. "No, it doesn't." She pushed the sheet aside and headed, one last time, to Eleanor's closet.

―――――――――――

Wedged between Emmy and Lorene, Lillian tried not to trip on one of the many broken boards of the pathetic, wooden excuse for a sidewalk they walked along. Emmy had suggested she wear a sweltering yellow crepe disaster featuring some truly horrid geometric shapes, and she was already sweating. It hadn't rained in days, which solved most of the unfortunate problem of the mud, but left the air unbearably heavy and humid. For the past twenty-four hours, one couldn't have a conversation without someone remarking: "We need a good thunderstorm to break this heat." Apparently that was the cycle: large rainstorms brought behind them cooler, lighter air—and the more violent the storm, the greater the relief. Lillian relished this tiny kernel of weather knowledge. It made her feel rustic, like a farmer.

In the distance, down the road, light and music poured from a long, wide building. The Recreation Hall stood out somewhat from the other squat, undecorated buildings in town because of the pine porch that circled it on all sides. At the front of the hall, the porch gave dancers a somewhat cool place to escape the heat indoors; at the back of the hall, it gave couples a place to neck in relative privacy. Now, it beckoned to Lillian almost menacingly—the jail that would keep her trapped within its borders for an unbearable few hours until she could go to bed, wake up, and then finally go home.

The evening, she already knew, would be an utter waste. She just had to endure it.

Lillian had never much enjoyed dances and furthermore did not understand how anyone could. How could two people get to know each other when the music was so loud and there was no place to talk? She knew that most people at these sorts of events *claimed* to be interested in something other than conversation, but she didn't quite believe this was possible. A person's physical charms could only bring about a short window of delight. And although Lillian's experience in that area was admittedly limited, she knew from what experience she did have that being a surprisingly good kisser did not make a man tolerable to be around.

Lorene, Sadie, and Emmy, however, eagerly squealed and giggled over every man who walked past them en route to the dance, displaying an obvious preference for the men in pressed army uniforms over the ones in slightly wrinkled white shirts and gray slacks. Was this indicative of some primitive, biological need to feel protected? Perhaps—but most of the army men weren't there to protect the women who worked at the engineer works. They were there to police them. They didn't walk around in their uniforms to make the workers feel safe; they did it to make the workers feel watched. Lillian still had no idea what this town was for or the need for its secrecy, but that much she had figured out rather quickly.

She tried, gently, to bring up this distinction to her companions, but it flew far above their heads, as expected.

"But wearing those uniforms means they're saving the country," said Sadie dreamily.

"We're all saving the country," pointed out Lillian. "And they were probably drafted. We volunteered."

"Huh," said Lorene. "I never thought of it that way before."

The group fell silent.

"I don't care at all about them saving the country. I just think those pants make their behinds look amazing," said Emmy after a moment. Lorene and Sadie wholeheartedly agreed, concluding Lillian's short dive into provocative conversation with Eleanor's friends.

"Look," Lorene whispered suddenly, tugging on Lillian's arm. "There's that crazy woman again, the one who was bothering you. That's her, right?"

Lillian couldn't tell which of the many figures on the road ahead of them Lorene was referring to, even if she had understood what Lorene was talking about. "Um, I'm not sure," she said, scanning the surroundings.

"Right there," said Lorene, pointing with a complete lack of discretion.

Lillian finally saw the woman: the only one heading away from the Rec Hall instead of toward it. She was Black, the first Black person Lillian had seen in Tennessee, although she'd heard many were employed as janitors in the engineer works. Distracted by studying this woman for signs of "crazy," of which there weren't any immediate ones, it took Lillian a few moments to realize the other three women were looking to her. "Do you want to go another way so she doesn't bother you?" said Emmy.

"Oh… No, it's all right," said Lillian, although even as she said it, she wasn't sure. The other women had such looks of alarm on their faces. *What on earth did Eleanor and this woman get into?* It wasn't like Eleanor to have made an enemy. "Besides, there's nowhere else to go." They were away from the center of town now, by at least a mile based on how long they had been walking, and the buildings were becoming fewer and farther between.

"We can duck into the woods until she passes," suggested Lorene.

"It's fine," Lillian insisted. Her curiosity was perking up. Maybe if this woman did confront Eleanor, she'd reveal something, some clue to think over so Lillian wouldn't be riding the train tomorrow completely empty-handed. Her mind raced with possibilities. Had this woman blackmailed Eleanor? Threatened her? Could it possibly have been the other way around?

"If she tries to say anything to you, we'll sock her," said Sadie.

Lillian raised an eyebrow. "I'm sure that won't be necessary."

She tried to study the woman without making it obvious that's what she was doing. Like all the women she'd encountered here, she looked incredibly young—no older than Lillian, at least. She wore a striped blue and white top that didn't quite match the paler blue on the skirt she'd chosen, a fact Lillian noticed and then felt silly for noticing. A charm bracelet with far too many charms on it dangled off her wrist, ringing like a bell as it smacked against the library book in her hand. For someone who all her friends were concerned would try to accost her, she seemed to be deliberately not making any eye contact with the group whatsoever, as if she'd seen them coming before they had seen her and was purposefully trying to ignore them.

"I can't believe she thinks they're kidnapping people," said Emmy with a bitter giggle.

Lillian's heart began to pound. She wondered if she'd heard correctly. "What?"

"That's what she said, right?" Emmy turned to Lillian with a glint in her eye. "She's insane."

"She said they might even be experimenting on them," added Lorene.

Kidnapping people. She thought of Eleanor, gone, her ID still in her nightstand drawer. She thought of Patricia, disappearing with no explanation from Y-12, and the terror that had crossed that other girl's face when Lillian had dared to speak her name.

"But they're not really doing that, right?" asked Lillian, knowing as she said it that she could not trust these women's reactions. They were fools.

Sadie scoffed. "If they were experimenting on people, I think we would know about it," she said. "Besides, doesn't the army have bigger things to worry about now?"

Those "bigger things" were exactly Lillian's concern. The army had one interest: winning a war, and it only made sense that they would justify anything they felt would help them do that. It made complete sense, a puzzle clicking into place. They were building a weapon. They had to be sure it worked on people. And here they had a whole city of them, a whole city where, if you asked where someone went, you'd get a dirty look until you shut your mouth and figured it wasn't any of your business.

Eleanor was here, Lillian realized. She wasn't in Chicago with Bev; she was here, right here, under her nose somewhere. Suddenly, every army man within a hundred yards was a threat. What if they knew, what if they all knew that she wasn't Eleanor, that she couldn't be, because Eleanor was in a cell somewhere, starving and screaming and—

Lillian's throat was coated in acid, and she felt so dazed she could hardly see. She had to talk to this woman now, had to break away from Eleanor's friends—but inconspicuously, always inconspicuously—and say *something*. Time was running out. The woman coming closer and closer, just inches from passing their group. Lillian cleared her throat. "Oh, I think I left something back at the room—"

None of her companions heard her meek excuse, because just as she said it, Sadie stuck out her left leg. The woman tripped, falling off the wooden sidewalk and collapsing into the road. A car slammed on its brakes with an awful noise, Sadie erupted in laughter, and several onlookers gasped and gawked at the drama. "Sadie!" scolded Emmy, but it was no use. Sadie raced ahead before the woman could regroup and retaliate, and Emmy fled after her.

Lorene grabbed Lillian's arm, and Lillian realized she'd stopped in her tracks. "Let's go," urged Lorene. "Hurry."

Lillian pulled her arm away and went to the woman's side. She offered the woman her outstretched hand, only to be met with a face full of dirt and twigs and rocks. Before she could recover and wipe the dust from her eyes, Lorene had dragged her out of there, a few minutes later arriving at the steps to the dance hall where Emmy and Sadie were waiting, looking quite pleased with themselves.

All Lillian wanted to do was smack the grin off Sadie's face, but Eleanor would never do such a thing. Besides, she had to get back, had to get out of here and see if she could find that woman again, before it was too late. "I'm going to go back and change," she said, wiping some of the dirt from her dress.

"I'll come with you," said Emmy.

"No!" Emmy raised her eyebrows in surprise, and Lillian quickly backtracked. "No, don't be silly. You enjoy the dance. I'll be fine."

Before Emmy could argue any more, Lillian was off the porch and back on the road. But the only traces she could find of the woman were the handprints she'd left in the dirt. She kicked at the dust, narrowly avoiding undue attention by swearing loudly.

She would not be going back to New York City tomorrow, she decided. If there was any chance Eleanor was here, she needed to stay.

Dear Mother,

I hope this letter finds you quite well. I am writing to let you know that I have heard from Lillian that her trip home has been unfortunately delayed. She knows this will inconvenience and upset you, and it's her wish that I inform you that it is a matter of urgency that cannot be put off. I hope you will make do on your own for a tiny bit longer—if not for her sake, then for mine.

Love,
Your darling Eleanor

Lillian stared at her penmanship. Even writing sloppy on purpose, it was nowhere near as bad as Eleanor's. Mother probably wouldn't notice, and Lillian hoped that the security apparatus that was sure to be monitoring outgoing mail wouldn't notice either. It stung her, a bit unexpectedly, to think that Mother *would* be more accepting, more forgiving of the bad news when delivered by Eleanor.

Next she wrote to Dot Greeley, again explaining that Lillian had been unfortunately delayed but would dip into the money saved for her final year at Columbia if only Dot would look after their mother just a little bit longer. Her two letters sealed and deposited in a mailbox, Lillian set out on the far more important task of finding out everything she could about the woman outside the Rec Hall.

After a few carefully placed questions, spaced out so as not to attract suspicion over the course of the weekend, Lillian had extracted more information about her from Emmy, Lorene, and Sadie. Her name was "something like Betty," according to Emmy, which Lillian took to mean "Betty" because what name on earth was "something like" Betty? "Betty" used to work as a janitor in the women's dormitories, which is how she found Eleanor and began "badgering her day and night," according to Lorene. After Eleanor complained, Betty was transferred to Y-12, which was a massive enough operation that their paths never crossed. The question no one could answer for Lillian was why Betty had been bothering Eleanor at all. What could Eleanor have done to stop a secret prison where human experiments were being conducted? Sing at it?

Now that Lillian had heard the rumor, she noticed traces of it everywhere over the next few days, the way that just after one learns about a new vegetable it seems to pop up on every menu in sight. First of all, there had been Patricia—gone from the stool next to her at Y-12 and everyone petrified to even consider discussing why. Then, a woman in the cafeteria line ahead of

Lillian scolded her friend: "Don't take so many carrots, they'll take you away for research." Then, a man clapped his friend on the back and said, "Don't feel down. At least the army hasn't come and plucked off your toes."

Lillian had never been one to believe in convoluted conspiracies, or any belief that lacked the requisite scientific proof. But a large organization like the army—that had proven time and again how little it cared for humanity—covering up something on this scale? It wasn't as far-fetched as it might have seemed.

Finally, Monday came, and Lillian could return to Y-12. After half an hour of pulling levers, she stepped away, murmuring casually to her neighbor that she was taking a bathroom break. For the next five minutes, she paced through as many halls as she could, covering ground, looking for Betty—or any janitor, for that matter, who might have some idea where she could find her. She saw no one. An hour and a half later, she spent another five minutes doing the same, with similar results.

By Wednesday afternoon, she'd been able to cover most of the building with no success. She hadn't even found a janitor's closet or a place where she might discreetly be able to leave Betty a note. She *had* managed to get a much closer look at the building's engineering works, but it provided no clues about what on earth they could be building. The facilities lacked the smokestacks and furnaces required to produce most metals, but Lillian couldn't imagine what else it could be.

Wednesday evening at dinner, she cautiously tried to probe

Emmy for information once more. "Gosh, I'm so lucky I've never run into Betty while at work," she said. It had taken nearly twenty minutes of conversation steering to get here naturally, from Thanksgiving traditions to siblings to disliking a sibling's wife to the awkwardness of having to see someone one dislikes in a place where one hadn't prepared to see them. "I'd be so uncomfortable."

"Well, you probably don't have to worry about that, right?" said Emmy. "I would think she works at night."

Of course. Lillian could have smacked herself. Of course the janitorial staff cleaned up at nights, when the building was quieter and a smaller shift of girls were managing the machines. Someone of her intelligence ought to have deduced that. Being Eleanor had really dulled her reasoning skills.

That night, Lillian lay quiet and still in the dark, and tried to breathe deeply and evenly like someone fast asleep, all the while digging a fingernail into her palm so she didn't drift off accidentally. As soon as Emmy began her light, breathy snore, Lillian threw off her sheet and slipped outside.

On her bus rides to work, she'd taken care to memorize the route south through the main stretch of town, past some single houses and lean-tos, down the dirt road to Y-12.

It was only about a half hour's walk, a distance shorter than the one she walked most days, from East 86th Street to Columbia University on the other side of the park. She'd done that walk in all sorts of weather and at all hours of the day or night, but Oak

Ridge (she was sorely reminded as she felt a mosquito attack her ankle) was not Manhattan. Streetlamps were far between, when they existed at all, and one of the few comforts was that no one was around to see the numerous times she stumbled on the dirt road.

A flash of an ID and a lie about leaving some medication in her locker was all it took to get past the guards and into the building. Once she was beyond their line of sight, she slipped past the door to the locker room and rounded a corner to a dark, empty corridor. An older Black woman mopped up the floor at the other end, and Lillian quickly made her way toward her. "Excuse me," said Lillian, and the woman instantly narrowed her eyes, looking Lillian up and down. "I'm looking for Betty. I think she works here. Do you know her?"

"Eleanor Kaufman," came a voice from behind her. "Who did you lose?"

Lillian turned around. Betty stood at the end of the hall, holding a mop of her own, but not even pretending to be using it as she smoked a cigarette and eyed Lillian.

"Pardon?" was the only thing Lillian could think to say.

"In here," said Betty, nodding toward a door.

They left the older woman and ducked into an empty break room, not much bigger than a broom closet and just as dreary. Betty settled on a bench as Lillian hovered nearby, holding her arms close to her chest so she wouldn't accidentally brush against the dusty walls. "Cigarette?" Betty asked.

Without thinking about it, Lillian replied, "Oh, I don't smoke."

Betty raised an eyebrow. Lillian immediately recognized her mistake. Eleanor, of course, could never resist a cigarette, especially when nervous or upset or feeling any emotion, really. It was Lillian who had always found the habit unseemly. "I'm trying to quit," Lillian added quickly.

Betty shrugged. "It doesn't matter. Who did you lose?"

"Why do you—why do you ask?" said Lillian.

Again, Betty shrugged. "I've been trying to talk to you for weeks, and you've done nothing but brush me off. You got me reassigned out of the dormitory and almost got me fired. Just two days ago, you and your friends were tripping me and laughing at me, and now you're here, tracking me down in the middle of the night. You must have lost someone, too."

Lillian hesitated. "I'm not sure that I have," she said finally. "It's possibly all a misunderstanding. But if it's not…"

Betty folded her hands on her lap. "And why did you come to me, instead of any of your famous friends?"

"I wanted to hear what you had to say."

"Oh, I see," said Betty, suddenly smug. "You and him aren't a thing anymore."

"Me and…?"

"Let me make this clear, Eleanor. I wasn't trying to enlist your help because of your superior detective skills. Without Dr. Ennis, you're no use to me."

Andrew Ennis. *Of course.* Betty had been badgering Eleanor because of who she knew.

Lillian started to talk before she knew for sure what she would say. "I could find a way talk to him," she said. "If you'd just tell me what happened—"

"Why should I?" snapped Betty. "How am I supposed to know this isn't another trick, that this won't end with me facedown in dirt again? Give me one good reason why I should trust you, Eleanor Kaufman."

"Because I'm not Eleanor Kaufman," said Lillian.

SEVEN

DECEMBER 1944

Tuesday was the one day a week Lillian didn't have to be at
Columbia at the crack of dawn for a 7:00 a.m. lecture. She
lingered in bed, drifting in and out of sleep to the sounds of
the winter wind outside and Eleanor rising and dressing. It
was nearly nine by the time Lillian, still yawning, made her way
downstairs where Eleanor was frantic in the kitchen. Pots and
pans clanged, something sizzled uncontrollably, and the air was
becoming thick with smoke. "Everything all right in there?"
called Lillian.

"I tried to make bread but I burned it," Eleanor shouted
back, just as the telephone rang in the hall. "Can you answer
that?"

"Sure," said Lillian, making her way to the little round table
that displayed the phone in the foyer—far too prominent a

setup for a device that was hardly ever used. She pressed the phone to her ear. "Kaufman residence."

"May I speak to Eleanor, please?" came the pleasant female voice from the other end of the line.

Lillian peered down the hall and into the kitchen. Eleanor had cracked open the oven, and curls of smoke were shooting out with alarming speed. She coughed and attempted to fan the air with an oven mitt. Fortunately, their voices were as identical as their faces. "This is Eleanor," said Lillian into the phone.

"Wonderful. This is Janet Mayberry calling from the Theatre Guild." Lillian reached for the notepad that perched by the telephone, only to find that its pen had dried up completely from lack of use. Lillian never used the telephone, and Eleanor could memorize a number as quickly as she could memorize a line. Janet Mayberry from the Theatre Guild prattled on unaware as Lillian scratched with the busted pen. "Unfortunately Mrs. Helburn had an unexpected commitment come up and needs to be out of town on Friday."

Lillian tried to plant these names in her brain. "I see," she said.

"So they're moving all the auditions to tomorrow morning, starting at ten. I'm dreadfully sorry for the late notice, but it is what it is. Can you come in then?"

Eleanor was still too distracted to pay Lillian or the phone call any mind. "Yes, that should be fine," said Lillian.

"Wonderful. If you need to reach us, we're at Spring-7-5600." Janet Mayberry hung up and the line clicked silent.

Lillian cradled the phone receiver to her ear for an extra moment before slowly lowering it.

The chaos erupting from the kitchen had calmed for a moment. "Come look at my efforts before I throw them in the trash," called Eleanor. Lillian followed her voice to find her sister staring down at a charred loaf of rye. It looked both flat and hollow, as if it had tried to rise only to be punctured like a balloon. "Such a sad little thing," said Eleanor.

"Why were you making bread anyway? Just go buy it."

"Didn't you hear?"

Lillian shook her head.

"Ed Blumenthal was drafted," continued Eleanor. "He leaves in a week." Ed Blumenthal ran the bakery around the corner. For a brief time about a year ago, he had courted Eleanor, but had kindly broken up with her when he realized his pies and cakes and breads brought him more joy than a wife and family ever could. Lillian had admired his resolve but recalled wishing it were put to better use than carbohydrates.

"How sad," said Lillian, in that way one does when they know something is sad but can't afford the emotional energy of lingering on the details.

"So I thought that with Ed gone, it might be a good time to learn how to bake these things myself," continued Eleanor.

"You could just go to the next bakery down," said Lillian. She didn't know off the top of her head, but she was pretty sure there was one only a few blocks away, just south of 81st Street.

"I suppose you're right," said Eleanor, wiping her hands on the light-pink apron she'd draped over her neck. "Who was on the phone?"

Lillian was about to answer, "*Janet Mayberry, from the Theatre Guild. Your audition's been rescheduled.*" It was on the tip of her tongue. But then a wild urge struck her. The urge to control her uncertain fate and Eleanor's unknown destiny by saying two simple words: *no one.* And as soon as the urge had arrived, she found her lips moving to form the words. "No one," she said.

Eleanor wrinkled her brow. "No one?"

"Just a classmate of mine, wanting to know if I could meet her for lunch today." It was so very easy to lie. Even as she was inventing the words, Lillian could see the imaginary conversation. *It was Irene,* she thought, *Irene, who had a Tuesday morning lecture. It went horribly and she wants to vent to someone. I don't know when that woman will learn that I'm not her mother, for goodness' sake.*

"Oh, how fun," said Eleanor, half-heartedly. She had already lost interest and was searching for something in the cupboard. "I'm thinking I'll make scrambled eggs. Do you want some?"

"No, thank you," said Lillian, who was suddenly quite eager to get out of the house. "I'll grab a bite on my way to school."

As she padded up the stairs and changed quickly into a gray wool skirt and thick, warm stockings, her heart began to pound. Lillian had told the occasional social lie before ("Why yes, Mrs. Teller, your new window decorations do look lovely") but this felt—this *was*—quite different. The feeling of calm that came with an uncertain situation finally being wrangled under control was fast replaced with the panic of this resolution not being the one she wanted. Quantum superposition dictated that an atom could exist in a number of different states all at once, only collapsing into one state upon observation. Lillian had observed, had changed the possible outcomes into one single possible outcome, had interfered.

She would find some other way to pass the message on to Eleanor. Yes, that's what she would do. When Eleanor was in the bath, or out with Max that night, or otherwise distracted, she'd pretend that Janet Mayberry had called then. That would be easy enough. She ran over the dialogue in her head. *"There was a phone call for you while you were at dinner. The Theatre Guild? They want you to come in tomorrow morning at ten…"*

In fact, telling her later might be *better*. It would give Eleanor less time to panic about the audition. She was already nervous— waking up early to bake bread was an obvious pretense to give her hands something to do. If Lillian told her now that the audition had been moved up, her darling sister would be a fit of nervous energy for the next twenty-four hours. The last time Eleanor had been anxious over a part, she'd scrubbed the grout in the tile of the kitchen floor with a toothbrush. The kitchen had never looked nicer, but the next day Eleanor had been so sore and grumpy and tired she'd completely flubbed her dance routine.

Yes, the more Lillian thought about it, the more she realized she was actually doing Eleanor a *favor* by not passing on the message right away. She was already as prepared as she could be. Knowing would just make things worse. It might even be for the best not to tell her until tomorrow morning, just so Eleanor would get an uninterrupted night's sleep.

Before heading outside into the chill December air, Lillian kissed her sister on the cheek, knowing that she loved her completely and that she always did what was in her best interest.

JUNE 1945

"Because I'm not Eleanor Kaufman."

Lillian's words hung in the air. Betty's first response, after a moment, was to laugh, then to squint, then to shake her head. "Well you look like her, and you sound like her, so if you're not her—"

"I'm her twin," said Lillian. "She's missing, and I came down here to find her. You asked who I lost, and that's the answer."

"How'd you get in?" asked Betty, eyes narrowing.

"I snuck in. Flirted with the bus driver."

Betty tsked. "That sounds about right."

"Listen. I was a physicist back in New York." Of course, she'd meant to say *physics student,* but her tongue mysteriously slipped. "I know one of the men on Dr. Ennis's team. If I explain what's going on—if you think Dr. Ennis can help—I can get to him. Please, just—just tell me what you know."

"I still don't see why I should trust you," said Betty.

"I've handed over my whole life to you, haven't I?" replied Lillian. "Only one other person here knows who I really am. You could have me arrested tonight, if you wanted to. Do you think the army would take very kindly to an outsider taking up residence in their secret facility?" As she said the words, it sank in for seemingly the first time that *no, they really, really would not.* Max had warned her about treason and prison, but after ten days among the Loose Lips Sink Ships signs, it seemed to Lillian more likely they'd just shoot her and spare the time and money.

Betty considered this, tilting her head to study a crack in the wall. "All right," she said finally. "I'll tell you what I know. If you tell me your name."

"Lillian," said Lillian.

Crawling back to Max Medelson was the last thing Lillian wanted to do, especially not with the way he'd left things. She could still see the cruel way his lips had curled around the words, *You're on your own, Lillian,* as if he had relished saying them, as if it's what he'd wanted all along.

She took her plate of gray-pink meat and limp green beans to the table where Max sat by himself, reading the newspaper. He didn't even look right reading a newspaper: instead of intelligent and worldly, he looked dwarfed by the size of the broadsheet. When he tried to turn the page, he was all elbows and

THE WOMAN WITH TWO SHADOWS

nearly knocked his glass of milk over. As she sat down in front of him, he didn't even bother to look up.

Fine. She deigned to speak first, even though it was obviously Max's turn since she had been the one to come over here. "Hi, Max," she said.

"You didn't go home," he replied, still not looking up.

"Obviously not."

"So you've come to your senses." His eyes finally flickered over to hers, clearly desperate to gauge her reaction. "Realized I was right about what's happened to her."

She longed to erase that smirk from his face. *Actually, I've stumbled onto something you never even thought of.* It took every ounce of self-restraint to swallow the words. Smirking or not, she needed Max. "I need to talk to Andrew Ennis."

Max laughed.

"It's important."

"I'm sure you think it is," he said. "What do you want, huh? A job on his team? It's not going to happen."

"I met a woman," said Lillian.

"We all knew you would eventually," Max sighed, lifting up the paper again.

Lillian swatted it away. "I know you don't give a damn about me, and I can assure you it's mutual. But this is about Eleanor."

Max went quiet for a moment. "You met a woman," he repeated eventually.

"Her boyfriend, a man named Martin, disappeared too,"

said Lillian. "Just like Eleanor. Completely mysterious circum-stances. He went into the hospital clinic building to have an infected tooth removed. The next day it was like he never even existed. Betty—that's her name—tried to get his records, and the nurse claimed they'd never had a patient by that name. He'd evaporated."

Max stabbed one of the green beans on his plate. "What does that have to do with Eleanor?"

"What if wherever Martin is, Eleanor's there, too?"

"So—what—they ran off together?"

Lillian could hardly believe how dense he was. "No," she said incredulously. "Is it possible that whatever they're building in Y-12, they need to test it on people?"

Max dropped his head and stabbed another green bean, chewing it at an agonizing pace. Lillian noted that he wasn't looking her in the eye. "Eleanor wasn't in the hospital."

"You didn't answer my question."

"So you think they're just grabbing people off the street? I thought Eleanor had run off. I thought you were certain."

"I was," said Lillian. "But when new information presents itself, we change our hypothesis. And besides, even if Eleanor is safe and sound somewhere, shouldn't we help *this* woman? Don't we have a moral imperative as scientists to discover the truth?"

"Not this truth." He finally lifted his eyes to meet hers again.

"So there is something," she breathed. "I'm right. There's something they want to test. Tell me I'm right."

"Andrew Ennis won't help you," said Max, his neat refusal to answer only confirming to Lillian that her hypothesis was correct. Whatever they were building around the clock in Y-12 required human test subjects. "He won't care that a man got kidnapped from the hospital."

"Betty thinks he's her only hope. She can't go to the army security, obviously, but he's not army."

"You can't meet him," said Max, slamming down his fork. "First of all, he'll know that you"—he snuck a look at the nearby table to make sure no one was eavesdropping before finishing with—"aren't who you say you are."

Lillian shrugged. "I assumed that he would."

"So your plan was to walk up to the head of the program out here and tell him you'd snuck into his facility?"

"Well, I was hoping that the people who have been kidnapped would take priority."

"You don't know everything," Max replied. "You don't know how things are around here. Trust me. Andrew Ennis is in charge, and the people in charge care more about spies sneaking things out than people stuck inside."

Lillian scowled. "I thought you wanted to investigate Andrew Ennis," she said. "I thought that's why you brought me down here."

"You're not talking about investigating him," said Max. "You want to *collaborate* with him. And I don't believe for one second you care about this crazy woman's boyfriend, or that you seriously believe Eleanor is wherever she thinks he is. If we were working on something the army needed to test, they could find damn better subjects than the *girlfriend of the head of the program,* and you know that! What you want is to meet a famous man and impress him. Maybe drop some mathematical skills once you've got him listening to your little theory. You want a promotion."

"Something's going on here, Max," said Lillian, trying to keep her cool. "I don't know what it is, but I know it's not good."

"There's no secret army conspiracy happening," said Max.

"This whole place is a secret army conspiracy," replied Lillian.

It was a stalemate. She closed her eyes and said a silent prayer for her sister's ability to flatter, to compromise. "Let's investigate him," she said.

Max seemed confused. "Really?"

"Yes, really. We're not at an impasse, here, Max. We both think there's something suspicious going on; we just disagree what it is and who's behind it. But I'll defer to you. You've been here longer, so you're the expert. Let's investigate Dr. Andrew Ennis. How do you want to begin?"

A surprised smile spread across Max's face, and Lillian marveled at how easy it was. Some mild flattery and a half compliment was all it took? To think, Max had tried to tell her being Eleanor would be difficult.

"I've got it all planned out," Max began. "Remember I told you he claimed Eleanor had left him an address where he could reach her?"

"Vaguely," Lillian answered.

"He was waving around some piece of paper when he did that, and then he put it in his desk drawer. I watched him do it. I've been thinking about how to get into that desk drawer for weeks, but there's no way for me to do it on my own. Most of us just work until five or six, and then call it quits. But he's in there all the goddamn time. After we finish for the day, he stays to work on some other secret pet project of his. Once he leaves, he locks up the building. There's no time of day that building is unlocked but he's not in it. But if I can distract him, late one night after everyone else has left, you can sneak in and search that desk."

This idea, to Lillian, did not seem promising. If she was going to be caught sneaking around a secret facility, it seemed prudent to at least strive for a lighter sentence than the one breaking into the head of the secret facility's office would produce. But the idea of a piece of paper that might have Eleanor's current address on it was hard to ignore. "I search the desk," she repeated. "And then what?"

"Well, if that piece of paper is there," said Max, "then we've got our answer, I'll admit to being wrong, and you can go home or come with me to track her down or whatever you please. But if it's not, well, why would a man who is innocent lie about something like that? He must be guilty."

"The absence of something can hardly prove guilt," Lillian pointed out. "He could have lost it, or thrown it away, or taken it home—"

"Yes, I'm aware, thank you," said Max. "But if you're so sure

I'm wrong, if you're so sure she lied to me about leaving him, then there's a decent chance that piece of paper does have her address on it, and it's sitting in his desk drawer, waiting for us to find it."

Lillian knew she should leave it alone. This plan would let her into Dr. Andrew Ennis's office, unsupervised. She could easily leave him a note detailing her and Betty's suspicions, ask him for help, tell him where to find her. She should shut her mouth and go along with Max's silly plan, but the whole thing seemed so ludicrous, she simply couldn't help pointing out the flaws. "But if it's not there, then what? We're exactly where we've started, where you suspect Dr. Ennis of something but neither of us can prove it. If it's not there—"

"I think it might be there, all right?" Max interrupted, unable to even look Lillian in the eye. "I didn't at first. I was sure he was lying. But after you got here, after we talked... I don't know. I've been less sure. So will you stop arguing with me about this and help?"

Lillian forced herself to bite her tongue and nod.

"Thank you." Max sighed. "Now I just need to find a math problem obscure enough that a man who does math problems for fun wouldn't have seen it before."

"I think I have one," said Lillian.

If an object weighing w lb. falls in a medium offering resistance proportional to the square of the velocity (ft./sec.), then

the differential equation of the motion is $\dfrac{w}{g}\dfrac{d^2y}{dt^2} = w - k\left(\dfrac{dy}{dt}\right)^2$
where the positive direction of the y-axis is downward and g is
the acceleration due to gravity (ft./sec.^{2}). Find y as a function of
t if (a) $\dfrac{dy}{dt} = V$ when $\dfrac{d^2y}{dt^2} = 0$; (b) $\dfrac{dy}{dt} = 0$ when t=0; (c) y=0
when t=0.

Lillian wrote quickly, not allowing herself to second-guess the words. She was certain she had memorized it—she memorized almost every math problem she saw—but that day in the lab all the way back at Columbia had been a rough one, with Irene breathing down her neck and the migraine hitting her deep in her skull. She finished writing and studied her work. Something about the shape of it looked off, the words not quite falling in the same order as the picture she could see in her mind of the piece of paper filled with Allerton problems.

It would have to do. She folded the paper, slipped it in her pocket, and headed for the door.

"Where are you going?" asked Emmy, looking up from the magazine she was reading. "It's almost curfew."

"Going to meet a boy," Lillian replied, in the most excited voice she could muster despite knowing the boy was Max Medelson.

Max was waiting outside the dormitory, and she followed him from a safe, inconspicuous distance of about twenty feet until they were out of the Townsite, and the streets were dark and empty.

"Did you bring the problem?" Max asked.

Lillian handed him the piece of paper. He immediately opened it to study it, as if he would catch a mistake that she hadn't. "And it's a real problem?" he asked after a moment. "It's solvable? He'll know right away if it's not solvable."

"Every problem is solvable," said Lillian, "if you accept that sometimes the solution is that the problem can't be solved."

"Jesus Christ," muttered Max. "Let's not talk anymore."

They walked in silence south along the same dark road Lillian had taken to Y-12 just two nights earlier. This time, however, just before reaching the plant, Max pointed out a small two-story building off to the right. It was so nondescript that even though she must have passed it going to and from the plant a dozen times, Lillian had never noticed it before. It seemed to blend completely into the mud surrounding it.

Sure enough, even though it was well past curfew by now, the doorknob turned in Max's hand, just as he said it would. Crossing the threshold as quietly as possible in two boots as heavy as textbooks, Lillian was suddenly struck with a cold jolt of fear. This was, objectively, the most dangerous thing she had ever done. Any quiet thrill she'd gotten from successfully pretending to be Eleanor was gone, leaving nothing but a pounding heart and a queasy stomach in its place.

"I'll bring him down the hall to my office," murmured Max as they made their slow, quiet way up the stairwell. "Whatever happens, you cannot let him see you."

She nodded, too afraid to be annoyed at the comment. Max met her gaze one last time and then quickly looked away, heading for Dr. Ennis's office.

Lillian tried to steady herself with a deep breath, and when that failed, she strained to listen to whatever was being said fifty feet down the hall. Max was keeping his voice frustratingly low, but it seemed to have worked, because a moment or two later the two men emerged and went down the hallway. Lillian wanted desperately to peek out of the stairwell, to get a glimpse of this man, but she remained paralyzed, flattened against the wall, until she heard a door shut on the other end of the building.

She moved more quickly than she probably should have, considering the shoes she was wearing, but Lillian wanted nothing more than to be out of this building as fast as possible. She went directly for the desk in the office, opening the drawer on the right that Max had claimed he'd seen the address stashed. It was stuffed to the brim with papers, sheet after sheet of yellow loose leaf, some folded and kept neat and others crumbled into balls. She took a moment to take in the rest of the office and saw it was equally a disaster. There were maybe a dozen empty cups strewn about the desk, and that assumed there was a desk somewhere under the stacks of legal pads and graphing paper and receipts and blueprints.

Every surface, including a wheeled-in chalkboard, was covered in a math problem of some kind, and Lillian had to stop herself from trying to solve a million things at once. It would be simply impossible to search this whole office to find one piece of paper; she would have more luck finding a particular grain of salt in the ocean. She quickly leafed through the open drawer and, finding nothing, did her best to wedge it shut again. It was time for plan B. She grabbed the nearest blank piece of paper and a pen and began to write.

Dear Dr. Ennis:

I need your help. I'm Eleanor Kaufman's

A sudden commotion in the hallway—Max shouting something, footsteps coming toward her—caused her to look up. She thought about ducking under the desk, even looked around for a window to jump out of, but it was no use. Ultimately she stood quite frozen, his pen still in her hand, as Dr. Ennis himself appeared in the doorframe.

EIGHT

JUNE 1945

The first thing Lillian noticed was that Dr. Andrew Ennis was quite tall. He practically had to duck to enter the office. She had assumed, given both that Eleanor had dated him and that he was a physicist, that he would look similar to Max—short, pale, unremarkable—but that couldn't have been further from the truth. The second thing she noticed, to her surprise, was that he was rather young. The gossip about him yelling at Niels Bohr had the air of a story passed on long enough to codify it into legend, but now that she was face-to-face with its leading player, she realized it couldn't have been more than a decade ago, if that.

The third thing Lillian noticed was that she wasn't afraid of him—not because she was particularly brave, but because he didn't actually seem angry to find her there. His expression, standing directly across the desk from her, was one of careful neutrality, but something in his eyes seemed to indicate that he was the one who was fearful of her.

"Can I help you?" he asked.

"As a matter of fact, you can," she answered.

Before she could elaborate, Max had stumbled inside, nearly tripping over himself to grab Lillian's wrist and drag her out from behind Dr. Ennis's desk. "Let's go," he said, as if maybe there was still a chance Dr. Ennis simply hadn't noticed her standing there, holding his black fountain pen.

Lillian shot Max an incredulous look. Dr. Ennis seemed to ignore the statement altogether. "Let me see if I've got this straight," Dr. Ennis said, pointing at Max. Even though there was nothing between Max and the door, nothing physically stopping him from making a run for it, he seemed frozen. "You distract me with some ridiculous math problem, and you break in here to—what?" He looked at Lillian.

"Did you solve that problem already?" she asked him.

"V-squared over g ln cosh gt over V," he replied, before adding nonchalantly after a beat or two, "I think. I came back for a pen." He nodded toward Lillian's left hand.

Lillian held out the pen. As he reached out to take it, his dark eyes met hers with such intensity that she had to look away, turning her gaze over to the blackboard in the corner. "Thanks, Eleanor," he murmured.

She could feel Max almost collapse with relief at the thought that they had fooled him, but Lillian did not believe it could be that simple. She cautioned a glance back at Dr. Ennis, seated now behind the desk, no longer even looking at the two of them as he scribbled in the margins of one of his many yellow loose-leaf pieces of paper. "I think it would be best for all of us if the two of you got the hell out of here and we forget this ever happened," he said.

Max was halfway out of the door before the sentence was over. But all Lillian could see was being right back where she was before. Two feet away from her, sitting eerily still, was the only man on the property who could help her.

"I'm not Eleanor," she said.

She could practically hear Max's stomach drop next to her, and half a beat later, he let out a chuckle that was both too loud and too late. "She's obviously kidding," said Max.

"I'm not," insisted Lillian. What, exactly, could the joke have been? "I'm her twin sister, Lillian."

Dr. Ennis hadn't moved, hadn't even raised an eyebrow. "Then why have you left a note on my desk saying, 'I'm Eleanor Kaufman'?" he asked, still not looking up.

"I hadn't finished writing it," she answered.

Dr. Ennis had already shoved the half-finished note into a desk drawer and was moving on. "You must understand," he half mumbled. "The paperwork required of me if that's the truth… I'd rather not…"

Max had managed to drag her almost to the doorway, not

exactly from his greater physical strength but because Lillian had let her body grow limp as she focused on the one thing that could possibly save her, could possibly prove her own identity. Seconds ticked away. She wasn't certain, but it would have to do.

"The problem on your blackboard is incorrect."

That got his attention. Dr. Ennis looked up, cocking his head toward the chalkboard, as Max mumbled an "oh god" under his breath. Lillian held still. A few more seconds passed, and now she was quite sure of it. It was a diffusion problem, a rather simple one, the kind she'd mastered for fun in her bedroom as a girl.

After a moment, Dr. Ennis smiled, a seemingly genuine one. "You're right," he said. "How exciting! Now I get to find out who did this and fire them." He paused, then tilted his head to look at Lillian out of the corner of his dark eyes. "That was fast," he said.

"I like problems," Lillian replied.

"Me too," he said, adding in a tone of pitch-perfect innocence a few heartbeats later, "Want to take a look at another one?"

There was so much about Oak Ridge that was strange and mysterious and foreign. The simplicity of a math problem, the precision of a solvable equation, was too much to resist. "I'll take a look at another one," said Lillian.

"Let me find a good one," Dr. Ennis replied, pulling a book out from one of his drawers and starting to leaf through it.

"We can race. If you beat me, I'll give you a prize. Fair warning, though: no one ever beats me."

Before Lillian could answer, Max interjected. "No. We're leaving," he said, this time grabbing Lillian's arm with an iron grasp.

"Ah well," said Dr. Ennis. "Like I said, for the best." He settled back into his desk chair and had already resumed scribbling down notes as Lillian allowed Max to drag her from the room.

DECEMBER 1944

Lillian resolved to tell Eleanor about the phone call from Janet Mayberry the first thing Wednesday morning, the day of the audition, giving Eleanor just enough time to dress and get to Spring Street without driving herself into a nervous tizzy. Lillian was rather proud of herself for being so sensitive to her sister's needs and so intelligently coming up with an optimal solution.

Tuesday evening, Lillian—as usual—was the last student left in the laboratory, working on an Allerton problem that she had expected to crack in forty-five minutes, but that was now stretching past the one-hour mark with no end in sight. She was a heartbeat away from giving up, calling it a night. In fact, she was reaching for her coat when she heard the voice.

"I should have known you'd be here, Lillian Kaufman."

Gabriel Meadows stood in the doorway, green eyes piercing her from across the room. Lillian didn't know Gabe very well. He was handsome and popular, the kind of broad-shouldered all-American boy who didn't see girls like Lillian. This was the first time she could remember him speaking a sentence to her that wasn't "*Could you pass me that notebook?*"

"I'm about to leave," she said defensively, her shoulders crouching toward her ears the way they did when she sensed she was about to be teased.

"Not because of me, I hope." He smiled. He had a face that would be especially charming in a few years, Lillian thought, once its boyish circles had hardened out into chiseled lines. Her shoulders relaxed.

"Not because of you," said Lillian. "Are you working? Should I leave the lights on?"

Gabe laughed as he reached into his coat pocket, producing a silver flask, which he shook devilishly. Liquid sloshed around inside. "Not exactly working."

"You're drinking alone in the laboratory?"

"I won't be alone," said Gabe, "if you join me."

Lillian considered this. She did not know Gabe Meadows, but she didn't dislike him. She had no place to be anytime soon—the Kaufmans never sat down to dinner together. Besides, she'd never actually been tipsy before, and she had to admit she was curious from a scientific standpoint. She'd heard so many stories of people's ridiculous behavior spurred on by drink. Lillian had always wondered if she—so outside society in many other ways—would be immune to alcohol's effects, but she'd never had a chance to find out.

"All right," she said.

Gabe reached over and flicked off the lights. Startled, Lillian laughed. "Why did you do that?"

"It's too harsh with the lights on. Besides, what do we need to see?" His dark outline moved toward her, pulling up a chair. A streetlight shining through the window flickered off the silver flask as he raised it to his lips. "Ah, disgusting," he said, handing it over to Lillian.

"Are you celebrating something?" she asked.

"I am," said Gabe. "Some very, very, *very* good news: I have been given the opportunity to give my life for Uncle Sam!"

Lillian inhaled sharply. "Oh, Gabe."

Gabe waved his arm. "It is what it is."

"I'm so sorry."

He forced a smile. "Enough about me. Drink up!"

Lillian lifted the flask to her mouth. She had no idea what the liquid inside was, but it smelled like death. She took a sip and nearly coughed it up. "Sorry about that," said Gabe. "I would have sprung for something better if I'd known I'd be drinking with a lady."

"It's fine," lied Lillian, handing over the flask.

"It's not," said Gabe.

They sat in silence for a moment, Lillian unsure what to say.

Gabe finally cleared his throat. "What were you working on so late? I'd have thought you'd be done with homework by now."

"I want to win the Allerton Prize," Lillian blurted out. She normally wasn't this forward with near strangers and wondered if the sip of liquor had been enough to have an effect. Did alcohol work that quickly?

"Impressive," said Gabe. "You could do it, you know. If any of us could, you would be the one."

Lillian was thankful he'd turned the lights off, so he wouldn't see her flush. Another surprise—she wasn't normally one to color with embarrassment, because she wasn't really one to be embarrassed. "Thank you."

"I wish I'd gotten to know you better, Lillian Kaufman," he said suddenly, sadly. "I always thought you were sexy as all hell. Hope that's not weird for me to say. If it is, well, the good news is you'll probably never see me again." He took another sip from the flask and passed it back to her.

She considered her response quite carefully. That was another area of human interaction that was of scientific interest to her, an area she was curious to explore but had never wanted to put in the requisite time with a boyfriend to get to.

"It's not weird for you to say that," she said finally. She added, "I think you are, too." This wasn't exactly a lie. She saw the potential in Gabe Meadows. Besides, it was dark enough in the lab that she could certainly fake it.

"You do?" asked Gabe.

The question annoyed her. Hadn't she just said that? "Yes."

"I'm glad to hear it," he whispered. Suddenly, she felt a warm weight on her knee. Gabe had placed his hand on her bare leg. He began to caress it with his thumb. She liked the motion of it but the sensation itself was nothing new. She wondered if there was a way to make sure the night progressed further than this.

"Do you live nearby?" she said, trying to make it sound innocent, as if she were merely inquiring about real estate.

"I do," said Gabe. "Do you want to come over?"

JUNE 1945

Lillian had no way to time herself solving the problem, since she had to work hunched on a toilet in the bathroom so as not to bother her sleeping roommate. This was probably for the best, as she was slightly encumbered by the fact that she had somehow misplaced the pack of stationery she'd purchased at the five-and-dime, so she had to work out a solution in pencil on the inside cover of Eleanor's dog-eared copy of *Little Women*. Lillian had read the book. She wasn't too distraught by the defacement.

By the time she arrived back at Building E, the morning sun was tinting the sky shades of pink and gold. She had expected needing to wait for someone to arrive, but the door was open. Whether it was open again or still, she didn't know.

Dr. Ennis was inside his office, his feet on the desk, staring at the ceiling and absentmindedly tossing a piece of crumbled paper. He looked over as Lillian appeared in his doorway and arched an eyebrow in a much milder expression of surprise than she would have expected.

"I thought I told you it would be better for all of us if you never came back here," he said.

She dropped the book on the desk. "You were right," she said. "V-squared over g ln cosh gt over V." Normally she would have said *lon* to represent the natural logarithm, but Dr. Ennis had said *ln* the night before, and she found herself repeating him without giving it much thought. (It did, she realized after saying it out loud, sound much more elegant.)

Dr. Ennis hesitated, but only for a moment. He reached over to pick up the book, unperturbed that she had defaced Louisa May Alcott's most beloved novel. There was a long silence during which he studied her work that Lillian found surprisingly hard to bear. "The math is good," he said finally. "There's a bit too much of it. At a certain point, you could have discarded a few of these unlikely solutions and worked a little faster, but otherwise, it's excellent."

"I wanted to be as thorough as I could," she said. "I had to convince you I'm not Eleanor."

"Come on, I knew that already. Give me some credit," he muttered, putting the book down and reaching for a cigarette case. "I just think it's a good idea for me to not be involved. That is to say... Hand me that lighter." He pointed to a silver lighter on the edge of his desk, which Lillian passed to him. He paused, taking his time to flick on the flame, light the cigarette, inhale. "That is to say, Eleanor made it extremely clear before she left that she wanted absolutely nothing to do with me ever again."

So Max had been right: Eleanor had dumped Dr. Ennis. "Neither Max nor I have heard from Eleanor since she left, but Max said she left you an address," said Lillian. "That's what we were in here last night looking for."

Dr. Ennis rolled his eyes. "Oh god, that. Max Medelson is an idiot. Sorry, I know he's a friend of yours, but—"

"He's not my friend," Lillian quickly clarified.

"Good. He's an idiot. I made up that whole thing about the address, obviously. Just wanted to see the look on his face. It was a good look, too, quite amusing. Almost worth how pathetic that story sounds, hearing it back now." He shook his head and took another drag on the cigarette. "So that's the truth. I'm just a sad man who knows nothing and can't help you. Sorry to disappoint."

"I think you can help me," said Lillian. "She's not the only person from this place who has gone missing."

He waved that away almost immediately. "The people in this town—the gossip—they can make a boogeyman out of their own shadows on the floor."

"It's not just gossip." She finally sat down, sliding into the single chair across from his desk. "I've found a woman who says her boyfriend disappeared from the hospital. They wouldn't give her his records, wouldn't even acknowledge he was ever there at all. She's worried that whatever they're making here, the army is testing it on people. Now this woman—she's convinced it's too late, that's he's already gone, but she thinks that perhaps you could get access to his medical records and help her prove what happened."

Dr. Ennis sat silently, cigarette slowly turning to ash in his hand. "I don't think that I…" he began.

"I know you're very important here, and you must be busy," said Lillian. "But it's because you're so important that you're the only person who can help. Is there anyone else here not from the army who could demand to see private medical files?"

"Probably not," Dr. Ennis admitted. "But I'll be honest. Everything you're alleging is possible, technically possible, that's true. However, it's so unlikely that it's… You have to understand. The trouble I could get in for even talking to you could ruin me, ruin my career. I ought to throw you out and call security."

"But you haven't," said Lillian.

"No," he said, as if surprised by his own actions. He stared down at the pages of *Little Women* that Lillian had defaced. "No, I haven't."

"Please, at least, come meet with her before you decide," said Lillian. "I know her story sounds unlikely. But this isn't a math problem, where you can discard an unlikely solution. We have a duty here, as scientists, to work this problem fully from the beginning, not to assume we know the solution. We have a duty to this woman, a duty to her boyfriend, and a duty to Eleanor. And while it certainly would be easier if you helped me, I'm going to keep looking, with or without you."

Her last sentence surprised her a little bit. She hadn't actually thought that far ahead yet, to what would happen were Dr. Ennis to say no, but she realized as she said the words that they were absolutely true. Of course they were.

After a moment, Dr. Ennis nodded, almost imperceptibly. Then he added in a quiet voice, "You know, Eleanor was in the hospital."

Lillian felt her heart jump. She tried to remain calm, focus on the facts. "She was? When she went missing?"

Dr. Ennis shook his head. "No, not when she went missing, but right before. Maybe two or three days...?" He shrugged. "I have no idea if it's related, but..."

"But it might be," said Lillian. She felt suddenly light-headed saying the words. *It might be.* This was something to follow, something to head toward. It felt like stepping off a ferry onto solid ground and only then realizing how much the motion of the boat had affected you.

Dr. Ennis went quiet as he extinguished his cigarette on the side of the desk, leaving a singed circular impression in the wood. He immediately reached for another. "I'll meet with her," he said finally. "Sure. What's the harm in that, I suppose."

Lillian sighed in relief. "Thank you," she said. "Thank you.

I can talk to her to set a time, pass that information back to you through Max—"

Dr. Ennis cut her off. "No, I don't trust Max. You'll come work here, for me."

Lillian blinked in surprise. "But I have to be Eleanor," she said. "Eleanor's not qualified to work here."

"No one needs to know that," said Dr. Ennis. "If I say she's qualified, people won't question it. And it'll give us an excuse to be seen together, more chances to talk. Plus..." He tapped his fingers on the desk for a moment before continuing. "You're new here, and you don't know how things work. If you work here, I can keep an eye on you."

Lillian was quite sure she did not need to have an eye kept on her. However, if she had to bide her time pretending to be Eleanor, surely whatever they were doing in this building would be more interesting than sitting on a stool and turning a dial for eight hours a day.

Dr. Ennis seemed to read her mind. "Forget I said that— 'Keep an eye on you.' Think of it as a promotion. I did promise you a prize if you beat me at a math problem."

"I didn't beat you," said Lillian. "You solved that problem almost instantly. I was there."

"Yes, technically you didn't beat me," said Dr. Ennis. "But you're the first person I've ever met who someday could. And that, to me, is..." He smiled. "Well, I like a challenge."

NINE

JUNE 1945

Lillian arrived early Monday morning, before the rest of Dr. Ennis's team (or, rather, Andrew's team—he had told her to call him Andrew) so he could brief her on the work that they were doing in the nondescript building known as Building E. That work turned out to be just a stack of index cards, bound together with a rubber band, and an adding machine. Lillian tried to hide the disappointed frown from her face as she thumbed through the disappointingly easy diffusion problems. The point of this job, she reminded herself, was to give her a reason to be seen talking to Andrew that wouldn't arouse suspicion. It wasn't supposed to be fun.

She must not have hid it very well, however. "I know, it's both dull and tedious," he said with a wry smile, perched on the desk of Lillian's absent office mate and fussing absentmindedly with the drawer pulls.

"I don't mind," she said, trying not to sound sarcastic. It was better, at least, than working in Y-12, where any second you could be scared off your stool by a machine going haywire. At least the chairs in this building had backs. "Betty's expecting us tonight."

"Good," said Andrew. "We can walk over together after work. There's just one more thing you need to know about this place. Do you see that safe?" Lillian looked down. The bottom right of her desk was a large metal box instead of a drawer, with a dial just above the handle. "Set a combination you'll remember, and then don't walk away from your desk for a second without locking up everything that's considered sensitive."

"What's considered sensitive?" she asked.

"Everything," he replied, before shoving some papers into his back pocket and leaving the room.

───────────

Lillian's office mate was a tall, gangly redhead named Sean. He spoke with a slight Midwestern accent and had the most freckles Lillian had ever seen on one person. They were the same age, but he seemed to her like a child. "This is my first job," he admitted to Lillian quietly, as if it were a secret. Technically, it was Lillian's first job, too, but she was fairly certain Sean was the type to spend his summers collecting rocks and playing baseball instead of taking a class or conducting research. For someone who had never collected a paycheck, Lillian felt as if she'd been working all her life.

In order to stall the dreadful diffusion problems for as long as possible, Lillian first turned her attention to the safe. Its numbers went from 0 to 60, allowing 216,000 possible combinations. Andrew had specified to choose something she would remember, so she entered 09-06-30 and pulled on the dial per the typed instructions to set the lock. September 6, 1930—the day of Father's suicide. Morbid, perhaps, but a number she'd never forget.

They worked in silence for most of the morning, the only sound their pens scratching against their respective papers until close to eleven, when Andrew and at least half a dozen other scientists appeared in the doorway. Lillian thought for a moment he might be bringing others around to introduce her, and felt slightly foolish when he ignored her entirely and went straight to Sean. "We need your charts from yesterday," he bellowed, his voice commanding the room.

Sean seemed to shrivel at the pressure of eight eyeballs directly on him. "Sure," he said, reaching over to his safe and opening it with a few flicks of his wrists. Then he stopped. Stopped moving, stopped speaking, stopped breathing, it seemed.

"Everything all right?" asked Andrew.

"Yes," answered Sean quickly, and then immediately, "No."

"Which is it?" asked Andrew. Little beads of sweat appeared on Sean's brow. When Sean didn't respond, Andrew pressed: "Because I can't help but note that 'yes' and 'no' are, in fact, contradictory answers—"

"My safe is empty," said Sean. "I put my charts in there last night, and now it's empty. I don't know what happened."

Andrew raised an eyebrow. For so small a gesture, it had such an air of menace. Perhaps it was because he'd stepped closer to Sean, with all his imposing frame. One of Andrew's hands was the size of Sean's tiny neck, thought Lillian. Everyone squeezed in the room was silent for some time, as sweat continued to pool on Sean's forehead. Finally, Andrew turned around to face the rest of the group. "Gentlemen, it appears as if Sean has lost our military secrets," he said, anger seething underneath his voice.

Poor Sean, for some reason that escaped Lillian, thought cracking a joke would be a wise course of action. "You'd think things you put in the safe would be safe, right?" he said with a little nervous laugh.

"Do you think this is funny?" yelled Andrew. A chill went down Lillian's back. The whole room seemed to drain of its color.

"No, sir," whispered Sean.

"Good," Andrew continued. "There's nothing funny here. The army has told me they suspect someone from this office of sneaking out sensitive information."

"It's not me," insisted Sean.

"Well, it might as well be you!" snapped Andrew. He reached for something in his pocket and slammed it down on Sean's desk. "Fortunately, this time, it wasn't. Here are your charts."

Sean stared down at the papers and, upon recognizing

them, hugged them to his chest. "Oh, thank god," he said, every muscle in his body visibly relaxing. "I'll never leave that safe unlocked again. I promise."

"You didn't," said Andrew.

Sean stammered in confusion. "I–I didn't?"

"No, you locked it. I cracked it." Andrew tapped the safe with his fingertips. "Very easy."

"You cracked it," said Sean. "That was just a prank?" He looked to his coworkers for support, but everyone avoided his gaze.

Andrew frowned. "It wasn't a *prank*. I cracked it, which is a physical *skill*. The real prank was yesterday when I told you these charts needed to be kept secret. Ninety-five percent of it is wrong, wrong, wrong. You *should* hand it over to the Germans. It'd set them back centuries."

"We're not fighting the Germans anymore," muttered Sean.

"What was that?" challenged Andrew.

Sean folded immediately. "Nothing, sir."

Andrew rounded on the assembled group of scientists. "This is a lesson. Do it right the first time, and you won't find yourself in a similar situation as your colleague here today." He paused for a moment, seeming to revel in the rest of the group cowering in fear. Then he snapped: "I don't know what we're all standing around for." The group scattered like a bunch of cockroaches when the light turned on, and within seconds the young men and Andrew had disappeared from the room.

"'Hand it over to the Germans.' Lots of use this shit will be to Hitler's blown-up head," mumbled Sean, crumpling the sheets of paper and throwing the ball across the room before sinking into his desk chair.

Lillian noticed he was shaking a bit. It was hardly her responsibility to comfort Sean, yet she knew this was one of those things humans weren't supposed to ignore. "Are you all right?" she asked.

"I'm fine," he answered. "I'll be fine."

"I think I saw him do it," mused Lillian. "He was in here, training me, and leaned up against your safe. It looked like he might have been playing with something behind his back. Then when he left, he stuffed something into his pocket. I wondered what it was."

Sean sighed. "So he wasn't even looking at it when he broke into my safe?"

Lillian was forced to respond, "No, I suppose he wasn't."

Sean closed his eyes, shook his head. "I shouldn't be surprised," he said a few moments later. "That guy... I swear to god, it's like he's not even human."

The incident didn't give Lillian pause, exactly. She had, after all, been warned that her new boss was temperamental, and she reckoned that the slightly uneasy feeling that had settled in her stomach was simply from witnessing it firsthand rather than from the events themselves being all that egregious. Still, she couldn't stand more than a few minutes of watching

Sean pretend to be all right enough to get back to work. She stood and made her way upstairs to Max's office.

Max's office mate was absent, so she slipped in and shut the door behind her. Max looked up expectantly, the *What do you want?* so clear in his eyes it didn't need to be said.

Lillian paused. What *did* she want? "Hi," she said and immediately felt ridiculous.

Max's eyes narrowed. "Let me guess. You just witnessed whatever little show just happened down there. Now you know what I was saying. He's mad."

"He's not mad," said Lillian. "Maybe a bit theatrical, but I hardly think you should be the one to hold that against a man."

"When have I ever been theatrical?" said Max, sweeping his arms open so forcefully he knocked a full glass of water on its side. "Ah, shoot. Can you grab some paper towels? There's a little kitchenette at the end of the hall."

That settled it, then. Max Medelson thought Dr. Andrew Ennis was not to be trusted. But Max Medelson was also—clearly, obviously—an idiot.

DECEMBER 1944

As they walked downtown on Broadway, Gabriel Meadows took Lillian's hand, which she found to be a nerve-racking experience. First she worried if she was holding too tight and then, after loosening her grip, agonized that it was not tight enough. She prayed the rest of the night wouldn't be filled with similar concerns. They walked in near silence, having exhausted all their topics of conversation during their three minutes together in the lab.

Finally, Gabe said something like, "Have you lived in New York all your life?" and Lillian replied that yes, yes she had. Through lots of feigned enthusiasm, they managed to stretch that conversation out for the remaining five blocks, finally arriving at Gabe's apartment on West 108th Street and Central Park West. "Shall we?" Gabe asked, standing on the stoop, and Lillian thought it a stupid question. She'd walked all the way here; she certainly wasn't calling a cab now.

Upstairs, in the cramped apartment on the third floor, Lillian sat on the couch and wondered what to do with her hands as Gabe made her a drink. This one tasted much better than whatever had been in the flask, and Lillian drank it quickly. Gabe sat next to her on the couch and continued the motion of rubbing her bare knee with his thumb. Lillian wondered how best to encourage this to move further, then wondered if she was even supposed to be the one doing that. Perhaps Gabe would find it odd if she leaned in to kiss him, or if she guided his hand to a different area. The rules for this sort of encounter were irritatingly indiscernible. Finally, Gabe leaned over to kiss her, and she breathed an (internal) sigh of relief. She leaned back, let his lips run over her neck, let his hands fuss with her blouse. It was nice if not particularly exceptional. She didn't mind it, but also wouldn't have minded being home in a warm bath.

Perhaps the actual act would be more life-changing. After a few minutes of fumbling with the tiny buttons of her blouse, Gabe led her toward his bedroom. The room was so small, the only furniture that fit inside was a bed and a small table. Lillian let out a clap of laughter when Gabe opened the door.

"What?" he asked, completely oblivious.

"I suppose there's no pretending that anything else could happen in here," said Lillian.

"What else could happen?" asked Gabe, his words slurring and his eyes cloudy with confusion.

"Never mind," said Lillian.

He made a motion as if to lay her on the bed, but he didn't quite have the upper-arm strength to lift her more than a centimeter off the ground for longer than half a second. Lillian ended up awkwardly collapsing herself onto the bed, while wrapping her arms around him and taking him down with her. It felt more like an ice-skating accident than a romantic encounter. They sloppily kissed for a few moments, then he buried his face into her neck and moaned softly, which surprised Lillian. He seemed to be enjoying this far more than she was. Shouldn't she be moaning, too?

"Lillian," he whispered, and she noticed a catch in his voice. He looked up at her, and she saw his eyes had welled with tears. "I'm sorry."

She hadn't the slightest idea what had gone wrong. "For what?" she asked.

"I'm so scared," he said and looked away. "I'm so scared I'm going to die over there."

Ah. There it was. He hadn't really wanted to be with her at all. Lillian had flattered herself into thinking she was a choice he was making, when the truth was he just didn't want to be alone. It was a disappointing revelation, but one she couldn't begrudge him, given the circumstances. "It's all right," she said.

He pressed his head to her chest, tears coming in full force now. She ran her fingers through his curls. His hair was smooth and soft, like a child. He *was* still a child, practically.

They lay there like that, partially undressed, the sounds of the city drifting up from the street three stories below, soothing them like a lullaby. Gabriel dozed off quickly, but Lillian lay awake, staring at the ceiling, for hours she couldn't count. Finally, she too fell into a quiet slumber.

The next morning, Lillian had to rush to campus for an early morning lecture (and make a stop at a Loehmann's to purchase a new blouse so no one would notice she hadn't made it home the night before). By the time she remembered Eleanor and the phone message she'd neglected to pass on, it was far too late. She thought about coming clean, but what could she say? That she'd failed her beloved twin so she could attempt a sexual tryst with a classmate she barely knew? Not only was that shameful, but it would break Eleanor's heart. There was no need for Lillian to explain, she decided. She could carry around this one secret. She could appear surprised when Eleanor told her she went in for her audition on Friday to find that Mrs. Helburn was out of town. It was the first time she'd ever failed her sister, and as long as she made a vow that it would be the very last, what could be the harm?

On her way home that afternoon, Lillian intended to stop at Ed Blumenthal's bakery for a loaf of bread, and of course found it closed. She kicked herself for not remembering, but only had to walk a few more blocks before finding the next bakery. It was run by a sweet Polish woman named Mrs. Grabinski, and Lillian and Eleanor both agreed at supper that evening that the bread was even softer and fluffier than Ed Blumenthal's (although nobody could replace Ed in kindness, of course).

Lillian hoped as she chewed that her error with Eleanor's message would resolve itself in a similar fashion by allowing her to experience another unexpected opportunity, a better one. It was Manhattan, after all. There was always another bakery down the road.

JUNE 1945

Lillian walked alongside Andrew as they headed north from Building E toward the main Townsite and then veered west along a road Lillian had not ventured down yet. They walked in silence, both knowing it wasn't wise to discuss what they wanted to discuss out in the open, but not knowing each other well enough to have any other topic of conversation.

She expected that the residences built for the Black workers would be roughly equivalent to the ones she had seen in her part of Oak Ridge: dormitories for single men and women, duplexes for families, houses for the important people. Yet the area they were rapidly approaching did not look anything like the rest of the town. Instead of buildings, there were row after row of tiny square huts of about twenty by twenty feet that appeared to be little more than four pieces of plywood leaning up against one another. Even more concerning, even though the entire facility was surrounded by a barbed-wire fence, this part of town was behind a separate barbed-wire fence.

"They have people living in there?" asked Lillian as they approached the security checkpoint.

"You want to hear something awful?" asked Andrew. "They had begun building real dormitories for the Black workers, but when they needed them for white workers, the army said that the Black residents preferred living here."

Lillian shook her head.

Andrew's security clearance got them through the checkpoint with no questions asked, and they made their way to Betty's hut. She greeted them at the door, looking back and forth from Lillian to Andrew as if she couldn't believe Lillian had actually done it.

"You have no idea how long I've been waiting to talk to you," Betty said to Andrew.

"Let's not waste any more time, then," he replied.

Lillian took in the small surroundings. She had believed the two beds in her dorm room seemed crammed in, but there were four in this tiny space, alongside a small stove, a few chairs, and not much else. There was no running water and no electricity. The idea that anyone would prefer to live here was ludicrous.

"Can you start from the beginning?" asked Andrew, leaning against a wall. His height stretched nearly to the ceiling, as if he were a support beam holding the roof away from their heads.

Betty nodded. "It started when Martin got this nasty infected tooth," she said. "I kept telling him to do something about it, but he refused. You know how men are," she said to Lillian.

Lillian hadn't expected to be addressed and looked up in surprise. "Sure," she agreed, even though she didn't have the faintest idea how men were about nearly anything.

"Finally I told him that if he didn't get it taken care of, it was only going to get worse and it would move to his brain and kill him. That did the trick. He finally went to see the dentist here, but instead of just taking it out, they told him he would need to come back in a week for surgery and stay overnight in the hospital. I thought that was strange. If it was bad enough that he needed to stay overnight in the hospital, why was it fine to wait a week? And who needs to stay overnight for a tooth removal anyway?"

"That is strange," remarked Andrew.

"They keep us separated by gender here. I don't know if you know that," Betty continued. "The women behind one barbed wire fence, the men behind another. So we always had to meet up in town. That got harder after I got in trouble and was moved to night shifts." She shot a pointed look at Lillian, who was halfway to apologizing before remembering it was Eleanor who had been the cause of that, not her. She shut her mouth again. "It was a few days after the surgery was scheduled when we both had our next night off. I waited at our spot and...he never showed up."

She sighed, and looked down at her hands. "This is the part I'm ashamed of," she said. "I thought he was maybe not feeling well, or tired or something. I wrote it off. I asked a few friends if they'd seen him, and when they hadn't, I wrote that off, too. He must be tired. Maybe they changed his shift around and he hadn't found a way to tell me. I didn't want it to be the bad thing, so I ignored it. And I worry that...if only I'd realized sooner..." She shook her head.

"You have nothing to be ashamed of," said Andrew. "Anyone reasonable would have done the same."

"Thank you," said Betty, although it was clear she didn't believe him. She cleared her throat. "A few days later, I finally went to the hospital clinic building. They told me..." She inhaled shakily. "Not only was he not there, but he'd never *been* there. There was never a Martin Hughes in their care." As if she knew what protests might come next, she held up a finger. "And he didn't run off on me or anything like that. I walked him over there. I watched him go inside. And everything between us was... He was the love of my life, you know?"

"I know," said Andrew, quietly and sadly.

"I asked for his records and they said they didn't have any. But I know they're lying, Dr. Ennis. They took him. The army, or someone. Someone took him. And he doesn't have a family, or anything. His parents are dead. He doesn't have any brothers or sisters. It's just me, just me that's looking for him, just me that remembers him, so I have to—I have to…" Her voice trailed off for a moment, and then she cleared her throat. "I'm not under any delusions that he's still alive," she continued. "That he can be saved, or anything like that. I just want some answers." She took a deep breath. "Do you think I'm crazy, Dr. Ennis?"

"I'll be honest," Andrew began. "I thought before coming here that you might be. But now, here, talking to you…" He shook his head. "No, I don't think you're crazy."

"So it is possible," Betty went on. "They're taking people. The army is taking people."

"But to what end?" asked Lillian. "What are they doing here that they need to test on human beings?"

Andrew frowned. "I'm not sure how much of that I can say."

"I know it's whatever they're making in Y-12," said Betty. "When I started working there, they told me about whole areas we're not supposed to go in, all this stuff we can't touch without gloves on. I figured whatever they're making there must be dangerous to people, and the army must want to know how much."

Andrew spoke slowly, choosing his words with care. "You're right. They're generating materials in Y-12 that are radioactive. We've known about radioactivity for a couple decades now, and scientists have suspected that the effects could be devastating to humans. But we don't know everything about how it works. How much exposure is safe, over what period of time. We have a team studying this slowly, safely, the goal being to prevent accidents from happening."

"I would assume the army doesn't like moving slowly and safely," said Lillian. "Especially when there's a war to win."

"They've taken matters into their own hands, then," said Betty.

"I can't say that for sure," said Andrew. "But it does concern me that..." Here his gaze slowly shifted from Betty to Lillian. "A few days before she disappeared, Eleanor was in the hospital clinic building, too."

"So it is possible," said Betty. "They're taking people from that building and experimenting on them."

At the very phrase—*experimenting on them*—Lillian felt ill. She looked down at her hands, at her clean, polished nails. *Did Eleanor's hands still look the same?*

"I'll ask some questions, poke in some corners," said Andrew. "I think I can get their medical records. I'll do everything I can. In the meantime, we need a way to get to you if we have to pass on a message. There's only so often we can walk out here before it gets suspicious."

Betty nodded. "I go to the Presbyterian service Sundays.

There's always lots of white people there. No one would think twice if we stood next to each other."

Andrew looked at Lillian. "Think you can pass for Presbyterian?"

"Is that the same as Christian?"

Her question went unanswered as Andrew turned back to Betty. "I have to stress…" He paused, pursed his lips together. "I'll try my hardest to find answers. But we could dig forever and not find anything. Can you accept that?"

His gaze had flickered back over to Lillian, who found herself nodding. She was sympathetic to where he was coming from, not wanting to raise Betty's hopes for a resolution only to have them dashed later on. But something in that moment told Lillian he was wrong. Between the two of them, they would find an answer. They had to.

"Everyone thought I was crazy," said Betty. "I'm the kind of person who… You know, I'll be a little chilly and immediately think I've got some horrible disease. When I first started talking about this, everyone thought I was just being dramatic again. Blowing things out of proportion. It really messed with my head. So to have you believe me, it…" She sighed. "It means a lot."

───────────────

After leaving Betty's hut, Andrew immediately reached into his pocket and took out a silver cigarette case. After taking one for himself, he automatically reached it out toward Lillian.

"I don't smoke," she said.

"Right," he replied through his clenched jaw, snapping the case away with an air of embarrassment. "I forgot you're not... Never mind." They took a few slow steps into the dusk. "You look just like her," he said, as if this could explain how he'd mistaken her for the woman whose kidnapping they had been discussing moments earlier.

"I know," replied Lillian.

The silence between them was agonizing. Lillian wondered if her very presence was torture for him and even considered apologizing for the unwelcome reminder her face must bring of the woman he wished were walking alongside him instead.

"It might take me awhile to find anyone at the hospital I can trust to get those records," said Andrew finally. "Just to warn you. I want to go about it delicately, if I can. Can't be going in there and throwing my weight around, or the army will get word of it for sure."

"What can I do to help?" asked Lillian.

"Nothing," said Andrew right away. "I've been in charge here for awhile. I have a better sense of who we can trust. You say the wrong thing to the wrong person and we're done."

"I want to do *something*," said Lillian.

"You are. Keeping a low profile, blending in, that's important."

"But I..." She fell silent, realizing she didn't have much of an argument to make. Betty had wanted her help in getting

Andrew's attention. She'd done her part. Now it was time to let Andrew do his.

"I'll walk you back to the dorms," Andrew said eventually—probably more out of a desire to break the silence than any inclination toward chivalry, Lillian figured.

"You don't have to do that," she said.

"It's not a problem," he replied.

"I don't really feel like going to the dormitory," said Lillian. "It's very loud there, lots of people around. I think I might go for a walk or something." She had a sudden longing to do what she normally did when she needed to clear her head: go for the long walk crosstown through Central Park to Columbia, and then head for the laboratory. She never thought she would miss that leaky old building with its rickety desks.

"You probably shouldn't do that," said Andrew. "Go walking alone without a destination? That's something these people consider suspicious."

"That's utterly absurd," said Lillian. "What do people do when they need to think about things?"

"It's the army. Thinking of any kind is strictly prohibited," said Andrew. Then after a moment he added, "You wouldn't want to come work on something with me, would you?"

"Not if it's more diffusion problems," said Lillian. She had meant it as a joke, but Andrew didn't smile.

"It's not," he said. "It's strictly extracurricular."

"Then, sure," said Lillian. "That would be…yes."

"I thought you might be that kind of person," said Andrew. "The kind of person who buries yourself in work to deal with things."

"How did you know?" she asked.

He cracked a small, guilty smile. "Because I'm the same way."

TEN

"I'm sure you noticed," said Andrew as he unlocked the door to Building E, "that about five years ago all mention of atomic research disappeared mysteriously from every scientific journal."

Lillian had noticed this, but had never thought much of it. Separating atoms had seemed, in those early days, like a terribly difficult business requiring complicated and expensive machinery. She had assumed that the research had stalled out, waiting for more funding or cheaper machinery. It seemed obvious now. No further research on the subject had been published because the fundamental workings of the building blocks of nature had become military secrets.

"I had noticed," she said. "I didn't think much of it."

They climbed the steps to his office, and he flicked on the

lights. It was nearly dark out by now, and even though the room had no windows, it still had an eerie, after-hours quality. "Let's see how quickly I can bring you up to speed on everything that would have been published if we hadn't had our hands tied. We spent a lot of time researching what elements would work the best if someone were to make a bomb from nuclear fission. Some uranium isotopes are decent, but we discovered if you shoot a lot of deuteron at uranium-238, it makes something we're calling plutonium. Actually we're not calling it plutonium; we're supposed to call it 'Element 49.'"

"Because its atomic number is 94?" guessed Lillian.

Andrew threw his hands up. "See? Cracked it in what, ten seconds?" He shook his head. "I'm of the opinion that if the codes we're going to use are so easy, we might as well just say *plutonium.* That's more likely to throw off any spies, I think. They'll spend more time debating if we're really stupid enough not to use a code word than it takes to crack that one."

"So that's what they're making here," said Lillian. "That's what all those cubicles were for. They're separating some isotope of plutonium as fissile material for a bomb."

"Plutonium 239, to be specific." He had begun pacing around the room. Lillian did her best to get out of the way, pushing a chair against the wall. "We tried 240, but it was too fissile. Burned out too fast before the thing could go critical. We tried a gun-type device, where we shoot one subcritical mass at a second subcritical mass, but same problem. We're working on an implosion model, with a subcritical core surrounded by a subcritical shell, which then collapses in on itself to create a critical mass of plutonium and then, god willing, an explosion."

"That sounds nearly impossible," said Lillian.

"Yes," replied Andrew.

"If it doesn't implode perfectly even, you'll have the same problem. It'll fizzle out before it goes critical."

"Indeed," said Andrew.

"So that's what you're working on."

Andrew shook his head. "No, that's what a lot of very smart people at a laboratory in New Mexico are working on. They sent me out here to be in charge of a bunch of children doing entry-level calculus—which I'm honored to do, don't get me wrong—but if they're going to drop me in the middle of nowhere with absolutely nobody interesting to talk to, I'm going to come back with the *next* thing." He stopped pacing and looked at her with a sigh.

"Look, I didn't mind telling you all that about the gadget because it's almost done. It's going to be public knowledge in the scientific community in a few months anyway. But what I've been working on—what I'm about to tell you next—has to stay a secret. This is the dangerous sort of knowledge. So if you won't be able to help yourself from blabbing about it to Max or whoever—"

"You don't need to worry about that," Lillian quickly interjected.

"Good," said Andrew. "I was hoping you'd say that. You're

the first person I've met out here who I thought could actually help me with this, and I—I need help with this. So, all right. Here and in New Mexico, they're working on a fission weapon. But I think the future is in a fusion weapon."

It took a moment for Lillian to catch up. "You'd create the heat needed for the fusion reaction with the fission weapon," she said.

"Precisely."

"So what this entire city is working twenty-four seven to build, that would just be igniter for your weapon."

"Yes. And the thing that's brilliant about it is: the fission bomb, it's always going to blow up about the same amount. The fusion bomb, you can pile more and more material on there and make it as big as you like. You could blow up the whole world, if you wanted to."

It was hard for Lillian to even wrap her mind around such a thing. She still hadn't quite wrapped her mind around the fission bomb, and now she had to comprehend the end of the world on top of it.

"To be clear, I don't actually want to blow up the world. Most of the time, anyway," said Andrew, before adding, "You think I'm nuts."

"I don't," she said, and she meant it. It was enormous, the potential for destruction of the thing he was suggesting, but on the other hand... "It's the logical next step, if the fission bomb is successful."

He excitedly smacked his hand down on his desk. "Thank you! The boys in New Mexico, I keep telling them that. I swear, I've used those exact words, 'the logical next step.' None of them wanted to hear it. They're smart men. Very smart. But I don't think they can see what I can see. I mean, I can see this thing, you know? Like I'm seeing the future. They kept telling me, 'Andrew, slow down, you gotta walk before you can run,' but I think—hell—you might as well try running first. Save you a whole lot of walking if it works out, know what I mean?" He shook his head. "Sometimes I think they sent me out here because I wouldn't stop yelling at them about it."

"You have a reputation for doing that, you know," said Lillian. "Niels Bohr?"

Andrew grinned. "That story has been wildly distorted."

"You didn't yell."

"Oh no, I definitely yelled," he said. "The part that's been distorted is that the bastard deserved it. He was showing us shoddy work, and I pointed it out—perhaps a bit loudly, but I care about this stuff. I care about getting it right. And you know, no one ever tells the second half of that story."

A little bit of lightness had returned to his voice, for the first time since they had returned from Betty's. They were talking more like colleagues now, the horror of what had brought them together receding into background noise for a moment. It was a welcome relief. "So tell me," said Lillian.

"All right. This all happened when I was an undergrad at

Caltech. After my disruption, I was personally removed from the conference hall by the dean of students. Idiotic fellow, actually named Dean. Dean Dean Evans. Can you believe that?" He laughed and shook his head. "So Bohr leaves Caltech and gets on a train up to Stanford to do the same presentation. He gets there and the Stanford boys are fawning over him. At the end of the presentation, he asks for questions, and all anyone has to say is, 'How do you do such flawless work?' Ass-kissing nonsense.

"But Bohr knows the work isn't flawless. In fact, it's so flawed a dumbass undergrad out of Caltech who'd barely begun his thesis saw a glaring error. So Niels Bohr does what any self-respecting man does when people lie to his face: he gets pissed off. He storms out of his lecture and goes to the little office they've prepared for him to work out of while he's in town. He picks up the phone and calls Dean Dean Evans of Caltech, who then had the delightful duty of finding the student he'd kicked out of a lecture just three days earlier and presenting him with a first-class train ticket to San Jose. Courtesy, of course, of Dr. Niels Bohr."

Lillian could hardly breathe. "That's unheard of," she said. "That doesn't happen. Niels Bohr working with a physics undergrad...?"

"Only for a few hours," Andrew clarified. "But we got through most of the rough bits."

"I always wondered if you had been right," she said. "When people told that story, I always wondered."

"People care more about the fame than they do the work."
Andrew shrugged. "That's the problem. When you're famous,
people become afraid of you. Afraid to disagree with you, afraid
to question you. But the best science only happens when you
question everything. Bohr saw the value in being challenged.
That's part of why..." Here he hesitated, but only for a moment.
"Why I want to work with you. When you came back here and
dropped that book on my desk and told me you wouldn't be
taking my no as an answer, I thought, here's someone who's
going to challenge me. That, and you're brilliant at math."

"In the spirit of being challenged, then," began Lillian,
"and with the caveat that I do agree, it is probably the future,
have you thought about this fusion bomb?"

"I've done nothing but think about it for the last three
years," he countered.

"I mean, as in..." She was having trouble thinking of the
words to use, but it was occurring to her that perhaps this was
what Eleanor had found out about Andrew that made her want
to leave him: he might blow up the world. "Morally, I suppose."

Lillian was a bit relieved to hear him answer, "Of course I
have," with no hesitation. "What I keep coming back to is...if it
is the future, it should be us. I'm not talking about the United
States or the army or any of that, I'm talking about us. Me,
you. Intelligent, hard-working, the kind of people who think
and overthink and analyze every possible outcome. Wouldn't
something of this magnitude be the safest with people like us

shepherding it into the world? In that sense, wouldn't it be immoral not to do it?"

It was, thought Lillian, an interesting point. She nodded. "All right," she said. "Let's work."

DECEMBER 1944

Lillian left for campus earlier than necessary Friday morning, not wanting to watch Eleanor painstakingly dress and groom for an audition that would not be happening. Knowing she'd come home to a heartbroken sister, she decided to plan something special for the two of them that night: a concert, perhaps, and then dinner on the town. Yes, that would raise Eleanor's spirits quite nicely. Feet kicked up on her laboratory desk, she consulted the *Times* to see what the Philharmonic would be playing that evening; fortunately, it wasn't Brahms, so she borrowed the department phone to call the box office to book two seats. Perhaps they could head to the Stork Club afterward. Lillian wasn't too fond of the place, but Eleanor found it amusing. She would get a kick out of that, and the whole disastrous day would be behind her, forgotten.

She was surprised, then, to arrive home just after five to find Max Medelson in her front room. "What are you doing here?" she said.

"Nice to see you too, Lillian," he replied.

Eleanor appeared from the kitchen shortly after. "Lil!" she

cried, throwing her arms around Lillian's neck. "I'm so glad you're here. I had the most wonderful audition!"

"You had your audition?" said Lillian, too dumbfounded to say anything else.

"Don't tell me you forgot. I'd be upset with you if I weren't in such a good mood. We were just going to toast! Max, get Lillian a glass."

Max rose from the couch, slapping his thighs. "Right."

Eleanor took her sister's hands and led her to the seat Max had just vacated. It was still warm, and Lillian hated the sensation. Who was Max Medelson to be sitting in her front room, warming her furniture?

"It was the most wonderful thing, Lil," began Eleanor. "But at first I thought it was going to be a disaster! The producer was out of town, so they'd moved the first round of auditions up a few days. I'd missed them completely. Apparently they'd meant to telephone, but my name must have been lost in the shuffle. Can you believe that?"

"No," said Lillian.

"Well, the secretary, Janet—who I know a bit, she's very sweet—felt so awful that she told me Mr. Rodgers was actually in the office that day, and if I would be willing to wait, she'd ask him to give me a few minutes after lunch."

"Mr. Rodgers, who's that?"

"The writer," said Eleanor. "Rodgers and Hammerstein. He's the Rodgers."

"Oh."

"He's *Richard Rodgers.*"

"Sure, all right." Eleanor was still looking at her imploringly, so Lillian added, "That's quite impressive."

"Impressive? It's unheard of, auditioning directly for Mr. Rodgers. So I sat there for a few hours, not thinking anything would come from it, but it did and—" She was so excited her mouth had started to move faster than she could produce words to come out of it. "And I sang for him and—they'd been unhappy with everyone else they saw—and he said my voice was a revelation, can you—a revelation!" She finally took a breath and reached for a cigarette, shaking her head. "It was unreal, Lillian. It was like I was…floating above the room the whole time, watching it happen. Like I wasn't myself."

"That's very exciting for you. Congratulations," said Lillian.

Eleanor beamed as she exhaled a puff of smoke. "That's not it, Lil. He cast me."

Lillian blinked, not sure if she was hearing correctly. "*Cast* you?"

Eleanor nodded. "I mean, I still have to audition for the rest of the team. For Mr. Hammerstein and the producers. But if Richard Rodgers likes me, I'm as good as in."

"That's…incredible," sputtered Lillian. And although she meant it, she wasn't quite sure why her heart felt like it had dropped into her stomach. "My goodness. Eleanor! That's…"

Max reappeared, his arms overflowing with three champagne flutes and an unopened bottle. "Shall we?" he said.

"Yes!" cried Eleanor, clapping as Max popped the cork. Lillian's head was swimming. Max handed her a glass, and she took a sip without waiting for the toast. She was suddenly parched.

"Max is taking me to the Berkshires for the weekend to celebrate," said Eleanor. Lillian noticed that Max had his arm around her sister's waist. Had they been going steady long enough for Max Medelson to put his arm around her sister's waist? "Max's family has a place up there."

"How lovely," said Lillian. "It will be nice for you to meet Max's family."

"Oh, they won't be there, actually," said Eleanor, looking at Max. "It'll just be the two of us."

"Separate bedrooms, though," Max added, far too quickly.

Eleanor laughed, giving him a playful hit on the arm before turning back to her sister, almost with pity. "Do you have any plans for the weekend, Lil?"

Lillian remembered her concert tickets, her plan to suffer through an evening at the Stork to please her heartbroken sister. "I'm going to the Philharmonic," she said.

"Oh, what are they playing?" asked Eleanor.

"I'm not sure," said Lillian.

"I hope it's something good, like Brahms," said Max.

Lillian smiled. "Me too." She hated the sight of Max's tiny, greasy hands on Eleanor's perfect waist, so she pulled her sister away in a hug. "I'm so proud of you, El."

She felt her sister smile into her shoulder. "Thank you."

Lillian hadn't the slightest idea what the Philharmonic performed that night. She stared at the empty seat next to her, considering how this was probably the first of many nights she'd spend alone at one event or another. She thought of the house in the Berkshires, of what Max and Eleanor were doing there together, alone. It made sense that Eleanor would cross that bridge before she did. Eleanor had a boyfriend first, had a kiss first, had her heart broken first. It wasn't a game Lillian was much interested in playing, so it never felt like she was losing—until now. Max Medelson was a drip, but it was certainly a victory compared to a sobbing Gabriel Meadows.

Everything was clicking into place for Eleanor, it seemed, and Lillian was being left behind to rot.

JUNE 1945

Monday, after yet another day .of only blending in and not drawing attention to herself, Lillian climbed the stairs to Andrew's office and shut the door behind her. "Did you get the records?" she asked.

"Not yet," he answered, then: "Want to help with my project again?"

"You mean, instead of sit around a tiny dorm room with people I hate and paint my fingernails while I pretend I'm not panicking inside?"

"Don't forget," said Andrew, "that if while painting your fingernails you fail to pretend you're not panicking inside adequately, you could be reported on as a spy and face treason charges."

"Yes, I would like to stay here and help with your project very much," said Lillian.

The conversation repeated itself on Tuesday, and on Wednesday, and while Lillian was grateful for the distraction and the intelligent company and the interesting work, by Thursday she was getting antsy. On Friday, when the answer to "Did you get the records?" was once again "Not yet," she decided to say something.

"It's taking a long time," she said.

Andrew looked up at her, surprised. "I said it would."

"I know, but…"

"But what?"

She sighed. "We spend hours in here every night. If what Betty says is true—"

"Which we don't know that it is—"

"But if it is, aren't we obligated to move with some urgency?"

He looked incredulous. "You don't trust me."

"I do," she insisted. "In fact, one could argue I trust you far more than is reasonable, given how little I know you. You could turn me in at any second; I have no choice but to trust you."

"But you don't think I have my priorities straight."

It was a fair assessment of what she believed, so she let it hang there. Andrew stood up and came around from behind his desk to stand just a few feet from her. "Here's what I've done," he said. "Monday at lunch, I drove to Knoxville to see a woman I know who used to work as a nurse in the hospital clinic building, to ask her if she knew anyone she trusted that still works there. Tuesday morning, while you were probably still asleep, I went to intercept her brother Dave, who works in the pharmacy, on his way to work. Dave said he didn't have access to what I was looking for, but he could discreetly ask around. Wednesday night, after I walked you home, I went to see him again and learned he'd found someone with access to those records, and we set up a rendezvous for last night." His voice started to grow in volume, and Lillian glanced a bit nervously at the closed door, hoping no one was listening behind it.

"Last night, again after I walked you home, I drove to Knoxville to meet with this guy at a bar because I thought it was too risky to meet anywhere on the property. Except a car followed me all the way out there, so I had to fuck around at Macy's for forty-five minutes and buy a bunch of shirts I didn't need. When I realized I was being followed the whole time, I skipped the meeting. So that's what I've been doing. And before you ask why I didn't just tell you all this sooner, consider that maybe *I* have my own reasons for not entirely trusting *you*."

"All right, I'm sorry," hissed Lillian, once again glancing toward the door in the hopes he would take the hint and lower his voice. "But you should have told me. You can trust me. You have to trust me."

He seemed to shrink a little bit as he softened. "No, I... You're right. I should. And there is something you can do, now that I think about it. Dave said that it might be helpful to have their birthdays, in case the names are redacted from their records. I know Eleanor's, but can you ask Betty for Martin's?"

Lillian nodded. "I can meet her at the church on Sunday and ask."

"Thanks," said Andrew.

They both fell silent for a few moments, until Lillian remembered why he wasn't asking her to stay and work. It was Friday, and Fridays in Oak Ridge meant a party.

It was not a party to Lillian, of course. A *party*, to Lillian, implied witty conversation and hors d'oeuvres. What transpired in the Rec Hall nearly every weekend seemed practically bacchanalian, and even that label felt too classy. Unfortunately, she had to be Eleanor, and if there was anything Eleanor couldn't resist, it was music and dancing. So Lillian retreated from Andrew's office, forced herself into a bright-yellow dress (Emmy insisted the color made her "stand out," but Lillian couldn't imagine it was for the right reasons), and marched to the Rec Hall.

The air was hot and still outside, and not much better inside. It had taken Lorene so long to decide how to do her hair that they'd arrived quite late, and the hall was already thick with people. The subpar band (Lillian recognized the drummer as Sean, her redheaded office mate) played a fast tune that Emmy squealed upon hearing. Lillian merely pressed a thumb to her temple. She could already feel the incoming migraine.

"Do you want to dance?" It took a few beats for Lillian to register that Emmy had addressed this question to her.

No would be the instantaneous Lillian reaction, but she had to filter it through Eleanor. "Oh, you don't want to dance with me."

Emmy laughed. "You're silly," she said, pulling her onto the dance floor anyway.

Lillian did her best to match the movements of the sea of bodies around her, not understanding how anyone found dancing enjoyable. For her, it was a constant worry that she was doing the incorrect thing. After confessing as much to her sister one night at the Stork Club, Eleanor had told Lillian that such a fear practically ensured that she would do the incorrect thing, which Lillian found infuriating. "You can't think about it," Eleanor had said. "Take a break from thinking so much." Lillian was of a mind that *thinking* was one of the best things a human being could do. *Shouldn't we be thinking all the time?* Were other people really so weak that they needed a break from *thinking*?

She noticed with a start that Emmy was looking at her with a piercing sort of gaze usually not reserved for one's dance partner. "What?" asked Lillian.

"Hmm?" responded Emmy.

"Why are you looking at me like that?" said Lillian.

"Like what?" said Emmy, her expression melting back into simple sweetness.

Thankfully, Lillian heard a throat clearing behind her. "May I cut in?" said a voice. Assuming no one would volunteer to dance with her, Lillian was about to step aside—until she realized who was speaking.

It was too late to make an escape from Max Medelson. Emmy practically shoved her into his arms, just as the band took an inopportune chance to switch from an upbeat number to a slow one. Max reached for Lillian's hand, and it took every ounce of strength she possessed not to snatch it away.

"We need to talk," said Max, swaying her gently.

"Do we?" countered Lillian.

"Are you having fun as Andrew Ennis's girl?"

"I'm not his girl."

"There's already rumors about what the two of you get up to, late nights in his office."

In spite of herself, Lillian flushed. She hated Max for making her display an emotion. "We're looking for Eleanor," she said.

"You're up there so often, would have thought you'd have found her by now." Max gave her a dainty little spin, twirling her around, then pressing her even closer to him. "Andrew's not a good man," he said.

"I've heard your spiel. Is there a reason you hate him so much? Besides the fact that Eleanor left you for him."

"There are plenty of reasons," Max insisted, "not the least of which is that he stole her from me."

There was that word again: *stole*. Lillian hated it. "Have you ever considered that Eleanor left you because of you, and it had nothing to do with anyone else?"

His eyes flared with anger, which told Lillian that he had considered it quite a lot. "Have you ever considered that you don't know everything?"

Lillian rolled her eyes. "Of course I have. I consider it nearly every day. Discovering the unknown is one of my primary motivations in pursuing theoretical physics."

"Oh, for god's sake—I didn't mean *literally*."

"How would you like me to interpret your words, if not at face value?"

"You are infuriating to talk to," muttered Max. "I'm trying to say... Look, he told you the Niels Bohr story. Didn't he?"

The question took Lillian aback. "I already knew the Niels Bohr story," she answered. "Everyone knows that story."

"Not the first part. That part everyone knows. I mean the second part, where Bohr thought he was special, brought him up to Stanford just to talk to him again."

"Yes, he told me that. Why?"

In spite of himself, Max smirked. "I figured. He tells that story to all his girls."

Lillian shook her head. "What do you mean?"

"Let me see if I can remember the exact line," said Max.

"'Bohr saw the value in being challenged. And you...you challenge me.' Something like that, no?"

"I don't remember every word he said," said Lillian.

"But that was in there, right?"

Lillian looked around, hoping to spot some sort of escape from this conversation. Maybe one of the lights would catch fire? Maybe the whole building would burn to the ground, leaving them trapped in a fiery inferno? That would certainly be convenient. "I said, I don't remember."

"Sure," said Max. "Well, just so you know, that thing you don't remember? He says to all the girls."

"I'm not sure why it's any of your business," snapped Lillian. "Why are you listening, anyway, to the things he says to 'all the girls'? How would you even know?"

"Doesn't matter," said Max. "I'm just saying. If you really think she's been kidnapped, why aren't you out searching the woods for secret torture chambers? Why are you trusting Andrew with everything? Why aren't you looking for her on your own?"

"Why aren't you?" snapped Lillian.

The song came to an end, and before Max could respond, Lillian broke off and headed for the drinks. She was incredibly pleased to find a familiar figure at the end of the table. "I've just had the most idiotic conversation with Max Medelson," she said.

Andrew turned around, drink in hand, and it was only then that Lillian noticed the woman on his arm. She was strawberry-blond, smiling, stunning. Her hair was pinned up in some elegant fashion that Lillian couldn't even begin to understand how to accomplish and decorated with flowers. Lillian had a better chance of solving the problem of quantum entanglement than she had of replicating that hairstyle.

"Max Medelson? Good god. You'd think someone who can single-handedly ruin a party would learn to stay away from one," Andrew replied, before turning to the woman at his side. "Annie, this is one of my colleagues, Eleanor."

Annie smiled at her warmly. "So nice to meet you, Eleanor."

Not a month out from losing my sister, my perfect sister, and he's already got some other woman on his arm? Lillian hated the flash of anger that crawled up the back of her throat. *If he were going to have some other woman, I would have at least thought it would be—* She stopped herself before she could think such an absurd thought. Faced with no idea what to do or say, she suddenly wished she were Eleanor. Eleanor would never have found herself in this situation. She'd be in the center of the dance floor, having a grand time, not doing all this pesky *thinking*. All Lillian could do was parrot back, "So nice to meet you, too," and flee the Rec Hall.

She wasn't entirely sure she made excuses before her sudden departure, but the dark, empty streets were such a relief that it hardly seemed to matter. In front of her stretched the road back toward the dormitories, and for a moment Lillian considered just calling it a night and heading there. But something drew her around to the back of the building, which was right next to a small patch of woods.

She knew, logically, that Andrew was right, that doing something like wandering around the woods alone was far more likely to produce suspicion and scrutiny than it was to produce answers. But she also knew that Max had a point, and she hated feeling like Max had a point. If she could get away with it—which she had no reason to believe she couldn't—why wasn't she out searching wherever she could?

The couples on the Rec Hall's porch back here were far too consumed with one another to take much notice of her, and no one else was around for miles, it seemed. Taking a cursory glance around, Lillian headed for the trees.

She had never been this direction, never traveled past the edge of the Townsite. She was sure that she would only be able to make it a few feet before encountering another barbed-wire fence, but the trees became denser and the sky darker, and still she was able to move forward. Soon she was completely alone, the sound of the dance replaced by complete silence except for a pair of owls duetting in the distance.

She stopped and stood still, observing how strange it felt to be unobserved. Had she ever been completely alone since coming to Oak Ridge? Even bathroom breaks were taken with another stall inches away, showers had while a row of girls scrubbed and rinsed nearby.

Lillian had been in Oak Ridge for nineteen days but had

only been *Lillian* a handful of times. A whispered conversation with Betty here, a sideways glance at Max there. She had thought that she had been Lillian with Andrew—but the ways his lips had curled so easily around the name *Eleanor* a few minutes ago made her wonder if perhaps he didn't see it that way.

She thought that maybe she ought to take advantage of this rare moment of solitude by doing something pure and wholly Lillian while she had the chance. Unfortunately, she hadn't the faintest idea what such a thing would look like. What was pure and wholly Lillian? Her mind was blank. Eventually, she felt silly for standing so long and turned around to head back.

Then she heard a noise.

It wasn't behind her, exactly, but off to her right. Exactly where someone who had been following her all the way from the Rec Hall might have stopped to observe her moment of stillness. Someone who had seen her turn around and hurried to get out of her line of sight, maybe in their haste stepping on a small branch—or was she being paranoid? How long could she stand here before the stranger, if he was out there, realized he'd been heard? Should she continue on as if nothing had happened, or would that put her in more danger?

Mind racing, she strained to listen for another noise—something, anything—but the night was still. Absurd, she was being absurd. It was probably a squirrel, or a raccoon, or one of those other wildlife creatures one tended to forget about while growing up in Manhattan. This had happened to her before.

Once, when staying with a friend outside of Philadelphia, she'd nearly fainted after looking out the window and finding a deer lazily munching on a plant less than ten feet away. *Such a city girl you are, Lillian,* the friend had teased. In return, Lillian reminded her that the greatest historical and cultural developments of human history had risen out of cities, and thanked her friend for the compliment.

It was a squirrel, just a silly little squirrel. And yet, although she felt confident in this knowledge, when she started back toward the road, it was at a quicker pace. She kept the spot behind the tree in the corner of her vision as she passed. Just as she'd suspected, there was nothing hiding behind its trunk. Nothing, nothing—and then—*something.*

Cursing Emmy for talking her into such a visible color, Lillian started to run as fast as she dared, given the darkness and the precarious roots and branches that covered the uneven ground. The sound of the dreadful band became louder and louder, and soon the Rec Hall was in sight, just up ahead, not too far away. Lillian was certain if she could reach the building, she'd be safe. She could find someone she knew and pretend she'd been with them all along. No one would recognize that she'd been the one off on her own, alone. For all whoever was following her knew, the girl from the woods would have disappeared into the night.

Another crack sounded out from behind her. Focusing all her energy on landing one foot in front of the other, she broke through the tree line with a relieved sigh. Quickly she climbed the steps to the hall's back porch, scanning the crowd, hoping to see a familiar face—any familiar face—

"Eleanor!"

It took a moment for her to realize the voice was talking to her. She turned slightly behind her to see Andrew, leaning up against the railing and smoking a cigarette. She ran to him and nearly collapsed. "You were right," she said. "I think someone is following me."

Andrew dropped his cigarette and look around wildly. "Who? Did you see who it was?"

"Don't," she said, grabbing his hand to pull him back. She dropped her voice to barely a whisper. "Just act like we were out here together this whole time. I don't think they saw me well."

She was speaking so quietly that he stepped in closer to hear her, and she realized that she hadn't let go of his hand. As the fear and adrenaline from the run wore off, she became quite conscious of their sudden proximity. Their eyes were locked, his dark eyes scanning hers with worry.

And then he kissed her.

Lillian was surprised to note that her first reaction was to consider that this did make logical sense. This is what couples come to the back of the Rec Hall to do, after all. It was probably the adrenaline that was making her heart beat like that. It was probably just fear that was making her feel like her knees might give out from under her and not the feeling of his hand, warm and heavy, on her neck. After a few moments that were both an eternity and an instant, he pulled away. "There," he whispered, his lips still inches from her face. "Now no one will believe you were anywhere but right here with me."

Lillian didn't understand, couldn't begin to fathom what was a ruse and what was genuine. She wanted to ask for clarification but felt like a general rule of thumb was probably that if you had to ask whether or not a kiss was real, it meant it wasn't. Besides, Andrew had already moved on. "If you figure out what creep was following you, you let me know and I'll take care of him."

"I think I'm going to go to bed now," she said.

"I'll walk you home," he said with a laugh. "That'll really sell it."

"What about your..." Lillian couldn't even remember the name of the woman, so she said simply, "Redhead?"

"Huh!" Andrew exclaimed with a smile. "I'd forgotten about her." He made a show of looking over his shoulders. "Do you think she's still around?"

In spite of herself, Lillian laughed. He chuckled a bit, too, and offered her his arm. For a moment she wanted to say something like *You know I'm not really Eleanor, don't you?*—but she let the inclination pass. Her worry seemed foolish now. Of course Andrew knew that. He knew it better than anyone.

As they walked away, Lillian still couldn't shake that feeling of the hairs on the back of her neck standing up, that notion that someone was watching her. She turned around again. There was no mysterious man, no dangerous army officer—only Emmy, standing on the porch of the Rec Hall, looking right at Lillian. She offered a little wave, which Lillian pretended not to notice as she turned back around, heading off with Andrew into the dark night.

ELEVEN

JUNE 1945

Lillian wasn't the least bit religious. Mother had made a few half-hearted attempts to take the family to temple, but that had ended quickly after Father died. Since then, Lillian hadn't much thought about religion at all—at least not until her sophomore year at Columbia, when a distracted secretary accidentally handed Lillian her admission records instead of her course history. She looked at what the dean of natural sciences had scrawled about her when considering the merits of her application: "*Miss Kaufman, despite being a woman, displays outstanding mathematical ability and would be an excellent candidate for the undergraduate physics department.*" She could put up with those four improper words, *despite being a woman.* She heard them so often they'd lost their meaning. And in a way, it was true, wasn't it? Women rarely took the same interest in mathematics that she did.

The next sentence, however, read: *"Kaufman, it must be noted, is Jewish."*

At first, it confused her. *No, I'm not.* And then: *Well, yes, I suppose, if you want to be technical about it.* And then: *Why on earth should that matter?*

She wasn't sure what she could do about it. She wasn't supposed to have seen the file in the first place, so she couldn't exactly tell anyone about it. And what would her complaint have been, anyway? Columbia had accepted her. Ultimately, it hadn't mattered.

Eleanor had been shocked by the sentence. "My god," she said. "You should come to the theater. Judaism is encouraged over there."

Lillian laughed it off, but again couldn't help but note the disparity between her path and her sister's. Eleanor was encouraged and applauded; Lillian was either mocked, regarded with suspicion, or—most commonly—ignored completely.

Now, in Oak Ridge, Lillian was going to be a Presbyterian. No one had bothered to clarify for her if this was the same as Christian; in fact, Andrew laughed rather loudly every time she tried to bring it up.

She wondered, as she slipped into the back of the service, whether this fact had been noted in a record about anyone, ever. *"So-and-so, it must be noted, is Presbyterian"* didn't have much of a ring to it. She found Betty in a pew near the back and pointed to the open space next to her. "Excuse me, is anyone sitting there?" she whispered. Betty shook her head no, and Lillian took the seat.

A large cross hung at the front of the church—Christian it was, then.

The service began with everyone rising (remarkably, all at the same time—had they rehearsed?) to sing a hymn. Lillian leaned over to Betty to pass along her message. "Andrew doesn't have the records yet. He thinks having Martin's birthday might help. Do you know it?"

"December 9, 1925," Betty rattled off, and Lillian was struck by the realization that he was younger than she was.

"Thanks." Lillian shifted uncomfortably. Nobody around her seemed much into the singing, droning on like a bunch of bored schoolchildren. If God existed, he certainly wasn't going to be pleased with this offering.

"How's it going?" asked Betty. "Getting the files. Is he close?"

Before Lillian could answer, she felt a tap on her shoulder.

"Eleanor Kaufman?" inquired a tall, slim man Lillian had never seen before. He wasn't in uniform, but he hardly needed to be. The straightness of his spinal column said it all.

"Yes," she replied.

"Come with me," he said. "Don't make a fuss."

Lillian stood, unable to stop the lump forming in her throat. She wanted nothing more than to glance at Betty but didn't dare, lest the man see that and decide to round Betty up, too.

I suppose the only thing left to do now is hope he doesn't interrogate me about Presbyterians, thought Lillian ruefully.

———

The man led Lillian outside the church and across the street, to the library. *How peculiar,* thought Lillian—although she had to admit that if she were destined to die in this strange town, the library would be a particularly atmospheric place to do so. He navigated expertly through the stacks, turning one way and another as if a map had been drawn on his palm. They reached a blank door, which he unlocked quickly with a key she hadn't even noticed him carrying.

Behind the door wasn't library storage—or, on the opposite end of what Lillian suspected, a torture chamber. Instead, it was a simple table with two chairs. The man motioned for her to sit, and just to be difficult about it, Lillian sat in the chair that was not the one he pointed to. It occurred to her that maybe she should be more afraid than she was, given that she was indeed trespassing on secret government property. But she wasn't Lillian, she was Eleanor. And Eleanor had nothing to be afraid of.

If Lillian's bit with the chair upset the man, his face didn't show it. He took the seat across from her without a second glance, pulling a small notebook and pen from his breast pocket. "Eleanor Kaufman," he repeated. He was not much older than she was, with painstakingly parted red-brown hair that didn't move an inch. She wondered if he sprayed it as much as Eleanor did.

"And what's your name?" she asked, knowing full well he wasn't going to tell her.

"Joe," he replied, so quickly she could tell that wasn't really his name. "About three weeks ago, you returned from an unexpected trip. Is that right, Eleanor?"

He hadn't provided a real name, a title, or any reason why he deserved to know any of Eleanor Kaufman's business. Had she been anywhere else, she would have refused to answer, but here her options were limited. "I was in New York," she said, adding only because she knew it would be his very next question: "Visiting my sister."

"I didn't know you had a sister," said "Joe."

"Why would you?" said Lillian. "We don't know each other."

The man tapped his pen and peered at her. "When you applied for a job with us, under 'siblings' you listed 'none.'"

Had Eleanor really done such a thing? Goodness. Eleanor could be so dramatic sometimes. Lillian pressed her tongue to her teeth as she tried to keep her expression neutral. "My sister and I were having an argument when I filled out my application, and I suppose I took some small satisfaction from pretending there was only one of us."

"What were you arguing about?" he asked.

Lillian sighed. That was the question, wasn't it? "She didn't like my boyfriend" was the best she could come up with for that moment. And then, just because she could, she added: "Although I've since realized she was right about him."

"And would that boyfriend be Dr. Ennis?"

The question took her aback. "No, a previous boyfriend."

"You've had a lot of boyfriends," mused Joe.

That got her temper flaring. "Two is a lot?" Of course to Lillian, whose number held steady at zero, two was quite a lot—but that was hardly the point.

"Are you still seeing Dr. Ennis?"

"No," said Lillian.

"Yet he recently got you a job on his team," said Joe.

"We're just colleagues," she replied.

"Interesting," he went on. "And Friday night, at the dance, you were necking on the back porch of the Rec Hall as colleagues, then?"

Lillian couldn't help but cross her arms at that. "*Yes*," she snarled defiantly.

Joe smiled, although it was quite clear from his pursed brow that he was not amused. "Well, Miss Kaufman, on behalf of the army, I'd like to warn you that it might not be in your best interest to get further involved with Dr. Ennis."

"I'm not sure why the army would care at all about my personal life," she said.

"Rest assured, it's not your personal life we care about," responded Joe. "Andrew Ennis is very important to this project."

"I'm aware. Is that all? May I go?"

Joe ignored the question. "If he gets you involved in something you shouldn't be involved in, you should know it's him we're going to protect. Not you."

"Don't worry," snapped Lillian, not waiting for permission to stand and head for the door. "I never held any illusions about the army protecting me."

JANUARY 1945

Things were delayed as the city shut down for the winter holidays—and then delayed again after a blistering, sudden snowstorm—but Eleanor was officially offered the leading role of Julie Jordan in the workshop production of Rodgers and Hammerstein's *Carousel* on January 13, 1945. Again, Lillian raised a glass to her sister in the front room; again, Max Medelson whisked her away for a weekend in the Berkshires to celebrate.

Eleanor would start a four-week rehearsal in Manhattan the following Monday. If the producers liked her enough to keep her around beyond that, the production would break for "some time" and then reconvene in Chicago for a tryout run that would last "indefinitely." Any pressing, no matter how delicate, done by Lillian on the subject of what exactly constituted "some time" and "indefinitely" was met with a scowl from Eleanor. Apparently, *artistes* of the theater didn't worry themselves with things like "the future" and "schedules."

Lillian, on the other hand, was very aware of the deadline to apply for spring admission to Harvard (postmarked by October 1), the day and time of the Allerton test (October 27, beginning precisely at ten o'clock in the morning), and the first day of what she hoped to be her postgraduate career (coincidentally, January 13, 1946). The chances of "some time" and "indefinitely" adding up to conflict with one of those dates was far, far too high for her liking.

There was one bit of good news, and it was that Max Medelson was shortly removing himself from the picture. Lillian had secretly hoped he'd be drafted (nothing like an ocean to wear down a floundering relationship), but always felt guilty for this quiet wish. Max was dull and a drip, but he didn't deserve to die, exactly. However, she hadn't calculated the effect Gabriel Meadows's unexpected departure would have on her male colleagues.

Suddenly the war, which of course had been all around and permeated their lives, but always in a removed sort of way—the way a thunderstorm would pound on the windows but never quite break through—collapsed from potential to reality. Student deferments really were a thing of the past, and the empty desk where Gabe used to sit and fling rubber bands at his classmates each day was the proof. The army no longer had patience for bright undergrads desperate to unlock the secrets of quantum mechanics. Gabe Meadows was off to Germany, leaving his classmates to wonder not only if they would see him again, but if they would be next.

Max was not the only one to ring up Lieutenant General Jones that winter, to submit eagerly the application for the Clinton Engineer Works that had been kept neatly in his desk drawer, just in case. He was hired almost instantly; apparently the army had a need for warm bodies who could do basic mathematics almost as desperately as it did for warm bodies who could fire a gun.

Lillian did not mean to eavesdrop on the conversation where he told Eleanor he'd be leaving soon, but they didn't know she was reading quietly in the study when they started talking in the front room. Once she realized the discussion was one of importance, it seemed rude to interrupt and draw attention to the fact she had been listening this whole time. She was stuck, their voices echoing around her whether she wanted them there or not.

"I suppose it's not as tragic as it could be," said Eleanor, a sentence Lillian would have nominated as *understatement of the whole goddamn century*. "I'll be going to Chicago soon"—soon, god, what did that mean?—"so we would be separated anyways."

"I pray to God I'm not away for too long," said Max. Eleanor was silent, and Lillian smiled triumphantly. The stakes of their separation were much higher for him, Lillian knew. Eleanor could forget about Max with a shift of the wind and a handsome new fellow, but Max would never forget about Eleanor.

Max cleared his throat. "I have to ask," he began hesitantly. "And I don't expect you to say yes. Or anything, really."

"Oh, Max," sighed Eleanor. Lillian could practically see her placing a hand on Max's shoulder. A gesture of consolation, rather than flirtation. They all knew what was coming.

"Well, they told me—I was told—there's housing available for families, for couples?" Max was clearing his throat an extraordinary number of times. "And there's work for women, too, down there—lots of it. That's what I was told."

"I already have a job," said Eleanor gently.

"I know," Max replied. "And that's why I don't expect you to agree to this. I really don't. It's more of a *Well, I had to ask* type of situation." He stopped to clear his throat one more time. "Eleanor Kaufman, will you marry me?"

Lillian wondered if Max had bothered to kneel for the occasion, or if he remained in his comfortable position on the couch. She wondered if he'd purchased a ring, and if so, what style he'd selected. She wondered almost everything except for what her sister's answer would be.

"I can't," said Eleanor. "Not now. I'm sorry."

"It's all right," said Max. "Really, it is! Like I said, just had to ask. It was one of the moments where I knew I'd be kicking myself later if I hadn't." He was talking so much that it was obvious, to Lillian at least, that he had hoped taking this risk might work out. "And don't think that means we're done, now that you've said no."

"I wouldn't dream of it," replied Eleanor.

"I'll be writing you letters every day," said Max.

"And I'll return each one."

"I'm going off to the war effort, you know," said Max. "You'll have to keep me going with pictures I can hang in my bunker."

"Oh, do I," said Eleanor with a laugh.

"Our success in Germany depends on it," Max said.

They went quiet, and it took Lillian an embarrassingly long few moments before she realized they were necking on the couch. She sulked. How could something as unromantic as a rejected proposal lead to necking? She hoped that at the very least they had taken the decency to shut the curtains first, so their lovemaking wouldn't be on display to the whole Upper East Side.

Trapped in the study for the foreseeable future, Lillian sank into Father's chair and stared at the fireplace that hadn't held a spark in years.

JUNE 1945

Lillian shook off the interrogation in the library rather quickly, and the next day—Monday—she climbed the steps to Andrew's office after work as always. It wasn't until she saw him—feet on his desk, shirtsleeves rolled up—that she remembered that the last time they had interacted, he had quite nearly put his tongue in her mouth. She halted in his doorway, mouth agape, simultaneously mortified, not mortified, and then mortified at not being mortified enough. After a few stammering moments, he looked over and furrowed his brow. "What's wrong with you?" he asked.

"Nothing." Clearly, he wasn't struck with the same embarrassing affliction. She shut the door behind her and took her usual seat. "I saw Betty yesterday. Martin's birthday is December 9th, 1925."

Andrew was staring up at the ceiling, squinting. "The army thinks I'm a spy." Before she could react, he went on. "Sorry, I skipped a few thoughts there. I almost have the records. The birthday will help. I have to go slowly because..."

"They don't think you're a spy," said Lillian, remembering what "Joe" had said. "You're important to them. They want to protect you."

"They think someone in this building is a spy, and they don't like my personality, ergo."

"That's ridiculous. How could anyone not love your personality?" said Lillian dryly. "Why, just this morning, I heard you scream at Max Medelson for using an adding machine."

"Max Medelson is the stupidest goddamn idiot I have ever met in my entire life," spat out Andrew.

Lillian snorted. "You know, he thought you..." The words had tumbled out of her mouth before she had considered if they were the wisest thing to say, an action that was completely unlike her.

Andrew looked down, eyes still narrow. "Max thought I *what?*"

She cleared her throat. "He, um, thought you had something to do with it. With Eleanor..."

Andrew's feet hit the floor with such force Lillian jumped in her chair. For a moment she feared he was going to march out of the building and fight Max this very instant, but he stayed put. "He thought I had something to do with it?"

"I know you didn't," Lillian said quickly.

"Of course you know," he said. "I'm putting everything on the line to help with this. What has he done?"

"Nothing," said Lillian. "I shouldn't have brought it up. Let's talk about shock waves."

After a moment, Andrew nodded, and the anger seemed to pass from his brow. "Only if you have good news for me," he said, although his voice stayed flat.

Lillian didn't get a chance to respond. A door banged open downstairs and an unfamiliar male voice thundered up: "Ennis! Get down here!"

Andrew's eyes met Lillian's, his expression unreadable. "Coming!" he shouted, before turning back to Lillian and whispering again. "Hide under the desk."

His tone and posture were so nonchalant, Lillian almost didn't believe those were the words that had come out of his mouth. "Hide under the—"

"The desk." He pointed underneath it. "Just in case." He flashed a smile as he backed out of the room. As she dropped to her knees and crawled under the desk, she could hear him whistling down the steps.

"Walter!" he cried jovially. "What can I do for you?"

The other man spoke lower, his voice not carrying enough for Lillian to hear. She thought he asked Andrew something like, "Are you alone?"

Andrew provided a wishy-washy response. Lillian felt a lump forming in her throat. Was the stranger there for her? Had she messed up in some way, said something to Joe to tip him off that she wasn't who she claimed to be? Her fears seemed confirmed when she heard the man's next question: "Who the hell did everyone see you kissing at that dance?"

Andrew laughed. "You'll have to be more specific."

The man's voice got even lower, more threatening. Lillian inched out from under the desk and crawled toward the door, hoping to hear a little better. "My subordinates have been running around talking about this Eleanor Kaufman girl. I swear to god, Ennis, after everything I've done for you, if you screw me over—"

"Oh, leave me alone, Walter. I've got work to do." She heard him start back up the steps, only to be stopped by another low threat from the other man. *What was he saying?*

Whatever it was, Andrew swore loudly in response and started stomping up the steps. Walter tried to speak again, but Andrew drowned him out. "Go fuck yourself," he shouted behind him. "Leave me the fuck alone so I can do my goddamn job." Reaching the office, he threw the door open. Lillian jumped to her feet, and they nearly collided in the doorframe.

He recoiled as if he'd completely forgotten she were there,

then narrowed his eyes. "Were you eavesdropping on me?" he hissed.

Lillian stammered. There was no use pretending she hadn't been. "I heard someone say Eleanor's name."

"And what? You think that's a reason to eavesdrop on me?"

She raised her eyebrows. "Yes, as a matter of fact, I do."

The downstairs door had clanged fully shut behind Walter, and Andrew took a step toward her, raising his voice. "Do you have any idea how stupid that is? That man was the head of army security—what if he'd heard you moving around?"

"He didn't. Why are you so angry about this? I have a right to know what people are saying about my sister."

"No, you don't!" cried Andrew. She was suddenly keenly aware of how his voice could overpower an entire room when he wanted it to, and in spite of herself, she winced. "You don't have rights here! You play by my rules, otherwise we'll both be locked up for sending information to the Germans—"

"Japanese," interrupted Lillian. As soon as she said it, she knew it was a mistake. Andrew went quiet, his pupils reduced to barely pinpricks. She tried to explain. "You've said that before, actually—to Sean one day, when—it doesn't matter. The point is, the Germans surrendered. So we're...fighting the Japanese."

"Get out," said Andrew.

"You can't be serious," said Lillian.

"Wouldn't be much of a joke" was his spat-out answer.

"Fine," she said, expecting him to step aside and let her pass. He didn't. His height took up almost the entire doorframe, one wooden piece of which was currently splintering under the intense pressure of his right hand. She kept her chin lifted as her heart began to pound. Surely he didn't intend to trap her in here, surely—

Not wanting to admit even a moment of fear, she stalked for the door. He held his ground until the last second, finally lowering his hand to allow her to squeeze by. She was halfway downstairs when his booming voice came after her, echoing off the stairwell as if he were right behind her, breathing down her neck. "I'm angry because you're not her. *That's why I'm so goddamn angry.*"

It wasn't until she was outside and alone that she allowed herself to feel afraid. Her heart still thumped against her chest, and even though it was a hot June evening, a shiver went up her spine. Taking a deep breath, she rubbed her arms in an attempt to warm herself and walked away from Building E as quickly as she could.

———

The dorm room was empty when Lillian reached it, which was a relief. She wasn't sure she'd be able to face Emmy with her heart still pounding and her mind racing impossibly fast. She had trusted Andrew largely because Max did *not* trust Andrew. Her eagerness to disagree with Max Medelson had led her to overlook a key piece of evidence, which was that Eleanor did not trust Andrew either. Eleanor had left him. Dumped him a few days before she disappeared. Why?

Had Andrew raised his voice to Eleanor the same way he had to her? Possibly, but unlikely. Eleanor was delicate and charming and had the social graces to say, "Yes, that's correct," when an already upset person misspoke the name of the country with which they were currently at war. She might have found out about Andrew's bomb, but Lillian had no proof that Andrew had ever told Eleanor, or that Eleanor would have even understood it enough to object to it. There couldn't have been another man involved: Lillian was certain Eleanor was not dating Dr. Andrew Ennis while pining away for the comfort of the arms of Max Medelson, and if there had been a third man involved, Max would have known of him, too.

What if Eleanor had found something out about Andrew? Something that he was now worried Lillian was on the verge of finding out, too?

She stared at her empty dormitory, and her instinct suddenly was to tear it all apart, top to bottom. There must have been something she'd missed. Some clue she hadn't come across these last three weeks. If Andrew were a spy—if Eleanor had proof—where would it be?

Lillian started in the trash, which hadn't been emptied since her arrival. She dumped its contents on the floor: a few Kleenex and that ridiculous nearly empty tube of lipstick Eleanor had held onto came tumbling out. Nothing of importance.

She moved on to the closet. All of Eleanor's blouses, all of Eleanor's dresses came tumbling off their hangers, one by one, creating a pile of clothes on the floor. Lillian turned each one inside out, running her fingers over the seams in case some secret was sewn up within them. She overturned shoes and boots, shaking each one, praying something would drop out besides a scrap of lint. She moved to the dresser, rummaging through Eleanor's collection of patched and well-worn stockings, holding each one to the light in case something could be revealed.

There was nothing here, she realized. The only thing out of the ordinary was Max's stupid wooden cat, tucked in the bottom of Eleanor's sock drawer like a casket laid to rest. It took everything in Lillian's power not to hurl the stupid thing against the wall. Her chest tightened, throat constricted. It felt as if she were gasping for air. Andrew Ennis wasn't a spy. She was being absolutely ridiculous. He just didn't *like* her. *I'm angry because you're not her. That's why I'm so goddamn angry.*

She had apparently tossed one of the stockings with surprising force. It had shot nearly to the ceiling and now clung to the light fixture above her. Lillian looked up just as it slid off and floated down—lilting—like a fallen petal—

She saw herself as if from above, drowning in the chaos she'd created in the room. A memory flashed in her mind:

Mother in the closet—Father's shirts, the threads floating down like snowflakes, like stockings—

Lillian collapsed into the pile of clothing.

───────────────

It was dark outside when Lillian came to. For a few heartbeats, in the darkness, she thought she was back in New York, on East 86th Street—but something felt wrong in a way she couldn't quite put her finger on, as if the earth's gravitational pull were affecting her slightly differently. It took a few moments for her to realize where she was, and a few moments longer for her to realize that the noise that had awakened her was in fact a knock on the door.

Rising to her feet, she tried to think of some excuse for the state of the room. She'd lost her…comb, perhaps? She reached for the door.

Andrew stood in front of her, his hair disheveled and shirt-sleeves still rolled up, carrying a stack of folders and yellow legal pads. She was so shocked to see him that she almost slammed the door in his face. The only thing she could think to say was, "You're not supposed to be in here."

He furrowed his brow, as if the fact were so mundane it was beneath him to be aware of it. "Who cares?" he replied. "Let me in."

Lillian stepped aside, only half-realizing this action might give her a certain reputation. He went immediately to sit on the bed, dumping the contents of his arms onto the pillow. "First I want to apologize," he began. "For yelling at you. What can I say? I'm Irish."

It took a few moments of silence for him to realize that Lillian would not be accepting *What can I say? I'm Irish* as an apology. "I'm under a lot of pressure here," he went on. "They put me in charge of this place, and I'm not even—I mean, I'm still not used to it when people call me 'Doctor.' I've got so many people watching me, and if I fail, it's my whole career. You can understand that. The pressure of your whole life riding on one thing."

Lillian stayed quiet. Her head was still spinning.

"And I'm sorry I said… Aw hell, don't make me say it again," Andrew continued after a moment. "Your sister broke my heart." It was so personal, all of a sudden, that Lillian was a bit surprised. But it stung in a way that seemed so true, so obvious. "And I'm still trying to work through all that. But I'm not angry that you're not her. I am angry. You are not her. The two facts are utterly unrelated. I had a stupid, cruel thought, and I'm sorry I said it out loud."

Lillian didn't believe that he could look at her without holding some anger in his heart for the person she wasn't, but she appreciated the kindness of lying to make her feel better nonetheless. He seemed so vulnerable just then, hunched over on her bed, suddenly so much smaller than he'd been only hours earlier. She was reminded of the way the storms in Tennessee brought behind them a break in the hot weather.

Lillian wondered if maybe—if she just asked the question on her mind—he might answer her now. "Why did she leave you?"

He considered his words carefully. "Because it was the right thing for her to do."

Lillian raised an eyebrow. "How bland a response."

"Because she found out I'm not a good man," said Andrew, throwing his hands up. "As you've found out tonight. As everyone finds out eventually. I've gotten this far this fast because I've put myself first and I don't intend on—" He stopped suddenly and collected himself. "Suffice to say, I've done things I regret. But I'm trying to make it up to her." He picked up a manila folder from the stack of papers on the pillow and held it out. Lillian took it, staring at the neatly typed label on the tabs. *Hughes, Martin.*

"I'm still working on Eleanor's," he said. "And to be honest, I only got this one because I yelled at a bunch of perfectly nice people, so let's hope I'm not fired for that first." He stood slowly, gathering the rest of his things. "Good night, Lillian."

"You shouldn't say my name," Lillian half murmured, still transfixed by the file in her hand.

"I know," said Andrew. "But sometimes I can't bear to say hers."

He headed for the door, pulled it open. Emmy was standing there, her key inches from the lock. She jumped a foot in fright.

"Hello," said Andrew cheerily, striding past her nonchalantly. "Goodbye."

Emmy stared at Lillian, her wide eyes taking in the file in Lillian's hands, the ransacked room. "What's going on?" she asked, her voice shaking. "Why was *Dr. Ennis* in here?"

"He's my boss," said Lillian, trying her best to keep her tone light. "He was dropping off something for work."

Emmy stepped over the pile of clothes, glancing at Lillian warily. "Why are your things everywhere?"

Lillian forced a laugh. "It's the silliest thing. I lost my comb."

After a moment, Emmy nodded and smiled. "I hate it when I lose things," she said. Lillian wholeheartedly agreed, clutching the file to her chest and feeling her heart beat rapidly against the pages.

———————————

Waiting out the rest of the week was agony, but Lillian knew she couldn't be the one to open Martin's file first. When Sunday finally arrived, Lillian didn't waste any time waiting for the cover of the first hymn to whisper to Betty. She carried Martin's file discreetly tucked away under her arm, and as soon as she sat down, she placed it on the empty space between them in the pew. After a few moments, Betty reached over and picked it up as if it were her own.

Lillian watched as Betty ran her fingers over the neatly typed *Hughes, Martin*. "Did you read it?" she murmured to Lillian.

"No," said Lillian.

With shaking hands, Betty opened the file. Lillian looked

away, trying to give her as much privacy as possible. She studied the unadorned windows. In any other church, in any other town, they'd be stained glass. The morning sun would be throwing patches of yellows and reds on the floor, instead of a square of bright, white light. Staring at that fine line between the lightness and the dark, Lillian did not see whatever it was that caused Betty to gasp.

Lillian wanted to look over, but kept her eyes fixed forward. Betty pushed the folder back toward her, laid open. A few moments later, Lillian cautioned a glance. It didn't take her long to locate the relevant phrase.

Deceased during procedure (tooth extraction, infected)

Remains located in 19A.

The hymn began, the congregation stood. Betty's eyes were glossed over with tears she knew she couldn't release just yet. "I suppose that's it, then," she said. "Tell Dr. Ennis I said thank you for his help."

"This isn't over," said Lillian.

"But it is," countered Betty. "I know some janitors who work in the hospital building. I tracked them down when I was first trying to find Martin. They have a morgue down there and a room where they're storing ashes until the war is over. He must have died during the procedure, and I invented a whole conspiracy about it."

Lillian had to push aside the frightening notion that apparently so many people died here, there was an entire bureaucracy set to deal with it. "Dying during a tooth extraction? It doesn't make sense. And why wouldn't they tell you, if it really was all routine? Why pretend he had never even been there?"

"Because they don't care about me," said Betty. "Because protocol says they can't. Because some stupid doctor messed up and now wants to cover his tracks. Choose a reason."

"They should at least let you have the remains," said Lillian.

"I know," said Betty. They fell silent. This particular hymn was about how man can achieve anything through God. Lillian hated it. If all they needed was God, where was he?

"I can get them," said Lillian. "If you can help get me in the building, I can get them for you."

TWELVE

FEBRUARY 1945

Eleanor's four weeks of workshop rehearsals practically flew by. Lillian seemed to spend all of her time at Columbia these days, between her extended classes and her laboratory work and practicing for the Allerton test. When Eleanor complained that the two hardly ever saw each other, Lillian retorted bitterly that it was good practice for the rest of their lives.

Eleanor still had no earthly idea if she'd be off to Chicago at all, let alone when. Lillian naturally assumed the cast would be told at the end of their four weeks, and came home that Friday night expecting the answer at last. But "Things don't work that way, Lil," said Eleanor, with a shrug.

Apparently the show had "major second-act problems" and was undergoing a "nearly complete rewrite," and the Chicago production was delayed "for now." They would call Eleanor if and when they decided to move forward.

"Can't *you* call *them?*" asked Lillian.

Eleanor laughed at the suggestion. "Oh goodness, no."

It seemed to Lillian that her darling sister was being far too kind. She was an *employee*, wasn't she? An employee—especially the most important, the *leading* employee—had a right to know if her employment was to continue, and when. Besides, what if other actresses were calling the Theatre Guild? She might lose out to someone being more proactive about the process. Eleanor was inconveniencing Lillian and potentially shooting herself in the foot out of *politeness*. Yet when Lillian brought up these quite reasonable points, Eleanor merely shook her head. "That's not how it's done."

That's not how it's done by you, thought Lillian.

The idea materialized in Lillian's head quite suddenly one morning, and before she fully realized what she was doing, she had pressed the telephone to her ear. "Could you place a call to Spring-7-5600?" she asked the operator.

Spring-7-5600. She hadn't remembered the number on purpose, but it was easy enough. *Spring*, where else would an office of artists be located? *756*, an easy combination of three numbers that were normally right next to each other anyway, just slightly reorganized. Followed by two zeros. It would have been harder to forget than remember.

The call connected. "The Theatre Guild, Janet Mayberry speaking," came the vaguely familiar voice.

Hearing another person on the line made this scheme

seem much more real to Lillian, and much more like a bad idea. She took a steadying breath and reminded herself that her request was ultimately quite reasonable, even if her methods were less than perfect. "Hello, Janet, this is Eleanor Kaufman," she began.

"Eleanor, darling, how are you?" said Janet. "I miss seeing your face around here!"

Of course, Eleanor had befriended the secretary. It was such an Eleanor thing to do, make friends with the administration. Lillian played along. "I miss you, too, dear! I'm quite well, and yourself?"

"I'm just splendid."

"How nice," said Lillian, hoping that would be the end of the pleasantries. "Darling, I was hoping I could ask you a favor."

"Name it, doll."

Lillian cleared her throat. "My, um, my boyfriend has been badgering me about the dates of the Chicago show." Blaming it on a boyfriend seemed like a wise choice. A boyfriend concerned about timing tended to add up to marriage, and who would begrudge a woman starting a family? "I was calling to see if there had been some update that I haven't heard yet."

There was a slight pause. "No updates yet," said Janet Mayberry. There was a hint of something in her voice—sarcasm? Frostiness? Or maybe it was simply Lillian's imagination.

"That's good to know," said Lillian, even though it wasn't.

"Anything else I can do for you?"

Lillian hesitated. She'd been carrying a suspicion for a while, and although she admitted the evidence was thin, part of her couldn't help but wonder if Eleanor had been lying about this whole scheduling drama. Or perhaps not *lying*, exactly, but leaving some things up in the air, letting Lillian dangle in the uncertainty of it all. Evidence in favor: how on earth could an office of any repute, scheduling a show on Broadway, be so damn disorganized? Evidence against: Eleanor would have no reason to do this. Argument against the evidence against: Lillian had been (quite rightfully) badgering her for the dates, and Eleanor was becoming more than a little annoyed. It *would* be like Eleanor to play a simple, harmless prank on her sister, by letting her hang on the line a little longer before cutting her loose.

"Still there?" said Janet Mayberry.

"Yes, sorry," said Lillian. *All I'm doing is gathering information,* she thought. She wasn't making an accusation against Eleanor by asking a few questions. Evidence gathering was well within reason. "I was wondering—is there any information on the dates that perhaps you told me already? I think something may have gone out of my brain. You know how forgetful I can be about the less creative parts of my job." She blanched at this last line (it was utterly untrue; Eleanor was a professional to the core), but she hoped it would slide by Janet Mayberry.

Janet was quiet. Lillian held her breath, her mind racing

through all the ways she could be caught. *I've heard you pronounce the word "creative" before and that's not how you say it, Eleanor.*

"Are you trying to trick me into telling you something?" said Janet finally.

It hadn't even occurred to Lillian that her inquiry might be read this way. "Oh goodness, no—"

"Because we know you're interested in the role, Miss Kaufman," continued Janet.

The sudden switch from "Eleanor" to "Miss Kaufman," caught Lillian by surprise. "Yes, of course," she said.

"There's no need to call this office and try to trick me into telling you private details of the production team's decisions."

Lillian almost cried out in shock. "That's not at all—"

"Especially under the guise of friendship," Janet went on. "Have a pleasant day."

The line clicked dead. Lillian kept the phone to her ear in stunned silence. How had that gone so wrong so fast?

"Hello?" The voice of the operator came back on. "May I connect you to another line?"

"Spring-7-5600," Lillian said without hesitation.

"One moment."

A pause, and Janet Mayberry was back on the line with a cheerful "The Theatre Guild, Janet Mayberry speaking."

"Janet, dear, it's Eleanor. I have to apologize. I shouldn't have asked, I'm deeply sorry."

Janet sighed. "It's all right. I promise, we'll let you know as soon as we're able."

"It's not all right," said Lillian. "I want you to know that I–I didn't mean it as a…as… I didn't mean to take advantage of our friendship. I hope you can forgive me, and that everything can remain between us just as it was, exactly as it was, before this conversation."

"Oh, Eleanor," said Janet. "Now I feel bad. I'm sure I over-reacted. We've been getting a million of these calls, each one more irritating than the last. I was taking some of that frustration out on you, I suppose."

Lillian exhaled in relief. "Still, I was quite out of line."

"It's perfectly fine, dear. Let's pretend it never happened."

Lillian was nearly shaking with relief. "Thank you, Janet. You're a doll."

She was about to hang up when Janet spoke again. "I do miss seeing you around the office. Are you free for lunch today? Why don't we meet someplace fun?"

When Lillian replayed this moment in her mind—as she did often in the following weeks—she could come up with a dozen reasons to decline, but at the time she saw no way out. She'd nearly ended Eleanor's career with one innocent telephone call. What if rejecting her lunch invitation sent Janet Mayberry off the rails again? Besides, what was the point of having your twin taking care of you if she couldn't slip into your shoes every now and then?

"I'd love to, Janet, darling," she said. "Where should we go?"

JULY 1945

Monday evening, just as everyone was preparing to leave for the day, Andrew stuck his head in Lillian's office and motioned for her to follow him upstairs. Lillian hadn't been to his office since he'd screamed her out of it, and though she wasn't keen on returning, she couldn't very well ignore a direct request from her boss. But her annoyance melted away when she crossed the threshold of his office and saw a second manila folder on her usual chair. She didn't need to look at the typed label to confirm what it was, but she did all the same: *Kaufman, Eleanor*.

Her stomach lurched. "You got it," she said, opening the cover. Immediately something hit her. "Why is so much redacted?"

Andrew shrugged as she flipped through page after page of scrawled, handwritten notes. At each turn, a marker's thick black strokes leapt out—sometimes a word or two, sometimes an entire paragraph had been completely erased from history. "This is ridiculous," said Lillian. "Martin's file wasn't blacked out like this."

"That's all they gave me," said Andrew. "What does it say?"

She sank into the chair as she turned back to the beginning, forcing herself to read more closely. Her eyes kept jumping ahead of her brain, finding the handful of relevant words among what was still available to read. *Nausea* popped out one page, *toothache* on another, *migraine headache* on another. She reached the end all too soon and returned a third time to the beginning. But it was already clear.

"Nothing," she said. "It says nothing."

"How about a drink?" said Andrew.

She didn't answer as she continued to read.

Eleanor had a fever and vomiting, diagnosed as food poisoning. Prescription: lots of fluids, bed rest.

Eleanor went in for a dental cleaning and complained she had been experiencing a toothache lately. The dentist saw nothing of note.

Eleanor fainted at work, diagnosed as migraine headache. She was prescribed pain medicine. The doctor wanted to keep her overnight for observation, believing she might have given herself a concussion when she hit the floor, but Eleanor insisted she felt fine and was released.

There were no more pages.

Lillian threw the file across the room. It knocked into the chalkboard and fell on the floor, its meager contents spilling onto the linoleum. "Nothing," she said again, so upset that she hadn't even noticed Andrew had left the room. He returned a moment later with two glasses from the kitchenette. As Lillian stewed, he reached into his desk drawer and produced a bottle of whiskey, pouring them each a few mouthfuls.

"I don't want any whiskey," said Lillian, although as soon as she said it, she realized whiskey was exactly what she wanted. She grabbed the glass. The night at Gabe's had taught her that a few sips from a flask left her devastatingly sober, so she let her cheeks puff full of the awful liquid before swallowing it all down in a huge gulp. This time, she felt its effects almost immediately. Fire spread through her lungs, and an involuntary shudder ran up her spine until her whole body shook, like a cat who had just been doused in water.

"Sorry I don't have ice," said Andrew.

"Can I have another?" said Lillian.

Andrew poured, and Lillian stared at the liquid as it splashed in the glass. The file had said nothing, and yet—it was so, so much. Each of these incidents would have been such a large drama, if things had stayed as they were, if they were still in New York. Lillian could practically hear her sister complaining: *The dentist said my toothache was nothing, but we both know he's full of it. How could "nothing" be causing me this much pain?*

Lillian could see it all, like some sick play in her mind that she couldn't turn away from—the way her sister would have reacted to each setback, each injury. Eleanor would have tried to muscle her way through the food poisoning. She hated being sick so much she dealt with it by pretending she was perfectly healthy. Lillian would have had to yell and yell to convince her to see a doctor, perhaps even going so far as to drag her there herself. "That's what the doctor is there for," Lillian would shout, and Eleanor would gather all her energy to shout back: "I don't want to bother him!"

Who did that for Eleanor in Lillian's absence? Who dragged

her to the doctor when she couldn't keep even water or crackers down? Was it Andrew? Max? Emmy? Lillian ached that she didn't know.

The migraine, the doctor recommending an overnight stay in the hospital—that would have frightened Eleanor most of all. A real fright, too, where she'd be too afraid to pretend to be anything else. *Will you stay with me for the night, Lil?* She could see Eleanor lying in a hospital bed, round eyes the size of dinner plates looking up at her. *Please, just the night?* And Lillian would make some excuse, *Come on, you know they won't allow it,* or *I'll be here first thing in the morning,* and Eleanor would tremble just a little bit and Lillian would give right in, crawling into the tiny twin bed, clutching her sister, so grateful she could do this, so grateful she had someone to protect from the world.

Lillian realized with a start that tears were streaming hot down her cheeks. She wiped them away matter-of-factly.

"I know it's a step backwards," said Andrew. "But we don't have to give up, not unless you want to."

Give up? That implied there was still something they could look for, some clue they could follow. What was there to give up, anymore? Eleanor hadn't gone in for a procedure and never came out, like Martin had. There were no answers in those sheets of paper; there weren't even questions. She was back where she started. The only reasonable conclusion left was that Eleanor was only missing in that she did not want Lillian to find her.

Andrew seemed to read her mind. "If you want to leave, it's not a failure," he said.

"I suppose I probably should," she mumbled. Mother was doubtless already falling apart without her, she couldn't afford to pay Dot Greeley forever, and the Allerton test was coming up in only a few months. She'd done nothing but waste her time here, as it turned out.

Andrew tapped his glass. "You know, this is very good whiskey. And I would know. Irish, and all that. This one in particular is aged for an entire decade in oak barrels on the coast. If you close your eyes, you can taste the salt of the Irish Sea."

She turned to look at him, trying to fathom why he was bringing this up now.

"You can, I'm not lying," he continued. "Try it."

"I'm all right."

"Miss Kaufman, you are clearly in a very distraught mood, and so I must insist as the project director of the Clinton Engineer Works that you close your eyes and taste the salt of the Irish Sea."

Lillian could feel the corners of her mouth creep upward, in spite of it all. She closed her eyes and took a sip, expecting it to taste like nothing more than burnt nail-polish remover—and yet—to her surprise—

"Oh my goodness," she exclaimed, opening her eyes.

"Did you taste it?" asked Andrew. "Did you taste the sea?"

"I did," said Lillian, shocked. It had been a faint taste, but unmistakable. The liquid had coursed over her tongue, bitter and sweet and smooth and salty. She could hardly believe it.

"I told you," said Andrew.

"Why didn't I taste it before?"

"Because you didn't know to look for it. Obviously." Andrew stood up. "In fact, this whiskey is far too good for us to be guzzling it down in a setting like this."

"Is this not where you usually drink it? It does live in your desk drawer," said Lillian.

"Hush," said Andrew with a smile, grabbing the jacket that hung from the back of his desk chair. "Follow me."

He led her down the hallway to a closed door, behind which was a small staircase Lillian didn't know existed. They climbed until they reached a wooden trapdoor, which Andrew pushed up and open before clambering through. Lillian started to follow. "Here," said Andrew, extending a hand.

Lillian only hesitated a moment before taking it.

He helped her up through the door, where she found herself on the flat, square roof. The sun was setting in one half of the sky, the other half already thrown into darkness and speckled with an impossible number of stars. "Where did all these stars come from?" she murmured, immediately cursing herself for how drunk a question it sounded. Was she drunk already? Was that how little it took?

"A thermonuclear fusion of hydrogen and helium," replied Andrew, without missing a beat. It was both the correct answer and the one Lillian most wanted to hear. He led her toward the ledge of the building, where he spread the jacket from his chair down on the roof for Lillian to sit on. He refilled both glasses before leaning back and exhaling. "Much, much better," he said, gazing out into the ever-growing darkness.

"I agree," Lillian said.

"So," he began after a moment. "When did you give up math for physics?"

Lillian frowned. "What a confusing question."

"Not really. Every one of us has that moment. We fall in love with math, and then realize math is a waste of our time."

Lillian scowled. "I wouldn't call math a waste of time."

"That's not what I mean, it's more—you can do math forever and ever and never accomplish anything, never build anything real. Hell, I'll just say it. Math is the girl who's gorgeous, but is never in a million years going to sleep with you. Physics is a little uglier, but she's no prude."

Lillian took a sip from her glass, smiling wickedly in the darkness. "Have you ever considered that maybe she won't sleep with you because you're not as good at it as you think you are? I'm talking about math, of course."

"Of course," said Andrew. "I have considered it, but it's impossible. I'm very, very good. At math."

To her surprise, Lillian didn't blush, didn't feel embarrassed at this thrillingly adult conversation. It was a wonder, she realized, how much the man next to her seemed like a completely different person from the one who yelled her out of his office just a week ago. "I always wanted to be a physicist," she said. "I knew the world had rules, and I wanted to know what they were."

"Why?"

"Why what?"

"Why did you want to know the rules of the world?"

Lillian had never considered anyone would require an answer beyond *They're the rules of the world.* "I don't know," she said.

"Is it so you could follow them?"

There had been a hint of a tease in his voice, and it struck a shudder of embarrassment into her gut, as if he thought her entire life's work had been the equivalent of a smarmy school-child wanting praise from Teacher. "Trust me, I don't have any particular love for rules."

"I met you when you snuck onto an army base pretending to be someone else. Trust *me,* I'm well aware of that." He reached into his pocket and procured a cigarette, twirling it between his fingers while adding, "But you do follow some set of rules, don't you? You do keep yourself tightly to some code."

"Doesn't everyone?"

He lit the cigarette, and in the flare from the lighter, Lillian could see him arch his eyebrows. "No."

The topic was veering dangerously close to a part she'd been keeping quite bottled up, to a shame in her stomach she did not want to take out and fully examine. Fortunately, Andrew seemed to feel the same way and quickly changed the subject. "You know, I'm a twin, too."

"Really?" said Lillian, and in spite of everything, she was suddenly imagining herself and Eleanor wed to two identical Andrews. She willed the thought away almost as quickly as it arrived.

"He passed when we were five," said Andrew.

"Oh, I'm sorry."

Andrew sort of shrugged, as if there were no other gesture that would be appropriate. "I don't think about it all that much anymore. Scarlet fever. We both had it. I lived, he didn't. It was random, it was chance."

Lillian inhaled. "After he was gone, did you feel…different?"

"Different how?"

She wished she could be more specific. Every night she'd taken stock of her physical state, lain in bed and tried to sense if something about the universe seemed shifted, seemed awry. If you share everything with someone and they disappear from the earth, you should feel it, shouldn't you? "I don't know," she said.

He answered slowly. "I became more aware of how quickly… how quickly it all can end. So very aware." His voice broke for a moment. Covering, he coughed a little and put out the cigarette. "It's a tough thing for a kid to learn, how close death is."

Lillian thought back to age six, to turning the corner onto

East 86th, the before and the after. She had revisited it so much she could see it perfectly in her mind. "It is," she said.

The silence between them suddenly seemed so potent, so intimate, Lillian felt as if she might explode if the subject weren't changed. "Can I ask you something else?" she said as lightly as possible.

"I'm an open book," said Andrew.

"Do you tell that Niels Bohr story to all the girls?"

Even in the dimming light, she could see the horror wash over Andrew's face, in a way that screamed that he absolutely did. Before tonight, before the whiskey, Lillian might have been mortified at the prospect. Instead, she screeched with laughter.

"That doesn't mean it's not true," said Andrew, skipping his glass to take a long, indignant sip directly from the bottle.

"I can't believe it!" She had practically doubled over with laughter. "That's so embarrassing!"

"Who ratted me out?"

"Max Medelson."

"Max? Well, I certainly never told the story to him."

That set her off cackling again. "All right, have your laugh," grumbled Andrew. "I don't care what you think. It's still a good story."

"Oh, I never said it wasn't a good story." She looked at him with a smile, and he smiled back, and all of a sudden, in the light reflecting from the moon and stars, he looked so handsome, his brown eyes so impossibly deep. She felt herself, almost against her own will, leaning in, and felt him—maybe, perhaps—doing the same.

"We should be going to bed," he said quietly, and it took Lillian a moment longer than she would have liked to realize it was a rebuke and not an invitation.

"Yes," she said. "We have work to do tomorrow."

"That, and the whiskey's gone."

"Shame."

"Yes, very."

They lingered awkwardly for another second before he stood up, looking out over the quiet town. Lillian suddenly felt quite foolish and cursed herself for being so shortsighted. Andrew had dated her sister, been in love with her sister—who was now gone without a trace, without a hint to her whereabouts. How could she even indulge the possibility?

Fortunately, nothing had transpired, so there was nothing for her to pack away, no secret shame to justify or reshape or hide away. Thank goodness, at least, for that.

THIRTEEN

JULY 1945

When Andrew walked Lillian to the women's dormitory the previous night, he'd told her not to worry if she came in late tomorrow morning. The comment made little sense at the time, but now she understood far too well. Her head pounded, and sweat pooled where her back met the scratchy sheet. Forcing herself to sit upright, she choked back a bit of bile. The room, she noted, was spinning around her.

None of this could stop her from smiling. She had enjoyed herself last night, she admitted through her nausea. She had never laughed like that with a friend before, nor shared so much of herself. She'd had fun nights with Eleanor, of course, but family was different. Family had a hierarchy.

It was nice, being someone's equal.

She stood up, wincing at the accompanying throb in her

head. "Are you all right?" asked Emmy from across the room, looking up from the letter she'd been scrawling in bed.

The question gave Lillian an unexpected opportunity. "No. I don't feel well at all."

Emmy sat up straighter, putting her letter aside. "What's wrong? Can I get you some water?"

Lillian sank back onto the bed as if standing were too much of an effort. The movement didn't require much acting. "I feel so faint," she moaned.

Emmy crossed the room to place a hand on Lillian's head. "You do feel a bit warm."

Of course I'm warm, thought Lillian. *It's Tennessee in summer. It's one hundred degrees, and the air is as thick as banana pudding.* "I feel like I'm burning up," she said.

"Lie back down," instructed Emmy, pulling the sheet back so Lillian could slide her feet down. Emmy disappeared down the hall, returning a few seconds later with a washcloth wet with cool water, which she pressed to Lillian's temples.

"Thank you," whispered Lillian. "You're being so kind to me."

"Of course I am," said Emmy, quite quickly. "We're friends."

"Of course," said Lillian.

"You should probably stay home from work today," Emmy went on. "This thing might be contagious."

Lillian pretended to murmur her agreement. "Do you think I should go to the hospital building?" she asked.

Emmy snorted. "After what that ridiculous dentist told you, I'm surprised you're even considering it."

Lillian fought the tiny twinge in her heart at the thought of not being Eleanor's confidant. "That's how awful I feel," she said.

"Close your eyes and try and get some more rest," said Emmy. "I'll come check on you during my lunch break. How's that?"

Lillian nodded, knowing full well she'd be gone by then. She wondered if she ought to leave some sort of note before slipping away: *Gone to doctor, hope to see you tomorrow, xoxo, Eleanor.* Whether that would be an expected courtesy or overkill, she couldn't say for sure.

She slept for a few more hours, the rest making her head infinitely clearer. She even felt cooler, for some reason, and wondered if drink could cause hot flashes in addition to nausea and a propensity for making poor decisions. She rose, dressed, and tried to ignore her sudden craving for a bagel as she headed for Betty's hut.

"Let's do it today," she said when Betty pulled open the door.

Betty nodded. "Let's go," she said.

"Hold on," said Lillian. "Have you anything to eat?"

After an interlude of some toast and jam, the two headed toward the imposing brick building near the outskirts of town. "You're going to have to really sell it," warned Betty.

"I know," replied Lillian.

"I mean, really sell it. They won't admit you overnight unless you're on the verge of death."

"They wanted to admit Eleanor after she'd only fallen off a stool," said Lillian.

"I know," said Betty. "I remember that fall. Everyone in Y-12 was talking about it. She hit her head something awful, and the doctor was worried she'd fall again. When you fall after you've already had a concussion like that, it's very dangerous."

"Of course, I knew that," said Lillian. She did not know that but felt that as a scientist she should appear to have a working knowledge of basic medicine. "All I mean is, they're cautious."

"That doesn't mean they let in anyone who has a stomach-ache," said Betty. "Worst-case scenario, you tell them that you feel like you're dying."

Lillian was so taken aback that she stopped in her tracks. "That I *what?*"

"Feel like you're dying." Lillian couldn't believe how nonchalantly the words slipped out of Betty's mouth. "I've heard dying feels like nothing else. You know when it's happening. You tell them you feel like you're dying, they'll take you seriously. At least for one night."

"But I'm not dying," said Lillian.

"They don't have to know that."

Lillian shook her head. "I'm not doing that. Not even as pretend." She couldn't help but remember Eleanor's words from so long ago: *If you pretend to feel the emotions for long enough, you just feel them. It's not pretend anymore.* What if she pretended she was dying for so long that she actually died? The thought made her shudder, even as she dismissed it as patently ridiculous.

They were nearing the front door of the hospital building. "You'd better let me carry you in," said Betty.

"Carry me in?"

"In fact, we'd better start now. Swoon."

"I don't know how—"

"Swoon!" Betty kicked Lillian in the shins, throwing her off balance and over into Betty's arms. "Oh my goodness, miss, are you all right?" Betty nearly shouted. If they had been in a theater, she'd be heard in the back of the stalls.

Betty guided her around the corner and through the doors, where a scrawny nurse working the dingy reception area looked deeply unprepared to deal with a wailing woman. "I found her collapsed outside," said Betty, not even a hitch of uncertainty in her voice. She was as good an actress as Eleanor, thought Lillian. "She must have tried to walk here on her own."

The nurse called for someone in the back as she pulled over a chair for Lillian to sink into. "You don't know her? Not even a name?" she asked Betty with an air of suspicion.

"No, ma'am. Like I said, I was passing by on my way to work," Betty replied.

The nurse was now prodding Lillian's lids to get a good look into her eyes. "We'll take it from here," she murmured, not even bothering to thank Betty.

Betty hesitated, then scurried out of the building without

another word. Lillian was on her own. Before Oak Ridge, she would have worried that she wasn't a good enough actress to pull this sort of thing off. But she'd been Eleanor successfully for a whole month now, hadn't she? Compared to regular Eleanor, invalid Eleanor would be easy.

A second, older nurse soon appeared from the back and took charge, shoving the younger woman out of the way with a gruff hand on the shoulder. Lillian was placed in a wheelchair and taken to an examination room. After it became clear that she was *simply too weak to do any talking*, her belongings were rooted through until her ID was procured. "Kaufman comma Eleanor," the older nurse read. "What brings you in here today?"

Lillian groaned and placed her hand on her temple. The nurse rolled her eyes, which Lillian found to be horrible bedside manner. "You're conscious, so I know you can talk. Out with it."

Of course, Lillian couldn't break that easily. She rubbed her temple again. The strange thing was, it was starting to throb a bit. *How funny,* thought Lillian. *I'm a good actress, too.*

Her success was short lived, as it soon became apparent that the throbbing was a very real migraine. The nurse shouted some words at her, but except for the movement of her lips, Lillian couldn't tell she was speaking at all. The noises of the room around her became only a dull, low hum, steadily growing louder and louder. Fear must have consumed her face because the nurse stopped her tirade to peer at her strangely. Lillian could see her lips forming the shapes *Miss Eleanor?*

And then everything went black.

FEBRUARY 1945

In a way, Lillian's lunch with Janet Mayberry was a considerable favor to Eleanor. Without *Carousel* rehearsals to rely on, Eleanor had returned to schlepping about town giving private singing lessons, a job that she found mostly unbearable. "If I have to teach 'Baby, Take a Bow' to another bored five-year-old whose mother thinks she's the next Shirley Temple, I'll rip my teeth out," she'd sworn.

Every day that Eleanor packed her sheet music and boarded the train took its emotional toll—but she had no choice. Her fate, her future, was completely in the hands of Misters Rodgers and Hammerstein. But Janet Mayberry had the ear of the three producers from nine to five, five days a week. Building a friendship with Janet Mayberry could only be good for Eleanor. And since Eleanor had no time for casual lunches herself, Lillian was just doing it *for* her. Never mind the fact that Lillian had put the whole friendship at risk in a three-minute telephone call; the lunch would make up for all that. In fact, she'd have to mess up quite desperately to make this anything but a net positive for Eleanor.

Besides, Eleanor would never know. Every second she wasn't

teaching the aspiring Shirley Temples of the Upper East Side, she was wasting time with Max, preparing for his departure for Tennessee. Their goodbye had stretched ages, and Lillian couldn't fathom why they didn't simply break up and be done with it. He'd asked Eleanor to marry him and she'd declined. The relationship was as good as dead. The breakup would be good even for Max, who would be losing the love of his life but gaining a wonderful romance to look back on wistfully in his elder years. Not everyone needed a someone, Lillian believed, but everyone needed a someone who got away.

Eleanor would never find out, and the lunch would be quite helpful. Confident in these two truths, Lillian cleared her schedule for the entire morning and headed upstairs.

The two had pretended to be each other before, in small, inconsequential ways. If a shop girl said, "How are you today, Eleanor?" when Lillian stopped in for a new dress, it was easier to respond to the name than it was to correct the error. But an entire lunch would require much more effort, starting with the preparation. Lillian sat in front of Eleanor's makeup mirror and stared at the array of foreign objects strewn about. She must have watched Eleanor do her makeup hundreds of times, but never with the care she would have given it if she could know she'd be tested. The tube of lipstick seemed the least frightening, so she reached for that first—only to end up with Eleanor's signature cherry-red shade inexplicably all over her teeth.

Her third attempt at lipstick, however, finally looked passable, and an impossibly silly device intended to curl one's eyelashes made a surprisingly noticeable difference in brightening her face. Lacking the time to curl and pin her hair properly, Lillian had to settle for pulling her unruly hair back in a snood—but the finished result, Lillian had to admit, looked startlingly chic.

Although she considered going for one of Eleanor's tamer outfits—perhaps the navy dress she sometimes borrowed to go to the symphony—Lillian ultimately decided that an article of Eleanor's she as Lillian would never wear would be the safer choice. She'd be less likely to slip up and forget the charade dressed completely as Eleanor. She eventually settled on a green silk dress that Eleanor had purchased secondhand and hemmed for herself, one that cinched at the waist and moved when she walked. Normally, Lillian would hate wearing a dress like this, one that called attention to itself, that hugged the hips and swished at the bottom. But putting this dress on, Lillian had to admit, made her feel—well—*beautiful.*

She studied her transformation in the mirror and couldn't help but smile at her reflection. She had become Eleanor.

Lillian had never wanted to *be* Eleanor. Eleanor got attention for being prettier and more put-together, but Lillian never *wanted* attention—not for her beauty, at least. Still, it bothered her that Eleanor was rewarded by society, it seemed, for spending her time the "correct" way. Lillian in her plain wool skirt and frizzy hair and unmade face could ask for a glass of water and be utterly ignored, but Eleanor in her green dress and painted lips and hair sprayed within an inch of its life could give one parched little cough and twenty strangers, men and women, would hold out a beverage for her to take a sip. So Lillian wanted to solve equations and Eleanor wanted to brush her eyebrows—what difference did it make? Why was one encouraged and praised and the other ignored and silenced?

It felt, sometimes, like the world was angry at her—for having the ability to be beautiful and then choosing not to, as if she were doing society some disservice, as if strangers on the street deserved her to look pleasing to their eye.

What was the harm, then, in enjoying this afternoon, in drinking in the glances she got on the elevated and letting people hold a door open for her rather than let it clang in her face? What could be the harm?

Just out of curiosity, before she left, she poked her head in Mother's room. "I'm heading out for the day," she said. "Do you need anything before I go?"

Mother wrinkled her brow. "Thought you already left."

"That was Lillian, Mother."

"Oh." Mother stiffened. "Can you rearrange these pillows before you go? Your sister never does anything right."

"Of course," said Lillian. The thrill of successfully pulling off the illusion took the edge off the insult's sting. "I'd be happy to."

JULY 1945

Lillian woke in a bed surrounded by a hanging curtain, one of likely dozens in a hall whose size she couldn't imagine. She lay perfectly still, trying to sense how long she'd been unconscious. Was it nighttime yet? Betty's janitor inside the building had promised to leave the door to the morgue unlocked, but whether it was time for Lillian to go down there, she couldn't say.

It was an unsettling feeling. Her migraines had caused her to faint before, but never like that. Normally she was conscious again practically as soon as she hit the ground, with her sister there to tell her exactly where she was and what had happened. But this room was empty. There wasn't a clock, weren't even any windows. She could have been asleep for half an hour or half a day. For all she knew, she could have missed the night altogether and slept until morning.

Panic started to rise in Lillian's chest. Being unconscious during the trip to this room meant she had no idea where she was in relation to the basement, would have no idea how to find this room again without being noticed. It had barely started, yet already her mission was doomed. Hell, for all she knew, she could have been taken to a different building, or even out of Oak Ridge altogether. She could be in a completely different part of the country. They could have taken her to the same place they had taken—

She had to push the thought from her mind, or she'd

devolve into uselessness. After a few agonizing minutes of lying in wait and hearing no sound from outside, she slowly lifted herself out of bed. Her clothing had been replaced with a hospital robe, and her boots and socks were missing altogether—her bare toes were cold on the linoleum. She reached a frightened hand up to the nape of her neck and was relieved to find the string of pearls still hanging there, thank goodness. She didn't know what she would have done if these people had gotten their hands on that.

Almost as soon as she stood up, a nurse parted the curtains and stepped inside. Seeing Lillian awake and out of bed, she remarked, "And where do you think you're going?" To Lillian's relief, it was a tease and not an admonishment.

"Sorry, I just woke up," Lillian said. "I wasn't sure if I should wait for someone to come to me or..."

"Let's get you back into bed; there's a good girl." The nurse—who seemed much kinder than the one who had interrogated Lillian upon her entry—helped Lillian lie back down and pulled a blanket over her waist. "I'm going to take your temperature now, all right?"

Lillian nodded as the nurse placed a thermometer under her tongue. "You were out for quite a bit there," the nurse chattered. Lillian longed to ask how long, but couldn't do anything but lie there patiently, waiting for the mercury to climb to the top. Finally, the nurse plucked the thermometer from her mouth. "One hundred and one," she said.

Lillian's jaw dropped in surprise. "I have a fever?" she asked without thinking.

"Yes, dear," said the nurse with a chuckle. "I imagine that's why you're here!"

"Right," said Lillian. "Sorry, I'm a bit out of it."

"Of course you are, dear. You must be exhausted. Don't worry, I've been instructed to give you something that will help you fall asleep." She gestured for Lillian to hold out her hand, then placed in her outstretched palm two round, white pills. "There you are. A good night's rest will do you wonders."

Lillian closed her hand around the pills. *Was that the same thing they'd told Martin Hughes when he'd checked in with his infected tooth?* She looked up at the smiling nurse, seemingly so kind, and yet she stared at Lillian's hand quite intently. "Go on, down the hatch," she urged. When Lillian didn't immediately move her hand to her mouth, the nurse went on. "Something the matter?"

"No, of course not," Lillian quickly assured her. "Would it be possible for me to have a glass of water?"

The nurse smiled. "Of course. I'll be right back."

As soon as she'd disappeared through the curtains, Lillian leaned over and stashed the pills under the pillow. Seconds later, the nurse returned, and Lillian clenched her empty fist shut. Taking the cup with a "thank you," Lillian pretended to dump the pills into her mouth and forced a gulp of water down her bone-dry throat.

"You should start relaxing any moment now," whispered the nurse, pushing aside a stray strand of Lillian's hair.

Lillian did her best to soften her eyes, let her muscles melt. "One more thing," she began, hesitating only slightly. "Would you mind telling me what time it is?"

The nurse, already headed for the curtains, turned and looked at Lillian with a puzzled expression. "Don't worry about that right now, dear."

"I'm just curious…"

But the nurse was already gone.

———————

Lillian lay still and quiet, her eyes studying the random patterns on the white ceiling, her body trying to ignore the bar of the bed frame that pressed through the paper-thin mattress and into her lower back. She tried to feel time passing, to count the seconds and minutes as best as she could, but her head (despite her pill-hiding efforts) was foggy. Did she really have a fever? Or were the nurses on to her, trying to frighten her into admitting she'd made everything up? She pressed her hand to her forehead to try to get a sense of things, to no use. She couldn't tell the truth of her own body.

Approximately one hour (her best guess, at least) after the nurse had come in, someone else came to check on her. She closed her eyes and pretended to be asleep, and whoever it was moved on without incident. Shortly after, the steady flow of footsteps in the area outside her curtained-off bed seemed to die down a bit, with people passing by less and less frequently. The sound of other curtains being pulled back, other patients being murmured to, became quieter and quieter. Another hour passed, another nurse poked her head in to find Lillian asleep. It had to be nighttime by now, surely? Or was she shaping the evidence to fit the conclusion she wanted to find?

She waited for another checkup, another hour to pass. Then she could wait no longer. If not now, when? If the mission was already doomed, might as well get it over with. She sat up, counting herself lucky that at least she hadn't been placed in a creaky bed. Her bare toes again touched the linoleum. She couldn't remember the last time she'd been completely barefoot and wasn't in the shower. It seemed indecent at best and unsanitary at worst, especially for someone whose destination was the morgue. But her boots were nowhere to be found, whisked off somewhere unseen with the rest of her clothes. Barefoot would have to do.

Tiptoeing to the curtain, she took a deep breath before drawing it open a few inches. She peeked outside.

As she suspected, she was at the end of a long line of similarly curtained areas, maybe a dozen or so, all lined up to her right like cabins in a train car. She dared to poke her head outside to get a good look around. There was no one in sight, no sound or movement.

This could be her only chance. Taking a deep breath, she stepped into the hallway.

Where she was going, she hadn't the faintest idea, but since to her left appeared to be a dead end, she headed right. Past the row of curtained rooms was a set of double doors; she pressed her ear to the metal before opening one slowly. Behind it, she found a more administrative-looking hallway, with doors that looked more likely to lead to offices, closets, and storage rather than patient rooms. To her right, however, were stairs. She still hadn't a clue as to what floor she was on, but either way, she needed to head down. So down she went, gaining momentum until she was practically running. She was surprised to find that she admired the feeling of running barefoot, the way the balls of her feet clung to the floor beneath her, both grounded and light. She counted the floors she passed, trying to tuck the number away in her still-foggy brain. *One...two...three...*

Four floors later (eight flights of steps, she repeated to herself—*Eight! Eight! Eight!*), she found herself with no lower to go.

The basement was practically pitch black. Betty had informed her that the morgue was in the east wing of the building, but Lillian could only hope that's where she was. Cardinal directions were hopelessly beyond her now. Drawing her nightgown closer to keep out a sudden chill, she looked around. She didn't see a way to any other wing, at least—so forward it was. She walked and walked and walked, passing nothing but blank white bricks, sweating nervously (or feverishly?). It felt like she had been walking for much longer than the hallway she'd walked on the third floor. (That's where she'd been, right? No, fourth floor. No, third floor. She'd gone down four floors total, including the one to the basement. Third floor.)

And then she spotted it. A single wooden door, its title emblazoned on it in block lettering. *Morgue.*

Lillian reached for the handle, turning it slowly. As promised, the door was unlocked. She expected to be hit with a gust of cool air, but the room was as hot and muggy as any other in town. She stepped inside, bracing herself for the sight of rows of corpses, hopefully shrouded in sheets—but found nothing nearly as dramatic. It looked more like a records room or a library. Shelves of boxes stretched back as far as the eye could see. As Lillian moved down the line, she realized each shelf was numbered.

The location *19A* suddenly made more sense, but she gaped as she passed stack after stack of cheap cardboard boxes. Were all these full of human remains? A shudder ran through her spine, settling itself in her jaw, which clenched in horror. If all these people had died the way that Martin had died... It was too awful to imagine.

She picked up the pace, desperate to be out of this nightmare room. She moved so quickly that she didn't even notice until she got to shelf 19 that somewhere in the stacks behind her, the cardboard boxes had been replaced with rows and rows of metal safes.

19A was not a location, not a tin or a box or something she could hide under her bed. 19A was a giant, locked safe.

How absurd. *Of course.* She was six inches away from the only thing she'd been able to find in this town, and it was impossible to reach. Somehow, the failure felt worse than if she'd passed out and slept twenty-four hours, or if she'd never made it into the hospital building at all. She'd come so close, only to fail at the end of things. Part of her wanted to collapse on the floor right there, not even bothering to climb back to her bed.

As it turned out, neither of these options would be the one she'd take. At that moment, she felt a hand on her shoulder. Lillian was too exhausted to even be properly frightened.

"Good evening, Miss Kaufman," said a voice. She recognized it as belonging to the older nurse she'd encountered when she arrived, the one who hadn't believed her weak and mute act. Being caught in the morgue at god knows what time of night probably wouldn't be doing much to help her credibility.

Lillian put a hand to her head. "Where am I? I tried to find a bathroom... I can't find my way..."

The nurse believed the gesture even less than Lillian believed herself. "Let's get you back to bed," she ordered, placing her other hand on Lillian's other shoulder and wheeling her around, marching her back toward the long basement hallway. She said nothing as they climbed the eight flights of steps, but she shoved Lillian into her bed with such force that Lillian almost hit the floor. The threat was clear: stay here or else. Without another word, the nurse was gone.

Lillian exhaled. It could have been a lot worse, all things

FOURTEEN

She was in complete whiteness—the painful sort of white that sent her squinting and her head throbbing. Blood pulsed through the vein in her right forehead with such force she worried it might burst.

"Lillian," she heard someone say, a pleasant female voice that echoed around the empty room. "Lillian. Lillian."

She recognized the voice, but couldn't place it. She tried to form a deduction, arrive at the most likely guess. Where had she been before here? The laboratory? It couldn't be Irene; her voice wasn't nearly as kind.

The voice seemed to sense her inner scrambling and got more forceful, as if to insist that whatever was distracting Lillian didn't matter. "Lillian!" it demanded. "Lillian! Wake up!"

The voice, she realized, was almost exactly like her own. *Eleanor?* she tried to say, but her frozen lips refused to budge.

Eleanor?

Eleanor?

FEBRUARY 1945

"Eleanor?"

Lillian blinked. "Oh goodness, I'm sorry. I didn't even see you there!"

The woman she presumed to be Janet Mayberry was dolled up and stylish, with a head full of amber curls and a sweet polka-dot dress. She laughed. "Such a daydreamer! Well, you see me now, so give me a hug, you goofball."

Within moments, Janet's arms were wrapped around Lillian. Lillian was not much of a hugger, but this embrace felt sweet, to her surprise. "So good to see you again," whispered Janet, rubbing Lillian's arm with a gloved hand.

"You too, darling," said Lillian. "It's been too long."

"Shall we head inside?"

"Let's."

Janet hooked her arm through Lillian's, and the two sashayed through the door of the restaurant. Lillian enjoyed the way it felt to move her hips that way, reveling in what a bombshell she could become if she wanted to.

JULY 1945

Lillian came to in a strange room.

Where am I? This isn't my bed, was her first thought. A heartbeat later she realized that the bed she thought of as "her bed" wasn't her bed but Eleanor's, and it wasn't even Eleanor's; it belonged to the women's dormitory. Had she been here that long, that she no longer thought of her bed in New York as *her* bed?

Pushing these thoughts aside, she focused on the realization that this bed was *not* her dormitory bed, nor was it the uncomfortable hospital bed she'd been shoved in the night before. This bed had a much thicker mattress—she could no longer feel the metal bar that had so painfully dug into her lower back. The sheets were smoother, the blanket fluffier. Her body was far more comfortable, but her head felt as if it had been reduced to mud, no better than the streets outside. She groaned.

It eventually occurred to her to open her eyes. To her surprise, when she did, she found someone sitting by her side.

Andrew looked up from the legal pad he was scribbling on. "You're awake," he said.

Lillian wasn't sure what to say. "Yes," she replied bluntly. "I certainly seem to be."

"How do you feel?"

"I don't know."

He tapped his pen on the yellow paper. "You don't know how you feel?"

"Are you interrogating me while I'm in the hospital?" She reached up to rub her aching right temple.

"Fair enough. I apologize."

He leaned back and resumed his writing. Lillian stared at the ceiling, contemplating closing her eyes but feeling a bit awkward about doing so. "What are you doing here?" she asked finally.

He looked up, as if surprised by the question. "You're in the hospital."

"Yes. But why are you here?"

"Because you're in the hospital."

He thought she was ill. He was being kind. The thought made her dizzy.

"I had them move you to a private room," he offered. "Much more comfortable."

Embarrassment clenched at Lillian's throat. "You didn't have to do that. You didn't have to do any of this," she managed to stammer.

He raised an eyebrow. "I can leave, if you'd prefer."

"No. It was quite kind of you, the private room and all," Lillian said, struggling to prop herself up on the many pillows available. "It's just—I should tell you—I'm not really ill. At least, I wasn't when I came in. I feel pretty terrible now but I think that's because of this medicine…" Her voice trailed off as she noticed Andrew smiling. "What?" she asked.

"Well, I must admit, I didn't exactly request the private room out of kindness," he replied. "I did it because the private rooms are all the way on the second floor of the west wing. And while the staff was distracted in moving you clear to the other side of the building, I was able to obtain this."

He reached down beside him and picked up a small metal canister. He handed it to Lillian. She turned it over to read the label affixed to the side. *Hughes.*

"You broke into the safe," she whispered.

He leaned back with a self-satisfied smirk. "It was a tricky one, I'll admit it. Much heavier-duty than the ones they provide in the offices. I practically had to slow my own heartbeat so I'd hear the pins drop. But I pulled it off."

Maybe it was the exhaustion, or the fact that her head still hadn't fully cleared up, or the sheer overwhelming nature of the past several months, at least, but Lillian felt her eyes well up with tears. "Thank you," she managed to say. "You have no idea what this means to me, what it will mean for Betty."

"It'll mean even more than all that," he replied. "Open it up."

Lillian looked up at him in horror. "I'm not going to open it," she said.

"Trust me. Open it."

Hesitating for only a moment, Lillian reluctantly gripped the top and peeled the canister open. She peered inside, frightened but admittedly curious.

Inside, rolling around at the bottom, were teeth. Six long, rotting teeth.

And that was all.

She looked up at Andrew. "He could still be alive," she said.

Andrew nodded.

———

Betty looked from Andrew to Lillian and back to Andrew. "I don't understand," she said. "The file you gave me said he was deceased."

"We can't know for certain," began Andrew, "but it's

possible they meant 'presumed deceased.' If he made it out, it'd be unlikely he'd find his way through the woods and the mountains on his own, without being caught and turned in. The army might have assumed he died, and moved on."

Betty shook her head. "No. He can't be alive. He... Do you really think so?"

"It's still a long shot," said Andrew. "The more likely reality, unfortunately, is that those were the only thing the army felt was worth keeping." He gestured toward Betty's left palm, where Martin's six teeth lay in a neat row. Betty touched each one gently, lovingly. "But we have to try. Do you know where he'd be if he managed to make it out?"

Betty nodded right away. "I know exactly where he'd be. Before this job, he was living at a church in Sevierville. But he's not there. I wrote a letter to the pastor ages ago, asking him to write me back if he saw Martin."

"The army censors every letter going in and out of here," said Andrew. "It's safe to say that message never made it. The only way to know for sure is to go and see for ourselves."

Betty furrowed her brow as she thought. "I can take the bus to Knoxville, maybe hitchhike from there—"

"We'll drive," interrupted Andrew. "I can borrow a car tomorrow. We'll leave first thing in the morning."

Lillian looked at him, both surprised and not surprised at all. He was the hardest working person at Oak Ridge, perhaps the hardest working person (besides herself) she'd ever met. He was the first in Building E in the morning, the last to leave at night. Sometimes she suspected he'd slept there, noting a similar coffee stain on his wrinkled shirtsleeves two days in a row. Yet he was still willing to drop everything to help a near stranger. Max had been dead wrong about him. Even she had underestimated him.

"You've done so much for me already," said Betty, shaking her head. "I can't ask for any more."

"You don't have to ask," Andrew replied. "I'll be honest. At first I wasn't sure if there was anything to your story. I'd like to think that if people were disappearing, I would know about it." He took a deep breath. "But I think you're right. There is something going on here, something so big the army is keeping it even from me. They took Martin and they probably took Eleanor too, and who knows how many others. If there's a chance Martin's alive, we have to find him. He's the only one who can help me shut this down for good."

"I never even thought there was a chance," Betty repeated. "Before I even tried to track you down, I assumed they killed him. I thought it was a given."

"Nothing's a given," said Lillian.

Betty nodded. "Tomorrow, then."

"Tomorrow."

When Lillian finally turned the knob to her dorm, she was practically assaulted by Emmy. "Where in god's name have you been?" she said, throwing her arms around Lillian. "Are you all right?"

She looked as if she'd been crying, and Lillian suddenly felt awful for deciding it was unnecessary to leave her roommate a note. "I'm fine," she said. "I didn't mean to frighten you."

"I heard you were in the hospital building," said Emmy. "Admitted overnight. But when I went to see you this morning, they told me you weren't there."

"They let me go right after breakfast," said Lillian. Her headache still hadn't fully cleared, but she managed to fake perfect health so she and Andrew could get to Betty as soon as possible.

"But it's nearly evening now," Emmy protested. "Where have you been?"

"I went to work," Lillian lied. She moved past Emmy to the dresser and began to prep her hair for the rollers.

"Work?" Emmy said. "You should have come home! And rested! And told me you were all right!"

She tried to place the strange lilt in Emmy's voice as she separated her hair into three sections, brushing in front of her eyes, a task for which she used to rely heavily on a mirror but now could practically accomplish in her sleep. Something was off about Emmy's outburst. It was too regretful, too impassioned, too involved. "I'm sorry. I didn't mean to frighten you."

"When the nurses told me you weren't there, I..." Emmy turned away quickly, but not fast enough to prevent Lillian from seeing her eyes begin to water. "I thought someone had reported you, and they had taken you away, or something," she mumbled.

"Taken me away?" Lillian forced a chuckle, as if the idea itself were absurd. "Why would they do that?"

Emmy wiped her eyes, as discreetly as possible. "They wouldn't, of course," she said, her voice as chipper as ever. "I'm being ridiculous, is all. I'm sorry." She gave Lillian another hug. "I'm glad you're all right."

"Me too," said Lillian quietly.

Emmy excused herself to the restroom, and Lillian continued to work the rollers into her hair. As she pinned the third one into place, it dawned on Lillian what that strange tone of voice had been. It was guilt.

"I think my roommate might be a spy."

Andrew didn't seemed concerned by this revelation. He lit a cigarette and leaned back against the station wagon, ignoring the fine layer of dirt that had gathered on the outside of the car. "Is she on our side, at least?"

"What do you mean?"

"Spying for the army or the Germans? Good guys or bad guys?"

"Good guys, I suppose. Technically, at least," said Lillian. "I think she turned me in to army security."

Andrew shook his head. "If she'd turned you in to army security…" He paused, not sure how to finish the sentence. "You wouldn't be here to have this conversation," he finally said.

"She seemed awfully guilty when I got home last night. When she couldn't find me at the hospital building, she panicked. Like she had some reason to believe I might have gone missing."

"I wouldn't worry about it too much," said Andrew. "You're smarter than her, right?"

"I'd like to think so," replied Lillian.

"Then think so."

She nodded, staring down at her dusty boots, letting a curl of hair fall into her eyes. "I just have this instinct, that's all. She was behaving so strangely. It felt off." She paused to flick away a mosquito that had settled on her arm. "I don't know. I certainly don't have any evidence."

Andrew was quiet. "Trust your instincts," he said after a moment. "If you're suspicious, be careful around her. This place isn't like the outside world. If you wait until you have evidence here, it might be too late."

Lillian considered this, and finally nodded. She absentmindedly played with one particularly springy curl as she watched Andrew press the cigarette to his lips and exhale another puff of smoke. Last night, around the fifth or sixth roller, it had occurred to her that she didn't have any real reason to curl her hair fresh for today. They had planned to leave Oak Ridge at five thirty in the morning, long before Emmy would be awake, and it wasn't necessary for her to pretend to be Eleanor around Betty and Andrew. Of course, by that time she was almost one-third of the way through her hair, and it seemed easier to just see the job through by that point. It had come out beautifully, perhaps her best effort yet.

"Can I have one of those?" she asked, pointing to Andrew's left hand.

His eyebrows lifted in surprise. "You don't smoke."

"I know. But I'm not used to getting up so early." It had still been dark when Lillian rose and dressed, and the sun was only just now beginning to creep up in the sky. "At the very least, it'll be better than the coffee."

"Can't be worse." Andrew lit her a cigarette and passed it over, snapping the lighter shut with a satisfying clank. Carefully she lifted it to her lips and inhaled. The smoke was hot and smooth and went right to her head in a very appealing fashion. It almost made her laugh. She'd always thought Eleanor's smoking habit was a bit low-brow. She had no idea what she'd been missing.

Andrew took a long drag from his cigarette. "I'm sure I've told you how the army thinks I'm a spy."

"You have. But you've never mentioned what side you're on."

He raised his eyebrows. "Wouldn't you like to know."

"No, you're not a spy," said Lillian, rolling her eyes. "If you were a spy, the Germans would have had the capability to blow us all up instead of surrendering."

"I'll take that as a compliment, thank you," said Andrew. "Alas, I am one of the good guys. How boring. Wouldn't it be so interesting if I were a spy?"

"I don't know," Lillian shrugged. "Arrogant young man, thinks he's better than everyone else, breaks into safes for fun—it would be a little trite."

He grinned. "Do you want to go on a trip with me?"

"Thought that's what we were doing," she replied, giving the tire of the station wagon a little kick.

"No, no," he said. The butt of his cigarette fell into the dirt between them. "A real trip. The army has another laboratory. Pretty soon there's going to be a test there, if they don't push it back again. I'm planning on going, presuming... Well, it depends on how everything today works out, of course. But you could come with me, if you'd like."

"A test?"

"Of the device."

All Lillian could think to say was, "Why?"

Andrew scoffed. "To see if it works, of course."

"But why?" She let her cigarette drop to the ground as well, where it still smoldered a bit on the dirt. "Germany's surrendered. Japan's on the way to it. What difference could it make now?"

"That's not the point," he said. "Do you think we're going to put all this effort into the thing and not see if it works?"

Lillian recognized the absurdity of this point and yet found herself unable to argue it. Hadn't she, just last night, rolled fifteen more sponge rollers into her hair after realizing there was no point in doing so? She did want to know, she realized. She wanted to know badly.

"When is it?" she asked.

"I can't tell you," he said.

"Is it far away?"

"I can provide you with almost no information."

"Why me?"

He looked at her, confused.

"Why are you inviting me?" she clarified.

He was silent for a moment. "You don't have to come, if you don't want to. I just thought I'd extend the invitation—"

"That's not what I meant. I was just wondering why not someone else on the team. Someone who's been here longer, someone who's not..." She wanted to avoid saying outright that she was the twin of his ex-girlfriend but wasn't sure how else to phrase it. "Someone who's not me."

He exhaled. "You have no idea how much I've been asking myself that question. I don't have a good answer, other than I want you to come, and I have a bad habit of always doing what I want without considering the consequences for anyone, even myself." He fixed her with a peculiar stare. "So what do you say?"

Lillian didn't get a chance to answer, as a figure appeared from around the corner. After glancing around to make sure no one was nearby watching, Betty approached the car. To Lillian's surprise, she was carrying a suitcase. "Sorry I'm late," she said. "It took me longer to pack up all my things than I thought it would."

"Not a problem," replied Andrew, reaching into his pocket for the keys.

"Why were you packing at all?" asked Lillian.

Andrew unlocked the trunk and Betty lifted the suitcase inside. She looked at Lillian with a hopeful smile. "Because if it all goes well, I won't be coming back," she replied.

Even though it was early enough that the town was mostly deserted, Andrew still drove them toward the gate on a back road and instructed Betty and Lillian to crouch down in the car in case they happened to pass a security officer. Lillian realized as the car bumped along that this would be her first time out of the facility in over a month. Did spending that much time behind the fence, hiding her identity, explain why she'd felt so compelled to finish curling her hair? If she pretended to be Eleanor long enough, would she eventually just become her?

"How are we going to get through the gate?" she asked suddenly, her forehead nearly knocking into Betty's. "Aren't they going to check the car?"

"Yes," said Andrew, bringing the car to a stop. "That's why you're not going through the gate. You can sit up now. No one's going to be coming down this road."

When Lillian sat up, she realized *road* was a generous term. It was more of a narrow dirt path, surrounded on both sides by dense woods. "I thought the gate was the only way out," she said. "Isn't there a fence?"

"There is," said Andrew. "And at this particular spot, the fence is just about a hundred yards that way."

"I'm not climbing a fence," said Lillian. "I'm wearing a skirt."

"Actually, you're not climbing the fence because it has barbed wire on top of it," Andrew replied. "This part of the fence, however, has a hole in it."

Betty and Lillian both stared at him.

"Are you serious?" Betty said finally.

Lillian added incredulously, "The army built millions of dollars' worth of top-secret engineer works and then left a hole in the fence."

"Of course they did." Andrew grinned. "That's why it's going to come down to us to win this war."

After begrudgingly agreeing to meet at a spot a mile down the road from the gate, Betty and Lillian clambered out of the car and waved a bitter farewell to Andrew. "Well this is an unexpected adventure, isn't it?" grumbled Betty. "I better not get bitten by anything out here."

"At least you won't have to make the return journey," said Lillian. "God willing."

They moved forward in silence. "It'll be a good day for

you, too," said Betty. "Martin will know where Eleanor is. He's been missing for four months now, a lot longer than her. If he's alive…" Her voice trailed off as she noticed Lillian pursing her lips. "What? Do you think Eleanor's not there?"

"I don't know," said Lillian quietly. She didn't know what to say, how to put words to the dread that had been slowly forming in her bones. They'd found traces of Martin, found records listing his location, found his teeth in 19A. They'd found nothing of Eleanor. It was as if she'd been wiped off the face of the earth, her existence entirely, carefully, purposefully erased—blacked out like the redacted bits in her medical file. "It's possible that after all this, she really is safe and sound in Chicago and simply wants nothing to do with me." She tried her best to keep her tone as bright as possible, to keep her voice ringing with optimism. But it wasn't easy. Lillian suddenly wondered if Eleanor's vanishing was her fault, as if Eleanor had disappeared because Lillian had become too good at being her, and both of them were no longer required.

"I hope she is in Chicago," said Betty. "I hope she's happy and healthy there and the two of you can make up and be sisters again."

"I don't know if that's possible," said Lillian.

"Of course it is." Now Betty was the one forcing optimism into her voice. "You're still her twin, no matter what you did to her." After a few beats she added nonchalantly, "What did you do to her?"

"Nothing," said Lillian instinctually. Then: "It was a misunderstanding."

"Was it nothing, or was it a misunderstanding?"

Lillian did not want to probe that question. Fortunately, Betty was distracted by the appearance of the fence in front of them. "Look, there it is," she said.

"I don't see a hole," said Lillian nervously.

They trekked closer, Betty agreeing that the fence looked rather secure. But sure enough, with a little pressure, the netting pushed easily away from the post, creating a hole large enough for a person to climb through.

"This must be how people get down to the river," said Betty.

"People go to the river?" asked Lillian.

Betty looked at her with a glimmer in her eye. "You haven't heard those stories?"

Lillian shook her head.

"It's a place men around here take their dates, or brag about taking them, anyway," Betty explained. "If you say yes to going down to the river with someone…" She let her voice trail off, raising her eyebrows suggestively. "Bet that's why the army doesn't close that hole. Then they won't have anywhere to take their lady friends."

"I thought the army officers lived in the houses," said Lillian.

Betty let out a peal of laughter. "Yeah, they live in the houses. With their wives."

Lillian blushed at her own naivete. "I would have hoped the people here would have more important things to do than all that."

"It's all the important things that make them want to do all that," said Betty. She paused and looked at Lillian, eyeing the curls she hadn't needed to put in her hair. "You've... Right?"

It took Lillian a minute to understand what Betty was asking, and as soon as she did, she felt nerves overtake her. It felt like Betty was taking a microscope to her insides, and if she answered incorrectly, Betty would know her whole past. "Yes, of course," she replied, focusing on the ground in front of her.

"You don't have a boyfriend, though," said Betty. That wasn't a question.

"It works the same even if he's not your boyfriend," said Lillian. "In fact, it works better." She didn't actually have evidence of this, but it seemed like a witty, worldly thing to say. It did get an approvingly loud laugh from Betty.

The sound of the river grew louder around them. "Figures Andrew Ennis would know exactly where that hole in the fence is," Betty mused. "Bet he takes women down here all the time." She paused before clapping a hand over her mouth. "Oh god, I shouldn't have said that. I forgot him and your sister—"

"It's all right," said Lillian, and just to prove how entirely all right she was with the idea of Andrew having affairs with multiple women, she added, "I'm sure you're right, that he's always down here. He's such a..." She was going to say that he was a catch, but suddenly she did not want to, so she allowed the thought to hang in the air, unresolved.

They stomped in silence, through the mud and the weeds,

the river babbling behind them. Betty was clearly turning over some question in her mind, deciding how to phrase it. "Your sister left him. Is that right?" she said finally.

"Yes," said Lillian, almost certain where this would be heading.

"And you and him…"

"I know for a fact that he's not interested," said Lillian curtly. Betty shut up after that.

Finally, they reached the side of the road where Andrew had parked. He sat inside, scribbling away on yet another yellow legal pad and smoking. As she pulled open the passenger's side door, he looked up at her and smiled, quickly shoving the legal pad underneath his seat. "Have a nice hike?" he asked.

"Lovely," said Lillian, not wanting to meet his gaze. "Let's go."

About an hour later, the three pulled up outside the First Methodist Church of Sevierville, Tennessee. She'd come along as a comfort to Betty, but Lillian realized as the car came to a stop that she was quite nervous as well.

"Do you want me to go with you?" she asked as Betty gripped the car door handle, gathering the strength to open it.

"No," said Betty immediately, but then she reconsidered. "Yes," she said with a nod. "Yes."

Lillian walked Betty to the door of the church, acutely aware of the crunch her feet made on the gravel. Betty knocked and then took Lillian's hand in her own, her pulse pounding through her palms.

The moment of stillness that followed seemed to last an eternity. A million thoughts raced through Lillian's head, and simultaneously not a single thought at all. Finally, there were footsteps inside the church, heading their way, and the door cracked open.

FIFTEEN

The pastor that opened the door was a tall, older man with a graying mustache and high cheekbones that lifted into a smile at the sight of Betty. He didn't have to say a word, nor did he get a chance to. Betty said, "He's here, isn't he?"

"Back in my office," said the pastor, but Betty had already taken off down the center aisle of the small sanctuary. She had almost reached the front of the church when a man emerged from a door off to the side. Betty stopped dead in her tracks to stare at him.

"You found me," he said.

"Are you a ghost?" she asked.

Martin shook his head. "I don't think so." This was proven quite true a few moments later, when Betty threw her arms around him and sobbed into his shirt.

Martin was desperately thin, his eyes sunken in and surrounded by dark circles, and when he spoke or smiled it was obvious he was missing most of his teeth. He did look a bit like a ghost, Lillian thought, but the more he held Betty in his arms as they settled in Pastor Brooks's office, the more he seemed to come back to life. Lillian fetched Andrew from the car, and Pastor Brooks made them all coffee, which Lillian felt too queasy to drink. She was thrilled that he was here, that he was alive, that Betty had found her Martin. But that joy came with a horrible pit in her stomach. It was all true.

"I know it must be painful for you to talk about what happened," Andrew began cautiously after they'd finished their introductions. "But I want you to know, myself and the other scientists in charge—we had no idea this was happening, and I'm going to do whatever I can to stop it. Any information you can give me would be helpful."

"I'm not sure you can stop it," said Martin. "Everyone there with me had died by the time I got out."

Lillian inhaled sharply, feeling the words like a punch to the stomach. If Andrew felt them, too, he didn't show it. "Can you start from the beginning?" he said. "Betty said you had an infected tooth…?"

Martin nodded. "I thought it would just fall out on its own," he said. "But Betty, she's a bit of a hypochondriac and it was making her nervous, so, fine, I said I'd go to the dentist. They told me I'd need to have it removed but I'd have to wait a week. She thought that was funny but I thought, it's fine, they're just busy, it's not a big deal. So I went back a week later, and the first thing they did was take me to a room and inject me with something. Didn't even ask, just—right in my vein. I asked what it was and they said don't worry about it, it was to help me relax. Then, boom, I was out."

Lillian nodded. "They gave that to me, too. I was asleep in seconds, it felt like."

"You're lucky you didn't wake up where I woke up." Martin shook his head. "They told me something had gone wrong with my surgery and that I was in a special part of the hospital clinic building for treatment, but I'm sure they were lying. What kind of hospital treatment locks its patients in their rooms? Besides, the other people there did not look like they had been receiving much treatment." He shuddered at the memory. "They gave us all something, every day. Some of the guys really did think it was medicine. One of them had stomach cancer, he said, and he thought they were giving him treatment for that. Different people got it different places…one in the arm, the other the foot, the man with cancer had to drink it. It was horrible. It made me sick to my stomach, dizzy, weak. But the others had it worse, it seemed. They started dying soon after I got there."

"How many?" asked Andrew.

"Five, when I got there," said Martin. "All but one dead by the time I escaped, but the last one…" He shook his head. "He wouldn't have made it by now."

"How did you get out?" asked Betty.

"It was partially just luck, I think," answered Martin. "They wanted to see if it would affect my teeth. I don't know if that's because I already had an infection or what. But I think they gave me less than some of the others got, since it was going in my gums. And it was horrible, don't get me wrong. My mouth began to rot, but they wouldn't even pull them out, just waited for them to fall out on their own. But I saw how sick and weak everyone else there was. So I let the doctors think I was going that way, too. I hoped I could use it to my advantage.

"I didn't have a plan or anything. Just one day as I was being taken to the bathroom, I saw an open door. I didn't think too much, or else I wouldn't have done it. I knocked over the lackey taking me and made a run for it. When I reached the fence, I climbed over it." He held out his hands, which were covered in cuts from the barbed wire. "I had so much adrenaline, I didn't even feel these. Until about thirty seconds later. Then I felt them."

Betty took his hands in hers and kissed them. "I tried to write here," she said. "It was the first place I thought to look. I didn't know the army made sure those letters never got here."

Martin shook his head. "Even if they had, I don't think I could have written you back without getting you in trouble. But I knew you'd be looking for me. Pastor Brooks let me stay in the parish house until you got here. We both knew you would get here."

Lillian gathered herself to ask the question she both did and didn't want to know the answer to. "Were there any women there? Perhaps one woman who looked like me?"

"Lillian's twin sister went missing, too," said Betty.

Martin shook his head. "No, I'm sorry," he said. "There weren't any women there at all."

She nodded, touching the pearls around her neck anxiously. "All right. Thank you," she managed to mumble, before making some excuse about needing air and heading outside.

It was afternoon now, and the sun was bright and hot. Lillian felt it beating down on her skin as she fought back tears. She tried to think rationally, like the scientist she was. This hypothesis had not led to Eleanor. What else, then, could she try? Surely this wasn't the only trail to be followed—surely, surely—

It was no use. It wasn't just that Eleanor didn't want to be found; she couldn't be.

Lillian wished, suddenly, that it had been her. That she had been the one who vanished, and Eleanor left behind. Eleanor had been the one everyone loved, the one whose face made Mother smile, the one whose fluttering eyelashes made boys trip over themselves. She would have married someone wonderful, started a family, had a good and long and happy life. That life, that legacy, would never be Lillian's. Who would care about Lillian's accomplishments, beyond a handful of other physicists? Who would even notice them? She'd never be loved as deeply as Eleanor had been loved. The life Eleanor would have led was gone, and Lillian—for all she'd pretended to be Eleanor, for all the hair she'd curled and the lipstick she'd applied and the dresses she'd zipped up—couldn't lead it.

Her knees buckled. She felt herself collapse on the stairs of the church, her head in her arms.

FEBRUARY 1945

Lunch with Janet Mayberry was delightfully uneventful, a turn of phrase that Lillian had never thought could be possible. Uneventful was boring, and boring was dreadful. But that had been Lillian's way of looking at the world, and she wasn't Lillian today.

While Lillian despised small talk, Lillian-as-Eleanor could dish about the weather for hours. As the conversation flowed between the safe, simple topics of Janet's stylish new boots and Eleanor's favorite recipes for vegetable soup, Lillian-as-Eleanor found she was having quite a bit of fun. Lillian would never order a glass of white wine at lunch; it never would have even occurred to her. But Eleanor and Eleanor's friends would order one just for fun, just to make a girls' lunch a bit more giggly, to make a gray winter day a bit easier to bear. It was quite amusing, she realized, to be a bit naughty just because she could get away with it.

Lillian was having such a ball that when their waiter came around to ask if the ladies would like another glass of wine, she wiggled her eyebrows at Janet suggestively. Janet laughed. "I can't, I have to get back to work!" she said.

"Oh gosh, I'd completely forgotten!" cried Lillian. "I was having so much fun!"

"Don't let me stop you," said Janet. "You should have one."

Lillian knew that even Eleanor would draw the line at drinking alone in the middle of the day. "No, no," she said with a wave of her hand. "We'll just take the check, please," she said to the waiter.

"Right away, miss," he said, adding a tiny wink before turning away.

As soon as he was out of earshot, Janet screeched. "He winked at you!"

"No, he did not," demurred Lillian, but she could still feel herself flush. Funny, she hadn't noticed before, but the waiter *was* quite handsome. He had black hair and large brown eyes, with just enough scruff on his chin to seem mysterious, but not so much he looked unkempt. Men had certainly winked at her before, but never one who was an actual romantic prospect.

"You think he's cute," said Janet, teasingly.

"Sure," admitted Lillian.

"You should stay and chat him up," Janet suggested.

Lillian was actually considering it—actually pondering sitting in a restaurant alone just to talk to a man who worked there—when Janet continued. "Oh, that's right, I forgot. You're seeing someone."

"Right." Lillian had nearly forgotten herself. The one stark downside to being Eleanor: Max Medelson.

"Well, if you ever find yourself single again, call me up. We can always come back," said Janet, grinning devilishly.

They split the check and departed the restaurant, arm in

arm once again. It had begun to snow, just a little bit—the perfect amount to flush their cheeks and make the street look like a snow globe. Lillian could have lingered in this afternoon forever, but Janet stopped in front of a brownstone just half a block later. "Well, back to real life," she said, rolling her eyes playfully. "It was so good to see you, Eleanor."

And just like that—with no one there to witness her—Lillian became Lillian once more, the street became gray, the snow became cold. She pulled her coat tight around her and shivered. Suddenly she was—suddenly she felt—quite alone.

She raised her hand for a taxi, but when one pulled up, she changed her mind and waved it off. It was true that Lillian had a lot of work to do today, but Lillian-as-Eleanor wasn't ready to go home, not yet. After such a wonderful afternoon, it would be wrong to leave it on a moment tinged with sadness, with emptiness.

She turned back.

As she returned to the restaurant's entrance, she was struck with a clever idea and tugged off one of her earrings as she pushed open the door. The lunch rush had ended, and the place was nearly empty. Her waiter lingered behind the bar, chatting with the bartender. She approached him without a second thought, just as Eleanor would have done.

"Excuse me," she said loudly, not even waiting for a break in their conversation.

The waiter looked at her, his annoyance at being interrupted melting quickly into a flirtatious smile. "You're back," he said.

"I think I lost an earring," she said, brushing back her hair to point to her bare right ear, making sure to extend her neck. Her neck, she'd been told by Mother, was one of her few pleasing features. "Did anyone happen to find it?"

"I'm sorry, I don't think so," he replied. "But I can help you take a look for it, if you'd like."

She smiled. "Thank you. How kind."

He stepped out from behind the bar and put a daring hand on Lillian's shoulder. Her skin tingled. "It's so warm in here. May I take your coat?" he said.

"Please," said Lillian, letting him slip the garment off her shoulders. The air between them seemed electric, every small gesture, every accidental touch full of meaning. He hung the coat on the back of one of the barstools, as if already inviting Lillian to stay for another drink.

Together, they examined the floor beneath the table where she and Janet had sat, coming up empty-handed as Lillian of course knew they would. "It must have come off on the street. Pity," she sighed as they finished their doomed hunt. "I really liked that set." She pushed back her hair on the left side of her face to show off the emerald cluster. It both matched the dress and made her usually muddy-brown eyes seem to sparkle green.

"I'm terribly sorry," said the waiter. "Maybe I can ease your pain with that second glass of wine."

Lillian smiled. "That would certainly help, I think," she said.

She settled in at the bar, and the waiter smiled as he opened a fresh bottle. "I've never seen you in here before," he said, pouring a glass and sliding it her direction.

"First time. My friend suggested it," said Lillian, eyeing the full glass. "You're not going to let me drink alone, are you?"

He grinned. "Wouldn't dream of it." After pouring a glass of his own, he raised it to Lillian's for a toast. "To trying something new."

"To trying something new." They clinked their glasses, and Lillian took a sip. It was exquisitely good, bright and light and dry.

"What's your name?" he asked.

"Eleanor," she replied. "And yours?"

"Dominic," he said.

"Pleasure to meet you, Dominic."

He winked again. "The pleasure's all mine."

They both took another sip from their glasses, Lillian admiring the way her refreshed lipstick left a bright-red lip print on the rim. For a stain, it was quite elegant.

"I bet you're wondering if I'm still here or if I've come back," said Dominic after a moment.

"I must admit, it crossed my mind," said Lillian. "I don't often get a chance to meet handsome men anymore."

Dominic grinned at the compliment. "I've come back," he said. "A little less of a man, I'm afraid."

Lillian had no idea what he could have meant by that, and worried for a moment that he could have lost his manhood in hand-to-hand combat. She blushed at the idea. Fortunately, Dominic dispelled this by coming around the bar and sitting on the stool next to Lillian. There, he raised his left pants leg to reveal a prosthetic foot.

"Oh, my," said Lillian, too taken aback to say much else. "I hadn't even noticed."

Dominic shrugged as he lowered the pant leg again. "It doesn't slow me down much," he said. "I can do everything any other man can do. Except fight in a war, apparently."

He paused, clearing his throat. "Eleanor, I hope this isn't too forward…" he began. She leaned in, her heart pounding. "But I'd love to take you out for dinner this evening."

She was so thrilled by the wine and the flirtation that it took her a moment to realize he had leaned in as well, and placed his hand on hers. "I would love that," she said.

"Eleanor?" shouted a voice, loud enough to be heard across the restaurant. Lillian looked toward the door.

Max Medelson was heading their way, quite quickly. And he looked pissed as all hell.

JULY 1945

Lillian didn't know how long she sat there outside the church, curled like a child, crying so many tears that she couldn't tell when she stopped. But eventually she heard the door open and close behind her, felt the presence of someone come out and sit on the steps next to her, not saying a word. She didn't look up. Soon the smell of cigarette smoke floated over to her.

She inhaled the scent deeply, felt it revive her a bit. She sat up, squinting in the bright sun, and looked at Andrew.

"Pastor Brooks invited us to stay for dinner," he said. "But we don't have to, if you'd rather just get back."

His eyes were full of sympathy, which Lillian couldn't stand. The cigarette dangled from his lips. She reached over and plucked it out.

"Do you want one?" he started to ask but didn't finish. Before she knew what she was doing, she was kissing him.

Her mind went completely blank. The cigarette dropped from her fingers onto the steps, unnoticed. She leaned in toward him, wrapped her arms around his neck. His hand pressed into the small of her back, heavy and strong. He tasted like tobacco and felt warm and safe. She thought of nothing but blank whiteness and the taste of him.

She could have stayed in that moment forever, but he pulled away after only a few seconds.

"Should I not have done that?" she asked.

He could barely look her in the eye as he exhaled shakily. "No," he said, but hastened to add, "I don't know."

With trembling fingers, he reached down for the cigarette that was still smoldering on the steps below. Dirt be damned, he lifted it to his mouth, inhaled, exhaled. "I've wanted to do that for...awhile," he finally said. "But it's complicated, of course, because of..."

She felt a pang of guilt for the unease she had caused in

him. "I know what you mean," she said. "And I wish it had been me, too. I wish it had been—but I—"

He looked to her, brow muddled in confusion. "What are you talking about?"

"I wish I were her," said Lillian. "I wish she were here, and I had died. I wish I could be her, for you, for me."

"Is that what you... Is that what you think of me?" He dropped the cigarette again, turning his whole body toward her. "That's not what I want. That's not why I can't... Oh god." He ran a hand through his already disheveled hair, throwing it even further askew. "I'm not a good person," he said finally.

"What does that mean?" asked Lillian.

"You don't want to know," he said. "Please, trust me. I'm not a good person to be around."

"And yet you keep me around."

He sighed. "Because I like you, and I'm selfish, and I always do what I damn well want to do. But I'm not good for you. And if you don't walk away from me..."

She considered this. Then she leaned in to kiss him again.

This time, their lips were only locked for a few desperate moments before he pulled away again. "What are you doing?" he said. "Are you even listening to me?"

"I'm perfectly capable of deciding who is good for me and who isn't on my own. I took what you had to say into consideration, but decided—"

"Lillian, for god's sake," he interrupted. There was

something in his eyes that she'd never noticed before, a glint of desperation that came from some deep place. He took a deep breath. "I hurt her. I hurt Eleanor."

Lillian didn't know what to make of this. "But she left you," she said. "She broke your heart."

"Because she found out how terrible I am," he replied. "Because she found out that I'm this—this monster…"

Lillian rolled her eyes. "Monster? For god's sake, what could you have done to be worth all that?"

"You really want to know?" he snapped.

"I do."

"Fine." He swallowed, looked away.

In the few empty seconds before he spoke again, Lillian's mind raced as she tried to imagine the possibilities. The options, she quickly deduced, were slim. In fact, there was really only *one* thing that was so desperately awful he would have hid it. And so she wasn't surprised when the words came out of his mouth to confirm it—wasn't surprised, but still went white-hot with anger and shame.

"I'm married."

SIXTEEN

Max stormed toward Lillian and Dominic, fury in his eyes.

Dominic yanked his hand away from hers. Without the weight on it, her skin felt cold and clammy. "Is that your—your—*husband?*" he spat, his voice quaking with either embarrassment or rage.

Lillian's mind raced as she tried to come up with some reasonable explanation in the precious few seconds before Max reached the bar. "No, he's—he's my twin sister's boyfriend. He must have me mistaken for her."

Dominic's face scrunched up in a disbelieving scowl. She couldn't blame him. She wouldn't buy the excuse if someone had given it to her.

It didn't help that Max had begun shouting the name which she'd just told Dominic belonged to her.

"Eleanor! What's going on here?" he demanded, looking between her and Dominic with disgust.

Dominic rose from his barstool. "And I suppose now you're going to tell me that your twin sister is *also* named Eleanor."

"I can explain, really," said Lillian, even though she couldn't. She cursed herself. Why hadn't she just given Dominic her real name? He didn't know that Lillian Kaufman was the name attached to a spinster, to a boring academic who preferred pressed white shirts and sensible shoes to slinky green dresses and emerald earrings. Why couldn't she have been Eleanor in personality and Lillian in name?

"Her twin is called Lillian," said Max, putting his hand on her shoulder possessively. The weight of it wasn't warm and electric like Dominic's had been, it was cold and dead like a fish. "Did she tell you she was Lillian?"

The whole situation was absurd, like something out of a Noël Coward play, or older, even—it was positively Shakespearean. Lillian would have laughed if her heart weren't pounding in fear. How could she explain to these men that claiming her name was Eleanor, even around someone who didn't know the difference at all, made her feel different? Better? That being Eleanor Kaufman gave her a confidence, a posture, that Lillian Kaufman could never have?

Dominic shook his head. "She told me she was Eleanor," he said. "I didn't know she had a husband."

"Let's go," said Max, grabbing Lillian's hand and practically dragging her from the stool. She stumbled forward, the force of Max's hand tight around her wrist the only thing keeping her from falling face-forward onto the carpeting.

She tried in vain to yank her arm away. "Let go of me," she demanded, her voice straining as her panic rose. "Max. Let me go."

No one paid them any mind as he dragged her from the restaurant, other than a few points and whispers. "Just caught his wife flirting with a waiter," Lillian heard one old lady mutter to a friend, which compelled Lillian to shout, "I am *not* his wife." It was useless. No one cared about her side of the story.

She was nearly out of breath, and on the edge of tears, when they emerged onto the street. God, she was so stupid. How could she have thought that pretending to be Eleanor would end any way but badly? Hadn't she almost ruined everything the last time she'd tried this, when she'd taken that message from Janet? What was wrong with her? She could never explain this to her sister. Eleanor would never understand that Lillian had pretended to be her to have a one-night stand with a waiter. No one in their right mind would. She didn't even understand it herself.

Even worse, she thought grimly, it had probably been her last shot. Young men weren't exactly in high supply at the moment, and when the war did end, the ones that remained would marry off quickly to the ones prettier than her, the quiet, polite girls who wanted families and didn't give one damn about quantum mechanics.

She was abnormal, different, some sort of unlovable, unwanted freak—and the thought made hot tears pour over the edge of her eyes and down her cheeks. She tried to wipe them away only to find that Max now had a hand grasped tightly around both of her wrists.

His rage hadn't gone away, but had focused itself into a white-hot pinpoint, all its energy directed at her. "Explain this to me," he muttered, his voice quiet and threatening and low.

She took a deep, steadying breath, trying to make herself sound as calm and believable as possible. "I'm not Eleanor," she whispered. "I'm Lillian. Please, you can't tell Eleanor about this. She can't ever know."

Max exhaled a forceful gust of hot air, right onto her face. "I know who you are. I can tell you two apart," he said. "Remember?"

She could remember Max claiming such a thing, but what was he saying now? That he'd known from the start she was Lillian? That he'd dragged her out of there—why? For the pure humiliation?

"What do you want from me?" she asked.

"An explanation."

"I don't have one." Her cheeks burned bright red.

"Of course you do. You want to be her so badly. You're so jealous of her, so obsessed with her."

"I don't. I'm not." The words sounded pleading, false.

"What are you jealous of? Huh?" Max's eyes glinted.

"It's not that." The more she denied it, the more desperate she sounded.

"Is it me?" Max continued. "Is it me you want so badly?"

"No," said Lillian. "You're her boyfriend. I would never—"

Before she could finish the thought, Max was kissing her.

She nearly gagged, reflexively. *Max Medelson has his lips on me* was a truly repulsive thought. Sensing her tense up, he pulled away. "No?" he said.

And suddenly, Lillian realized, her lips felt so cold without him near them. So without much thinking about it—at least, that's how it felt, in the moment—Lillian leaned in and kissed her sister's boyfriend.

She was immediately revolted at her own action, but revulsion was quickly replaced with enjoyment of the reality of it. Max, it turned out, was an exceptional kisser. That was an objective fact, one she could observe and note while still despising him as a person. Their embrace quickly elevated to a level of passion that she'd never witnessed between Max and the real Eleanor. Maybe it was the wine going to her head, but she enjoyed the way he seemed to hunger for her.

Her heart began to pound. What on earth was she doing? She pulled away, but—for reasons that escaped her—stayed in his arms.

"So it is me," he murmured, brushing away the snowflakes that had accumulated from her hair.

"It is you," she found herself saying. It was absolutely

untrue, and yet it had passed through her lips without a second thought. She kissed him again, marveling at how much easier it was to tolerate him when he wasn't talking.

"Let's go," said Max, pulling away, breathless. He nuzzled his nose against Lillian's cheek. "Let's go back to my place."

Her head was so, so cloudy, but she still knew what her answer should be. *I would never.* She tried to will her mouth to form the words. *You're scum for even suggesting it.*

Instead, Lillian nodded, allowing Max to take her hand and usher her into a taxi. Eleanor would never find out, she reasoned. Max certainly wouldn't be telling her.

She let him run his fingers up her legs in the back of the cab, letting the idea that it felt good push out the thought that it was wrong. No—it *wasn't* wrong. Max and Eleanor were as good as over. He was off to Tennessee in a matter of days—his apartment, when they reached it, was all suitcases and boxes. Eleanor would be off to Chicago, would forget about this dreadful, cheating man soon enough. She'd never have to know, thought Lillian, and what she wouldn't ever know couldn't possibly hurt her. And besides, it might be—it was shaping up to be—Lillian's only chance at an experience so basic, so fundamentally human. Wouldn't Eleanor have *wanted* her to have that?

And so Lillian let Max Medelson lead her into his bedroom and close the blinds. And if she felt any guilt when he accidentally moaned her sister's name instead of her own, she pushed it down into some dark, unexamined place and let it rot.

SEVENTEEN

JULY 1945

Lillian bid farewell to Betty in a daze. She longed to take her friend aside and tell her what she'd just learned about Andrew, but even if they'd had the time, she knew that Betty quite understandably would no longer care. Oak Ridge's problems, the secrets and lies of its residents, were far behind her now. Lillian hugged Betty tightly in what they knew but didn't want to admit was goodbye forever, then opened the door to the station wagon and settled inside.

Andrew hadn't met her gaze all through dinner, and he didn't now. "Ready?" he asked, looking steadfastly out the windshield. Lilian said nothing. Eventually he figured out she wouldn't be answering and provided his own response. "Right." The engine lurched to a start.

They drove in silence, the sun burning their eyes as it

slowly set ahead of them. Lillian had a million things to say and nothing to say at all. She was so lost in her own thoughts that she hardly noticed when Andrew pulled to the side of the road and shut off the car. "Let's go," he said.

"Go where?" she asked.

"Back through the fence," came the answer.

She'd completely forgotten she would need to reenter Oak Ridge through the damned hole in the fence. Trudging through the woods was the last thing she wanted to do at the moment, but she didn't have much of a choice. At least it would give her a chance to be out of this miserable car, away from him. "Don't bother picking me up on the other side," she said as she climbed out of the vehicle. "I'll make it back to the dormitory on my own."

"Don't be absurd," Andrew replied, exiting the car himself and heading for its trunk. "I'm coming with you."

Lillian stopped, stunned into silence. "No," was all she could manage.

"Yes," he said. He popped the trunk, reached inside for a silver-handled flashlight. "It's about to get dark. I'm not letting you wander through the woods alone."

"But the car," she protested lamely.

"I'll go with you, and then come back on my own for the car."

She snorted. How very *kind*. "Where was this chivalry when you were using my sister as your whore?"

He sighed. "I'm not letting you go alone. It's dangerous."

"I'm going on my own, whether you approve of it or not."

"And I'm following you, whether *you* approve of it or not." He slammed the trunk shut. "So, are you going to do this easy way, or the difficult way?"

"What do you think?" said Lillian, turning on her heel and heading across the road toward the woods.

Andrew groaned and trotted after her. "It'll be dark soon. You could at least take the flashlight."

"I'm not taking anything from you."

"Just because you're a bit upset doesn't mean there's any reason to be impractical."

She hated that this point made a bit of sense, hated him for being right. She stopped in her tracks and whirled around. "I am not *a bit upset.* I've never been angrier at someone in my life. You lied to my sister. You lied to…" She let her voice trail off momentarily, not wanting to say the words *to me.* "You lied to everyone."

"I told you, I'm not a good person. I've never pretended to be otherwise."

"As if that makes it any better, that you *never pretended to be otherwise!* My god." Her fingernails dug into her palms. "And the worst of it is, you are. That's why it's so awful. You are a good person, and you *know* that. You've helped me, you've helped Betty. You're smart and I've seen the way you've poured every-thing into this project. That's not what a bad person does, pour their whole self into something that way. So don't give me this nonsense about how you had no choice and you're tragic and flawed and broken. You're not. You made a choice. You lied to her."

Andrew merely stood there, absorbing Lillian's tirade, not saying a word. She turned around in frustration and headed for the woods once again.

He followed. *Fine, let him,* thought Lillian. She would pay him no mind.

They trekked further, the woods growing thicker around them. The sun seemed to slip below the horizon all at once, leaving them in near darkness quite quickly. Andrew clicked on the flashlight behind her—the little circle of light bobbed about at her feet. Still, she said nothing.

"Are you sure you don't want to carry this?" he said finally. "Especially if you insist on walking in front of me?"

"Please shut up about the flashlight," she snapped in response.

"Look, I didn't mean to lie," he said. "To her, to you... I didn't mean to lie."

She almost laughed, it was so absurd. "Oh, so you just forgot you had a wife, then?"

"I didn't tell anyone," he answered bitterly. "No one at Oak Ridge knows."

"So you lied to *all* the women you wanted to sleep with, and not just my sister. How charming."

He sighed in exasperation. "I didn't lie intentionally. I just didn't bring it up." He paused. Lillian could sense his hesitation to continue, but refused to let it soften her. "My wife and I haven't spoken in years," he added eventually.

"Is that because you cheat on her?" snarled Lillian.

He didn't answer. Suddenly the white light bobbing at her feet came to a halt, and she realized he'd stopped a few paces back. "What's wrong?" she asked, reluctantly stopping as well. As much as she hated to admit it, she was starting to rely on the small white circle.

"I need a cigarette," he said. "Hold on." She could hear him patting at his pockets. "I don't have my case. I must have left it—fuck." He started walking again, abruptly, and Lillian hurried to stay in front of him.

"Why haven't you spoken to your wife in years?" she asked after a few seconds of silence.

"Well, she lives with another man in a ranch house in Pasadena, so it's difficult," he snapped.

Lillian didn't know how to respond to that. "Oh."

"She left me for my best friend at Caltech. And that's the whole story."

She blinked. "I'm sorry," she said lamely, not really meaning it.

"No, you're not. I suppose you think it's what I deserve."

"Why don't you divorce her?" she asked.

"A divorce, gee, why didn't I think of that?" he replied sarcastically. "We're Catholic. We don't divorce. We shove all our problems inside and try to pretend they don't exist until one day, hopefully, we die." He took a deep, angry breath. "I need a cigarette. Do you have one?"

"I don't smoke," she reminded him.

He muttered some unintelligible curse.

"What's her name?" Lillian asked.

She heard him huff, fuming quietly behind her. "Does it matter?"

"It likely matters to her."

"My apologies," he grumbled. "It's hard for me to have much sympathy, given that she got a goddamn ranch house and my life was ruined."

"Ruined?" scoffed Lillian. "You seem to be doing just fine."

"Fine. That's exactly how I'm doing. *Fine*. It took three brutal years to get to *fine*," he said. "Everyone knew, Lillian. All my classmates, my future colleagues, *everyone*. I was the last... I was the last to know. The last person to find out. It was all the gossip at Caltech, 'Hear what's happening to Ennis? His life is about to explode underneath him and he has no idea.' Do you know how many rooms I've walked into that have instantly gone quiet? So yes, when I came to Oak Ridge, it was a new place where no one knew me and so I didn't bring it up. I didn't think about how it might hurt someone else. I only thought about how—how nice it felt for me."

Lillian was quiet, trying desperately not to think about the time she had made a similar choice.

They continued in silence for a moment, the only sound the river babbling up ahead. Then Andrew said softly, "Her name is Kathleen." Speaking the name seemed to break his heart.

"Kathleen," Lillian repeated. She wondered what Kathleen looked like, how she and Andrew had met.

"I never thought I'd meet someone I would care about enough for it to matter." There was a hitch in his voice. After a moment he added, "And then after I lost Eleanor, I didn't think I'd meet someone else."

"I don't think I care for that statement," she replied under her breath.

"Lillian, you kissed me."

She was surprised to think that had only been a few hours ago. It felt like an eternity. "I wasn't in my right mind. I was upset."

"I'm upset a lot, but it never ends with me kissing someone I wouldn't have kissed otherwise."

"Well, it has for me," she said.

"What about on the roof? You almost kissed me that night on the roof, didn't you?"

Why were they talking about this? "But I didn't."

"But you almost did."

"Fine," said Lillian. "I kissed you, I almost kissed you, and then I kissed you. Not because I needed you or I wanted you, but because I knew you would kiss me back. I know you want me because I remind you of her. I've heard all your slipups, the times you accidentally call me by her name. Not two minutes ago you forgot that she's the one who smokes, not me. Normally, it hurts, knowing someone only cares about you because of who you remind them of, but today I didn't care. I wanted to be wanted and I didn't care what the reason was, so I kissed you."

Andrew again went quiet. "That's not why I want you," he said finally, so softly she could barely hear him over the sound of the river and wind rustling through the trees.

"I'm not stupid," she replied, under her breath. "And I'm not upset about it. Not anymore, at least. I understand it. It's not right or wrong; it's just the way things are. I'm your second chance with her."

"That's not why I want you," he repeated. "You're nothing like her."

"I recognize that I'm an inferior choice, but better than nothing at all."

He practically chuckled. "Inferior? You're not inferior. Is that what you think?"

"No," Lillian admitted. "But everyone else says so. Eleanor is sweet and willing to pretend that boring things are interesting and likes to go dancing and drink white wine during the day but never too much of it, and those are the sorts of traits that people admire."

"Well, I'm not sweet," began Andrew. "And I hate white wine. I do like to go dancing, but it's not the end of my interests. And if you ever pretended I was being interesting when I was in fact being boring, I'd be pissed as all hell. Lillian, I care about you for no reason other than who you are."

She crossed her arms. "But you lied to me."

"Yes," he said. "I did." He paused before stopping in his tracks. "How would you like to punish me?" he asked. With a sigh, Lillian turned around to face him and found he was holding the flashlight out to her. "Would you like to take this and beat me over the head with it?"

"Stop," she said.

"Or if that's too unpleasant for you, would you like me to beat myself with it? I don't know if I can do that, but if all else fails, I can go to the river and drown myself."

"You're not funny."

"I'm not laughing," he said. "I don't like living with what I've done, and you don't like me living at all. We both get what we want."

"That's not what I want," she said.

"Then what do you want, Lillian?" He asked it gently, his voice cracking. She could see even in the darkness his round eyes, his disheveled hair. "Because I'll do it. That's how much I care about you. Whatever can be done, whatever I can do to prove myself to you again, name it."

She tried to run the various scenarios in her head, tried to rationalize one outcome against another, but her mind was far too jumbled. She took a step toward him. "What do *you* want, Andrew?"

"Have I not made that clear?" he answered. "I want you. I want you, Lillian."

She'd never heard the words before, never thought she would. Gabe had wanted anyone, wanted comfort, and she had been the warm body he'd stumbled upon that night. Max had claimed to want her but only as a shameful secret. He had never pursued her until he had her caught in a lie. He would never have chosen her—he couldn't even bring himself to say her name. She hadn't wanted to admit how much that had stung, tried to forget about the tears she'd cried in the taxi on her way home. Everyone else in the world, it had seemed, was wanted—there was something terribly, terribly wrong with her—

She closed the space between her and Andrew with a few short steps, and he understood immediately. There was no gentle brush, no sweet embrace. Their lips locked eagerly, or maybe it was angrily—Lillian couldn't quite tell. Instead of her mind going blank, it went white-hot. She wanted to touch him, wanted him to touch her.

He pulled away but not in regret. "Over here," he said, taking Lillian's hand and leading her off to their left, toward the sound of the river. Only a few yards further, the trees fell away and were replaced by long, green grass. The ground beneath them slopped down to the river, which cut through the earth like a gash in a piece of fabric.

Andrew turned off the flashlight and dropped it to the ground with a dull thud, then wrapped his arms around her and lowered her to the ground as well. Her fingers wove through the soft grass, clutching at it as Andrew kissed the soft, sensitive spot of skin just below her ear. He made his way lower and lower, pausing to unbutton the top of her navy button-up blouse. He inhaled deeply at the sight of her exposed skin. Lillian looked to find she was nearly glowing in the moonlight.

"You are so beautiful," he murmured, and for the first time in her life, she agreed.

With Gabe, she'd been quite concerned about seeming too eager or not eager enough, but no such thoughts filled her head now. She sat up and reached for the buttons on his shirt. He eagerly helped, pulling it off with a few quick motions, exposing the hair on his chest above his white undershirt, the lines of the muscles in his arms. Max had been so hairless and bland that she almost started to laugh in surprise. She reached out to pull him close to her again.

Then she heard it: a cracking noise, not unlike the one she'd heard when she had last gone into the woods, alone during the dance.

They looked at each other: *Did you hear that, too?*

"Someone's here," she whispered.

Andrew pulled away, reaching for his discarded shirt. "Stay here," he whispered back. "Keep low, and stay quiet. Don't be seen."

He stood and crept forward in the dark, grabbing the flashlight but keeping it off. Lillian searched the grass for her own shirt and pulled it over her shoulders as best she could while keeping low to the ground. She tried to smooth her hair and, as she did, noticed that one of her earrings had slipped off. She patted the grass around her, trying to feel for any metal, to no avail.

Suddenly, she heard a startled scream. To her surprise, the voice belonged to a woman. Earring forgotten, Lillian dropped flat in the grass. Ahead of her by only a few yards, Andrew clicked on the flashlight, illuminating an older man in a disheveled army uniform. "The hell, Ennis!" the man shouted.

Lillian strained to look at him, but saw nothing she recognized. Had this been the man that had followed her last time? Was the army on to her all along?

Andrew brought his free hand to his head, laughing. "Oh, this is too good."

"Fuck you." The man charged toward Andrew. Lillian held in a gasp as Andrew shoved him backwards. The man stumbled back into the grass, his hands on his knees, breathing heavily.

"Fuck you, Walter," Andrew spat back. "After the shit you gave me…! I can't believe this."

"The shit you deserved!" Walter stumbled toward Andrew again. Again, Andrew shoved him down.

"Walter!" shouted the woman, still unseen somewhere in the weeds.

"Get out of here," Walter shouted back at her. "I've gotta take care of something." The woman started to protest, but

Walter shouted again, "Get the fuck out of here!" Lillian heard the woman stumble off into the darkness.

Walter squared his shoulders toward Andrew. "Where is she?"

"What?"

"Who are you here with?"

Lillian snapped her head down, lying as flat as possible, barely even breathing.

"I'm not here with anyone," said Andrew.

"Fuck you," replied Walter. "Where is she?"

He must have tried to push past Andrew a third time— Lillian heard someone fall into the grass. Walter shouted, "I'm just doing my job here."

"Oh, is that what you're doing, out here with your secretary? Your job?" snarled Andrew. "Just going over the calendar, were you?"

"My job is to protect this place," Walter shouted back. "Your inability to keep your pants zipped makes that difficult for me."

"Of the two of us, I'm the one with my pants zipped."

"But I'm not the one with the *nuclear secrets*!" cried Walter. "Every time you bring a girl out here, you compromise our project! Do you get that?" The smell of tobacco wafted over toward Lillian. Walter must have lit a cigarette. She heard Andrew inhale the scent eagerly. "Your *situation* makes you uniquely positioned to be blackmailed—"

"For god's sake, I'm not a spy."

"Don't piss me off, Ennis," said Walter. "You may be some

young hotshot, but I could get you booted from here in a second. I bet your bosses out there would love to know how reckless you are."

"I bet they'd also love to know that you've been testing radioactive materials on human subjects," Andrew snapped back.

Lillian saw something out of the corner of her eye: a glint of metal. Her earring. Terrified of leaving any trace, she tried to scoot over to retrieve it without rustling the grass.

Walter laughed. "You didn't know about that?"

"I know now."

"Well shit, Ennis. Guess you're not as important to them as you thought you were."

"What does that mean?"

Lillian's fingers found the object, and she was surprised to find—for something that had fallen from her ear only moments earlier—it was nearly entirely buried in the dirt.

Walter continued to mutter at Andrew in a low, threatening voice as Lillian pried the object free from the ground. It wasn't her earring at all, she realized—it was much smaller, a thin oval, not much longer than a kidney bean. Her heart began to pound in her head. The noises of Walter and Andrew arguing, the river rushing nearby, everything faded away. In her hand was a clasp, a thin diamond-adorned fishhook clasp that remained fastened, although there was no longer a necklace attached to its ends. She drew it closer, studied it. Two broken threads dangled from each side, as if it had been yanked off someone quite violently.

She would have recognized it anywhere, instantly. It was identical to the clasp on the string of pearls Lillian wore around her neck.

Any instinct to stay silent and hidden flew from her mind, which pounded sharply with a sudden migraine. The night seemed to close in on her, darkness creeping so only a pinpoint of the world was still visible, a tiny circle of light glinting from the clasp in her hand. She stumbled to her feet.

"Who's that?" she heard Walter shout. The anger in his voice brought her present danger into sharp focus again. He stomped past Andrew, shoving him aside, toward Lillian.

She stood frozen. All she could do was close her palm around the clasp tightly, pressing it into her flesh. Walter's eyes widened as he got closer, as she came into his view. "You son of a bitch," he said, turning back to Andrew, who was clambering to his feet. "Is that...her *twin?*"

Lillian unfroze with a start. Then she ran.

She wasn't sure what direction she was going: to the road? To the fence? It didn't matter. She just had to survive this, just had to find some place to stay out of sight, just had to keep running.

The man who chased her knew she was not Eleanor.

The man who chased her knew there was no way she could be Eleanor.

He knew Eleanor was dead, knew it with certainty, knew it as if he'd done it himself.

Somehow, she didn't fall. It was pitch-black, the ground uneven underneath her, and even so her feet remained sure. It didn't matter. He caught up anyway.

Grabbing at her arm, he pulled her down. She screamed, half out of fright and half because the force was so painful, it felt as if her shoulder had been wrenched out of its socket.

He wrestled her to the ground, pinning her. "Who are you?" he shouted. "What are you doing here?"

She said nothing—she would say nothing to this monster who had killed her sister. Although her throat was dry with exhaustion and fright, she dug deep into her stomach and found the moisture to heave a ball of spit directly at his face.

"You little bitch!" he cried out, tightening his grip around her arms.

It was only a heartbeat later that Andrew appeared, tall above Walter. With his left hand he grabbed Walter by the shoulder. Walter only gripped Lillian's wrists tighter. She cried out in pain again, feeling the blood vessels popping in her forearms. Her fingers began to go numb.

Then Andrew raised his right arm and brought the handle of his silver flashlight down into Walter's skull.

EIGHTEEN

FEBRUARY 1945

Max lay next to her afterward, his head buried in the small of her neck. His breath was annoyingly heavy, blowing the same strand of hair back and forth across her face. She wondered how long she was required by politeness to lie here before she could extricate herself. She desperately had to pee, and by now what was supposed to be a lunch outing had stretched until sundown. She'd have to put in dreadful hours at the lab over the next few days in order to make up for the lost time.

Part of her was proud. She'd done it, at last. She still didn't quite understand what all the fuss was about, but at least now she was approaching the conversation from an informed point of view. She was glad to have the experience, as it was so unlike any other. Nothing could have prepared her for it; there was nothing to compare it to.

But another part of her felt...*ashamed* wasn't exactly the right word, but *ashamed* seemed less severe than *guilty*, and she had no reason to feel guilty. It didn't quite count, what she'd done, not enough to feel guilt over. Eleanor and Max's relationship was headed for the grave. Max was to leave for Tennessee in a few days. Eleanor would forget about him soon enough. And yet Lillian's stomach still churned. *It was all for science,* she reassured herself. *Just an experiment. To see what it was it was like.*

She only lay there for a second or two more before pushing Max's arm off her and sliding out of the bed. He didn't even wake up as she finally relieved herself and pulled the green dress back on. She left the apartment, paying attention to her body as she moved down the steps and onto the street, trying to ascertain if she felt any different physically. It was a bit disappointing, she had to admit, when she realized she didn't.

JULY 1945

Lillian found packing for the trip difficult. None of her clothes seemed right for the occasion, which was complicated by not knowing exactly what the occasion would be or how long she would be away for. They would watch the test, yes—but how long would that take? An hour? What did one wear to a test of a new army weapon? And what would she wear for the rest of her time there? She had plenty of white shirts and professional skirts, but hardly anything for the evenings.

The door to the dormitory creaked open. Lillian did not bother to look up.

"Eleanor?" came Emmy's timid squeak. The death of an important army official in the woods (and Dr. Ennis and Eleanor Kaufman's involvement in it) had been the latest gossip around Oak Ridge, and ever since, Lillian's roommate had spoken to her so delicately, like she was a flower that might snap in half at too strong a breeze. Lillian despised this treatment. She did not answer Emmy's greeting, as she saw no need to do so. Emmy could see for herself that she was in the room, and if she had further inquiries beyond that, she was free to voice them.

"Eleanor?" Emmy repeated. "There's someone here to see you."

Again, Lillian did not look up. She hated the sound of her sister's name now. *Eleanor's dead,* she wanted to say.

A male voice cleared his throat. "Do you mind if Eleanor and I talk alone, Emmy?"

Lillian refused to give him the satisfaction of letting *that* voice startle her into paying attention. She rolled her eyes and continued her packing as Emmy acquiesced and scuttled from the room, pulling the door shut behind her.

Max watched her fold shirts in silence. She wondered how long he could keep it up, how long he could go without talking. She could fold shirts happily for hours—but there was not a doubt in her mind that he would break first.

Sure enough, not even one minute later, he coughed a bit, then asked, "So you really are leaving, then?"

"This is the women's dormitory. You're not supposed to be here." She would certainly not be having a heart-to-heart with Max Medelson.

"Is it true that when they asked why he did it, Andrew answered, 'I needed a cigarette'?"

That got Lillian's attention, which of course had been Max's intent. Angry it had worked, she let the pair of boots in her hand thud to the floor. "What if it were?"

"I'd believe it. It's a good line." Max sucked on his teeth to emphasize his point. "Clever and cruel, just like him."

Admittedly, Lillian had wondered if the night would have escalated the way it did if all parties involved had access to a cigarette and a nip of whiskey. But that was hardly the point. As far as she (and an official army commission) was concerned, Andrew had acted entirely in self-defense when he killed the Oak Ridge head of security in the dark woods.

"So what did happen, then?" asked Max.

It appeared that she wouldn't be rid of him without a bit of gossip he could take back to the boys in Building E. With a sigh, she launched into the spiel she'd been compelled to deliver to every person she'd come across in the last few days. "Andrew caught Walter by the river with a woman who was not Walter's wife." Walter. She'd learned so much about Walter the past seventy-two hours. How he'd seemed to have had it out for Andrew from the moment he arrived at Oak Ridge. Always monitoring the younger man's movements, showing up at his office in the middle of the night to interrogate him, desperate to prove Andrew was some kind of spy. "Walter tried to kill us both to keep us quiet." Of course, this was not the entire truth, but she and Andrew had decided that informing the army of her real identity would put her in undue jeopardy, not to mention would likely take her away from the project at a critical time.

Max responded with a sarcastic little clap. "Wow, you've got that story down," he said. "It almost sounds believable."

She hated that he saw through her, but she wouldn't be telling him the truth. Besides, what made Max believe he was entitled to her honesty? "It was awful, and scary, and I don't appreciate being made to discuss it," she said. That part was quite true, at least.

"You left out what you were doing down by the river with Andrew in the first place," Max pointed out.

"None of your business," Lillian said.

"Don't be upset with me for asking an innocent question. I'm just trying to get to the bottom of things before you run off to god-knows-where with a dangerous man."

"He's not dangerous." She had to grip the edge of the bed momentarily to keep her voice from getting loud and defensive. "He saved my life."

"I know you don't want to hear this, but Andrew—"

"Don't start," said Lillian.

"Listen to me—" Max insisted.

She cut him off. "Why? You're running a biased experiment. You have been from day one. You want him to be a bad guy. You'd love nothing more than to see the man who 'stole' my sister away from you punished. To prove once and for all that you're better than him, I suppose."

"We know he's violent," Max persisted. "He's arrogant, a hothead. And now with this business in the woods? He's proven himself capable of murder."

"Fine. You want the truth?"

"I think I've made it clear that's what I want, yes," said Max.

Lillian lowered her voice. "It was Walter. Walter killed her, and that's why he was coming after me. Eleanor's dead. That's the truth and that's the end of it."

His eyes were so wide she wondered for a moment if she'd been too harsh, sharing the horrible news this way—but if she could handle it, so could he. He recovered quickly, his adversarial tone returning. "Why?" he said finally. "Why would Walter kill—? Eleanor wasn't involved in anything bad. She wouldn't have been in trouble with the head of security—"

"I know it's what happened. Does it matter why?" she asked.

"Of course it does," he responded. "We might not have the whole story."

It had all made perfect sense to Andrew, when she told him about finding the clasp to Eleanor's necklace in the woods. Walter must have taken Eleanor out to the woods to frighten her into giving a confession. To scare her into agreeing that Andrew was the spy Walter wanted him to be. Whether her death was an accident or a consequence, they'd probably never know. As army head of security, Andrew pointed out, Walter had the power to keep whatever he wanted from the official files.

"Sometimes you don't get the whole story," she said.

Max threw up his hands in disbelief. "So you think we should just stop trying?"

She looked at him, hardly believing this man—after everything he had done with Lillian—was claiming the moral high ground. "It's an imperfect world, Max. I thought you would know that."

He studied her for a moment, then shook his head. "You don't sound like yourself," he said. "You don't sound like the Lillian I knew, outside of this place. Andrew's got you eating out of his hand."

"Grow up. Eleanor rejected you for Andrew, and she was right to do so. That doesn't make him a murderer."

"He's feeding you lies and got you lying on his behalf. You are walking into a lion's den with this man and insisting it's full of kitty cats!"

"Please lower your voice," said Lillian calmly. "The walls here are thin."

Max sighed. "Did I love her? Yes. Does that affect what I think of Andrew? Perhaps. I don't know. But even if it does, I'm not the only one here guilty of letting love change how I see Andrew." He paused to look at her and shake his head one more time. "I hope he's worth it."

"He's more worth it than you were," said Lillian.

"What was that?" Max shot back.

She shook her head. It wasn't worth getting into that with Max, not anymore. "You should go."

Instead of leaving, Max began to plead. "Please don't leave with Andrew. Wherever he's taking you, please don't go."

"Are you jealous of that, too? I got invited to the big test and you didn't?"

"No," he said, his voice cracking. "I'm worried you're going to go and not come back."

The pain in his voice surprised her. She looked at him and realized he was holding something out toward her. "If you insist on going, please. Take this," he said.

It was his pocketknife, the one she'd seen him use countless times at Columbia carving his stupid woodwork. The sight of it took her far away. Max had held it in his hand the day he'd met Eleanor, the day Lillian first saw them across the quad. Even then, she'd known he would bring nothing but trouble into her and Eleanor's lives. She stared at the knife in his outstretched hand. "I don't need that," she said. It was small, almost pathetically so—more useful for opening mail than it would be in any sort of self-defense. A butter knife would be just as dangerous.

"Just take it? Please?" he insisted.

It was easier to acquiesce than to argue any longer. She took the pocketknife, which was cool and surprisingly heavy in her hands. "Good luck, Lillian," he said, before turning away and heading for the door.

Something caught his eyes, and he stopped. "Was that there?"

He pointed at the wooden cat, which Lillian had found in the bottom of one of Eleanor's drawers. She'd placed it on top of the dresser, not bothering to hide it away. "Was that there?" he asked again, his tone crushingly hopeful. "When you got here? Did Eleanor keep that out, in her room?"

"No, I found it in a drawer and put it out myself," she replied. "Always had a thing for kitty cats."

Lillian hadn't the slightest idea what to do with Max's pocketknife. She had no use for it and no reason to take it with her, but it didn't feel right just leaving an abandoned knife in a nearly empty drawer for anyone to find and become suspicious over. Eventually she gave up looking for somewhere to stash it, and slipped it into the zipper compartment on the top of her suitcase. The outline of it stuck out in a defiant little lump.

Finally packed and believing she had a moment to herself, Lillian sank onto the bed and closed her eyes. For a happy moment, it was dark and quiet, and she thought about nothing.

"Are you leaving tonight?"

Lillian's eyes fluttered open. Emmy was standing in front of her, looking nervously down at the closed suitcase.

"Tomorrow morning," Lillian replied. "The airplane takes off right at dawn."

"My goodness, an airplane," said Emmy. "You must be going far."

If she was trying indirectly to ask where Lillian would be going, it wasn't going to work, both because Lillian wasn't in the mood for a chat and because she didn't technically know herself. She allowed the silence to hang in the air as Emmy's right middle finger curled over to pick at the skin around her thumb. The hollow snapping noise it made with each flick made Lillian rather nauseous. "I'll miss you, you know," Emmy went on eventually. "It won't be the same without you."

Lillian knew the polite thing would be to respond how she would miss Emmy as well, but it would have been a lie, so she said nothing.

Emmy went on. "I was thinking"—*snap, snap, snap* went the skin around her thumb—"there's something I ought to tell you."

"What is it?" asked Lillian.

Swallowing, Emmy nervously began, "I..." But her voice trailed off.

Lillian rolled her eyes. "What?" she asked again.

"I...reported on you," said Emmy finally. "I thought you might be a spy."

Lillian had once been quite concerned about this, she recalled. Worried that someone at Oak Ridge was following her, fearful her roommate was keeping too close an eye on her. How little any of that mattered now. She'd figured out what she came to figure out. Eleanor was dead. Anything that might happen to Lillian now would at least be less severe than that. "That's all right," said Lillian with a shrug. "I'm sure you had your reasons."

"I'm worried I might have put you in danger," said Emmy. "If that man in the woods if he was there to look for you—if all this happened because of me—"

"Emmy," Lillian said, putting her hand up. "Please drop it."

"I can't," said Emmy. "I know you weren't doing anything wrong in those woods, but you were still pulled into something so awful." She paused. "You weren't doing anything wrong, were you?"

Lillian sighed. "It's all over. It doesn't matter now."

"Are you sure it's over?" said Emmy. *Snap, snap, snap.* "Because if you weren't doing anything wrong, and I set this man on you when you were innocent—I would just feel awful about the whole thing."

"Yes," interrupted Lillian. "I'm quite sure. It's all over now."

NINETEEN

After the humidity of Tennessee, stepping off the plane in New Mexico was a welcome relief. Lillian breathed in the dry air with joy, realizing for the first time how much pressure the constant humidity had been putting on her sinuses. She tilted her face to the sun, feeling its exquisite warmth on her. It was intoxicating.

"Look at that," breathed Andrew, gazing out over the horizon. Nothing but desert stretched back as far as the eye could see.

"Look at what?" asked Lillian, shielding her eyes to gaze far into the distance. "I don't see anything."

"Precisely," replied Andrew.

Lillian did her best to smooth out her skirt, which was severely wrinkled from several hours on the cramped, terrifying flight, and then they were off, carrying their suitcases to the dusty Jeep that awaited them a few yards away. The driver, a thirtysomething man with rolled-up white shirtsleeves, leaned against it. "Welcome back, Drew," he shouted with a grin as the two approached.

"Eat shit, Carl," Andrew called back.

When they got a little closer, somewhat more proper introductions were made. "This is Dr. Carl Wolfe," said Andrew. Lillian recognized the name and immediately felt conscious about her wrinkled attire. If she had known she was going to be meeting prominent physicists as soon as she left the plane, she would have chosen a better outfit.

Dr. Wolfe stuck out his hand, and Lillian tried to maintain her composure as she shook it. "It's an honor to meet you, Dr. Wolfe," she said.

"Please, call me Carl."

"Carl, this is my colleague from Oak Ridge, Dr. Lillian Kaufman," continued Andrew.

Lillian froze. She'd always imagined the title *doctor* in front of her name, of course, but never heard it out loud. More important, she wasn't a real doctor yet, not even close. She was sure that Dr. Wolfe—Carl—would sense this immediately. She glanced at Andrew nervously, not sure if she should correct him.

"Pleasure to meet you, Dr. Kaufman," said Carl, extending his hand. Lillian shook it, saying nothing.

"Lillian's been instrumental in helping me develop the

fusion bomb," Andrew continued. "We've almost cracked it. Just a few more weeks of work and—"

"Are you still banging on about that? Christ."

"It's the future, Carl," said Andrew.

"We'll see. Here, let me take that suitcase from you," said Carl, pointing to the bag Lillian still clutched in her left hand. "Drew, I can't believe you made the lady carry her own suitcase."

Andrew scoffed. "She's perfectly capable."

It wasn't until they were settled in the Jeep and speeding down the road that she realized Andrew had also introduced her as *Lillian*.

Her throat went dry as she quietly panicked. Did Andrew realize what he had done? She sneaked a look over. He was happily gazing out of the Jeep, watching the mesas and the orange sand with quiet glee. She put her hand on his knee, gently. He looked over with a smile. "I missed this!" he said, practically shouting so he could be heard over the noise of the road. "Nothing but mud in Tennessee!"

"You called me Lillian," she whispered back, as loudly as she dared, hoping that Carl in the front seat wouldn't be able to hear in the noisy car.

"I know," he said, putting his hand on top of hers and patting it. "You're going to want the people here to know your real name." Lillian must have looked uneasy at that because he leaned in and added, "You don't want to be Eleanor for the rest of your life, do you?"

Lillian didn't quite know what to say. After a moment she shook her head, but Andrew had already turned away, his gaze back out toward the horizon.

"There's a party tonight," Carl yelled from the front seat, completely unaware of the conversation happening behind him. "At Oppenheimer's."

"Of course there is," said Andrew.

"Will you be there, Lillian?" asked Carl.

Lillian was taken aback. She hardly felt up for a party, given the circumstances of the last few days. "I'm not sure," she mumbled, struggling to come up with any of the excuses she'd used to get out of parties in the past. "I'm rather exhausted from the flight." Then she realized what exactly she had just been asked. "Are you talking about *Robert* Oppenheimer?"

"No, the other Oppenheimer," quipped Andrew. "He's a self-important bastard but he throws the best parties. God, it's been ages since I've been to a proper party."

"Tennessee parties not your scene, Drew?"

"Not really. I found them wanting."

"Yeah, I heard you didn't play so nice out there."

Andrew grinned. "Hearsay."

"Sure, sure." Carl drummed his fingers on the steering wheel. "Remind me not to piss you off."

"I always do," replied Andrew.

He sort of likes this, Lillian realized, immediately followed with, *Well, why shouldn't he?* He'd saved her life. Now in addition to being the hotshot young physicist, he was a hero. It was all right for him to enjoy it a bit, especially after what he'd been through over his wife. It must be nice, she mused, for him to have something new to be infamous over.

And maybe it was all right for her to enjoy this all a bit as well: being called a doctor, meeting Carl Wolfe, being invited to fancy parties at the homes of famous scientists. Eleanor was gone—but being miserable wouldn't change that. Perhaps the logical approach was to enjoy all this while she could, before she was back in New York, where the only scientist she saw was Irene and the only interesting conversations she had were with herself.

The New Mexico facility, she soon observed, was like an older cousin to its Tennessee counterpart: still in the middle of nowhere, still surrounded by an ominous fence and an armed gate, but much more built up (or at least, far less muddy). Carl dropped Andrew and Lillian off at a one-story house on a street of similar small houses that would have been right at home in any number of quaint small towns. Lillian was surprised to see bricks, walls, doors, different styles of architecture—and then noted how amusing it was to find any of these things novel. But after a few weeks in the land of overflowing dormitories and shoddy lean-tos, it was a welcome relief.

"Do you have a whole house to yourself?" she asked, looking at the porch and the front door and the pebbled lawn.

"I share it with a few terrifying insects, but largely yes," he replied, heading up the cobblestone path.

"You get a whole house? You don't even live here."

"I was here a whole year before they sent me to Oak Ridge," he replied.

A whole year—that would have put him here basically at the inception of the project. She'd almost forgotten that before her, before even Eleanor or Max Medelson, there were thousands of others working for months, years, in secrecy.

Seemingly reading her thoughts, Andrew smiled and reached for the doorknob. "Don't be too impressed yet," he warned. "You still haven't seen it."

He opened the door and they stepped inside. The place wasn't much: it opened into a small den, with a kitchen and dining room table in the back and a bedroom off to the right. The furniture didn't have much more charm than the pieces found at Oak Ridge, but the warm lights and carpeting made it seem far more comfortable—like an actual home.

"I'll, um, I'll sleep on the couch, of course," said Andrew, scratching his head.

"Oh!" Lillian genuinely hadn't considered the sleeping arrangements. "You don't have to do that," she said.

"Oh," said Andrew.

"Or I could sleep on the couch?" Lillian offered, suddenly worried she'd been too forward. Perhaps the way the last time had played out had ruined the mood sufficiently for him. Perhaps it should have ruined it for her, as well.

"Why don't we just play it by ear?" said Andrew.

Lillian nodded. "Sure, all right."

When their plane had taken off from Oak Ridge, the test had been scheduled to take place in two days' time. By the time they were wheels down, the test had already been pushed back another two days, and nobody seemed optimistic about sticking to that schedule either. Apparently it was a matter of materials and assembly, not one of calculations, although that didn't stop Andrew from saying he needed to get some work done. After providing her with a corner to stash her suitcase and making sure she knew where to find the clean towels, Andrew disappeared to some secret building, leaving Lillian alone.

The first thing she did, of course, was go through all his things, but there wasn't much. The bookshelf, which she thought would be the most interesting part, on closer examination did not contain any book that wasn't a physics or mathematics textbook. Most of the bookshelf was packed with Andrew's old yellow legal pads, page after page covered in doodles and nonsense calculations. She flipped through a few on the hunt for anything interesting, but came up empty. She turned on the radio but found it nearly impossible to bring in any station clearly and quickly gave up on that, too. She took a nap, she took a shower.

She hoped there would be room to hang her clothes up in the closet and found there was plenty of room, because the only thing hanging in the closet was a single tie on a coat hanger, dangling toward the floor like a snake hanging from a tree branch. Her stomach began to rumble and she went to the kitchen, where she found no food except some canned beans that had been placed under the sink, of all places. After moving the beans to one of the many empty cupboards, she laced up her boots and headed for the small shopping area they'd passed on their way to the house.

She found a cafeteria quickly, even though it was much smaller and quieter than the one in Tennessee. Although she'd avoided the limp, old vegetables that were served at Oak Ridge, she took a chance on the tuna Niçoise salad here and found it more than adequate. It occurred to her that Andrew might be hungry when he returned home and so she found a small grocer, where she bought food that wasn't beans in a can and carried it back to the house in a little tote provided by the store.

Lillian didn't really know how to do any cooking, of course, but she figured it couldn't be that difficult. By the time she'd finished peeling potatoes and chopping vegetables, the sun was starting to go down. Potatoes and vegetables went on a pan in the oven, chicken in a skillet on the stovetop with lemon and olive oil and rosemary. It all looked perfectly respectable, even if it might not necessarily taste good. While everything was roasting and sizzling away, she took some needle-nose pliers to the back of the radio and fiddled with its components, hoping to extend the receiver to pick up some channels somewhere.

She was delighted to find, just as Andrew returned, that she was able to pick up a classical station out of Albuquerque.

"You fixed it," said Andrew.

"It was easy. I'm surprised you couldn't do it," she replied.

"Fix it?" said Andrew. "I'm the one who broke it." He paused as the scent of roasted potatoes hit him. "Did you cook?"

"Yes. What did you do for meals before me? All I found in the whole house were a can of beans and a bottle of whiskey."

He grinned. "Well most nights, let's see, I'd have...a can of beans and a bottle of whiskey."

After dinner, which was delightfully adequate, Lillian shut herself in the bedroom and tried to decide what was appropriate to wear to a party full of everyone in her field she'd ever wanted to impress. None of the clothes she had brought felt right, and she ended up back in her daily uniform of a white blouse tucked neatly into a gray skirt.

"Is this all right?" she asked Andrew. "I don't feel like wearing anything else."

"That's perfect," he said.

Lillian was rather surprised to find that the home of J. Robert Oppenheimer himself was not much bigger than Andrew's. They were greeted at the door by the famous scientist's wife, who kissed them both on the cheek and had vodka martinis in their hands within seconds. Lillian had never had a vodka martini before and took her first sip quite cautiously. It was the best cocktail she had ever tasted, in that it tasted like nothing, but with a hint of salt.

Kitty Oppenheimer was only the beginning. Every time Lillian turned around, it seemed, there was someone else she was eager to meet. Everyone in attendance was someone whose name she had once read in the *Physical Review*. And each one of them shook her hand with kindness, laughed at her jokes, remarked how Andrew had raved about her abilities. She and Dr. Wolfe had a long conversation about Noël Coward, and she even exchanged a pleasant few words with Dr. Oppenheimer himself about the New York Philharmonic.

She planned, mentally, on staying for an hour at most, then making excuses to Andrew and ducking out. She ended up staying five. Truly, she could have easily stayed five more.

It was nearly two in the morning when they stumbled back to Andrew's house. "I've never been to a party like that," she gushed. "So many intelligent people, all in one room. Do you know how rare that sort of thing is?"

"It's really not," said Andrew, fiddling with the radio.

Lillian collapsed onto the couch. "I've never experienced anything like it," she said.

"Of course, you haven't," Andrew mumbled.

"What's that supposed to mean?"

"Only that you're just starting out."

"So are you," Lillian blurted out. The vodka martinis made

her feel bold but not sloppy. It was a wonderful rush. "How old are you? Thirty? You've only had a PhD for a few years."

Andrew laughed. "I forgot, I haven't told you."

"Told me what?"

"I don't have a PhD."

Lillian sat up straight on the couch. "What?"

"They took me away from my thesis to work on this, two years ago. Never finished the dang thing. I'll get around to it one of these days." He grinned. "And I'm twenty-six, by the way."

"So anytime you called yourself Dr. Ennis, you were lying."

"It was a lie in fact but not in spirit." He settled down next to her on the couch, having found a station playing something suitably jazzy and fun.

"Any other secrets I should know about?"

He looked away, down at the floor, and smiled a little nervously. "I don't know if I should tell you this."

Lillian couldn't imagine what would require such an ominous tone. "Tell me what?"

"You're going to think I'm awful," he said. "But I can't crack safes."

"What?" said Lillian.

He put his head in hands. "God, it's so embarrassing. I was so desperate to impress you. Well, everyone, really, but especially you. I pretended I could crack safes—"

"You did crack safes," said Lillian. "I saw you. The one in my office—Sean's—you scared the daylights out of him."

"Well, you see, it's the same with safes as it is with anything else. Whoever goes right for the most complicated path has already lost," he said. "I don't know how to feel the vibrations of the locks falling with my fingertips, or whatever it is I told you. But I do know that if you ask a scientist to select a series of numbers on his own, at least a third of them will choose 27-18-28."

"The natural logarithm," said Lillian. It seemed so obvious, now, but it had never occurred to her.

"Sean is more of a basic type, so his was even less obscure. 31-41-59."

"The first digits of pi."

"A couple rounds of guesswork is much easier than listening to locks falling. And surprisingly, rather interesting. You can tell a lot about a person by the numbers they choose. I learned to fire anyone immediately who chose his own birthday and promote anyone who chose the birthday of his mother. One is an idiot; the other's an idiot but a loyal one." He paused, looking slyly at Lillian. "What did you choose?"

Lillian went quiet, remembering her selection of 09-06-30. "The day my father died," she said after a moment, then in a half-hearted attempt to lighten the tension added: "What does that say about me?"

"That you're smart," said Andrew immediately. "Only the highly intelligent consider death all the time, no matter where they are, no matter what they're doing. The rest of the world can go about living and forget it. Other people can be consumed with the silly daily business of being alive. But us—we never can shake the thought that it's all ultimately pointless, can we?"

A hush fell over Lillian.

After a moment, Andrew cleared his throat. "The only people you can't crack are the ones who choose something truly random. But most people don't do that. Human beings aren't designed well for randomness."

"But you didn't know who set the safe in the morgue," said Lillian. Realizing that it wasn't impossible, she added, "Did you?"

"That one was the easiest of them all," he said. "Government bureaucracy? They never even set the lock. It was 00-00-00."

"Oh my god," Lillian said with a laugh. "I can't believe it was all a trick."

"Did you fall for it?" he asked.

"I did."

He smiled. "Good."

Then he leaned in to kiss her.

The last time they were in each other's arms, she'd enjoyed the sensation of her mind, which was always on, finally going blank. Of not having a worry in the world beyond that moment, of not feeling anything of the world around her. This time, she wanted the opposite. As his hands eagerly wandered over her hips, her waist, as his lips caressed every sensitive spot on her body, as she ran her fingers through his hair, and down his arms, and across his back, she wanted to remember each moment exactly, have each look and each sensation burned into the folds of her brain.

———————

"This is ridiculous. Drag us out of bed and all the way up here for nothing." Andrew tapped his thumbs on the steering wheel of the parked car anxiously.

"I wonder if they changed the time," said Lillian.

Andrew cranked down the window. Little drops of water splashed onto his forearm. He hollered to the car parked next to theirs, "Carl!"

Carl Wolfe, sitting in the passenger's seat, rolled down his window. "What's taking them so long?" Andrew asked.

"Don't you have your radio on?" asked Carl.

"We kept picking up static," said Lillian, leaning over. "Yours working?"

"Loud and clear. They're holding for the rain," said Carl.

Andrew rolled his eyes. "Three years harnessing the power of nuclear fission, and they're worried it might not work if it's damp?"

Carl shrugged. "Don't look at me. I'm not in charge. They're gonna send up a flare at one minute."

"Think it'll be a good explosion?" asked Andrew.

Carl cracked his knuckles. "Wanna bet on it?"

"You know I do," said Andrew. "Tons TNT equivalent. Who has a guess?"

"You first," said Lillian.

Andrew considered, his tongue rolling over his teeth thoughtfully. "Three hundred," he said after a moment.

Carl whistled. "Bold. Put me down for zero."

"Aw, come on."

"We did good work, but if those molds were one millimeter off…"

"You're so boring, Carl," Andrew scolded. "Lil?"

Lillian ran some numbers in her head. "You said three hundred?"

Andrew nodded.

"He's nuts," commented Carl. "Don't base your answer off him."

"I'm not," said Lillian. "Ten thousand."

Both Andrew and Carl went wide-eyed. "Ten thousand?" said Carl.

"It's three hundred," said Andrew.

Somewhere in the valley below them, a spark went off. "There's the flare," said Carl. "Guess we'll find out soon enough."

Carl and Andrew rolled up their windows. Lillian reached again for the radio, flicking it on. A voice spoke through the static, counting down. "Fifty-seven. Fifty-six."

"Hey, there we go!" said Andrew, but as soon as he did the voice fizzled into static again. Another station took over, a dramatic crescendo of violins bursting into the space between them. Andrew cursed as he reached for the switch.

"Leave it on," said Lillian. "I like this piece."

"What is it?" he asked, withdrawing his hand.

"It's Tchaikovsky, of course."

"Oh, *of course.*"

"It's his Serenade for Strings."

Andrew glanced over at the car to his right, where Carl and the others were putting on large welding masks. Dark metal covered their faces and dark glasses protected their eyes. "We have two of those, if you want," he said.

"If the blast reaches up here, a welder's mask isn't going to help too much," said Lillian.

"Fair point."

"Besides," she went on, "I want to see it."

"Me too," said Andrew.

The countdown continued to flicker in and out, overtaken by the tide of Tchaikovsky, and the seconds seemed to contain centuries within them. It surprised Lillian to note that once a moment was broken open this way, it was found to have so much nothingness contained within it. *Atoms are mostly empty space,* she thought. *The world is mostly a void.*

And then: white light.

It hit Lillian like a migraine. She felt herself gasp—seemed almost to watch herself gasping, from some far-above place—as the white light quickly faded into blackness. She tried to search the brightness before it was too late, to stare deep into it, certain she would see there—what? some vision of the gods, perhaps, absurdly—but before long the white became nothing but a dark cloud, billowing higher and higher, as tall as any building in Manhattan and then up further still, gathering up dirt and debris and then casting it all aside, raining its contents down upon the empty desert.

It was still only the first movement of Tchaikovsky's Serenade for Strings, she realized, as the cello cried, its strings vibrating with a resonance Lillian felt suddenly in her chest. Only the first movement—absurd. Absurd! She had to laugh. She was laughing—she could feel herself laughing (she could see it, from some far-above place)—alone in the car (had she been alone, before?), a cello ringing in her ears, the world split open in front of her eyes.

Her laughter was not the only noise she could hear— whoops and cheers and hoots were coming from outside of the car, from all around her. She discovered the door had been opened; she saw men cheering, one of whom was familiar. She recognized (of course) the line of the muscle along Andrew's forearm, his rolled-up white shirtsleeves stained with blotches of coffee and ink. She wanted to laugh again, or perhaps continue laughing—as there was no way to be certain if she was still laughing. How foolish she had been, all her life. She remembered not being sure if she should kiss him, on the roof in Tennessee. (Oh goodness, she had gone to Tennessee—what a lark that all had been.) How could she not have known that it could make no possible difference in the universe if she had kissed him or not. It didn't matter! Her face tilted toward the sky as she laughed. Nothing, truly nothing could have mattered less! And Max—Max had given her a knife, Max had worried she was in danger. As if Andrew were the biggest danger she could meet, as if it weren't herself, as if it weren't all of them! As if it mattered at all!

"Can you believe it?"

She managed to turn her head and found him looking at her, standing outside the car, bending over to peer inside with a light in his eyes and a wide smile across his face. He was so handsome, his smile so charming, those eyes so brown—it was really such a waste. Lillian laughed, again and still.

"What's so funny?" he asked.

"It's Tchaikovsky," she answered.

"Serenade for Strings," he said. "Didn't realize it was so hilarious."

"It's only the first movement," she said. "Can you imagine?"

He shook his head. "I don't think I understand."

"If he knew what we were going to do here today..." She could barely finish the sentence, she was so overcome with laughter. "He never would have written the other three."

———

Truly, Lillian thought they'd never be caught, that what had transpired between her and Max on the Upper West Side a handful of nights before his departure would disappear into eternity. It wasn't good or bad that it would never be unearthed; it just was. To prepare for the burial, she dismissed it from her own heart, from her body, from her memory. Papered over it with recollections that painted her in a better light. She balled it up and threw it aside and made it so small that when Eleanor did find out, Lillian really did think she was spiraling nothing into something, making an explosion where one didn't need to exist.

"He knew it was me," Lillian had said, as if that mattered. She couldn't see it at the time.

"He told me that he didn't," said Eleanor. "He said you dressed up as me and seduced him."

"He's lying," said Lillian, although she couldn't help but be struck by the memory of Max saying Eleanor's name instead of hers. That had been a mistake, hadn't it? "He's scum."

"That doesn't matter! *You* knew it was *him*."

"I thought…" What had she thought? It seemed so faint. "I thought you didn't love him, not really."

"I do."

"I thought he was beneath you."

"He wasn't."

"I thought it would be my only chance."

"Enough! I get it!" Tears were streaming down Eleanor's face. All the mascara she'd so lovingly applied that morning—wiped away. "You thought, and you thought, and you thought. You thought so many little things, and you never once thought about the big thing, the very big thing."

She was right, of course. She had been so right. Every small step had seemed so logical, at the time. Once Lillian had answered the phone as Eleanor, it made sense to go out as Eleanor, too. Each small step made the next small step seem reasonable. It was only stopping to look back that she realized she'd walked a mile.

"I've spent my whole life protecting you," Lillian had shot back. "Do you really think I would do something like this on purpose?"

"Yes," said Eleanor. "You're getting exactly what you always wanted."

"That doesn't make sense."

"I have to go to Tennessee now. Do you understand that?"

"Why?"

"Because my relationship is *ruined*," Eleanor shouted. (Lillian had rolled her eyes at that. God, her sister could be so dramatic.) "I have to go where Max is going so I can try to fix this. I'm not going to be in *Carousel*, I'm not going to Chicago. You get everything you wanted. You get to go to Harvard next year without any interference from me."

(Lillian had actually replied to that, "Well, what if you're not back from Tennessee in time?" Eleanor had thrown a shoe at her.)

"Don't go to Tennessee," said Lillian. "You're being ridiculous." She tried not to add that a relationship with Max wasn't worth saving. Instead she said, "You and Max will be fine."

"I have to be with him right now," she said. "I have to know that he loves me and not you." A paranoid glint sparked in Eleanor's eyes. "Is that why you did this?"

"Of course not. The last thing I want is for you to throw away your career for that idiot," snapped Lillian.

"Some things are more important than a career," Eleanor said. "But I suppose I shouldn't expect you to understand that." She didn't stick around to hear Lillian's rebuttal, which would have been something like: *Sure, some things are but not Max Medelson.* It wouldn't have mattered. She'd taken too many small steps.

She'd sent Eleanor off to Oak Ridge, and Eleanor had died at Oak Ridge.

She'd spent six weeks denying it, but she couldn't anymore.

Eleanor was dead because of her.

TWENTY

JULY 1945

Despite the oppressive heat, the party that night was the most raucous Lillian had ever seen. Champagne bottles popped every few minutes, each one met with a new round of cheers and laughter. Everyone was kissing, hugging, laughing. Backs were clapped, hands shook, congratulations shared all around. Nearly every ten minutes, it seemed, someone clanged on his glass with a fork to silence the room for a speech, each successive speaker becoming less and less eloquent as the night wore on. Big-band music crackled through the air, and everyone seemed to be dancing even as they stood still. Lillian drank too much champagne, mostly to stop it from growing warm in her hands. Andrew wrapped his arms around her as another red-faced scientist gushed, and she felt nothing except uncomfortably hot.

When that physicist was followed immediately by another, even rosier-cheeked fellow, Lillian whispered to Andrew that she needed some air. He looked at her with worry. She could feel his concern bouncing against her exterior and slipping off, like water on a tile. She did not need his concern; there was no point for it. What did it matter if she felt ill; what did it matter if he felt bad about it? She slipped away without another word.

Outside, she tilted her head up to look at the stars, so much brighter here than in New York. Her curls, limp with dry heat, clung to the sweat that had gathered on the back of her neck inside the packed house. She didn't stare long before looking back down to the ground. The luminosity of the stars didn't matter much either.

Andrew appeared by her side after a few moments. He must have followed her, must have been concerned. She didn't care. "Is everything all right?" he asked, wiping the sweat off his own forehead with the rolled-up sleeve of his white shirt.

"I was too warm," she said.

"Yeah, it's an oven in there. I'll get you some water."

Lillian didn't want water, but couldn't be bothered to say so. Andrew disappeared into the house, emerging shortly with a long-stemmed champagne flute filled with water. "This is the only glass I could find," he said with a laugh. "Kitty must have assumed no one would want any other refreshment tonight."

Unaffected by the quip, Lillian took the glass in her hands but didn't raise it to her lips.

"You seem tired," he said.

"I am tired." Tired didn't even begin to cover it. She was weary.

"We could call it a night, if you'd like," he said. When she didn't respond, he glanced at his watch. "How about we stay for fifteen more minutes and then find a reason to leave?"

Making plans felt unnecessary, even absurd. It seemed to Lillian that there wasn't going to be any future to plan for, not even in fifteen minutes. She didn't see the point in saying all that to Andrew, however. Why bother explaining? "Whatever you want," she said.

"What do you want?" he asked, gently emphasizing the word *you* as he reached out to touch her hair.

She didn't answer.

He put his arms around her, bent down to lower his lips to hers. It almost shocked Lillian, how little she felt in those lips that had once been her only comfort. Just a few days ago, Andrew had been everything to her. She had cooked a chicken for him, fixed his radio. It felt so far away.

After a moment he pulled away. "Today was incredible," he said. "After all that work, we pulled it off. You should be proud of yourself."

"I'm not," said Lillian. "I don't think any of us should be proud."

Andrew was taken aback. He lifted an eyebrow in surprise. "Come on. If we hadn't done it, someone else would. You're smart enough to know that. It was only a matter of time, only a matter of some other country getting the materials before us."

It was an excuse, and a poor one at that. She wondered if there was any chance at all of making him see, of pointing out how the tiny reasonable steps became the large mistakes. "You mean Germany? You kept saying—several times, if I recall—we were racing against Germany to build this thing. And yet Germany surrendered, months ago. Why didn't we stop?"

"Germany might have been the reason we started the project, but reasons can change."

"Did your reason change?"

"I don't know—I—why are you interrogating me?"

"You joined this project to fight Germany, maybe. But you kept going because it was fun." She took a shaky breath. She wasn't sure if she was talking about Andrew anymore, or Germany for that matter. "Because you wanted to see if you could do it, if you could get away with it, if you could pull it off."

Andrew shrugged. "Is that so wrong?"

"We built something terrible. We've made the world terrible. How can you not see that? How can you not feel the weight of that inside you?"

"The world's always been terrible," he said. "And if we hadn't done it, someone else would."

To her own surprise, she let out a laugh as his words sank in. "You're right," she said finally. "You are."

"I don't think I've ever been surprised to hear that before," he replied.

"Someone else would have done it if we hadn't. It was always going to end this way." She shook her head. "I thought science was about finding the truth, and the truth is that human beings will destroy each other, as long as they can rationalize it away."

"That's absurd," he said, then added, "Are you still talking about the project?"

"It's a bomb," she replied, shoving the champagne glass full of water back into his hand. It sloshed over the edges, onto his white shirt. "Call it a bomb."

As he tried to wipe up the spill, she turned and walked away. "Where are you going?" he shouted after her.

"I'm going home," she answered.

He looked around for a place to stash the glass, eventually dumping the remaining water onto the ground and trotting after her with it dangling from his hand. "Well, wait for me," he said.

"You don't need to come."

"We've both been drinking. We shouldn't go wandering off alone," he said, catching up to her. "Truth be told, I'm ready to go home, too. If I have to hear another drunken toast to the inevitable march of progress, I'll lose my mind."

"I don't mean back to your house," said Lillian. "I'm leaving Los Alamos."

"Hold on, hold on, hold on." He reached for her hand,

pulling her to a halt. "Stop for a second. We can't leave. Not now. It's past midnight."

"By the time I pack, it will be close enough to morning."

"The army hasn't chartered us a plane."

"I'll take the bus into Albuquerque and take a train from there."

"From Albuquerque? That will take *weeks*."

She shrugged. It didn't matter to her how long it took; time was a useless measurement anyway. "It'll take what it takes."

She tried to walk off, but he tugged at her arm again, holding her still. "But I have to stay," he said. "The business in Tennessee is done for the moment. I have to stay here."

"I'm not going to Tennessee," she said. "I said home. New York."

He was so surprised that he let go of her hand, and Lillian wasted no time in continuing to walk away. Regaining his composure a moment later, he followed. "I don't understand," he said. "Why would you go back to New York?"

She didn't respond, just kept walking. What did it matter if he understood or not? Finally, he threw himself in front of her, blocking her path, forcing her to come to a halt. He was so much taller than she that Lillian had to look up to meet his eyes. They'd come far enough that the sounds of the party had faded completely into the thick night air. They were entirely alone.

"Why would you go back to New York?" he repeated.

"It's where I live," she replied. "My mother is there, my school is there…"

"But what about me?"

His eyes were so wide, so open. She could see his every emotion, from flickering hope to dreadful fear to horrible pain. She wanted to say that he didn't matter, because she didn't matter either—nothing at all mattered—there was no point in them being together, other than the temporary distraction from the knowledge that they'd ruined the world.

That was the difference between her and Eleanor, she realized. That was the thing that had made them even less identical than Eleanor's hair sprays and lipsticks. Eleanor could tolerate the temporary distractions of life: the theater, men, dancing, white wine at lunch. She could embrace them, even. Lillian never could, as much as she pretended. Not before, and especially not now. She had seen some truth in that bright-white light—she could never again pretend the world was normal, or sane, or just. She could never pretend that there was some truth underneath it all worth looking for.

His eyes darted desperately around her face, and there he read something far more sinister. When he spoke, his throat was dry and his voice was low. "Is there someone else?"

"No," said Lillian. "Of course not." But she could already see the gears clicking away in his head, putting together pieces, finding evidence for his hypothesis.

"There's someone in New York," he said. "Of course there

is. How could I be so stupid to think that a woman like you would be single?"

How could you think that a woman like me would be married? she wanted to say. "There's no one in New York."

"That's why you forgave me," he went on. "That's why you don't care that I'm married, because you're doing the same thing to me."

"That's absurd," said Lillian. She tried to push past him, but he grabbed her shoulders. "What are you doing?"

"Tell me there's no one else," he said. "Tell me you're not leaving me for someone else."

She could see the desperation in his eyes and smell the sour stale champagne on his breath. His fingers clung so tightly to her shoulders that his nails dug through her shirt into her skin. She began to sweat, although it was far cooler out here than it had been in the party. "There's no one else," she said, trying to sound as calm as she could.

"I love you," he said. "Do you love me?"

Yesterday the answer would have been *yes*, but too much had changed since then. She hesitated, her silence only adding more evidence to the accusation being built in Andrew's mind. "Not again," he mumbled. "I can't go through this again."

He wouldn't loosen his grip on her shoulders even as he looked away. Lillian's heart started to pound, so loudly she began to worry Andrew would hear it, that it would somehow be seen as evidence of a guilty conscience and upset him more.

She wanted to explain, but didn't know how to put the words together. *I would love you, but I don't see the point* couldn't be all that comforting.

"I can't go through this again," he repeated, looking back to her, a strange glint in his dark eyes. "You can't do this to me."

"Andrew," she whispered, "it was real. It was. But it's not anymore. It can't be."

A sharp sting of pain rang out on her left cheek. It wasn't until she heard something crash near her right foot that she realized she'd been hit. He had hit her, his hand still holding the empty champagne flute, which had shattered and dug its shards across her cheek. The force of it sent her reeling, stumbling back a few steps. She felt more glass crumbling beneath her feet, cracking and sending her off balance. Putting her hand to her cheek she felt cool blood, white-hot pain.

Andrew had let go of her, seemingly in shock at what he'd just done. "Fuck!" he shouted. "Oh god. *Fuck.* I'm so sorry." His voice seemed far away. "I have no goddamn self-control. I'm sorry."

He stumbled toward her. Lillian barely heard his words. All she noticed was that his grip on her shoulders was gone. She didn't think, she ran.

She was sure he was shouting out to her, but she could not focus enough to make out the words. It had not occurred to her that he could be capable of hitting her, a notion which now felt foolish. She had, after all, watched him kill a man. And yet—

Maybe she should stop. Maybe it was an accident, maybe it

was a mistake. He was probably concerned about the blood that was now dripping heavily from her wound, leaving a little trail of dots behind her. Maybe she should stop—and yet her feet, too, seemed beyond her control—

It wasn't until she reached Andrew's small house, almost out of breath, that she realized he hadn't followed her. He was nowhere to be seen. The night was completely quiet and still, except for her heavy breaths and gasps for air. She pushed open the door and went immediately to her suitcase stashed in its corner, retrieving the pocketknife tucked into the front zippered pocket. *He's feeding you lies and got you lying on his behalf,* Max had said. As soon as she touched the cool, heavy handle she could hear the words as if he were there in the room.

Shaking off the phantom sound, she went into the bathroom, where she ran a washcloth under the warm faucet and pressed it to her cheek. It stung like mad. Blood and water ran down her chin in swirls of red and beige, the water washing away the powder on her face. The wound was deep, she realized. She was lucky it hadn't cut straight through to the teeth. It would need stitches, but that was the least of her concern, for now.

With the first washcloth discarded (it was quickly ruined) and a second pressed to her cheek, Lillian returned to the bedroom. There was no time to pack any of her things. She grabbed her small purse from the nightstand and slipped the few bills inside into her pocket, praying it would be enough to either get her a taxi to a train station or to a hospital—whichever she determined she would need first. Just as she was heading for the front door, she heard someone else open it.

She whipped around and, without thinking, opened the knife, hiding the blade behind her back. The washcloth tumbled to the floor.

He appeared in the doorframe within moments. "Lillian." His voice cracked. "I'm sorry. But please, don't do this. Don't leave. It's not what's best for you."

It was almost exactly the sentence she had said when Eleanor told her she wouldn't be in *Carousel*, that she would be going to Tennessee to be with Max. She felt the weight of the pearls that still hung around her neck and remembered how Eleanor's were probably stuck in the mud and grass near a river in Tennessee.

"If I don't listen to you," she began slowly, her cheek aching with every movement, "what will you do?"

Andrew ignored the question. "Let me see your cut," he said gently. "Is it bad?"

"What will you do?" she asked again. "Will you kill me, too?"

No surprise, or anger, or emotion of any kind flickered over his face. "What makes you say that?" he asked, not moving from the frame of the door, which happened to be her only way out.

"When you thought for one moment that I might be leaving you for another man, you slashed my face with a wineglass," she said.

"It was a champagne flute."

"That's hardly the point."

"You're smart," he said.

"I know."

"Then don't ask more questions. End this now." His hands gripped the molding around the edge of the door. "We've both had too much to drink. Let me take you to the hospital building, they'll look at that cut, then we can both go to bed."

She almost laughed—a cut! It wasn't a *cut,* some harmless little slice from a piece of paper. It was a wound, an injury—done to her *by him*—and yet, remarkably, it actually flickered through her mind to consider what he was saying. *It would be easier,* whispered some seductive voice. *He seems much calmer now—maybe you were only imagining things—*

She shook her head, tried to dispel the thought from her now-woozy brain. "Will you kill me, too?" she repeated.

"I didn't kill her," he said. "She wouldn't have died if she hadn't—" He brought his hands to his head, practically beating his temples. "Fuck. Fuck. Fuck."

"She wouldn't have died if *what?*"

Andrew slowly lowered his hands. "She fell," he began, then corrected himself. "She had fallen. Earlier that day, at work, she'd fainted and hit her head. She should have stayed overnight in the hospital. They wanted her to stay. If she had just listened to them, none of this would have happened."

"None of what would have happened?" asked Lillian.

"She insisted she was fine," Andrew went on. "She told them she needed to go home because she had to talk to me."

Lillian remembered reading this in Eleanor's file, the one Andrew had given to her. He'd handed her a huge piece of the puzzle and she'd dismissed it as nothing.

"She'd found out about Kathleen that morning, and she was determined to end it with me that night." Andrew shook his head. Lillian, it seemed, had evaporated from the room. He talked mostly to himself, in a low voice. "I have no goddamn self-control. I got angry. We were down by the river. We fought. She fought back, mind you. I wasn't alone in this. I pushed her. Not hard. She hit her head. It wasn't even that bad. If she hadn't already hurt herself, she would have been fine."

"Walter knew about it," Lillian said. "The man in the woods, the head of security, he knew—"

"I had to tell him," Andrew said. "He had to help me—" His sentence ended abruptly.

"Cover it up?" filled in Lillian. "Help you get away with it."

"*No*," said Andrew forcefully. "It wasn't like that. I was needed—by the project, by the country—"

"I suppose if they've already hired you to murder millions of people, what difference does one more make," said Lillian.

Andrew's eyes met hers, just as sad and confused and dark as ever. "It wasn't like that," he repeated. "It wasn't my fault. If I hadn't asked Walter to help me, if I'd gone to the police, or something, I'd be arrested. I'd be ruined. Why should my life be ruined for something that wasn't my fault? Ruined *again*?"

Lillian said nothing.

After a moment, her silence angered him. "I suppose you feel all better now that you know that," he spat out. "Happier, now that you know the truth."

They had spent weeks studying chain reactions, optimizing the release of neutrons from fissioning uranium in order to induce more and more fission reactions. Calculating the precise measurements of the plates that would surround the core. Millimeters made a difference. It was so easy for a fission reaction to fizzle out, so rare for one chain to link perfectly to the next. One caused nothing; the other a giant release of energy. This moment felt similar to the explosions they'd tried to induce, except for the first time Lillian didn't have to calculate the outcome. She could create it.

She gripped the pocketknife she'd concealed behind her back. The world was already blown apart. As good as gone, once the thing they'd created was put to use. Why not blow up some more things with it?

She ran suddenly toward Andrew.

It took more work that she expected, stabbing someone, more effort than she would have thought to drive the blade through his flesh. Perhaps this knife wasn't the right sort for self-defense, or perhaps it was dull from all the misshapen cats that had been carved with it.

Andrew must have seen it coming, surely knew or guessed in those few milliseconds what Lillian's intent was, but he didn't stop her. Still, his eyes grew wide in shock. Lillian reckoned that perhaps that part couldn't be helped, that even expecting to be stabbed didn't prepare one for the feeling of it. He stumbled a few steps back, hands over his chest. Blood spread quickly, running through the water that already covered his white shirt.

As he backed away, Lillian let go of the knife. It fell to the floor between them, leaving a stripe of dark blood on the carpet. Lillian suddenly felt paralyzed, even as she feared Andrew would pick up the knife and attack her. Even wounded and bleeding, he was bigger and stronger. All she'd had to her advantage was the element of surprise. She still couldn't move. He could easily kill her. Was that what she wanted?

Andrew looked at her, and she was surprised to see he looked tired. "Pick it up," he said.

Lillian hesitated. Was it a trick? Was his plan to wait until she bent over, wait until she'd taken her eyes off him to attack?

He seemed to read her mind. "I'm trying to help. It's not a very deep wound, and you didn't hit any of the important organs. I'm not dying from this, at least not for a while." Even as he said it, his voice took on a slight rattle. He coughed a little.

Lillian still didn't move for the knife, was still unsure she could have even if she wanted to. "What if I wanted it to take a while?" she said, trying to keep her voice steady.

He nodded. "Sure, sure. To make me suffer and all. That makes sense. In that case, do you mind if I sit down? This is going to get dreadfully boring." Lowering himself to the floor, he leaned against the doorframe and looked up at Lillian. "In a way, this is how I wanted it to end."

"Shut up," she snapped. "You're so damn clever, and you always have something to say. I don't want to hear what you have to say anymore."

"Pick up that knife and slit my throat, then."

"I said, shut up."

"We're similar, you know. Smart enough to know what's best for everyone. Doomed to watch the rest of the world fail to live up to their potential. Smart enough to build an atomic bomb, cursed to watch that atomic bomb handed over to politicians."

"I'm nothing like you," said Lillian. "I never would have killed someone."

"Oh, that's fantastic news. I'll be off to Pasadena, then."

"You know what I mean. I never would have—"

"She told me what you did, you know." He looked at her and seemed to smile. "With Max and all that. Pretending to be your twin sister to sleep with her boyfriend! I think that's when I knew. *You* were the twin I should be with. We deserve each other."

"I'm nothing like you," said Lillian, although her voice wavered. "I made a mistake. I never would have done what you did."

"Slit my throat," Andrew said.

"If you're trying to play some game right now, prove something to me—"

"I'm not. I'm changing the subject. I've been thinking all this through, running the various outcomes, and you have to slit my throat. Look at it objectively." He stopped to cough, and a little fleck of blood splatted from his throat and onto the carpet. "Oh!" he cried with an excited little laugh. "Look at that! That's neat, at least. What was I saying?"

Before Lillian could answer, he remembered. "Ah! Right. Look at it objectively. If I were in a murderous rage now, I'd have had plenty of time and strength and energy to keep attacking you. You haven't even bothered to pick the knife back up, so I have a convenient weapon right there."

"But you're not attacking me."

"Lillian, Lillian. Think." He sounded just as he always had in his office, explaining some advanced aspect of the bomb he hoped to build. "What you've done is murder. Sort of. Really delayed, exceptionally boring murder—unless I'm attacking you, unless you fear for your life."

"I know," she said. "I don't care if it is murder. I don't care what they do me."

He rolled his eyes. "Life in jail? Over me? That's ridiculous. I'm not worth it. I don't even want to live." He started to laugh. "I've never wanted to live. That's probably why I kept working with you, even though you were the only person in that town I should have kept away from. I should have…" The laugh turned into a cough, which knocked him over onto his side. "I had a choice, the night she died, a choice to call the hospital, try to help her, or call Walter and help myself. I chose me. I chose… I have no goddamn self-control. I hate what I've done, everything, I hate it all. It hurts, being so broken."

"You're not broken," said Lillian. "You don't get to be broken. You did exactly as you always pleased and didn't care who you hurt."

"Yes," he said sadly. "That's cleaner. But I did love…" He paused, and then shakily cleared his throat. "Here's what we'll do, all right? You grab that knife, run out of here, and start screaming. I'll chase after you. Once you've screamed enough to wake people up, once witnesses come outside, I'll come at you again and you can stab me for good. How does that sound?"

"Ridiculous," said Lillian. She spat the word out with such force she felt a small little tear in the flesh of her cheek wound. She winced in pain.

"I'll do this the hard way, if I have to."

"Is that a threat? Because you're not very intimidating when you're coughing up—"

Before she finished her sentence, he dove forward. In an instant, he had the knife in his hands, was on his feet, towering over Lillian as if he didn't have a wound of several inches in his stomach. Lillian watched, frozen, almost in awe of the sudden transformation from the injured man drawing haggard breaths moments earlier.

"What are you doing?" he said after she still didn't move. "Run."

He let her bolt past him and into the living room, but he followed with surprising speed. In the foyer, she fumbled with the door. He was close behind her as the door banged open and she flew outside.

Her brain was a clattering mess of thoughts. *Noise. Witnesses.* "Help!" she screamed, or at least tried to scream. The empty air seemed to swallow her sounds. "Help me!"

A few lights flickered on in the quiet homes nearby as she ran into the street. And then suddenly he wasn't behind her anymore. She heard a cry out from behind her and looked down to see him facedown on the small walkway leading to the house. He'd fallen—tripped, maybe?—and lay still on the ground.

She froze on the street, unsure if she should keep running— but for only a heartbeat until someone, some strange neighbor she had never met and never would, wrapped an arm around her and began to ask if she was okay. "He was coming after me," she managed to say. She felt a deep stinging on her cheek and was surprised when she realized that a tear had dripped in to the cut there. Why was she crying? "He was coming after me."

The stranger pulled her into an embrace. Others, men, started to crowd the scene. Everything began to grow hazy, and she wondered how much blood she had lost from the wound on her face, if it was enough to make a person pass out. The men crowded around Andrew, shouting incomprehensible things. A few of them managed to turn him over. The knife protruded from his chest, on the right side, a few inches away from where she had aimed. The neighbor forced her away before she could see more.

His eyes had been closed, but Lillian knew he was still alive. She also knew it would not be for long. The doctors would do everything they could to save him, knew they would try with unprecedented desperation to save their future of physics, their genius. Dr. Carl Wolfe would be one of several to offer a kidney to replace the one he'd inevitably torn apart, but it was a pointless gesture. Dr. Andrew Ennis accomplished everything he set his mind to. She wouldn't have been surprised to know that in the moments he'd pursued her, he'd been running calculations in his head. The precise angle, the perfect spot. How to bleed out quickly, how to send an irreversible stream of toxins into his bloodstream.

He accomplished everything he set his mind to, which meant he could have killed her, easily, and probably gotten away with it, too. He'd done it twice before. Why didn't he?

Maybe Andrew Ennis was even smarter than all the credit he'd been given. Maybe he knew the worst fate for Lillian would be leaving her alive, that the best option in this world they'd burst open was death.

Lillian could never know for sure. She could only make educated hypotheses for the rest of her days.

TWENTY-ONE

JULY 1945

As the plane descended from that clear world above the clouds to fog and dark and whiteness, Lillian wondered what to say to Max. What *could* she say? Should she apologize for not believing him, or finally smack him across the face, like she should have done that afternoon in February? She ran her tongue over the stitches on the inside of her mouth (somewhere in the confusion, the wound had ripped itself all the way open, exposing a hole in her cheek that the doctor warned would be numb and stiff for the rest of her life) and tried not to think of how she owed her life to the man who had ruined it.

The army officer who helped her off the plane refused to look at her, even as he offered her his hand. She wasn't surprised.

Already, it seemed, everyone had forgotten about the part where she'd run screaming into the night, pursued by an angry man with a knife. She had been involved in the death of an important man, and that was all anyone cared about. There was no use in being bothered by it.

To her surprise, it wasn't Max waiting for her when she disembarked and the hot Tennessee air assaulted her sinuses once again. In fact, it was someone so unexpected Lillian would have been less shocked to see a ghost.

In front of her stood Emmy, her dull roommate, but wearing an army uniform instead of the pastel dresses she normally donned. "Hello, Lillian," she said. "It is Lillian, right?"

Lillian nodded. "So you work for the army," she said, glancing down at her roommate's stark uniform. "You're a spy." She wondered if she ought to feel something—betrayal? Anger? Although the news was unexpected, Lillian couldn't quite bring herself to care.

"Sort of," Emmy replied. "Undercover security officer." She paused, and Lillian could tell she was just aching to have a pick at the skin around her fingernails again. "I was assigned to be Eleanor's roommate once she started dating Andrew Ennis because he was considered an important asset. Which means I should have figured it all out much sooner."

I should have, too, thought Lillian, although she said nothing.

"I'm going to be taking over this case," Emmy went on. "We'll have to keep you at Oak Ridge until this is all settled, but you should be going home soon, Miss Kaufman. The army wants very much to keep this unfortunate business out of civilian courts."

Unfortunate business. It was quite the euphemism. "I killed him," she said. "That's the unfortunate business?"

"We'll get to the bottom of all that, I promise you," said Emmy with a sympathetic smile. Lillian hated this. She did not need or want Emmy's sympathy. "For now," continued Emmy, "let's just get you something to eat."

———————

Lillian was taken by Emmy to an empty room with only a table inside, where she was given a bowl of watery tomato soup and some lime Jell-O, the most solid food her fresh stitches permitted her to eat. Neither of these options seemed appealing, but she got the sense from Emmy's insistent gaze that none of this would be moving along until she ate everything that was in front of her. The tomato soup settled nastily in her already acidic stomach, the lime Jell-O seemed to slither down her throat whole and plunk on top of it. And yet, after managing to choke it all down, she found that she did feel slightly better.

"Is your wound all right?" asked Emmy, and Lillian ruefully pondered if she should quip in response, "Of course not," or "Which one?" Thankfully, Emmy continued before she could decide. "I can send for some medicine, if you'd like."

"What about a whiskey?" asked Lillian.

Emmy raised an eyebrow. Perhaps, thought Lillian, it was

not a good idea to ask during your interrogation for the signature drink of the man you'd just murdered.

"How about a coffee?" asked Emmy.

Lillian shrugged.

A black coffee was speedily procured and placed in front of Lillian with two painkillers resting on the rim of the saucer like special after-coffee mints. She took both and swallowed them dry.

Emmy smiled at her. She'd been doing that all throughout the mostly silent lunch, and Lillian longed to ask her why. It hardly seemed like the occasion. "Feeling better?" Emmy asked.

Lillian stared into her coffee cup. The black liquid had a thin film on it that made the mug's contents look more like an oil spill. She decided against raising it to her lips. "Not much," she replied.

"Is there something else we can get you?" asked Emmy, her brow furrowing with concern.

Lillian shook her head. She'd made a mistake with that slip of honesty, clearly. If she wanted to be out of the room as soon as possible, she'd have to force a smile. "No, thank you, actually. I think I am feeling much better."

Emmy breathed a sigh of relief. "This is going to be difficult," she began, kindly and gently. "If you need to stop at any point, it's not a problem."

"Why would I need to stop?" asked Lillian.

"In case it…" Emmy fumbled for the words, clearly not expecting to have to explain. "If it's too much."

"Oh," said Lillian. She was certain it wasn't going to be too much, but it seemed useless to protest.

"Can you start from the beginning?" Emmy raised a pen, hovered it above an empty page of yellow legal paper. The same kind Andrew had favored, mused Lillian. How was it Emmy could write on his favorite type of yellow legal paper but she couldn't ask for a whiskey?

"What happened the night Dr. Ennis died?" began Emmy.

"I stabbed him," replied Lillian.

Emmy blinked, then reclined back in her chair and let out a nervous laugh. "I meant...from the beginning."

"Sure," said Lillian. "I found out he killed my sister, and then I stabbed him."

Emmy sighed. "We're going to need a bit more detail than that, I'm afraid."

Lillian did not want to go into more detail. She wanted to go home, to go to sleep, to wait for the world to end.

"Perhaps you could start with why you stabbed him," Emmy said after a moment.

Lillian was confused. She thought, at least, that part had been adequately covered. "Because I wanted him to be dead. Because he killed my sister, and I wanted him to die."

She thought the harshness of these words might fluster Emmy, but her former roommate didn't even blink. "And?" Emmy said after a moment.

And? And what? "That's it," said Lillian.

Emmy leaned in, her eyes gazing into Lillian's imploringly. "We have several witnesses who say they saw him chasing you with a knife. Is that true?"

"If you have witnesses saying it, it must be," said Lillian.

"Lillian, I'm on your side here," Emmy muttered, her voice betraying her frustration. From concern to annoyance in under three minutes—that had to be some kind of record.

"You shouldn't be on my side," Lillian replied. "No one else is. To the doctors, to the men on the plane, to everyone else—I'm the woman who ruined the future of physics." She had to chuckle as the full irony dawned on her. "They've all spent years making an atomic bomb, and I'm the one who has ruined physics."

"Well, the army knows several things that the doctors and the men on the plane don't," said Emmy. "We know that Dr. Ennis was…" Her voice trailed off as she searched for the correct word to describe what Dr. Ennis was. Lillian herself tried to think how she would finish the sentence. Inhuman? Evil? Disturbed? "Troubled," Emmy finally settled on. "I thought he might have been a spy. I thought for sure he'd killed Walter in the woods that night because Walter caught the two of you sneaking secrets out of here. But that wasn't the case.

"When the two of you left for Los Alamos, I went through Walter's things and learned that after your sister's death, Andrew convinced Walter to help him keep it all quiet. And Walter was happy to do it, it seemed. Because Dr. Ennis was 'special.'

'Necessary to the project.' But I don't think that. I don't think someone who does bad things gets to be special and necessary because they can do a few math problems quickly."

The words burned in Lillian's ears as Emmy continued. "But I need your help to change that. I need you to tell me the truth. Dr. Ennis gave you that wound, didn't he?"

Lillian reached up to touch the stitches in her cheek. "Yes," she answered.

"So he was coming after you," Emmy said. "He'd hurt you, and you had to defend yourself before he hurt you again."

"No," said Lillian. "He hurt me earlier in the night. He'd calmed down by the time I stabbed him. I stabbed him because I wanted him to die."

"Lillian," Emmy said, desperation building in her voice. "If this is a clear-cut case of self-defense, we don't have to go through the civilian courts. If that's not what it is, I don't know what will happen to you."

"So you want me to lie," said Lillian.

Emmy sighed in frustration. "Andrew Ennis is dead, whether you go to jail for this or not. The outcome is the same, and from where I'm sitting, it's the right outcome. I have to imagine from where you're sitting, it's the right outcome, too. Don't punish yourself for this."

"Maybe I..." In spite of her resolution to be strong-willed, unemotional, Lillian felt her voice tremble as it trailed off. "Maybe I deserve to be punished."

"For this?" asked Emmy.

Lillian didn't answer.

"You know, it's interesting," mused Emmy after a moment. "We were both sharing that dormitory room, sleeping ten feet away from one another, and both lying to each other about our identities. I thought you were hiding something. I thought you were a criminal—helping Dr. Ennis smuggle out blueprints, maybe. I never for a moment suspected you were anyone but Eleanor Kaufman. Just goes to show, you can never really know the people around you, huh?"

"The atom is mostly empty space," thought Lillian, and without thinking, she was saying it aloud, too. "Even when you touch another person, there's so much nothing between you."

Emmy took this in with a nod. After a moment, she added gently, "Perhaps there's something the army could do that would make it…easier for you to call this self-defense."

"I don't want the army's money," Lillian shot back.

"I'm not talking about paying you off," replied Emmy. "But we are a powerful institution. If there's something you're interested in, maybe we can help."

Lillian shook her head, which Emmy deftly pretended not to notice. "I'll give you a chance to think about it," she said.

And before Lillian could protest that there was really no need, she was escorted from the room into a narrow hallway, where a figure jumped up from his crouched position on the floor.

Although she'd spent most of the plane ride pondering what to say to Max Medelson, when she saw him, Lillian was suddenly at a loss for words. "Lillian," he said, his blue eyes widening as if he were surprised to see her, although surely he had camped outside there waiting for her.

"Hi, Max," she said. Her greeting hung in the air, so lame and incomplete.

He cleared his throat. "I'm glad you're...well, alive, I suppose."

Was she alive? It hardly felt that way. A moment that felt like an eternity passed. Finally, Lillian said: "I lost your knife."

"That's all right," he said. "That's quite all right."

"Surely there's something you want from the army," said Max. "Isn't there?"

Lillian shook her head.

Even though she was desperate to be alone, Emmy insisted on giving her and Max a private little room where they could talk. More coffee was brought out—and then tea, once it was discovered this coffee was just as unpleasant-looking as the cup Lillian had been offered earlier—and then Lillian filled Max in on her conversation with Emmy, partially out of a sense he had a right to know about it and partially as something to fill the nearly unbearable silence.

"Well, I can think of something," said Max.

"A job? I don't want to work for the army," mumbled Lillian. She wasn't sure how much Max knew about her father, but thought he at least knew enough not to suggest such a thing.

"Not a job," Max clarified. "Harvard."

Lillian stared into the depths of her too-weak tea. *Harvard.* She'd almost forgotten the place existed. "Harvard," she said out loud. Speaking the name was comforting in a strange way, like her body remembered that the last time her mouth had formed the word, she was in a happier time and place. "Do you think the army could do that?" she asked, more curious than hopeful.

"Of course," Max replied instantly. "I mean, I don't suppose they can tell Harvard what to do, but they can tell J. Robert Oppenheimer what to do, and a letter from him about how talented you are would do the rest."

Lillian shook her head. "That's not going to work," she said.

"Why?" asked Max.

She wasn't even surprised that after all this time, Max could still be so hopelessly naive. "Because J. Robert Oppenheimer doesn't know me as a physicist," she said. "To anyone who could help me, ever, I'll only be the woman who murdered Andrew Ennis."

"Not to me," said Max.

There was such kindness, gentleness in his voice that Lillian stopped in spite of herself, in spite of every fiber of her being wanting nothing more than to sit in a dark room, alone, for the rest of her surely numbered days. She felt a tear roll down her face. "I don't want to go to Harvard anymore. All I want is to not have hurt her the way we did," she confessed. "The way I did," she clarified a moment later. She was done with downplaying her own guilt, with pretending she somehow wasn't complicit in her own actions.

"The way we did," said Max, which surprised her into looking up. "I wish I hadn't lied to her. I told her I thought you were her and...the funny thing was, it didn't even feel like a lie by the time I said it, because I spent so long convincing myself it was true. Because I didn't want to be the bad guy. I didn't want to be..." He hung his head. "Sorry. I sound ridiculous."

"No," said Lillian, quite truthfully. "You pretended for so long you started to believe it. It didn't feel like pretending anymore."

"Yes," said Max sadly.

"I don't think there's anything quite like humanity's capacity to delude ourselves if it makes us feel better," said Lillian. "And look where that's gotten me. She died wanting me gone from her life forever. She never wanted to see me again, speak to me, wouldn't even write me a letter. She didn't want to think about me. I'll never be able to explain to you how much that hurts."

"That's not what she wanted," said Max. "She wrote you all the time. I saw her."

Lillian felt her nose running and wiped it with the edge of her sleeve. "No, she didn't. Not once."

"Almost every day." Max furrowed his brow. "You never got them?"

"Never," answered Lillian. Thinking of her own stack of unmailed letters in her room back in New York, she added: "Maybe she threw them away."

"No," said Max, sounding quite sure of himself. "She might not have been ready to send them, but I know she wrote them, and she wouldn't have thrown them away."

"But I searched her whole room," said Lillian. "Up and down. There was nowhere she could have put them where I wouldn't have seen."

As the words were leaving her mouth, Lillian realized they weren't true. There was one place of Eleanor's that Lillian had never found a way into, that she'd considered a dead end from the beginning.

Max seemed to read the realization on her face, and his protests died away.

"Do you think the army will let me into Y-12 one more time?" she asked him.

———

Building Y-12 still teemed with activity as Emmy escorted Lillian and Max inside. Max, for his part, seemed confused by the regular stream of people entering and exiting. "Why are they all still here?" he asked. "The thing's built, isn't it? What's left for them to do?"

Emmy responded with a non-answer: "We have to be ready."

Max shrugged, as if to say, *Well, if you insist.* Lillian wasn't surprised. They'd figured out how to make a bomb capable of flattening out a three-mile radius. The army wasn't going to be cautious with its production. They'd make as much fissile material as they could.

As they continued on through the double doors, Max leaned over to whisper to Lillian, "I heard that some guys are already working on a thermonuclear fusion bomb."

Lillian felt her heart drop.

"The fission bomb we made would be the igniter for the new one," Max went on. "I thought it was just theoretical, but apparently they've almost got it cracked."

"I know," said Lillian. "That was Andrew. That's what he was always working on, late at night. He knew once the fission bomb was successful, they'd move on to the next thing." The fission bomb had burned so hotly it turned the sand of the New Mexico desert into shards of green glass, only a shade or two lighter than the silk of Eleanor's green silk dress. That that would only be the igniter for the next bomb was unthinkable and inevitable, both at once.

Andrew had given the world the blueprints to blow itself up, and then left it. He always had been two steps ahead.

They took the first right into the women's locker room, just as Lillian had done on her first day lifetimes ago. Max hesitated at the door, not sure if he should follow, but Emmy assured him they were hours away from the shift change and the room would be empty.

It had been a month since Lillian had stepped inside this enormous building, yet she remembered exactly which twists and turns led her to Eleanor's locker. It was as if her heart were leading her, as if she were drawn by some supernatural force far outside herself. The three stopped in front of the locker, silent and reverent.

E. Kaufman.

"They have to be in there," said Max. "The letters. They've gotta be."

Lillian didn't want to voice her optimism, so she only nodded.

Emmy studied the locker. "I'll have someone come to break the lock off," she concluded. "Can you wait here?"

"I think I can do it," said Lillian suddenly. She wasn't sure what prompted this swell of confidence, but she felt more than capable. She stepped to the locker, ran her fingers over the dial, then twirled it a few times. It was stiff at first, but turned easily after a moment.

"Not you, too," Max muttered under his breath. Instantly regretting even a sideways mention of Andrew, he winced. "Sorry," he added.

Lillian didn't answer. She slowed down her twirling. *Whoever goes right for the most complicated path is already lost.* She didn't want to hear his voice, but she did, as loudly and as clearly as if his ghost stood just behind her left shoulder. She wondered what combination Eleanor would choose, alone in front of this locker, away from everything she'd ever known for the first time in her life.

Lillian turned the dial again. *06.* June. *07.* The 7th. *19.* Their birthday, Lillian's seven minutes sooner. She pulled on the handle.

Nothing.

It couldn't be the variation 67-19-19, as the dial only went up to 60. Lillian searched her memory, scanning every date that could have been significant to her sister. The birthdays of their parents wouldn't fit, but there was no way Eleanor had left it at nothing either.

"It's no problem to have maintenance come," Emmy said, trying to sound helpful.

"One more minute," said Lillian. She thought as hard as she could. Codes had never been her specialty, and neither was reading people—even her own twin, apparently.

She could feel Emmy and Max's eyes on her. Why had she thought she could do this? She was not Andrew, would never be Andrew, would never have that uncanny ability to size someone up instantly, effortlessly. *What if it wasn't a number at all, but a series of letters coded in numbers?* This was a good thing, of course—*A could equal 1, B equals 2, C equals 3*—the same thing that made Andrew understand someone instantly also made them disposable to him. *But that's a Lillian way to code a message. You need to find the Eleanor way. But what method of encoding letters into numbers would Eleanor be familiar with?*

The answer struck her as clean and crystal as the chime of a bell. This time, she knew it was correct just from the way the dial turned beneath her fingers.

54.

54.

26.

The latch sprang open.

"Oh my god," exclaimed Max. "How on earth…? Do you really hear the pins dropping?"

"No," replied Lillian. "It's a trick. That's all."

The three fell silent for a moment, until Emmy said quietly, "Open it."

Lillian reached for the opened latch and pulled the locker open, for the first time in days allowing her heart to feel some hope. Inside was a neat stack of white envelopes—at least thirty, maybe more.

For a moment, Lillian felt like her eyes must be deceiving her, like the papers would dissolve as soon as she reached out and touched them. But that wasn't the case. Her fingers ran across the top envelope, smooth and solid. In Eleanor's terrible handwriting, the outside read: *Lillian.*

"Open one," said Max.

Lillian shook her head. "It's not the right time. I don't know if it will be the right time for a while." She noticed as the words left her mouth that it was the first time she had thought about the future as anything other than a void that would swallow them whole any minute now. The future held unspeakable pain, but it did exist.

"I thought you wanted to know," said Max. "Know that she did love you."

"I do," said Lillian, taking the letters in her hands and closing the locker. "I'm ready to go home now."

They left Y-12 through the cubicles, with their women and stools and telephones. Telephones identical to the one Eleanor, the social butterfly of the family, would have been infinitely familiar with. She knew everyone's phone number by heart, never needed to write anything down on the little pad of paper left next to the receiver.

When Lillian returned to New York, to East 86th Street, the first thing she did was run her fingers over the numbers of the telephone in her foyer. *54-54-26*. The corresponding letters over which her fingers grazed were *LI-LI-AN*.

Eleanor had never forgotten her, never stopped loving her. Now all Lillian could do was the same.

AUTHOR'S NOTE

By the summer of 1945, 75,000 people were living in Oak Ridge, Tennessee. An additional 20,000 commuted from nearby cities like Knoxville to work at the Clinton Engineer Works. Many worked, like Eleanor, as calutron girls—controlling the machines that were generating fissile uranium and plutonium for the atomic bomb. Most of them would not know the nature of their work until the first atomic bomb was detonated by the U.S. Army Air Forces over Hiroshima on August 6, 1945.

The following books were invaluable to me as I wrote this story: *City Behind a Fence* by Charles W. John and Charles O. Jackson, *The Girls of Atomic City* by Denise Kiernan, *The Making of the Atomic Bomb* by Richard Rhodes, *Brotherhood of the Bomb* by Gregg Herken, and the lecture "Los Alamos from Below" by Richard Feynman.

Lillian, Eleanor, Andrew, Max, and Betty are all fictional, although Andrew's obsession with the fusion or thermonuclear bomb is based on Edward Teller, and his safe-cracking is based on Richard Feynman.

After the end of World War II, Edward Teller (with Stanislaw

Ulam) developed a thermonuclear bomb that was tested by the United States on November 1, 1952. The test destroyed the island of Elugelab, where the detonation occurred.

The Allerton test is based on the real William Lowell Putnam Mathematical Competition, which has been given annually by the Mathematical Association of America since 1938. The Allerton problem Lillian works on is from *Calculus* by Alfred L. Nelson, William Martin Borgman, and Karl W. Folley (revised edition, Boston: D.C. Heath and Company, 1946). This work is in the public domain and provided by the Hathi Trust Digital Library, hathitrust.org.

From 1945 to 1947, eighteen patients were given plutonium, most without their knowledge or full informed consent, at four separate sites associated with the Manhattan Project, including Oak Ridge. These patients ranged in age from four years to sixty-nine years old. Some were facing (or believed to be facing) terminal illnesses; others were hospitalized for other reasons. Fifty-five-year-old Ebb Cabe had been injured in a car crash, and treatment of his injuries was delayed so the experiment could be conducted. Of the eighteen patients, half died within two and a half years of their injection. More information on these experiments can be found in "The Human Plutonium Injection Experiments" by William Moss and Roger Eckhardt, published in *Los Alamos Science,* Issue Number 23, 1995.

READING GROUP GUIDE

1. In the early days of Eleanor's relationship with Max, Lillian is extremely irritated with her. How does she justify this frustration?

2. Describe Lillian's relationship to femininity. If all expectations for women to look, dress, and think a certain way were gone, do you think she would behave differently?

3. What does Lillian gain from lying about Eleanor's rescheduled audition? What would you have done in her position?

4. Why didn't Andrew have Lillian immediately escorted from Oak Ridge after realizing who she was?

5. How does pretending to be Eleanor change Lillian's habits and ideas? Do you think she'll maintain any of Eleanor's traits when she's back to living as herself full time?

6. Andrew is comfortable with being a "bad person," but Lillian insists he's good, at least in some ways. Whom do you agree with? Does that change the way you think about Andrew's fate?

7. Due to his scientific expertise, Andrew is protected from the consequences of his actions. How can we stop letting talent excuse dangerous behavior?

8. What causes the difference between Andrew's and Lillian's reaction to the Los Alamos test? If you witnessed that historic explosion, how would you feel?

9. Throughout the book, Lillian makes decisions thinking that the outcome will justify her choices, but when Emmy says something similar about claiming self-defense, she hesitates. Why?

10. The true goal of the many branches of the Manhattan Project was a carefully guarded secret, even from the people who were helping achieve it. How do you think history would be different if everyone—from the calutron girls to the scientists perfecting fusion reactions—knew what they were developing?

A CONVERSATION WITH THE AUTHOR

What was your inspiration for *The Woman with Two Shadows?* When I was in college, I read Richard Feynman's lecture about working on the Manhattan Project as a young man just at the start of his career. The day of the Trinity Test, he describes how everyone was celebrating except for one person, who seemed acutely aware of the terrible thing they had made. He reflects that everyone got so excited and so wrapped up in the project, in solving this unsolvable thing, that they'd stopped thinking about what it is they were actually doing.

I thought that was fascinating, that this group of people who were supposedly the smartest people in our country, people whose profession requires them to question everything and never accept a hypothesis without evidence, could still so easily "stop thinking" when it suited them. That's what I wanted to explore.

How much planning do you do before you start writing? Do you prefer to know the end of your story right away? At one point in this book, Andrew says, "You might as well try

running first. Save you a whole lot of walking if it works out."
Regrettably, this is also my approach to writing.

When I was working on the first draft of this story in my
MFA class at USC, the professor, Mark Shepherd, told me I
should write down the entire solution to the mystery and how
it all happened. That way, I would know everything, even if I
decided later to not let the audience in on all the details. It was
great advice that I completely ignored. I wish I hadn't.

**How did you navigate the difference between Lillian's idealized
role as Eleanor's caretaker and her often detrimental interference in Eleanor's life?**

I think Lillian's role as her sister's caretaker became folded
up in Lillian's narrative about herself. It started as a principle, a standard to follow: "I want to protect my sister." But it
warped into "I'm the kind of person who wants to protect my
sister, therefore every decision I make must be to protect my
sister." She stopped using the idea of protecting Eleanor to
guide her decision-making and started using it to *justify* her
decision-making.

**Andrew Ennis meets a very dark but avoidable end. Was it chal-
lenging to get into his headspace in his final moments?**

No, because his last moments are his most honest.

Despite the army's best efforts to keep the secret, Andrew is quick to connect his own work in Oak Ridge to the development of the nuclear bomb. If you were in his position, would you continue working on its development?

I think this question is asking if I would continue working on my own projects while being paid to do an office job I thought was boring, and my answer is: no comment.

ACKNOWLEDGMENTS

This book would not exist without my parents, Jim and Judi Rogers. Thank you for supporting my dreams and always having the History Channel on during my formative years.

I have been so grateful during this process to work with two women who understood this story in such a deep and meaningful way: my agent, Abby Saul, and my editor, Shana Drehs. Thank you for never asking me to make Lillian less difficult.

Thanks to the entire team at Sourcebooks for making this such a pleasant experience. Thanks to production editor Jessica Thelander, proofreader Aimee Algas Alker, art director Heather VenHuizen, senior graphic designer Stephanie Rocha, production designer Danielle McNaughton, and the marketing and publicity team, including Molly Waxman and Cristina Arreola. Copy editor Diane Dannenfeldt had the unenviable task of correcting my southwestern Pennsylvania grammar.

A million thanks to Matt Mahaffey for the beautiful author photos.

To my Gumps—Audrey Beauchamp, Taylor Dariarow, Jake

Farrington, Adrienne Teeley, and Taylor Wolfe—I would be lost
without you. Welcome to Hollywood.

I am pleased to call some of the most brilliant people I know
my friends: Brittany Axworthy, Alex Baia, Laurie Bolewitz, Ross
Brenneman, Kristen Damiani, Tiffany Ho, Ibet Inyang, Audrey
Wong Kennedy, Rebecca Munley, Jeremy Palmer, Lyndsay Palmer,
Becky Rosenberg, Mary Sette, and many more. Thanks for inspir-
ing me and supporting me. Amanda Freechack, thanks for the
all the rooftop beers. Katie Avery, thanks for telling me how this
book should end. Christy McElhinny, thanks for the cat pictures.

Thanks to all my fellow Lark Group writers for being so
supportive. I can't wait to meet you all at the company picnic
Abby doesn't know I'm forcing her to host.

The first version of this story was written in Professor Mark
Shepherd's screenplay class in the USC writing for screen
and television MFA program. Mark, thank you for encourag-
ing me to keep going with this story when I was ready to give
up. Thanks to my (wildly talented) classmates for their notes
on that draft: Alyson Nichols, Lauren Moon, Jovan Robinson,
Christopher Sullivan, Mellori Vasquez, and especially, Michael
Patrick Clarkson, who said after my first pitch, "What if she had
a twin?"

I have been lucky to have so many incredible writing teach-
ers, including Daphne Pollon and David Isaacs at USC, Daniel
Alexander Jones at Fordham College at Lincoln Center, and
Peg Seifert at Woodland Hills High School in Turtle Creek,

Pennsylvania. Thank you for never batting an eye when I cried in your offices.

Thanks to my favorite place in the world, the Los Angeles Public Library.

Finally, thanks to my cat, Lucille.

ABOUT THE AUTHOR

Sarah James is a public transit enthusiast, bird watcher, and former theater kid. *The Woman with Two Shadows* is her debut novel. Originally from Pittsburgh, Pennsylvania, Sarah received an MFA in writing for screen and television from the University of Southern California. She currently lives in Los Angeles, California, with her cat, Lucille.